Thomas Talbot Bury

Rudimentary Architecture

for the use of beginners - The history and description of the styles of architecture of
various countries, from the earliest to the present period

Thomas Talbot Bury

Rudimentary Architecture
for the use of beginners - The history and description of the styles of architecture of various countries, from the earliest to the present period

ISBN/EAN: 9783337388317

Printed in Europe, USA, Canada, Australia, Japan

Cover: Foto ©Andreas Hilbeck / pixelio.de

More available books at **www.hansebooks.com**

RUDIMENTARY

ARCHITECTURE

For the Use of Beginners and Students

THE STYLES

OF

ARCHITECTURE OF VARIOUS COUNTRIES

FROM THE EARLIEST TO THE PRESENT PERIOD

With Illustrative Engravings

By T. TALBOT BURY, Architect

FELLOW OF THE ROYAL INSTITUTE OF BRITISH ARCHITECTS, ASSOCIATE OF THE
INSTITUTE OF CIVIL ENGINEERS, AND AUTHOR OF "THE REMAINS OF
ECCLESIASTICAL WOODWORK"

SIXTH EDITION, WITH NUMEROUS ADDITIONAL ENGRAVINGS

Capio Lumen

LONDON

LOCKWOOD & CO., 7, STATIONERS' HALL COURT

LUDGATE HILL

1874

CONTENTS.

PREFACE TO THE FIRST EDITION.

THERE is, perhaps, no art or science which possesses more extensive or prolific means of instruction and entertainment, or which has greater claims on the consideration of the world at large, than that of Architecture. To consider properly and appreciate fully the importance of the art, we must first take its history from the earliest period, wherein we shall find that every invention has had its origin in the wants of man, and every improvement in the science of building has resulted from the requirements of various nations advancing towards a more powerful position or a higher degree of civilization.

The architecture of a country is therefore inseparable from its history; it is the external and enduring form of a people's habit — an index of their state of knowledge and social progress. But it may safely be asserted, that to the influence of religious systems is mainly to be attributed the advances and perfection in the arts of design and decoration, as well as their perpetuity to veneration for the purposes of their erection.

The present small work on the History of Architecture is intended to serve as an introduction to the study of the art,— to assist the student in the distinction and classification of the various styles which have been practised in different countries, —and to point out their derivation or application. In some

instances, for want of positive evidence, conclusions are formed
from similarities of combinations or comparative history, but
avoiding all reference to speculative theories.   The origin of
Grecian architecture is, and always has been, a *rexata quæstio*:
whether the forms of the temples built in durable materials
were derived from the timber erections of their own country,
or from the stone temples of Egypt, is difficult to determine ;
but we know that from the earliest period there was a connection and intercourse carried on between the two nations ; and
as the climate of Egypt was not favourable for the growth of
timber, we are certain that no country was called upon earlier
to adopt stone or granite as a building material.   Thus there
is every probability that the architecture of the Greeks was
formed on those pre-existent structural buildings of the Egyptians having columns and entablatures, and which had no
relation to a wooden edifice.   To the dissimilarities of the constituent principles of sculpture, or the general properties of
moulding and ornament, no importance can be attached in
deciding the origin of any style ; for we know that the essential elements of a class of architecture may be borrowed by
men of a different property of mind, who may have the power
of adopting and improving what others have invented so as to
make the invention their own, and produce so great a difference
that it is scarcely possible to discover the growth of one style
of architecture from another.   To instance this, we need not
go beyond our own country,—where, in five centuries, the
same race of men produced varieties of design much more
antagonistic to each other than those of Egypt and Greece.

 It has been the main object in the following treatise, to give
a continuous history of architecture, from the time of its perfection in Greece to the present period, describing its various
peculiarities and gradual transitions from one style to another;
and it is to be regretted, that the comparatively restricted
space has necessitated an undue compression of the vast mass
of information connected with this subject, and to which circumstance some omissions may be attributed.   It is, however,

to be hoped that this Introduction to the Art of Architecture, divested of unnecessary technicalities, may be instrumental in producing a more general appreciation of its beauties, and be the means of leading the general reader to more extensive researches.

T. TALBOT BURY.

26, Golden Square, June, 1849.

IN producing a Third edition of Mr. BURY's Treatise on the History of Architecture, which has been demanded by the sale of an extensive impression since its publication in 1849, it has been deemed advisable to make some considerable additions to the number of its illustrations: engravings of several of the most interesting examples of the various styles of architecture which prevailed at different periods are therefore inserted, with a view to enhance the intrinsic merits of the work. The supplementary remarks now first added, and commencing at page 170, are from the pen of that well-known architectural writer and critic Mr. W. H. LEEDS, who alone is answerable for the opinions there expressed.

An APPENDIX, containing some additional remarks on the churches of Wren, Hawksmoor, Gibbs, and others, is also added.

February, 1856.

LIST OF ILLUSTRATIONS.

RUDIMENTARY ARCHITECTURE.

CHAPTER I.

ARCHITECTURE OF VARIOUS COUNTRIES.

In an attempt to trace the origin of Architecture, with a view to a history of the Styles that prevailed in this and other countries, it will be quite unnecessary to give any account of the different kinds of tents, huts, and other timber erections used as the early habitations of mankind, resulting from the necessity of protection from the inclemency of the seasons, and which required little skill or knowledge of construction. Our purpose is to refer only to such ancient erections of durable materials as evince a knowledge of some systematic construction, or were the source from which proceeded all that properly can be called Architecture.

NINEVEH, BABYLON, AND EGYPT.

The first city that contained solid and durable edifices was Nineveh, the capital of the Assyrian empire and the residence of the Assyrian kings, founded by Asshur, the great-grandson of Noah.* Jonah speaks of it as "an exceeding great city of three days' journey:" † it is described by Strabo as larger than Babylon: the walls, according to Diodorus, were 100 feet high, and so broad that three chariots might be driven on them abreast: upon the walls stood 1500 towers, each 200 feet in height; and the whole was so strong as to be deemed impregnable. That this city must have been one of great gran-

* Genesis x. 11. "Out of that land went forth Asshur, and builded Nineveh." † Chap. iii. 3.

A

deur at a very early period, there can be little doubt.   It
is mentioned as a place of great commercial importance, and
"its merchants as more than the stars of heaven."   Nineveh
was taken by the Medes under Arbaces, in the eighth century
B. C., when it was nearly destroyed ; and quite so, when taken
by Cyaxares, 625 B. C.   All that now remains, on each side
of the Tigris, of this once splendid city, has the appearance of
a range of hills, from which large stones and bricks connected
by bitumen, on which are inscriptions, are frequently dug up.

The next city noted for its early origin was Babylon, founded
by Nimrod, son of Cush, and grandson of Ham.*   It is described by the ancient writers, Strabo and Quintus Curtius, as
a city of great strength and magnificence: so great was the
circuit of its walls, that there was pasture and arable land
within them sufficient to support the whole population during a
long siege.   According to Herodotus, the walls were 50 cubits
thick and 200 in height, built of bricks made from the earth
which was dug out of the ditch that surrounded the city.   In
the walls were 100 gates made of brass, as well as the jambs
and lintels.   It has been said, that if ever there was a city
which seemed to bid defiance to any predictions of its fall,
that city was Babylon,—for a long time the most famous city
of the old world, whose walls were reckoned amongst its
wonders.

The ruins that have been discovered on each side of the
Euphrates confirm the accounts which have descended to us of
its splendour ; although nothing now remains but large masses
of brick-work laid on lime mortar of good quality.   On the
eastern side, it is supposed, are the remains of the great
temple of Belus,† which, according to Diodorus, was higher
than the largest pyramid.   Among the ruins are to be found

* Genesis x. 10. "And the beginning of his kingdom was Babel."
† The temple of Belus, as described by Herodotus, was of a pyramidal
form, similar to the Hindoo temple at Tanjore, and the great Mexican
temples.   It was founded by Semiramis, 1650 B. C.

fragments of alabaster vessels, fine earthenware, marble, and great quantities of varnished tiles whose glazing and colouring are still fresh.

Of what date these are it is impossible to conjecture, as so little information exists on this interesting subject. We are told that in the time of Semiramis, Queen of Assyria 1665 B. C., an extensive and splendid palace existed on each side of the Euphrates, connected by a tunnel under the river, and likewise that a bridge was built by Nitocris to connect the two parts of the city divided by the Euphrates. The piers were of large hewn stones, in order to erect which the course of the river was diverted, and its bed left dry.

The city was brought to its highest degree of perfection by Nebuchadnezzar, about 600 years before the Christian era; but its splendour must have been of short duration, as about 60 years after the death of that monarch, and during the reign of Belshazzar, it was taken by Cyrus. From that time it gradually declined, and afterwards became a part of the great Persian monarchy.

The Egyptian Thebes,* situated near the southern extremity of that empire, is the most ancient city of whose buildings any remains exist at the present time. The period of its foundation ascends, probably, to the same antiquity as that of Nineveh and Babylon. It was the first seat of the Egyptian government,† which at an early period was transferred to Memphis, near the northern extremity of the empire. From this time its importance declined, but the imperishable nature of the materials and the immensity of its masses have preserved the buildings for more than three thousand years. Memphis, less fortunately situated, by being nearer the line of

* The most ancient name of Thebes is Pathros, and it was so called from Pathrusim, son of Mizraim and son of Ham. Mizraim was the first occupier of the country of Egypt.

† The first king mentioned is Menes, who is supposed to have lived above 2000 years B. C., and contemporary with the era of the Chinese emperor Gao, with whom the historical period of China begins.

communication between Asia and Africa, has been more subject to the destructive caprices of man, and has disappeared
from the face of the earth.*　At present the site of the city
of Thebes is occupied by four principal villages,—Luxor and
Karnac on the eastern side, Gournah and Medinet-A'zou on
the western side of the river.　The buildings and sculpture of
this gigantic 'city of a hundred gates,' still extant, are the most
ancient that exist in Egypt, and are the best and most genuine
specimens of Egyptian art and architecture; for there is every
reason to believe that by far the greater part were executed
before Egypt had yet experienced the influence of the Greeks,
and long before the Persian invasion.

The ruins, chiefly consisting of temples, colossi, sphinxes,
and obelisks, occupy nearly the whole extent of the valley of
the Nile, a space of six miles from east to west.　On the
western side, where the ruins of this vast city terminate, those
of the City of the Dead commence, among which there are
tombs excavated in the rocks, and decorated with paintings
still as fresh as though the artist's hand had been engaged
upon them but a few weeks past.

The principal remains of Egyptian architecture (chiefly
temples) are to be found on the banks of the Nile, and extend
from Cairo to Nubia, a distance of 500 miles.　The peculiarity
observable in all that was erected by the Egyptians is the great
sublimity of the masses, the grandeur and severity of every
line, by which their buildings bear the stamp of that sentiment
of eternal duration which they were always so anxious to
realize in their monuments.

At a very early period the Egyptians were extremely skilful
in working stone, an art in which they have never been surpassed.　The large blocks of stone of which their temples are
composed are well squared, and so laid that the joints are
scarcely visible.

The most interesting and complete temple in the whole

* Egypt was conquered by Cambyses, 525 years B. C.; after which time
it became a province of Persia.

val'ey of the Nile is that of Edfou, about 25 miles above Thebes. This great and magnificent temple is one of the largest in Egypt, and is in comparatively good preservation. Its form is rectangular, and its general dimensions 450 feet by 140 feet. In the centre of one of the sides is the entrance between two sloping towers, 100 feet in length by 32 feet in width, on the surface of which are represented some colossal figures; and above these are two rows of smaller ones, supposed to be the divinities of the temple receiving the offerings of the Ptolemies. Within is a court surrounded by a colonnade on three sides, and on the side facing the entrance is a beautiful pronaos, or portico, of eighteen columns: beyond this is another of smaller dimensions; and further on are the walls which protect the sanctuary and its dependencies: these are so completely filled up with sand and soil, that it is nearly impossible to reach them. All the columns, friezes, cornices, and the whole surface of the walls, inside as well as out, both of the pronaos and court, are covered with symbolical sculptures, hieroglyphical inscriptions, and representations of offerings to their divinities.

Of all the works of the ancient Egyptians, those which have caused the greatest wonder to the world at large are the Pyramids of Gizeh, supposed by Sir Gardner Wilkinson to have been erected 2120 years B.C.* Herodotus dates the Great Pyramid about 900 years B.C., or about 450 years before he visited Egypt. Chevalier Bunsen places them about 2000 years before that period; and this is confirmed by the opinions of Champollion and Rosellini.

The Great Pyramid, said to have been built by Cheops,† is 700 feet square at the base, and 470 feet in height; the second is 650 feet square, and 280 feet in height; the third, 400 feet square, and 160 feet in height. About 300 paces from the second pyramid stands the gigantic statue of the Sphinx, whose length, from the forepart to the tail, has been found to

* And attributed by him to Suphis and Sen-suphis.
† The other two by Cephrenes and Mycerinus.

be 125 feet. Belzoni cleared away the sand, and found a temple between the legs, and another in one of its paws.

The mechanical skill of the Egyptians is shown in their quarrying and working stone; and the means that must have been used to convey such immense blocks of stone as we find in their works, from quarries situated at a distance from them, naturally surprise us.

The obelisks of Thebes and Heliopolis vary in size from 70 to 93 feet in length,* and are built of one stone. The largest in Egypt, which is at the great temple at Karnac, is calculated to weigh 297 tons, and was brought about 138 miles from the quarry. Those at Heliopolis passed over a space of 800 miles.

The two colossal statues in a sitting attitude (one of which is the vocal Memnon) are each of a single block, 47 feet in height, and contain 11,500 cubic feet; they are carved from stone not known within several days' journey from the place where the statues are found; and at Memnonium is a colossal statue, which, when entire, weighed 887 tons. The raising of the obelisks is considered a far greater test of mechanical skill than the transport of these prodigious weights; but into the mode that was adopted we have no insight from any representations yet discovered.

Of the taste, style, and character of Egyptian Architecture, little can be said, beyond admiration at the immensity of the works and the patience with which they must have been accomplished. The masses of material which the country produced measured their efforts and conceptions, and their invention was exhausted by a very restricted number of combinations.

Their monuments are admirable for grandeur and solidity, and they have a truly imposing effect; but we can only consider them as part of the history of Architecture and Art, because the ornaments and sculpture, originating from a

* Sir Gardner Wilkinson's 'Manners and Customs of the Ancient Egyptians.

symbolical religion peculiar to the Egyptians, admit of no revival, even were art more immediately connected with them.

The columns are evidently a representation of a bundle of
reeds or lotus stems, tied together at the top and base, the
leaves of which, as well as those of the palm, are chiefly used
in ornamenting the capitals.

CHAPTER II.

GRECIAN ARCHITECTURE.

THAT Architecture and Art always have been progressive,
and have not appeared at once in full perfection, is a truism
that need scarcely be advanced; yet in our admiration of their
perfection we do not always consider the history of their progression, or the sources from whence they sprang. No style,
with the exception of the Egyptian, was the spontaneous
growth of the soil on which it flourished, or proceeded directly
from the nations that practised it: the germs of all other
styles were borrowed from people whose habits and religious
customs were totally dissimilar; and its advances or improvements were the natural results of civilization, caused by intercourse with other nations in times of peace, or by the adoption
of all that was worthy of imitation in conquered states, during
the incessant wars that were carried on in the eastern parts of
the world.

Thus was it with the much admired Architecture and Arts
of Greece and Rome, so that centuries elapsed ere anything
worthy of those terms was to be found in either empire.

The most ancient writings and traditions inform us (and
reason itself assists us to the same conclusion) that the various
tribes of human beings diffused over the face of the earth led
a wandering life until a period when, increasing in number and
uniting together for mutual protection, they were obliged to
surround their abodes by walls and fortifications, in order to
secure themselves from hordes that lived by plunder only.

Such was the origin of the earliest societies, and the foundation of the first towns and cities.

Greece was divided into a number of petty states, which, independent of each other, and therefore necessarily rivals, surrounded themselves, as a means of protection, with thick walls, long before they had learned the art of building temples, and when their huts or houses were of the rudest character. The first erections were their acropoles, invariably situated on eminences which were converted into citadels, and served for places of security when the population became too numerous to remain in them, and had spread themselves over the surrounding plains. The acropoles usually contained all things of the greatest value to the community, such as the public treasures, the archives, and the temples of the tutelary divinities; indeed, they were to the Greeks what the capitol was to the Romans.

The oldest remains of walls and acropoles exist at Tiryns or Tirynthus and Mycenæ, near Argos, in the Morea, and are said to have been built by the Cyclopes, a tribe which is supposed to have arrived from Thrace or Phœnicia, and settled in Asia Minor. The date of the masonry is supposed to be coeval with the time of Abraham, who arrived in Canaan B.C. 1917.* Sir William Gell makes the date of the buildings B.C. 1379. All that at present exists of Tiryns consists of portions of the walls of the acropolis, which are from 21 to 25 feet in thickness, and 45 feet in height, built of tremendous blocks of stone from 10 to 13 feet long, and 4 feet 4 inches thick. In the thickness of these walls are two ranges of galleries, each 5 feet broad and about 12 feet high: the shape of these passages is triangular, the sides sloping upwards until they meet. This form was obtained by making the horizontal courses of masonry project one beyond the other, the edge of each course being splayed off so as to give, from the interior, very much the appearance of a kind of arch having been constructed. They probably conducted round the whole of the citadel, and were

* Fosbroke.

used as shelters for the garrison during the night or bad weather. Mr. Woods* says that no tool seems to have been applied to the stone, but that the rude masses are merely heaped on one another, taking care in the position of each successive block to place it where it would most exactly fit into the work, and most probably keeping the smoothest side outwards to form the face of the work. The workmanship of these walls is nothing more than that of the modern fencing without mortar, the interstices between the larger stones being filled up with others of smaller size, unworked, and merely heaped on one another. Pausanias informs us, that when the Argives attempted to destroy Tiryns, the walls were so strong that they could not throw them down: he also describes them to be equally worthy of admiration with the Pyramids of Egypt.†

The next city connected with Greece that demands our notice, on account of its early fortifications and acropolis, of which parts exist at the present time, is Mycenæ, near Argos, likewise built by the Cyclopes, or by Mycenæus, B. C. 1700, and considerably enlarged by Perseus about B. C. 1390. The walls of this city, like those of Tiryns, are in some places built of rough stones, from 8 to 9 feet in length: when entire, they must have been 60 feet high, although at present, in the most perfect part, their height is only 43 feet. The general thickness is 21 feet, but in some places 25 feet, and they are mostly constructed of well-jointed polygonal stone. Some remains of towers are discernible.

One of the most interesting objects in the history of Art still remains here, generally known as 'the Gate of the Lions:' it is the principal entrance to the acropolis. This gate owes its celebrity to the basso-relievo by which it is surmounted,

* 'Letters on Architecture,' 2 vols. 4to.

† Sir William Gell states that on the centre of the architraves of the gates are holes, which leads him to suppose that the gates were hung from large central pivots, so that one side opened inwards while the other advanced.

the subject of which is two lions, with their fore-paws resting on a pedestal : from this the gateway takes its name. This sculpture (on a triangular stone over the architrave) is the most ancient specimen of this kind of Grecian art ; it is 10 feet 6 inches wide at the base, and 9 feet in height : between the lions is a semicircular pillar, bearing some resemblance to the Doric Order, although, contrary to the general usage, it increases in size from the bottom to the top. The date of this sculpture is supposed by some to be nearly coeval with the other part. Pausanias mentions, that in his day it was reported to be the work of the Cyclopes : however this may be, there can be little doubt but that it is the oldest specimen of Grecian sculpture now existing. The architrave over this gate is of one stone, 15 feet long, and 4 feet 4 inches in height, and in it are visible sockets of about 3 inches in diameter, which received the pivots upon which the gates turned.

We may here mention a subterranean building at Mycenæ, known as the Treasury of Atreus, the father of Agamemnon : * the principal chamber is of a circular form, 48 feet in diameter, and about 49 feet in height. The covering of this building has the appearance of the inside of a dome, which has led some authors to suppose that the arch was known in Greece at a very early period ; but it is now ascertained that the principle of the arch does not exist in it, as the construction is the same as in the arched passages at Tiryns : the courses are horizontal, each projecting beyond the other, with the lower angles cut away until they meet at the apex, which consists of one very large stone. Beyond this is a vault or inner chamber, in the walls of which, as well as those of the larger chamber, are a number of bronze nails, which in all probability were used to fasten plates of metal to the walls ; a custom doubtless resorted to on some occasions, as we read of " brazen chambers" and " brazen temples." †   The courses of stone in this build-

---

* Atreus came to the throne of Argos 927 B. C.

† There are other instances of subterraneous chambers being lined with thin plates of metal : that at Argos, in which Acrisius confined his

ing are regular, although of unequal size, and laid without cement: the lintel of the door is of one piece of stone, of about 27 feet long, 17 feet wide, and 3 feet 9 inches thick, and is calculated to weigh about 133 tons; a mass of stone to which none can be compared, excepting those used in Egypt.*

Having given a slight description of the earliest erections of stone in Greece, which are considered as specimens of Cyclopean or Pelasgic Architecture, we will now proceed to notice that style of Architecture which has with justice been deemed the purest that

---

daughter, was probably similar to those of the adjacent rival city.—*Vide* Donaldson's ' Description of the Subterranean Chamber at Mycenæ.'

* Mr. Donaldson states that "there are numerous buildings and excavations in Egypt, Sicily, and Italy, constructed in a manner similar to this subterraneous chamber. In the Memnonium at Thebes is an oblong chamber, covered by a semicircular vaulting, the stones of which have horizontal courses projecting beyond each other as they advance in height,

the mind of man has invented, and to adorn which has
originated a class of sculpture which, for composition and
execution, has never been surpassed.

The accounts of the earliest temples of Greece or Asia
Minor are chiefly founded on inferences, and so unsatisfactory
that it would be useless to dwell on them at any length. The
sacerdotal office, which at first was possessed by the head of
each family, became in some countries, by the establishment
of a monarchical government, vested in the prince ; and where
this happened, there is every reason to believe that some part
of the palace was set apart for the offices of religion ;—but subsequently, when a regular order of priesthood was formed, it was
found necessary to have places appointed for performing the
sacrifices, and therefore temples were erected for that purpose.

Before the time of Homer, 900 B.C., there were few temples
in Greece. Those mentioned by him are, the temple of
Minerva at Athens, that of Apollo at Delphi, and of Neptune
at Ægæ. He represents the sacrifices to have been performed on altars in the open air; and it is obvious from
the terms which he employs, that the temples of Minerva
and Apollo were roofless. That temples existed on the
Asiatic coast is certain, for Hecuba is described by him as
leading a procession of matrons to the temple of Minerva, in
the city of Troy, in order to propitiate the goddess.

There is every reason to suppose, however, that until after
the time of Homer there was no regular priesthood in Greece,
and that the office of priest was vested in the kings. The
altar appears to have been the only structure for sacred use at
this period, and the tops of the mountains were selected, not

so as to produce that curvilinear form. Near Noto in Sicily, in the district
of Falconara, on the road from Mititello to Vizzi ; also in Sardinia, where
these chambers are known by the name of Norages ; and at Tusculum,
near Rome, the same construction exists ; but in none of these do we
possess such correct dates as Pausanias and history itself furnish of those of
Orcomenus and Mycenæ."—*Vide* supplementary volume to the 'Antiquities
of Athens.'

only by the Greeks, but by other nations,* for the worship of their gods; and we read in the Iliad that Hector sacrificed on the top of Ida. The altars erected on the hills were at first only enclosed by walls and the abodes of the priests, but when the forms of their worship became more mysterious, and to them more sacred, these altars were concealed from the public view by more lofty erections, which, in the first place, were composed of wood. The temple of Delphi, mentioned by Homer, is supposed by Bryant to have been founded by Egyptians, and was, according to Pausanias, a mere hut covered with laurel and branches.

That temples of wood, in Greece, preceded those of stone, is certain; and considerable ingenuity has been exercised to prove that they were the types of the latter,—that each part of the stone building corresponds with and was copied from that previously constructed in wood. The greatest dissimilarity between the wood and stone buildings must have been in the space between the upright supports. It is scarcely to be supposed that where timber was to be obtained in good lengths and thicknesses, they would have placed the supports so near each other as we find in every example of a columnar temple of stone: further, it is not probable that, however prodigal they might have been of their material, they would have placed their tie-beams so near each other, as must have been the case if the ends of them are to be compared to the triglyphs of the frieze. However, after the admission of this theory by so many writers on Architecture, it would be profitless to wander from the path they have trodden, and would occupy more space than we can give to the subject.

It is still a matter of conjecture in what city the first Grecian Doric temple was erected; but we are informed by Vitruvius that Dorus, the son of Hellen, reigned over Achaia and Peloponnesus, and that he built a temple of the Doric Order on a spot sacred to Juno, in the ancient city of Argos, 1200 years

* *Vide* Numbers xxiii. 14. Strabo informs us that the Persians always performed their worship upon the hills.

before Christ. Many temples similar to it were afterwards raised in the other parts of Achaia.

There exists no doubt but that the temples in Asia Minor were far in advance, in an architectural point of view, of those in Greece Proper, and that the art of erecting substantial structures was derived directly or indirectly from the Egyptians, as many of their religious rites and ceremonies were similar to those of Egypt.* The columns in front of a tomb at Beni-hassen, in Egypt, bear a strong resemblance to the Doric column; they have twenty shallow flutes, and a simple abacus, without any base or plinth. The date is supposed to be 1740 B. C. The Dorians, Æolians, Achæans, and Ionians (descendants of Hellen), are said to have acquired considerable knowledge of the arts and sciences, which they must have derived from the surrounding nations, and afterwards imparted to the Grecian states from whom they originated. From the buildings that were raised by these tribes were taken the two Grecian Orders of Architecture, viz. the Doric and the Ionic, which have been called after their originators, and by them introduced into the other Grecian states. Architecture, as well as all the other arts, could only be carried to perfection by very slow steps, and many changes and improvements must have taken place in their temples before they could have arrived at that beauty of proportion and excellence of design which are evinced in the works of the time of Pericles (about 460 B. C.).

History furnishes us with few means of ascertaining the progress and condition of the Fine Arts among the Greeks between the period commonly assigned to the siege of Troy (1180 B.C.) and that of the time of Solon and Pisistratus, 594 B.C. One of the earliest temples of the Greeks, that of Jupiter at Olympia, must, according to Pausanias, have been built about 630 years before the Christian era; that of Diana at Ephesus was begun at a period a little less remote. After this time

* Cadmus, son of Agenor, King of Phœnicia, who is supposed to have lived 1530 B. C., is said to have instructed the Greeks in the worship of the Egyptian and Phœnician deities, and to have taught them various useful arts.

temples were reared at Samos, Priene, Magnesia, and other places, up to that age when, under the administration of Pericles, the Architecture of Greece attained perfection; and the highest beauty whereof it is supposed to be susceptible was displayed in the Parthenon at Athens.*

Notwithstanding the magnitude of these works, the science of Mechanics was in its infancy, and the Greeks bestowed but little attention on their private houses: all the splendour and magnificence of art was reserved for the embellishment of their temples and other public buildings.†

The most splendid period of the Grecian history was between the sixth and fourth centuries before the Christian era, during the time of the wars that were carried on between the Persians and the principal states of Greece, and to which the greatest prosperity of the Athenians may be attributed: literature was cultivated, and the arts of architecture and sculpture, which were employed to ornament the city, were carried to a degree of excellence that has never been surpassed. Greece was conquered by the Romans 146 B. C., and became a Roman province, although Athens and Delphi were declared as free towns. Its history from this period is without interest to us in our inquiry into the progress of art. It was overrun by the Goths in 267 A. D., and again in 398 A. D. under Alaric; and after being occupied by the Crusaders and Venetians, at last fell into the power of the Turks, on the conquest of Constantinople.‡

* This temple, dedicated to Minerva, was built by Ictinus, under the direction of Phidias, who enjoyed the most exalted reputation, and executed the unrivalled sculpture which adorned it.

† One remark may not be out of place here, which will explain the mode of deciding on the date of the temples, viz. that in the earliest the diameter of the columns was greater in proportion to their height, and the intercolumniations were less, than those of a later period.

‡ We have been compelled to go into the general history of the nations in which Architecture has originated, as it is nearly impossible to give the history of one without the other. An improvement in art has invariably been caused by some great change in the policy or religion of nations.

CHAPTER III.

ROMAN ARCHITECTURE.

THE Architecture of the Romans can scarcely be said to be original; it was unquestionably borrowed from the Etruscans. Etruria, a city of Italy now called Tuscany, is supposed to have been a colony of Greece. This opinion has been formed by the great solidity of the walls that surround their cities, consisting of enormous blocks of stone, similar to the masonry of the Cyclopes, and said to be coeval with the walls of Tiryns, Mycenæ, and other works of a very early age. The instruction in the art of building that the Romans received from the Etruscans was not probably before the time of the Tarquins, 540 B. C., when their edifices began to be constructed on fixed principles. The first Tarquin, who was a native of Etruria, did much towards the improvement of Rome, and brought from his native country a taste for that grandeur and solidity which prevailed in the Etruscan works. Under his reign the city was fortified, and the walls built of hewn stone. The reign of the second Tarquin was distinguished by the erection of temples, schools for both sexes, and halls for the administration of justice; this was about 508 B. C.: but to Tarquinius Superbus, the seventh and last king, Rome was indebted for its greatest improvements; he continued the building of the temple of Jupiter Capitolinus, finished the Circus and other public buildings, and made a regular drainage of the city to the Tiber.*

It will be impossible to trace the Architecture of the Romans through its various stages between the time of the last king, 508 B. C., and the subjugation of Greece by that people in 145 B. C., a period of 363 years. The disputes in which they were continually engaged left little leisure for the arts of peace.

---

* The cloacæ, or sewers, which extended under the whole of Rome, were a work on which time and expense were not spared; they were of wrought stone, and in height and breadth were so considerable that a cart loaded with hay could pass through them. How insignificant must our own drainage appear in comparison with this stupendous work!

During the time that Appius Claudius was Censor, about 309 B. C., the earliest paved road was made by the Romans: it was first carried to Capua, and afterwards continued to a length altogether of 350 miles: it was paved with the hardest stone, and it remains entire at the present day. To Appius Claudius belongs the honour of raising the first aqueduct: the water with which it supplied the city was collected from the neighbourhood of Frascati, about 100 feet above the level of Rome.

The materials for carrying on a continuous investigation of the styles of the Roman buildings are so scanty, (as in the case of Grecian Architecture, without examples whereon we can reason,) that we will not detain the reader with useless speculations, but at once proceed to that period when Greece was reduced to a Roman province, 145 B. C. Art, in the strict application of that word, was not properly understood by the victorious Romans at this time; but after a succession of triumphant wars, when immense treasure was brought to Rome, and they wished to celebrate their victories, there became a necessity for erections to record them, and the riches that were amassed were expended in the adornment of Rome.

The Greek Architects who settled in Italy executed works of great beauty; they founded a school of art, and modified that which was practised in their own country, to suit the habits, taste, and climate of the Romans. The Romans were at all times anxious to subjugate, for their own purposes, those nations that successfully cultivated the arts; a motive which, joined to the desire of aggrandizement, induced them at a very early period to carry their arms against the Etruscans, who were in a far higher state of civilization than themselves. We find that they drew supplies of artists from Sicily, Asia Minor, and Greece, instead of employing their own citizens. Although, in Rome, Architecture lost its simplicity, it gained in magnificence: it there took a deeper root than the other arts, from its affording, by the dimensions of its monuments, more splendour to the character of so dominating a nation.

The first effort of Architecture was shown in the temple reared to Minerva at Rome, by Pompey the Great, about 60 years B. C. The villas of the Romans were at this period of considerable extent: the statues of Greece had been required for their decoration, besides a plentiful supply of all that Greek art afforded. We find that Cicero was in the habit of employing two Greek architects, Chrysippus and Cluatius, on his buildings.

The first permanent theatre that existed in Rome was built by Pompey, 54 B. C., and was capable of containing 40,000 persons.

In the time of Augustus (from 30 B. C. to 14 A. D.) we find that the Italian buildings attained a point of magnificence far beyond all that preceded. The conquest of nearly the whole of the then known world, added to a general peace, allowed the sovereign to turn his thoughts to the improvement of his country ; and a constellation of illustrious philosophers and poets, who shone at this time in the metropolis of the empire, gave the minds of the people an inclination towards subjects more useful and honourable than the conquest of remote and unoffending nations. The patronage of literature with the fine arts by Augustus produced the most brilliant results, and has caused a veneration for the age in which he lived. The perfection which literature and architecture attained during his dominion effected more towards immortalizing Rome than all the conquests of its emperors, and raised its inhabitants to a state of civilization never before equalled. By him was erected the temple and forum of Mars the Avenger, the theatre of Marcellus, and a large number of other public buildings. His boast was not a vain one, when he asserted that he found his capital built of brick, and he left it of marble.

Nero was the next emperor (with the exception of Claudius*) who seemed to have given his attention to Architecture, but his buildings must be considered more as monuments of

* During the reign of Claudius, one of the finest aqueducts of Rome was completed, whose length is 46 miles, and the water passes over arches

his prodigality and expenditure than of correct taste. A palace was erected for him, than which nothing could be more gorgeous, nor could the pomp of decoration be carried further.

The reigns of Vespasian and Titus are justly celebrated by the erection of baths and amphitheatres of such magnitude as to astonish the world, and to which nothing of their kind, either before or since, will bear comparison. The Coliseum, so named from its gigantic dimensions, was commenced and finished by Vespasian and Titus: it was capable of containing 109,000 spectators, who could view the sports and combats in the arena. The baths of Titus were among the wonders of the age; but their remains are not so perfect as those of others, although they are still majestic.* The temple of Peace, the largest covered building of antiquity, and another temple dedicated to Minerva, of the richest and most exquisite workmanship, were erected at this time, from 70 to 81 A. D.

To give a further description of the buildings of ancient Rome would be unnecessary, as our object is only to treat of the history of the Styles of Architecture, to show the periods at which they attained their greatest excellence, and to trace, as far as possible, the connection of one with the other. We therefore pass over the reigns of Trajan and Hadrian, celebrated for some fine architectural works, and proceed to the styles that sprung up, on the decline of the empire, among those nations who borrowed their first principles of art from the Romans. For a description of the Roman Orders, with remarks on their application to our present buildings, the reader is referred to the Treatise on 'Ancient and Classical Architecture,' by W. H. Leeds, Esq., published as the sixteenth volume of this series.

---

raised more than 100 feet from the surface of the ground for nearly 10 miles of it.

* The baths of Diocletian, erected 294 A. D., were of great extent and magnificence, and are in a better state of preservation than those of Titus.

CHAPTER IV.

BYZANTINE AND ROMANESQUE ARCHITECTURE.

FROM the time of Hadrian, 117 A. D., to that of Constantine, 306, a general decline in the Arts took place, which, however, seemed to revive during the reign of the latter emperor.

The Christians at Rome, who, during the time of Diocletian, had borne persecution and the destruction of their religious buildings, were now permitted openly to avow their creed.

In 324, Constantine, who, if he had not embraced Christianity, was favourable to its followers, extended his laws, and ordered that the churches which had been demolished during the former reigns should be rebuilt, and the property of the church restored; he exempted the Christian clergy from personal taxes, and granted donations and privileges to the churches.*

The Christian religion may be said to have rendered the most essential service to the Arts, and contributed to the revival of the genius of the artists, after a period of barbarism, by the preservation of many remains of Ancient Architecture,

---

* By an edict of March, 321, he ordered the observance of the Sunday and abstinence from work on that day: he published an edict addressed to all the subjects of the empire, in which he exhorted them to renounce the old superstitions, and to adore only one God, the Saviour of the Christians. In 313 A. D. he abolished the punishment of the cross, which had existed until then.

In 325 he assembled and attended in person the first universal council of Niceæa, the object of which was to oppose the Arian heresy, then gaining ground in the East, although in 328 he recalled several Arian bishops who had been exiled by the council. This change is said to have happened at the instigation of Constantia, his sister, who was herself in the Arian communion.

Athanasius, Bishop of Alexandria, opposed the re-admission of the Arians into the orthodox church, which led to a controversy between him and the Emperor, which lasted until the death of the latter, 337 A. D

which became embodied in the buildings they erected for religious purposes.

The style of building employed by the Christians in the churches they erected, during the time of Constantine and his immediate successors, would necessarily resemble that of the basilicæ themselves; for the materials employed must have influenced the design, and columns taken from other buildings could only be applied in a manner somewhat similar to that in which they had been previously used.

The basilicæ, or halls of justice of the ancient Romans, were undoubtedly the types from which the early Christian places of worship were taken; and the ruins of these buildings were the chief materials used. In several instances the columns that divide the centre part of the church from the aisles have been taken from other edifices, either on account of the want of artists capable of executing anything equal to them, or the haste with which they were erected.

The expedient that was adopted tends to show that proportion was not considered; some columns were reduced from their former height, and others mounted on pedestals to suit the purposes to which they were applied. Besides this total disregard to proportion in the shafts of the columns, capitals and bases were applied without any consideration to their fitness. In addition to the reasons we have given for these inconsistencies, another probably may be added, viz. want of means, which might well be the case, when we see the state to which the Christians at Rome were reduced prior to their emancipation by Constantine.

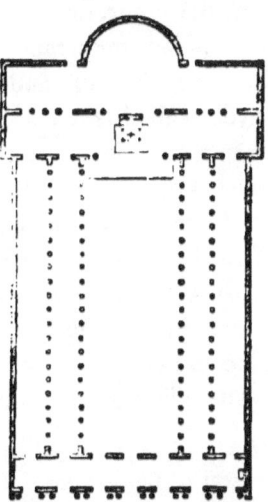

Plan of the Basilica of St. Paul's, without the walls.

The heathen basilicæ, generally situated in the forums, were of rectangular form, and divided into three or five parts by rows of columns parallel to the length of the building; another colonnade at the extremity crossed the former at right angles, and in the middle of the end wall was a semicircular recess, in which was situated the tribune of the judge. These basilicæ had likewise galleries over the aisles, in which commercial or other business was transacted; but in the Christian churches this was appropriated to the women, who (as in the Jewish synagogues) were not allowed to join with the men in the lower parts of the building. These galleries were omitted in the after basilicæ, and one of the aisles was retained solely for their use.*

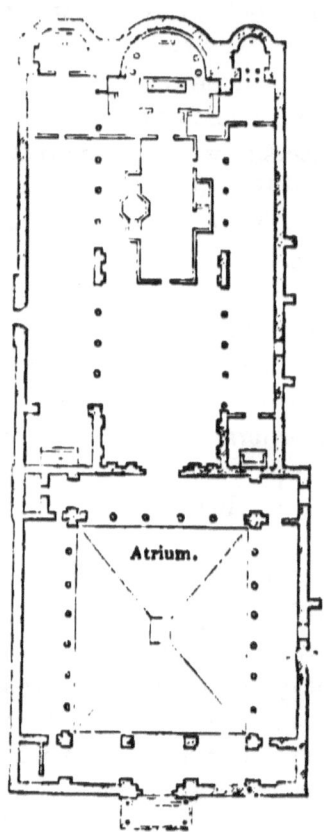

Plan of St. Clement's.

The basilica of St. Clement at Rome demands our attention from its antiquity and the peculiar character of some parts of its plan. It is stated to have been built on the very spot formerly occupied by the house of St. Clement, the immediate successor of St. Peter. It acquired importance under Leo the Great in 449, and was afterwards embellished by John II. During the eighth and ninth centuries, Popes Adrian I. and Nicholas I. restored this basilica. In 1112 the church was repaired by Cardinal Anastasius, by whose orders the mosaics and the marble episcopal chair were added.

The plan of this building re-

* Six of the principal churches or basilicæ at Rome are attributed to the zeal of Constantine. The basilicæ of St. John de Lateran, St. Peter, St. Laurentius, St. Paul, St. Agnes, and St. Stephen, were built by him, besides the baptisterium that bears his name.

sembles, more particularly than any others, that of the earliest basilicæ. It is entered by a court, which is surrounded by porticoes supported by columns and piers; on the sides parallel to the front of the church arches spring from the columns, but on the others there are only architraves. Under the portico nearest the temple were placed the holy water vases, for the purpose of purification, (a custom taken from the Jewish and Pagan rites,) until in after-times they were removed into the body of the church, near the western door. Here, like-wise, the penitents, and those who were not permitted to share in the holy sacrifice, used to remain during its performance.

The centre part of the atrium or court was used for the pur-pose of burial after the custom of interring 'extra muros' fell into disuse. Some remains of ancient sculpture tend to a belief that the atrium was at an early period used for this purpose.

The sanctuary of this church, as in all the Christian temples of the first ages, is semicircular in plan, and contains the altar, the cathedra, or throne for the bishop, and exedræ, or benches for the priests. It is surmounted by a half-cupola, the front of which is richly ornamented with marble and paintings, representing our Saviour, the Apostles, and the emblems of the Evangelists. The cupola is covered with paintings of foliage on a gold ground; the remainder of this semicircular part, known by the name of 'apsis,' is richly ornamented with figures of the Saints. On each side of the great apsis were secondary apsides, which are now used as chapels, although in the primitive church they were appropriated to a different purpose. One of them was called the vestiarium, and contained the priests' robes and the consecrated vessels, and was the origin of our vestries; the other, the evangelium, received the sacred books, charters, &c., and gave rise to charter-houses and libraries.

This ancient arrangement still exists among the Greeks. In the church of San Dimitri at Smyrna there are two apsides, closed by curtains only, devoted to these purposes.

The chancel, which was used by the inferior order of acclesiastics, and contained the pulpits and ambones, is situated in front of the apsis, and enclosed by a low partition of marble: it is raised one step from the level of the church. The floor is decorated with mosaics, composed of a combination of various sorts of precious marbles and porphyry.

The arrangement of this basilica is nearly the same as all that followed it, although in later examples sculpture, painting, and mosaics were much introduced to decorate the walls above the side arches, as well as those of the aisles.

The women here were placed in the north aisle, the men in the south aisle,* and the centre part or nave was reserved for processions.

About the year 328 A. D., Constantine, who had hitherto, when at peace, resided at Rome, commenced his new capital in the East, which was called after his name, and in May, 330, was solemnly dedicated to the Virgin Mary. He adorned it with so many stately edifices that it nearly equalled the ancient capital itself; he here built a cathedral dedicated to Santa Sophia or the Eternal Wisdom, and a church to the Apostles.† This cathedral, having been twice destroyed by fire, was finally rebuilt about 532 A. D., by Justinian, who had invited the celebrated architect Anthemius to Constantinople for that purpose. It was completed in six years from the time of laying the first stone.

The emperor, in his admiration of this magnificent edifice, is said to have exclaimed, "I have vanquished thee, O Solomon :" and with justice might he glorify himself; for the dome of St. Sophia is the largest in the world, and the more

---

* This observance is still retained in many churches in Greece, by partitions between the columns with curtains hanging above them, so as to intercept all communication between the sexes.

† Helena, the mother of Constantine, caused several churches to be erected in the East; the most celebrated was that of the Holy Sepulchre, at Jerusalem. The Church of the Nativity, at Bethlehem, supposed to have been erected on the site where our Saviour was born, has been likewise attributed to her.

to be admired in its construction from the lowness of the curvature.

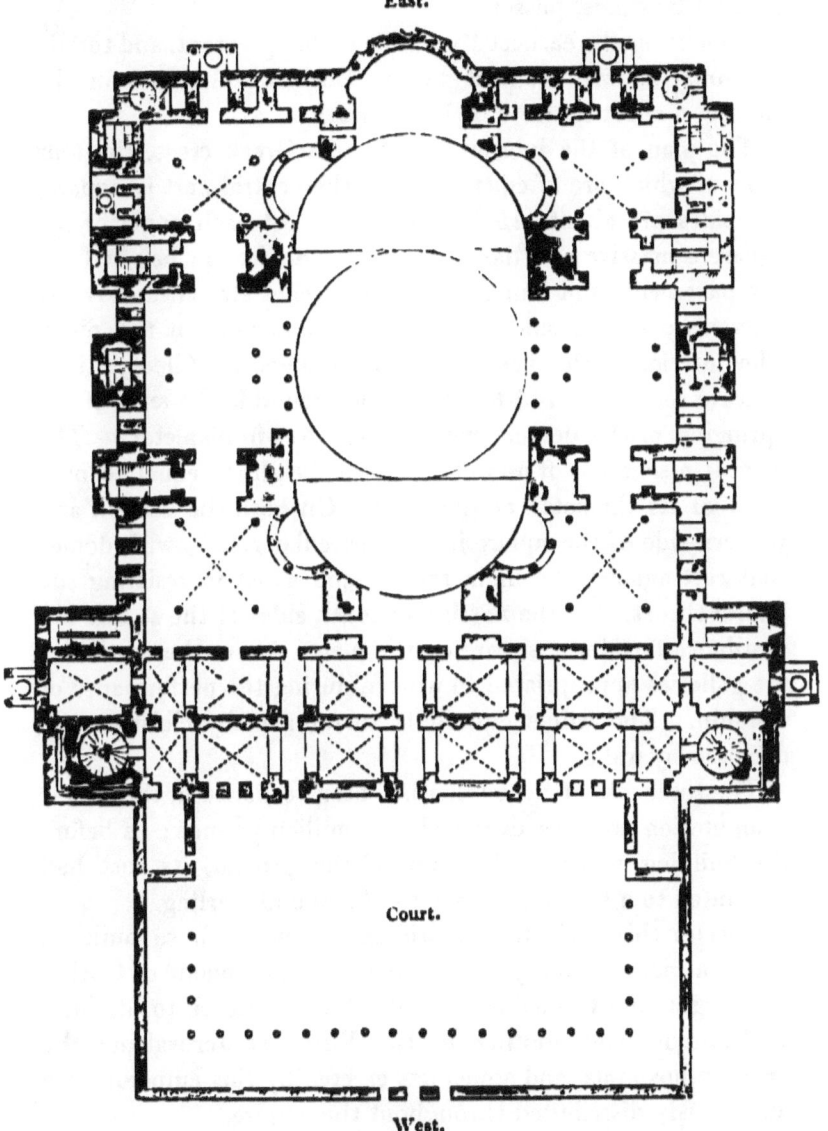

East.

West.

St. Sophia.

This church, after twelve centuries, remains the same, with

the exception of the mode of worship to which it is devoted. It still retains its former name, but the Mohammedans, instead of the Christians, possess it.

This being the earliest Byzantine building extant, and totally dissimilar in arrangement to the Christian churches in the empire, a short notice of it is necessary.

The plan of the interior is that of a Greek cross, the four arms of which are of equal length ; the central part is square, the sides are about 115 feet in length. At each angle of the square a massive pier has been carried 86 feet in height from the pavement, and four semicircular arches stretch across the intervals over the sides of the square and rest on the piers The interior angles between the four piers are filled up in a concave form. At 145 feet from the ground is the level of the springing of the dome,* which is 115 feet in diameter. The form is a segment of a circle, and the height is equal to one-sixth of its diameter at the base. On both the eastern and western side of the square is a semicircular recess, with domes that rest against the main arches, and assist in resisting the lateral thrust. On the north and south sides of the square are vestibules forming a square on the plan. Above the vestibules are galleries appropriated to women during the performance of worship. The whole church is surrounded by cloisters and enclosed by walls.

The total cost of St. Sophia has been reckoned at the lowest computation to have exceeded one million pounds; as before the building was four feet out of the ground, its cost had amounted to a sum equivalent to £200,000 sterling.

Besides this cathedral, Justinian is said to have built, at Constantinople, twenty-five churches to the honour of Christ, the Virgin, and the Saints; he also built a church to St. John at Ephesus, and another to the Virgin at Jerusalem : the bridges, hospitals, and aqueducts erected by this emperor were numerously distributed throughout the empire.

* This dome is constructed of pumice-stone and very light bricks from the isle of Rhodes.

To give a connected description of the architecture between the sixth and eighth centuries would be as difficult as unsatisfactory; the irruptions of the Goths and other nations caused a division of the empire. Those who settled in various cities in Italy, erected buildings partaking of the Roman character, yet possessing both novelty of arrangement and purpose.

One of the most interesting churches of the Byzantine or Romanesque style is that of St. Vital at Ravenna,* built by Justinian, when he expelled the Goths from Italy: this church is much embellished with mosaics.

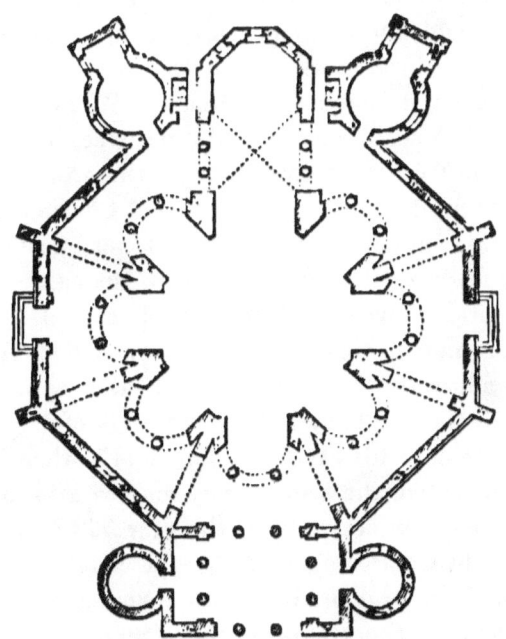

Plan of St. Vital at Ravenna.

* The Goths, after the conquest of Italy, established the seat of their power at Ravenna. Theodoric, one of their kings, and a lover of the arts, restored its ancient edifices; and numerous altars were erected for the religion he had embraced.

The striking similarity between the plan of St. Vital and that of the churches of St. Sophia and Sergius is sufficient to induce the supposition that its founders employed architects from Constantinople. The plan is an octagon, to which several round towers and a semicircular apsis are added. One great peculiarity, which shows a deviation from the Roman work, is seen in the double window, having a column in the centre, from which spring two semicircular arches forming the heads to both openings, which are encircled by another arch extending across the whole width of the window.*

Whatever may be said against the Goths for the manner in which those large hordes overran Italy, and caused a change in its policy, yet it would be most unjust to consider them as a people who could not appreciate art, simply because some of the fine architectural works were destroyed in the excesses that succeeded the conquest of Rome. When Rome was in possession of Odoacer, chief of a Gothic tribe, in 476, he exerted his utmost for the preservation of the arts. Theodoric, his successor in 493, who was educated at Constantinople and established his residence chiefly at Ravenna, passed laws to prevent the neglect of, or depredations of the citizens of Rome upon, the works of art still existing in the capital. Under his reign, Rome and Ravenna, as well as many of the Italian cities, were adorned by the erection of churches, palaces, porticoes, aqueducts, and baths. The successors of Theodoric did not, however, follow his example ; for in 547, when Rome was plundered by Totila, the arts in Italy may be said to have become completely extinct. From the year 568 up to the conquest of Italy by Charlemagne in 774, the country was overrun by the Lombards, who brought with them no style of their own, but employed the architects they found in Italy. From 774 to 813, Charlemagne caused to be erected, in different parts of his extensive dominions, many grand buildings dedicated to Christianity.

* This indicates a great feature in the style which in a few centuries was distributed throughout the northern parts of Europe.

Among others, we may mention the cathedral of Aix-la-Chapelle in Germany, which the marbles brought from Ravenna and Rome served to decorate. The portico of another of his churches exists at Lorsch, near Worms, in Germany. In France, all the churches of that period have been subsequently rebuilt, and it is impossible to determine with certainty if any parts remain in their original state.

We now arrive at a period when the dominion of Charlemagne extended from Italy to the Baltic. He established cities in different parts of Germany and France, and naturally carried the architecture of Italy to the northern parts of Europe, which in the general outline conformed to the Italian models, although the details might have varied considerably.

In consequence of the intercourse which still subsisted between Italy and Greece after the fall of the Western Empire, the natives of Greece are supposed to have been employed to construct the ecclesiastical edifices of the former. Thus in the ninth, tenth, and eleventh centuries the cathedrals of Venice and Pisa, as well as that at Ravenna, were built.

The most important of the Italian churches built in the Constantinopolitan or Byzantine style is the cathedral of St. Mark at Venice, which is said to have been erected in the ninth century by a Greek artist. Its plan is that of a Greek cross, and each arm is roofed with a semicircular vault ; these terminate against four semicircular arches on the sides of a square, about 42 feet long ; above this is a circle, containing a row of windows which light the interior ; and on this is raised the central or principal dome, which is of a hemispherical form. The church is divided longitudinally and transversely by rows of columns supporting semicircular arches. Over each of the arms of the cross are domes of equal size, but rather smaller than that in the centre. The exteriors of these domes are covered with lead, and surmounted by crosses. This building has undergone many alterations since its original construction, and the ornaments are of a much later date than the rest of the edifice. The plans of this church and of St. Sophia are very similar.

Before we turn to the churches of the northern parts of Europe, we must notice the buildings of Pisa, in Italy, which retain the distinguishing features of the Byzantine and Roma-nesque styles : they consist of the cathedral, built in 1016 by Baschetto ; the baptistery, in 1152, by Dioti Salvi ; and the campanile or belfry, which was built in 1174 by two architects, a German and an Italian,—William of Inspruck, and Bonnani of Pisa.

The cathedral of Pisa, with the baptistery and belfry belong-ing to it, form a group of buildings to which as much interest is attached as to any in Italy. The cathedral in plan resem-bles the Latin cross, which differs from the Greek in having one of its arms longer than the other three : this is one of the oldest of the Christian churches of this form, which has been followed in all the cathedrals of the north-western part of Europe.* The length is 304 feet, and the width 107 ; the transverse branch is 234 feet by 55 feet in width.

The plan is divided longitudinally into five parts ; the nave is 40 feet broad, and 128 feet in height ; this is separated from the aisles by twelve Corinthian columns, of oriental granite, on each side : from the capitals spring semicircular arches, which carry smaller columns, forming the front of an upper gallery, appropriated to women. The columns that separate the aisles are smaller than those of the nave, but are raised on pedestals to an equal height. The nave is roofed with timber, but the aisles are vaulted and painted.

The western façade consists of five stories : the lower one is composed of seven arches, supported by Corinthian columns and two pilasters ; under three of these arches are the entrance doors : the second tier contains nineteen arches ; the third has nine arches in the centre of equal height, but on each side they diminish in height, following the *slope* of the roof of the aisles :

* The cathedral at Worms, built in 1016, is similar in this respect.

above this is another row of columns and arches of equal height, surmounted by columns and arches diminishing with the inclination of the roof of the nave. The arches and columns in the lowest tier are attached to the wall, and all above are detached from it, and have a narrow open gallery in their rear. This arrangement of arcades in the façades is a feature peculiar to churches of this date in Italy, and was partially copied in other parts of Europe.

The baptistery, close to the cathedral, is a cylindrical building of marble : it is 100 feet in diameter within the walls, which are 8 feet 6 inches thick. On the exterior are two orders of Corinthian columns, supporting semicircular arches; the columns of the upper order are less in height than the lower, each intercolumniation below being equal to three above it. These smaller arches are finished by pediments and pinnacles.* From this springs the dome, divided by twelve ribs, between which are small dormer windows; the cupola rises above this in similar divisions. The total height is 179 feet. The dome is double, and built of brick; the inner one being pedimental, resting on granite columns and piers, and supporting the cupola, which is covered with lead and tiles.

The campanile or bell-tower, likewise near the cathedral, is of a cylindrical form, 50 feet in diameter, and 180 feet high. This consists of eight tiers of columns, supporting semicircular arches, forming open galleries : the roof is flat, and the upper story contains some bells. A remarkable circumstance in this tower is, that the top overhangs the base upwards of 13 feet. This peculiarity is observable in several other Italian belfries, and has doubtless resulted from defective foundations. In this instance we have conclusive evidence that the failure exhibited itself before the building was completed; for on one side the columns are higher than on the other, thus showing that the builders endeavoured to bring the upper part of the tower

---

* The pediments and pinnacles are supposed to have been introduced subsequently to the original construction of the edifice.

nearer to a vertical direction, or at least to lessen the inclination of that which deviated from its horizontal position.

Having now given a general description of the peculiarities of the churches of Italy which appear to have been the work of Greek artists, similar in arrangement and mode of execution to the Byzantine churches of the East, as well as of those that are specimens of the Lombardic style, we will now proceed with a few observations on the ecclesiastical buildings of Germany, France, and Normandy, which were the direct sources from which the architecture in our own country proceeded.

CHAPTER V.

THE ARCHITECTURE OF GERMANY, FRANCE, AND NORMANDY.

THE difficulties attendant on the historical part of our present inquiry are such as to hinder our taking a chronological survey of the different variations of styles of architecture that prevailed in different parts of the Continent up to the twelfth century. The poverty and indistinctness of the notices of the erection of early buildings, — the difficulty of identifying those described with those that exist, — the confusion of works protracted, suspended, and built in imitation of others, which was frequently the case, or in accommodation to them, — would tend, if they were properly examined, to make this part of our inquiry too lengthy; and after every care, very unsatisfactory conclusions would be arrived at. We therefore confine ourselves to notices of such buildings as bear upon our purpose, or which may have some peculiarity of character.

The edifices erected for the purposes of religion are nearly the only records of architecture that have been spared to us; other buildings were demolished in the course of events, but the sacredness of their intent preserved them from the hand of the destroyer, when idolatry had ceased to exist, and the Christian worship was practised throughout Europe.

Germany lays claim to churches of antiquity, superior to those of any other country on this side of the Alps: those existing of the tenth and eleventh centuries are very important in the history of art, and testify extraordinary solidity and magnificence. Such are the churches of Spire, Mentz, and Worms. That of Spire was founded by Conrad II., in 1030; the east end of that at Worms, still earlier, was commenced in 996, and the building was consecrated in 1016: the oldest part of the cathedral of Mentz is said to be of the date of Archbishop Willigris, between 978 and 1009.

One of the most instructive as well as the most ancient of these churches is that at Worms, now in a very perfect state of preservation. The plan is strongly distinguished by the cross: the piers separating the nave from the aisles are square, with columns at alternate piers, to carry the stone vaulting, which embraces two compartments of the lateral arches between each groin or rib. The east end is square on the face externally, but semicircular inside; thus retaining one of the principal features of the Romanesque basilicæ. On each side are circular turrets containing staircases, and corresponding with two at the west end, although of somewhat larger dimensions. The entrances are in the north and south sides, and nearer the transepts than the west end. This arrangement is quite at variance with all preceding buildings; as instead of the three doorways at the west front, there is an apsis of the form of three sides of an octagon, which is used as a chapel. At the intersection of the nave and transepts springs an octagonal tower, which is scarcely higher than the nave roof, and covered with a cupola: the turrets are carried to a great height, and terminate conically. This church, as well as those of the same date, is vaulted with stone throughout, which caused the introduction of the shaft on the face of the piers, and is one great deviation from the arrangement of the Roman basilicæ, which were covered with horizontal ceilings; or else the wooden roofs were left exposed, which rested on the walls, without having any relation vertically to the substructure.

The church of St. Castor at Coblentz, part of which was built in the eleventh century, is likewise executed with semi-circular arches, which spring from square piers, to each face of which a half-column is attached. This may be considered as one of the steps leading towards the clustered columns, which gradually were introduced in the naves of all churches throughout the western part of Europe.

The early German churches, although differing considerably from each other in their general plan, still retain peculiarities that are not to be seen in those of other countries, though erected about the same period, or rather later. The octagonal form of the aspides and turrets, and their enrichments generally retaining a primitive character, make their Lombardic origin perceptible. The square piers which support the nave arches evince a direct departure from their Italian types; there is likewise a prevalence of rectangular faces and square-edged projections. This general simplicity may be well accounted for, when we consider that the chief impressions were received from Romanesque examples, which were simplified from necessity; as there was great deficiency in knowledge of art, although no inferiority in mechanical skill.

In the cathedral of Worms we find the pointed arch, which was not introduced generally until a century after the erection of that building; therefore if this was not added subsequently, it confutes many of the theories as to the causes and dates of its introduction.

The church of Gelnhausen, in Suabia, which was built in the beginning of the thirteenth century, is one of the earliest German churches in which a positive change of style is perceptible throughout; although in many of those of the eleventh and twelfth centuries there exist deviations from the unity of the designs which are difficult to be accounted for.

The heads of the windows, instead of being semicircular, are of the lancet form, with cusps, and differ from the proportions before adopted by being long and narrow. The arches and windows in the nave have trefoiled heads, and the windows of the central tower possess a marked distinction from the earlier arrangements, having the three apertures with trefoils inscribed in a semicircular top, and separated by mullions.

The church of St. Catherine at Oppenheim, commenced in 1262, resembles in plan that of Worms, being in the form of a Latin cross, and having semi-octagonal chancels at the east and west ends. The latter is of a subsequent date, and was not consecrated before 1439. This peculiarity is observable in several other churches in Germany: the entrances are on the north and south sides.

The cathedral of Strasburg, which was begun in 1277, and brought to its present state in 1439, holds the first rank among the Gothic churches of the Continent, in point of the high degree of enrichment which prevails throughout. The length of the body of the church is 324 feet, and the height of the nave vault is 98 feet. The western façade is divided into three parts, vertically, by buttresses richly ornamented with canopies and statues. The three entrances are crowned by crocketed gables, and the diverging sides of the doorways are completely filled with niches and statues.

This cathedral has but one of its spires completed, which is at the north-west angle: it is perforated in the richest manner, and in height it exceeds any other church in Europe, being 414 feet from the ground.

Before we bring our view of the architecture of Germany to a close, we must not omit to notice the cathedral of Cologne, which, if it had been completed, would have been the most magnificent and exquisitely ornamented ecclesiastical building ever erected. The plan exhibits a symmetry not surpassed by any of the works of the best days of Greece or Rome: it consists of the nave and two aisles on

each side, and two western towers; the eastern end is com
posed of seven engaged chapels.   Charlemagne erected *
church on the present site, which was destroyed by fire in
1248.   Conrad, who filled the archiepiscopal throne of the
city at this time, resolved on the erection of a new church;
and on the 14th of August in the year following the destruction of the old edifice, laid the first stone of the new fabric
with every possible solemnity.

The magnitude of Conrad's intention, or rather of Gerard's
design, may be arrived at by a consideration of its general
dimensions.   The whole length is upwards of 500 feet; the
width of the aisles, 180 feet; the width across the transepts,
290 feet: the roofs are more than 210 feet in height; and the
height of the western towers, when finished, would have
exceeded 500 feet; they are 100 feet wide at the base.   For
carrying out this extensive design, collections were made
throughout Europe; and nearly the whole wealth of Cologne
itself was applied to make this the finest building in the
world.   Notwithstanding the large sums of money that were
raised, and all the industry and activity of a large number of
workmen, this gigantic structure could only proceed slowly,
as all the stone was wrought, and had to be conveyed from
Kœnigswainter and Unckel-Bruch, on the Rhine.   The foundations alone of the southern tower were laid at least 44 feet
below the surface.

The unprofitable wars of the bishops of Cologne tended
to dissipate their treasures; and although the works were
not interrupted, they made but little progress.   In the year
1322, seventy-four years after the first stone was laid, the
choir was consecrated.   The zeal of those who contributed was
much damped by the misappropriation of the funds; for about
1370, little activity seems to have been evinced on the works,
as the nave and southern tower were only a few feet above the
ground.   In 1437, Thiery de Moers carried up the latter to
the third story.   In the early part of the sixteenth century, the
nave was brought up to the capitals of the aisles, the northern

tower carried up to a corresponding height; and after the windows on the north aisle had been ornamented with painted glass, the works stopped altogether.

That this work of genius and art should have remained three centuries without anything having been done, except for its preservation, must be a matter of deep regret to all who feel an interest in architecture; and more particularly so as the suspension of its works was caused by civil discords, which diverted the funds that ought to have been applied to it. But there is one other cause to which its non-completion is to be attributed: the style in which it was designed was passing away; new ideas of art prevailed, owing to the revival of the Italian styles; and the love of variety and change alone produced a distaste for that style of art whose beauties could not be denied, although the sublimity of its origin and development was forgotten. Thus centuries have passed, and with apathy the civilized world has looked on this neglected building with a feeling of its being little more than a monument of something that was to have been, without any effort towards its completion.

The late King of Prussia, desirous for the continuance of this stupendous work, lent his aid in 1824, which, however liberal in amount, was small in comparison with the requirements for its completion. In ten years the expenditure was under £ 28,000, or about £ 2720 for each year, of which the greater part was consumed in keeping the building in repair: we have therefore but little hope of more than its preservation.

Another of the celebrated cathedrals of Germany is that at Ulm, commenced in 1377. Its length is 416 feet, its width 166 feet, and its height, including the thickness of the vaulting, 141 feet. The height of the tower, if it had been completed according to the original design, would have been 491 feet: it is placed in the centre of the western façade.

Ratisbon cathedral, which was built about 1480, possesses great claims on our admiration. The west front is flanked by two towers, and, like the former, left unfinished.

The greatest variety of forms, both in traceries and ornaments, prevails throughout most of the larger churches of Germany that were built in the later period of the Gothic era; and it is to be regretted that our limited space will not permit us to describe the peculiarities of this class of design and carving. Their interesting mouldings and ornaments are of the most florid nature, and totally dissimilar to anything that exists in our own country.

The buildings in France of the ninth and tenth centuries were, like those of Germany, in the Byzantine or Romanesque styles, and decorated with a profusion of mosaic and other ornamental work. These were undoubtedly copied from the basilican churches, or else from those erected by Charlemagne in Germany, where he first introduced the arts that he acquired in Italy. Nothing, however, remains of the churches prior to the eleventh century which would assist in our present inquiry, as no certain date can be assigned to portions of early buildings that still exist, and which possess little interest, except to the critical antiquary.

The invasions of France by the Normans, in the ninth and tenth centuries, caused the destruction of the greater part of the ecclesiastical buildings; and after that period we find a very similar style of architecture to have prevailed in both countries at nearly the same time, although presenting many variations, both in the general design and subordinate details.

On the termination of the ravages of the Northmen or Danes, under Rollo, in the early part of the tenth century, the Duchy of Normandy was ceded to him by the French king, whose daughter he married on condition of his embracing the Christian religion. Peace being now established between them, the French commenced rebuilding their churches, which was zealously followed by their converted neighbours. The influence of Christianity, or their settled position in their newly-acquired territory, induced a civilization which strongly contrasted with their previous piratical habits; and Normandy, both under Rollo and his successor William I., vied

with France in the erection of churches. The principles of
the architecture that prevailed in both countries were identical,
being modifications of the Lombardic styles, and were characterized by the general use of the semicircular forms in arches
or windows.

One of the earliest of the French churches that presents
any features that require our notice is that of St. Germain
des Prés, which was rebuilt by Abbot Morard, in 1014. The
nave of the church still remains in its primitive state; the
capitals of some of the columns possess much of the character
of the Corinthian order, whilst others are composed of birds
and griffins. In the churches of Normandy, more particularly
those of the Holy Trinity and St. Stephen at Caen, the capitals of the columns are direct imitations of the Corinthian
order, with the exception of the abaci, which are more massive: they have the volutes at the angles, and two rows of
solid leaves above the astragal.*

In the beginning of the eleventh century two of the greatest
ecclesiastical buildings of France were erected, viz. the cathedral of Chartres, and the abbey of Cluny. Both are cruciform
in plan: the first is 420 feet in length and 108 in breadth, and
on the east side of the choir the aisles are double. The abbey
church of Cluny, which is perhaps one of the most interesting
ecclesiastical monuments in France, was erected in 1056. The
style of these buildings is similar to that which prevailed
throughout Europe at nearly the same time, and is more familiar to us under the name of Norman.

The buildings in Normandy of the eleventh and twelfth
centuries are undeniably the models from which those in our
own country were copied; it will therefore only be necessary
to give one description of their peculiarities, which will be
included in our notes of the Anglo-Norman churches.

* The monastery and church of the Holy Trinity, or Abbaye aux
Dames, was founded by Queen Matilda, and consecrated in 1066. St.
Stephen's, or Abbaye aux Hommes, was founded by William the Conqueror in 1066, and dedicated in 1077. The upper parts of the towers
in the west front were built about 1200.

Towards the end of the twelfth century an important change took place in the architecture of the western parts of Europe, by the introduction of the pointed arch, which was substituted for the semicircular. Although the cause of this deviation has engaged the attention of many men whose whole time has been devoted to studying the history and practice of architecture, yet, hitherto, no definite conclusion has been arrived at. To describe fully the different hypotheses in which various writers have indulged, would be a matter of curiosity more than advantage, as many seem to result from an effort of imagination, rather than from a careful inquiry into probabilities.*

It has been supposed that the pointed arch is of Eastern extraction, and that it was introduced by the first crusaders on their return into the West.† This opinion is founded on the fact that arches of a pointed form exist in various parts of the

---

* Mr. Lascelles traces the origin of the pointed arch to the curves of Noah's ark; but from what he takes his authority that it was curved at all is somewhat puzzling. Murphy, the author of a work on the Batalha, is equally mystical in bestowing the parentage of it on the aspiring lines of the pyramids of Egypt. That it was derived from the forms of groves of trees and their branches, as another party asserts, becomes a probability in comparison.

† "Sir Christopher Wren was of opinion that what we now vulgarly call Gothic ought properly and truly to be named the Saracenic architecture refined by the Christians; which first of all began in the East, after the fall of the Greek empire." (Britton's 'Chronological History.') In refutation of this opinion, Dr. Milner asserts that the crusaders did not bring with them into England or Europe a single feature of that style, "since the churches built subsequent to that period do not, in their original works, exhibit one of the features; as, for example, the ancient parts of Exeter and Rochester cathedrals, and the abbey church of Reading. Gundulph, a monk of Bec abbey, afterwards Bishop of Rochester, was the most celebrated practical architect of the age in which he lived. He made a journey of devotion to the Holy Land, a little before the first crusade, and of course had an opportunity of surveying its buildings; yet in the various structures erected by him after his return, we find no traits of the style under consideration."—Milner's 'Treatise on Ecclesiastical Architecture,' and 'Vita Gundulphi.'

East, and some of these in buildings of great antiquity, such
as the tomb or chapel of the Virgin at Jerusalem, the remains
of a church at Acre, the tomb of Abdallah, and the hall of
Joseph at Cairo. In the façade of the first is a Gothic pointed
arch, springing from columns, and there are also two others
on the staircase in the interior. This edifice is supposed to
have been erected in the time of Constantine, but it is very
probable that the arches were constructed at a later period
than the body of the building. The antiquity of the church of
Acre ascends only to the time of the existence of the Saracenic
empire, and it was undoubtedly built by the Christians, whilst
in possession of that part of Syria; consequently the pointed
arch found in this erection is as likely to have been copied from
similar works executed in Europe before that time, as from any
building constructed by the Arabians.

It is to be remarked that the form of the pointed arch employed in the Saracenic works differs from that adopted in the
west of Europe, in being very slightly pointed, and the aper-
ture being narrower at the foot than a little above it. If,
therefore, we suppose that the pointed arch originated in the
East, it appears surprising that those who introduced it into
France and England should have so far altered its form as to
make it spring from the capitals of the columns which support
it, and that not one example should exist in this part of
Europe similar to those which are found in the Moorish
buildings. By this theory it is inferred that its introduction
into the West was solely a matter of taste, and not of necessity; but we have numerous instances, both in England and
France, which prove that the pointed style was not introduced
at once with all its distinctive features, but that pointed arches
were intermixed with those of semicircular form in the same
building, from constructive causes. This is the case in the
church of St. Germain des Prés, described by Mr. Whittington
(who advocates the Saracenic origin): "The columns support
a series of round arches, except in the semicircular arcade at
the eastern end, where they are pointed, in consequence of the

arrangement of the pillars, which are placed in the bow, nearer
to each other than where the colonnade proceeds in a straight
direction; and the arches rising from them, when brought to
an equal height with those of a round shape, become necessarily pointed." This is among the number of instances where
the pointed arch was used from accident or necessity. The
same arrangement occurs in the crypt of St. Denis, and also in
the chapel and crypt of the Holy Trinity at Canterbury.
There is one objection to the opinion that the pointed arch
originated from this circumstance, viz. that those which are so
employed appear to have been erected subsequently to its
introduction in some other manner; and that this method was
not generally adopted is certain, for in the Tower of London,
as well as in some foreign buildings, where there are wide and
narrow arches intermixed, the latter are not pointed, although
they are of equal height with the others.

The hypothesis of Dr. Milner, if not altogether satisfactory,
is entitled to our best consideration, provided the principle is
to be entertained that the form was originally a matter of
taste, uninfluenced by necessity. It is attributed by him to
the intersection of semicircular arches, which were frequently
introduced on the surface of the
walls in the Norman styles, but
placed there solely for ornament,
as in St. Botolph's, Colchester,
built in 1120; St. John's, Devizes,
in 1160, and in numerous other
churches. The former is built of
brick, and the latter has a flat

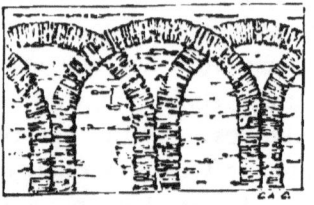
St. Botolph's, Colchester.

ziz-zag on the face. At Castle Acre priory, Bristol cathedral,
Croyland abbey, and St. Joseph's chapel at Glastonbury, the
transition of style is evident, as the mouldings do not altogether cross each other, but are stopped on the inside at the
apex; and if the upper part of the semicircle were taken away,
the pointed arch would be complete. At St. James's church,
Bristol, is one of the most convincing proofs of the correct-

Castle Acre Priory.

Bristol Cathedral.

St. James's Church, Bristol.

ness of Dr. Milner's theory, for within the interlacing mouldings there is a lancet window, the arch of which is struck from the same centres, and follows the inside lines: pointed arches are likewise found interlaced with those of semicircular form, as seen at St. James's, Bristol.

In the instances above referred to, these intersecting semicircular mouldings are not detached from the wall, and therefore must be looked upon rather as an ornamental than a constructive feature; but at Christ Church, Oxford, erected about 1180, there is an instance of an interlacing arcade, supported by columns entirely disengaged from the wall, and from its construction, as well as its form, may be considered as a transition between the semicircular and the pointed styles.

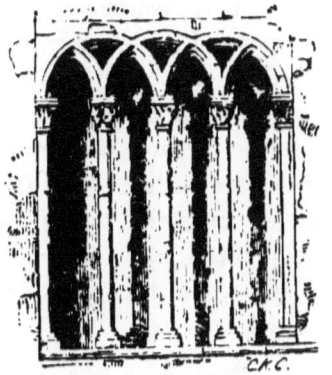

Christ Church, Oxford.

So numerous are instances of the use of the pointed in

close connection with
the semicircular form,
that it is difficult to
reconcile the mind to
any other opinion,
than that the one
proceeded from the
other, although by

Christ Church, Oxford.

those progressive steps which mark all advancements in
the arts of design or construction.* It is more observable
in the buildings of our own country than in those of any
other, and more particularly so from the time of the
Conquest in 1066 to the year 1200, during which period we
trace a gradual improvement in the style first introduced by
the Normans, until, in the course of attaining the full capabilities of its enrichment, new combinations of forms and
details arose that were naturally suggestive of what we consider to be a new style of architecture, although it cannot con-
sistently be regarded otherwise than as a continuous current of
design, progressing towards that perfection which it afterwards
achieved.

We may reasonably conclude that this is the history of
the pointed arch, or rather the pointed window, which preceded it, and that it was not an abstract invention of any
class of men or people, but simply the result of attempting
a more elegant or novel application of the former style.
But afterwards, when this new principle was more fully
carried out, the traces of its direct origin were lost, and
the pointed style became quite distinct from the circular,
except when the whole chain of its progression was considered.

* In the west front of Croyland abbey there are four tiers of engaged
arcades. The lowest is semicircular, with zig-zag ornaments : that above
it has pointed arches on Norman columns, with a pointed window between; the next above has interlacing mouldings, and the uppermost has
semicircular arches on a larger scale. The date is about 1177.

The advantages of the pointed form over the semicircular were at once apparent, and every endeavour was made by the introduction of mouldings and columns to give all possible lightness and enrichment to a mode of building of itself massive and grand, but the capabilities of which to produce new effects had now become exhausted. The pointed form suggested a greater loftiness and elegance in composition, and to a certain extent the principles of arrangement became different: these again, in their turn, gradually gave place to others, apparently as much at variance with them as they were from the parent source.

With every veneration for the opinion of Sir Christopher Wren, we are at a loss to find anything that is at all satisfactory to prove that either the Saracens of the East or the Moors in Spain were the originators of the pointed style, much less of the arch, which is quite dissimilar, as the Moorish arches which we find in Spain are of the horse-shoe shape; the columns generally single, and not connected in groups; the windows small; the roofs flat, and the general forms horizontal; whereas in the early pointed buildings the roofs and gables are particularly lofty, the pillars high, and composed of beads and columns, and the general character vertical.

Having now given a general account of the opinions on this subject which are most entitled to our consideration, or at all necessary in our inquiry, we must refer the curious reader to the fifth volume of Britton's 'Ancient Architecture' for a full description of the theories of the different writers.

CHAPTER VI.

SYRIAN, PERSIAN, AND PERSEPOLITAN ARCHITECTURE.

THE ancient edifices of Syria were undoubtedly of a character
very similar to those of the Egyptians, if we may judge from
the intercourse that existed between these nations.   The principal cities of the Canaanites, or Phœnicians, who settled on the
coast of Palestine, were Tyre and Sidon ; the latter originally
the capital, and Tyre, although at first only a colony, became
afterwards greater than the parent city itself.   Judging from
the wealth of a people "whose merchants were princes, and
whose traffickers were the honourable of the earth," there can
be little doubt but that their buildings corresponded with their
resources : it is therefore to be deplored that the entire
destruction of the ancient works of their cities leaves us no
monument of Phœnician architecture.

When Solomon ascended the throne of Israel, and was desirous of fulfilling the wish that his father had entertained of
building a temple for the reception of the Ark of the Covenant,
he was obliged to send to Tyre for an architect, as well as for
workmen. The description of this temple is to be found in the
sixth chapter of the first book of Kings. Its plan was a parallelogram of about 109½ feet by 36 feet ;* in front was a pronaos
or portico extending along the whole width of the temple, the
depth of which was half its extent.   The cell or main body of
the temple was 54¾ feet deep, and the sanctuary beyond 36½
feet.   The height of the sanctuary was 36½ feet, the middle
part or cell 54¾, and the portico 36½. The body of the temple
was surrounded by three tiers of chambers, to which there was
an ascent by stairs, and the central space was a court open to
the sky.   Bells were suspended about the temple, and were
probably intended, by the sound they produced on being agi-
tated by the wind, to keep off the birds from the consecrated

* Taking a cubit at 1·824 feet.

edifice.* The ends of the beams of the upper floors rested on stone corbels, and were not inserted into the walls, which were lined with cedar, on which were figures of cherubim and sculptured palm-trees, covered with gilding: within the sanctuary were two figures of cherubim made of wood and covered with gold; these were 10 cubits high, and their expanded wings extended across the width of the temple.

In front of the portico were two pillars of brass, each 18 cubits high, and nearly 4 cubits in diameter. The chapiters or capitals, also of brass, were 5 cubits high; one was ornamented with lilies on a net-work ground, the other with pomegranates.

The 'house of the forest of Lebanon' seems in style to have been similar to the temple, but more extensive, being 100 cubits long by 50 cubits in breadth. From the proportion of the columns they must have borne considerable resemblance to the Egyptian or early Greek examples, as the height was only equal to five diameters; indeed, from the description given, as well as the fact of Phœnician workmen being employed, there is every reason to suppose that the temple was very similar to those of Egypt.

Persia was the seat of one of the most powerful empires of Asia from a very early period until the invasion of the country by Alexander the Great, 330 B. C., during which time the art of building must have been practised to a great extent; but in consequence of the invasions to which the empire was subjected, and the frequent internal commotions, which were doubtless accompanied with their usual devastations, nearly all the monuments of this celebrated and civilized nation have passed away, and, with the exception of the ruins that exist in one place, not a vestige of any ancient building remains. These ruins, situated in the great and fertile plain of Merdasht or Istaker, in the province of Farsistan, are all that is left to

* The like means are known to have been adopted on the roofs of the Grecian temples.

mark the spot where the city of Persepolis once stood. This city, the ancient capital of the Persian kings, is supposed to have been built or embellished by Cambyses, or his successors, Darius and Xerxes, in the sixth century B. C. ; but its prosperity must have been of short duration, for, with the other cities of the empire, it declined after the death of Alexander and the division of the territories he had conquered.

The ruins are supposed by Le Brun to be those of the palace of Darius that was destroyed by Alexander in one of his revels: the inequality of the ground, together with the appearance of distinct apartments for men and women, seem to favour the opinion that they formed part of a palace rather than a temple. The edifice has been founded on a marble rock, and extends 400 yards from north to south, and 200 yards from east to west.

The western platform is elevated 22 feet above the plain in front, and is ascended by flights of steps, which meet at the top. The two great masses of masonry, resembling those in front of the temples of Egypt,* diminish upwards, and are crowned by a hollow member. Their length is 22 feet, and their thickness 13 feet, but they vary from each other in height, that of the one being 39 feet, while the other measures only 29 : on the sides are sculptured winged horses or bulls with human heads,† wearing Persian dresses: in these are doorways, which, no doubt, led to the front courts of the palace, the magnificence of which is attested by the number of broken columns which lie scattered about.

Beyond these ruins is another assemblage upon more elevated ground, apparently forming the principal part of the palace. This terrace is supported by walls on which are

---

* Le Brun, who visited these ruins in 1704, conceives, from their similarity to the works of Egypt, that they must have been derived from the same source, and that they are not many removes from one common parent.

† The sculpture of these very much resembles the figures lately discovered by Mr. Layard at Nimroud, and are probably of the same date.

numerous sculptures, representing processions and sacrifices of horses and oxen : the figures wear the head-dress and robes worn by the Persians and Medes. The columns are of grey marble, from 70 to 72 feet in height, and 5¼ feet in diameter ; each column has a base 4⅓ feet high, with sculptured mouldings ; some of the columns are decorated with zig-zag ornaments, others have small scrolls at the top, and some of them are fluted, with fillets between the flutes.* These ruins possess great interest, from the number of groups of these large columns, which show the arrangement of the palace, the extensive staircases, many of which are 51 feet in width, and the remains of portals, windows, and sculpture, which are everywhere scattered around.

About two leagues from Persepolis are some excavations supposed to be the tombs of the early kings of Persia. The sculpture on the lower tombs show them to be the work of the Parthians.

No person can look at the style of composition and details of Persepolis without feeling the conviction that some intimate connection must have existed between the architects of Persia and those of Egypt, the principles of both being identical ; indeed, according to Mr. J. Gwilt's opinion,† "there appears to be sufficient evidence to convince us that the arts travelled in every direction from some Asiatic point, and that the Egyptian style had its origin in Asia," though conjecture has assigned the erection of this stupendous palace to Egyptian captives at a comparatively late period, after the conquest of Egypt by Cambyses.‡ On one of the portals are arrow-headed characters, similar to those of Ancient Babylon.

A great resemblance exists between the present architecture

---

* Niebuhr and Sir R. K. Porter inform us that these buildings were of marble. No cement seems to have been used, but the blocks were connected by cramps. The joints are so well wrought as to be scarcely perceptible.

† Mr. J. Gwilt's 'Encyclopædia of Architecture,' page 22.

‡ B. C. 525.

of Persia and other Mohammedan countries, and it therefore requires no description of its peculiarities.

CHAPTER VII.

THE ANCIENT ARCHITECTURE OF INDIA.

Of all the remains of ancient buildings that have attracted the curiosity or attention of the traveller devoted to antiquarian research, none have been investigated with less satisfaction, as regards their history or chronology, than those of India. No attempt at classification has been made until lately, doubtless in consequence of its difficulties ; for it was quite impossible to form any conclusive opinion, without a careful examination of a considerable portion of the excavated and constructed monuments scattered over an immense country, and which in some places are difficult of access. All the information that we have hitherto obtained on this subject has been from picturesque views, or else from descriptions of particular caves or buildings hastily or imperfectly examined, and which throw little light on their origin.

This task, which required a thorough knowledge of architecture, and a careful study of the forms of religion, as well as of the earlier history of India, has been accomplished by Mr. James Fergusson, who visited the principal caves and temples in different parts of India, and with great industry and enthusiasm has collected a mass of information ; for the publication of which, all must be grateful who are engaged or interested in the history of art.*

---

* Fergusson's ' Rock-cut Temples of India,' 1845; and ' Illustrations, with Descriptions, of the Ancient Architecture of Hindostan,' 1848. The following descriptions of the ancient buildings of India, and the conclusions as to their dates, are chiefly abridged from those contained in the above works, to which the reader is referred for a more careful study of these interesting monuments.

An impression has generally prevailed, that the cave temples of India are of a date anterior to any existing remains of antiquity, with the exception of those of Mexico, which still remain unexplained; and that the arts of Persia and Egypt proceeded from India: whereas it has been clearly ascertained that Egypt had ceased to be a nation before the earliest of the cave temples were excavated; and if we except the copies of the earlier structures by the Ptolemies and Cæsars, there is nothing on the banks of the Nile which does not belong to a different and far more ancient epoch than anything in India.

The inference that the Persians derived their forms of architecture and ornaments from those of the temples of India, has been founded on the similarity of the capitals and columns of Persepolis to some of the Hindoo temples, which it has been supposed were built in an older style than that which prevailed at the time of their erection. Of this, however, there is no positive evidence; and, if the similarity is admitted, the more reasonable cause of it may be, that the Persians during their migrations or traffic with India imparted, to a certain extent, some of the ornamental features of their buildings; and this is confirmed by the date of the building of Persepolis, which took place more than ten centuries before the oldest structural temple at present existing in India.

The ancient monuments of India are of two kinds, the excavated and the structural; the one being cut out of the rocks, while the others are erected of different materials in the usual way. The former are the most ancient, and were made by the Buddhists, a sect whose earliest existence cannot be dated prior to the sixth century before the Christian era.*

---

* Brahminism was a religion which existed antecedently to Buddhism, and was much purer in its forms than the faith which is at present followed, bearing the same name, or that of Hindooism. It seems to have been Monotheism, with a mixture of elemental worship, and had resemblance to the fire worship of the ancient Persians; but image worship, or idolatry in any shape, was quite unknown. It is extremely doubtful whether they ever built temples, or made them a part of their system: it

The founder Buddha is ascertained from the best authorities to have died in the year 543 B. C., though the trans-Himalayan chronologers concur in placing him about 500 years earlier.*   Mr. Fergusson considers that there is no cave anterior to the middle of the third century B. C.

The caves consist of three classes : the first of these are the Vihara or monastery caves, the earliest of which are natural caverns slightly improved by art, appropriated to religious purposes : those which followed had a verandah opening into the cells for the abodes of the priests,† but without sanctuaries or images of any kind.   The simplest form of these consists of merely one square cell with a porch, sometimes nearly 30 feet in length ; in others the arrangement is extended by the verandah opening into a square hall, on three sides of which the cells are placed.   Another subdivision of the Vihara caves consists in the enlargement of the hall, and the consequent necessity of the use of pillars.‡   In these, besides the cells, there was always a deep recess facing the entrance, in which the statue of Buddha, with his attendants, was usually placed ;

---

however is certain that no trace of any of their buildings now exists in India, nor is any description of them found in the works of native or foreign writers.

* Sakya Sinha, or Buddha (the sage), devoted himself to a life of ascetic contemplation and teaching, and died at the age of 80.   His doctrines were reduced to writing ; and 110 years after, a convocation was held at Nisali to settle disputed matters, but not until 300 years after his death was the faith firmly established in India: it was afterwards propagated nearly throughout the whole of India, China, Ceylon, and Japan.   Though in its native country it has now ceased to exist, the number of its followers exceeds that of any other known religion, being computed at 315 millions.

† The Buddhist priesthood was taken from all classes, and congregated, under vows of celibacy, in monasteries.   Nunneries were established for female devotees, in a manner resembling the ascetic Monachism that existed in Egypt and Syria in the earlier centuries of Christianity.

‡ The earliest caves were merely cells for the dwelling of an ascetic, which afterwards expanded into monasteries, and contained cells for a number to reside in.

thus making the cave not only an abode for the priests, but a place of worship. To this division by far the greater number of Buddhist excavations belong: those at Ajunta are the finest, though good specimens exist at Ellora and Salsette.

The second class consists of Buddhist Chaitya caves: these must be considered as the temples or churches, and one or more of them is attached to every set of caves in the west of India: the plan and arrangement of them are exactly the same, though the details and sculpture vary with the age in which they were erected. These, unlike the Viharas, seem to have taken the same form at once, as is seen in that of Karli, which is the most perfect, and believed to be the oldest in India. It has been supposed from this circumstance that, they were copies of the interiors of structural buildings, though no traces of such buildings exist in India, Ceylon, or beyond the Ganges. In all these caves there is an external porch, or music-gallery, and an internal gallery over the entrance; the centre part of the temple is surrounded by circular or octagonal pillars that divide it from the aisles, and are carried round the semicircular part at the farthest end, and which may be considered as an apsis: the whole bears a strong resemblance to the arrangement of the early Norman churches. The nave or centre part is twice its width, and is roofed by a waggon vault; the roof of the aisles is generally flat. In the centre of the semicircular part stands the Daghopa, in part of which there is always a sculptured niche containing a figure of Buddha and his attendants.* The third class consists of Brahminical caves, many of which have a great resemblance to the Vihara, though the arrangement of the pillars and the position of the sanctuary are in no instance the same. The walls are nearly always covered with sculpture, while the Viharas are generally decorated with painting and inscriptions. The finest specimens are at Elephanta and Ellora; others are to be found in the island of Salsette, near

* The Daghopa consists of a plain circular drum, surmounted by a hemispherical dome, and containing some sacred relic.

Bombay.* The excavated temple at Elephanta is 130 feet long by 110 feet wide, and 14½ in height. The ceiling is flat, and supported by four rows of columns connected by a fascia, or simple architrave: the columns are 9 feet high, standing on pedestals: they are reeded or ribbed, and have projecting capitals of a semicircular form in profile, from which spring the brackets of the ceiling. Against the walls are sculptured colossal human figures in high relief, which differ from each other by a variety of symbols, representing the attributes of the deities whom they worshipped. At the farthest end there is a square recess, supposed to be the sanctuary; on either side of the doors by which it is entered there are large figures. Our space will not admit of more than a general description of these very interesting monuments, which are numerously scattered about; in some places they are in large numbers; those at Kannari are nearly 100, and consist of three stories cut out of the face of the rock: the excavated caves at Ajunta are at an altitude of 150 feet above the ravine in which they are situated.† It has been observed that the form of the arch was unknown, in a structural point, to the Buddhists, yet they nearly always adopted that form in their Chaitya temples, while in the Brahminical caves no such form exists, as the ceilings are invariably flat.

Besides these cave temples and Viharas, there is another distinct and curious class of excavations cut out of the rock, and which seem to be imitations of structural Brahminical temples; they are of one block of stone, though executed in a manner

* The cave temple at Elephanta is supposed to have been excavated in the tenth century of our era.

† In many of the caves there are remains of painting and inscriptions; but they cannot be depended on to regulate their dates, as the characters were often in an older style than that which prevailed at the time they were executed. In none of the caves excavated before the Christian era is there any image or symbol of worship found; but gradually, during the ten and eleven centuries that their religion extended, we find images of all kinds; first Buddha; afterwards of Bodisatwas, or inferior Buddhas; then saints of all kinds, male and female.

to convey the impression that they are erected of jointed masonry. These temples, to which so much care has been given in their excavation, have the appearance of standing in pits, as all the surrounding parts have been cut away, and the present level of the ground is, of course, higher than the temples. The most remarkable of this class is the Kylas at Ellora, which is one of the most modern specimens of excavation in India, and can scarcely be considered earlier than the tenth century, A.D. The whole extent of this excavation is 401 feet long by 247 feet wide, and is at the north-east angle 104 feet deep; round the sides of this area is a cloister supported on square pillars, which are covered with subjects from the Indian mythology. The centre part is occupied with the entrance pavilion, the chapel of Nandi, and the grand temple and sanctuary, round which are balconies supposed to have been used by the musicians on solemn occasions. The approach to it is by a bridge, from which you descend to the chapel by nine steps; and, passing on over another bridge, you arrive at staircases on each side, which lead to the inner court, the temple, and cloisters. On each side of the bridge are gigantic representations of elephants, and beyond are two richly-carved pillars or obelisks. It is with regret that we are compelled to curtail our description of this wonderful monument, which appears to impress all who see it with feelings of something more than admiration: this is not caused by its height, its forms, the regularity of its lines, or the profuse number of ornaments and enrichments with which it is covered, but by its great peculiarity of situation, and which conveys an impression of its originating from superhuman efforts. The suddenness with which it opens to the view may account for the feeling; being so much below the level of the ground, it is not visible until within a few yards of it.*

To trace chronologically the history of the constructive

---

* For further description, see 6th vol. 'Asiatic Researches,' by Sir C. Malet; 'Tracts of the Literary Society of Bombay;' Capt. Sykes's 'Memoir;' and 'The Wonders of Ellora,' by J. B. Seely, 1825.

buildings of Hindostan is a matter of greater difficulty than that of the caves that preceded them, in which there is a visible progression from their originals, the natural caverns. There is no characteristic which can be produced with certainty of all the styles of architecture of Hindostan, except the melancholy one, that their history is written in decay ; for wherever we meet with two buildings, or two specimens of art of any sort, in the whole country between Cape Comorin and the Hima- layas, if the one is more perfect or of a higher class than the other, we may at once feel certain that it is also the more ancient of the two ; and it only requires sufficient familiarity with the rate of downward progress to be enabled to use it as a graduated scale, by which to measure the time that must have elapsed before the more perfect could have sunk into the more debased specimen.

The absence of the arch in all constructions of every age is general throughout India, as the principle was quite unknown. This is observable in a pointed arch at Kutub, near Delhi (built A.D. 1210 to 1235), of 22 feet in diameter by 60 feet in height, constructed in horizontal courses, which it would not have been, had more scientific principles been known. This inconvenience must have been great to a people who in their ornamental buildings employed stone roofs ; they were therefore compelled to resort to the bracket principle, to supply its place.

The upper parts of the buildings were supported on square piers or pillars, and from all sides of their capitals brackets projected equal to their width, and leaving generally a space equal to three diameters between their greatest projection, thus leaving only one-half of the whole length of the architrave un- supported ; but when a greater space was required, a succes- sion of projecting brackets placed above each other was adopted, sometimes meeting in the centre, thus having the effect of a horizontal arch. The effect of this is undoubtedly pleasing, as the projecting brackets on all the sides of the square capital produce in perspective a variety of lines, and great play of light and shade.

One of the oldest structural monuments or temples is that of Bobaneswar, which is 60 feet square at the base and 180 feet in height, built about the middle of the seventh century,* and in a style of art for which it is extremely difficult to find explanatory terms, the details being so far removed from all the ordinary forms of architecture. There can be little doubt but that great and progressive changes must have occurred before building could have arrived at the forms that are here developed, but at what period or from what sources their impressions were derived is at present a mystery.†

In plan, the Indian temples or pagodas are square : the only light that is admitted is by the door : the gloom of their caverns was followed, and solemn darkness seems to have been considered as necessary to the sacredness of the building. Temples were frequently placed in groups : those at Barelli are the most perfect of their age, and are covered with the most elaborate detail ; in size they give place to those of Cuttack : the date given by Colonel Todd is somewhere between the eighth and tenth centuries of our era.

One of the largest of the Hindoo temples is that at Chillambaram, on the Coromandel coast, which from its dimensions and antiquity is held in high veneration. This cluster of pagodas is enclosed in a rectangular space of 1332 feet in length by 936 in width, by walls 30 feet in height. This area contains a variety of temples, much decorated with sculpture of figures and ornaments, more curious than beautiful : these are connected by extensive colonnades and porticoes.

---

* About the same date as the pillars in the Mokemdra Pass. Pillars and obelisks occur frequently in India : they were set up for the purpose of receiving inscriptions or records of native offerings and gifts to temples : six of them set up by Asoka about 240 years B. C. are still known to exist.

† The Mohammedan invasions took place in the eleventh and thirteenth centuries ; therefore the art of decoration cannot have been influenced by these events : besides, some very elaborate temples exist in the most southern parts of India, far removed from the scene of conquest, and therefore not likely to have been erected in any foreign style.

Pyramids stand over the entrances of the outer enclosures, and consist of several floors. Other pagodas of very large dimensions exist at Tanjore, on the island of Seringham, near Trichinopoly, and at Madurah; but our limits will not permit us to extend this section for any observations on them.

Among the interesting works of the Hindoos are the Bunds or dams, which are made for the purpose of intercepting the course of small rivers, so as to form an artificial lake for the purpose of irrigation : on these dams, which are constructed of stone, palaces and temples are generally placed, and between them are very broad flights of steps leading down to the water, which are ornamented frequently with figures of elephants, and were used as fountains. That at Raj-Sing, at Oddypore, is 376 paces in length, and was built in 1653.

In concluding this interesting subject, we have to remark, that nothing can be more erroneous than to compare the architecture of India with that of Egypt, or even with classic styles, to which there is not the slightest resemblance or ornamental affinity. The essential principles of their composition and sculpture are totally different: in that of Egypt the chief character is the uninterrupted solidity of the masses, to which the enrichment is subservient; whereas in that of India the principal form is lost in the perplexity of the ornaments, which so completely preponderate as to destroy the scale, and project without any consideration to the general effect. In the former, even the smallest edifices are grand; whereas in the latter the unmeaning subdivision of its parts gives an air of littleness to those of the largest dimensions : there can scarcely be a greater contrast than the extreme solidity of the one with the total absence of its appearance in the other.

The Indian styles, whatever their defects may be, have at least the merit of being original; for there can be little doubt but that they were invented in the country where we find them.

CHAPTER VIII.

CHINESE ARCHITECTURE.

THE architecture of China, unlike that of other nations, has retained its particular character during all times without any mutation, aud uninfluenced by that of other countries. Their native historians ascribe the origin of building to their Emperor Fou-Hi, who first taught his subjects that art about 368 B.C.: however, there does not exist any building of that date, probably from their being generally constructed of wood. Besides, in the year 246 A.D. the Emperor Tsin-Chi-Hoang-Ti demolished all the existing buildings of importance, so as to remove all records of the grandeur and power of his predecessors: beyond a few temples and tombs in the mountains, which are supposed to be of a prior date, nothing remains of a higher antiquity.

The type of all Chinese buildings, whether they are used for the purposes of religion or as residences, is undoubtedly a tent; and the convex form of their roofs shows that they are a copy of those made of more pliant materials, sustained at different points from brackets at the top of vertical supports. The material generally employed is wood; that most in use is the nan-mon, which is said to last more than a thousand years: stone, marble, bricks, bamboo, and porcelain tiles, are also used.

In all other countries, however strong their prejudices may have been in favour of their peculiar or natural style of architecture, yet still we find proofs of a continuous current of invention and visible steps of improvement, both in the constructive and decorative portions of their buildings. In other parts of Asia, where bigotry to religion existed, and its natural attendant, the greatest veneration for the edifices devoted to its rites, still in all their caves and temples we find progressive changes towards a more elaborate or impressive class of monuments. In China, on the contrary, a totally different feeling prevails, and improvement seems to have been considered an innovation and direct breach of the laws, which are looked upon as something more than human ordinances, from their supposed perfection and antiquity.

One great hindrance to any advance in architecture is caused by the construction of their private houses and public buildings being subject to the restrictions of public functionaries (who may be properly designated district surveyors), backed by most arbitrary laws: under their supervision every one is obliged to build according to his rank, and for every house a certain size as well as details are fixed. These officers seem to govern the arts in China, and the laws regulate the magnitude and arrangement of residences of the various degrees,—for a noble family, for a president of a tribune, for a mandarin, and for all classes who can afford the luxury of a house. The size of public buildings likewise comes under their management. The merchant, whatever the amount of his wealth may be, is compelled by this regulation to restrict the dimensions and decorations of his house to his exact grade or standing: this refers only to the external part of his dwelling; the interior arrangements are unfettered. According to these prohibitions (for they cannot be considered in any other light), the level of the ground floor, the length of the frontage of the building, and the height of the roofs, are in an advancing scale from the citizen to the emperor, and their limits must be attended to without appeal.

The buildings generally are only of one story; and in Pekin the shopkeepers are obliged to sleep under their pent-houses in the open air in summer. One reason perhaps justifies their houses generally being only of one story, which is the slightness of their construction, and which renders them incapable of bearing anything above them. The general character and arrangement of the Chinese houses is so well understood, that no object will be gained by enlarging on the subject. In every part, nothing is seen but a succession of combinations of frame-work and trellises painted in all the primitive colours, which has caused the impression that the Chinese houses bear a greater affinity to bird-cages than to anything under the sun : the form of some of their doors is sometimes circular or octagonal, and tends to strengthen them, as in no other country are apertures of that form used for entrances.

The palaces resemble a number of tents united; and the highest pagodas are nothing else than a succession of them piled on one another, instead of side by side : in short, from the smallest village to the imperial residence at Pekin, no other form but that of a permanent encampment prevails.   Lord Macartney, who travelled the whole empire from the farthest part of the great wall to Canton, observed that there was but very little variation in the buildings to be seen.

Amidst the substantial works of the Chinese the most remarkable are the bridges : that at Loyau, in the province of Fod-Kien, is composed of 250 piers built with very large stones, which support enormous granite lintels, or stones placed horizontally; these are crowned by a balustrade. A considerable number of bridges have been constructed in China, and they are considered to be works of great magnitude and importance. To the Chinese is attributed the earliest application of the suspension bridge, which has been so much adopted in modern times in situations where no other means of passage could have been applied.

The temples of the Chinese are generally small, and consist of only one chamber, which is the sanctuary of their idols; on the outside is a gallery : others stand in a court surrounded by corridors.   In some instances the interior is spacious : that at Ho-Nang, near Canton, is 590 feet in length by 250 in width; the temple is constructed of wood, and covered with painted and varnished porcelain. It has been estimated that Pekin and its environs contain nearly 10,000 mido or idol temples, some of which are superior in decoration to those at Canton.

Amongst the buildings that are peculiar to China are the pagodas, or towers of from six to ten stories, diminishing upwards: the projecting top of each story presents the concave form before referred to; and the plan of these buildings is generally an octagon. The most celebrated is that of Nang-King, which is called 'the tower of porcelain;' it is 40 feet in diameter at the base and 200 feet in height; in the centre is a staircase connecting each stage, and which is lighted by windows on four sides; the openings do not occur over each other, but in alternate stories: the whole is cased with porcelain. The age of this pagoda is little more than three centuries.

Commemorative buildings and triumphal arches or doors are very numerous throughout China: they are placed at the entrances of streets as well as before principal buildings; the better class of which consist of a central and two side openings: the lower part is generally of stone, without any mouldings; the upper part is of wood, and supported on horizontal lintels, the constructive arch being as little known in China as in other Eastern nations.

The great wall, which extends for 1500 miles, has perhaps caused a much higher opinion to be formed of the monuments of the Chinese than a careful survey justifies. It is (with an exception in favour of their bridges) the only work of any importance that can give the Chinese any position as a constructive people.* It consists of an earthen mound faced by walls of brick and masonry; its total height is 20 feet. The platform on the top is 15 feet broad, and increases to 25 feet

---

* From the architecture as well as the ornamental works, the impression is conveyed that mechanical skill and imitation are the only faculties that are possessed by the Chinese, as their arts seem to be confined to servile copies of the works of Nature, without any feeling of composition or invention. The ancient people must indeed have been widely different in their composition, as they have credit for the discovery of the magnetic compass before 121 A. D.; the art of printing in the tenth century; the earliest manufacture of silk and porcelain; and last, though not least, the composition of gunpowder, which their descendants of the present day use to so little purpose.

at the base of the wall; at intervals of 200 paces are towers of
40 feet square, which diminish to 30 feet at the top; their
height in some places is 37 feet, in others 48.   This wall,
which commences in the sea to the east of Pekin, extends along
the frontiers of their provinces, over rivers, mountains, villages,
and often in places that are of themselves sufficient protections
from any hostile invasion: it engaged   million of persons for
ten years in its erection.*

CHAPTER IX.

ARABIAN, SARACENIC, OR MOORISH ARCHITECTURE.

In consequence of the very few examples remaining, we have
little evidence of the ancient architecture of the Arabians.
The Caaba at Mecca is the only temple existing in which the
Arabians worshipped their idols; this, however, was much
repaired by Mohammed, and it is extremely difficult to trace
the portions of the prior erections.   Since the death of the
Prophet, the veneration in which it has been held has preserved it from material alteration, in consequence of its containing his tomb.

From the appearance of Mohammed, in the seventh century,† may be dated the commencement of a style of architec-

* The first emperor of the Tsin dynasty caused this wall to be built as
a protection against the Tartars, though it has been supposed that the
employment of a large mass of people, who were in a state of excitement
at his tyranny, was the more direct cause of its erection, or it would not
have been carried over places that were quite inaccessible to an enemy,
and therefore in these situations useless.   It has now stood nearly sixteen
hundred years.   He ordered all the books of the learned, including the
writings of Confucius, to be cast into the flames, for the same reason that
caused the destruction of all the principal existing buildings.

† Mohammed was born in A. D. 570, and died in 632.   It was not
until 610 that he assumed the name of the Prophet.   His flight from

ture which extended from the Indus along the northern coasts of Africa, and to a considerable portion of Spain. In the latter country it attained its greatest excellence; and it is remarkable that the most splendid specimens of Arabian arts should be found so far from the seat of their government.

There is every reason to suppose that the Arabians were indebted to their Egyptian or Babylonian neighbours for the forms of architecture that were adopted in their temples prior to the time of Mohammed. Their unsettled habits were a hindrance to improvement in their mode of building beyond what their requirements induced. Their extensive conquests under Mohammed and the succeeding caliphs brought them in contact with nations more civilized than themselves, and from whom they acquired a knowledge of the arts and sciences.

The mosque which was built at Jerusalem by Omar, the second caliph, about A. D. 640, is supposed to have been the first of their erections beyond the limits of Arabia. Of the nature of this edifice we are ignorant, in consequence of the numerous additions made to it at subsequent periods.* When Damascus became the seat of the empire, it was considerably improved; and among its splendid buildings was the celebrated mosque founded by Alwalid II. In the year A. D. 762, the foundations of Bagdad were laid; and this city remained the imperial seat for 500 years. The magnificence of the palace of the caliphs could only be exceeded by that of the Persian kings; and the pious and charitable works of those days have

---

Mecca, on the 16th of July, 622, has become the era from which his followers count their years; and his precepts are observed from the Ganges to the Atlantic by more than 120 millions of people.

* The mosque of Omar is considered by the Mohammedans as next in sanctity to that at Mecca. For an account of it, see Fergusson's ' Temple of Jerusalem,' and ' Itinéraire à Jérusalem,' by Chateaubriand. The whole is contained in a quadrangular area of 500 paces long and 460 paces wide, surrounded by walls in which there are twelve entrances. The edifices within the enclosure consist of two temples, or mosques, respectively called El Achsa and El Sachara.

never been equalled, as water cisterns and caravanseras were built along several hundred miles of road.

It is surprising that so few public buildings remain, when we consider the extent of the dominions acquired by the Arabians after the establishment of the religion of Mohammed, the magnificence of the cities of Cairo and Bagdad, and the patronage bestowed on men of science by their caliphs. This scarcity of their earliest buildings can hardly be attributed to any devastations caused by wars in the eastern part of their dominions ; for, with the exception of the crusaders, whose conquests, and consequent destruction of religious edifices, did not extend beyond the sea-coasts of Syria, all other invaders of the Saracen empire were men of the same faith, and would have considered the public edifices as property common to all the moslems, and have retained them for their original purpose.

Nearly all that remains of the ancient architecture of the Eastern Saracens are the mosques at Mecca and Jerusalem : to these may be added the castle of Cairo, and the ruins of the hall of Joseph ; although both the latter are supposed to be the works of Saladin in the latter part of the twelfth century.

The architecture of Byzantium, as we have already shown, was the groundwork from which all new styles sprung up in Italy ; and its development was the basis of all modern art. The Saracenic styles of architecture proceeded from the same source as that practised in the western parts of Europe, and hence the similarity that has caused the supposition that the pointed form was actually taken from the Eastern nations, instead of its resulting from alterations which have always marked the progress of art.

The most splendid specimens of Arabian or Saracenic architecture are to be found in Spain, of which the most ancient is the mosque at Cordova, begun in A. D. 780 by Abd-el-rahman, then king of this part of the Moorish dominions. The style of this building was, without doubt, copied from those then existing in the East, as it was erected within the first century after the Moors had established themselves in Spain.* It is an insulated parallelogram of 620 feet in length by 420 feet in breadth, and is divided into two parts; one of them is an open court, in which worshippers performed their ablutions before entering into the body of the temple: on three sides there is a colonnade 25 feet wide, and on the other are the several doors communicating with the mosque. This consists of nineteen naves divided by seventeen rows of columns: thus the interior presents an appearance of a forest of columns composed of jasper and other marbles; they are 18 inches in diameter, and surmounted by capitals which bear a strong resemblance to the Corinthian and Composite orders;† these are connected by segmental arches. The ceilings are of wood, painted; the enrichments are of stucco, also painted in various colours, decorated with legends, and occasionally gilt. After the conquest of the city by San Ferdinand, in 1238, the mosque was converted into a cathedral; and the character has since been greatly injured by erections that were necessary for its adaptation to the service of the Christian religion.

The most perfect example existing, that can convey an idea of the extent to which sumptuousness of ornament and enrichment can be carried, is to be found in the Alhambra, the residence of the Moorish kings of Granada, erected between the years A. D. 1240 and 1348. In this there are no traces of art peculiar to any other nation; the composition and distribution of the ornaments being arranged with consummate skill. To

---

* The Moors, under Mùsa Ibn Nosseyr, the viceroy of the northern part of Africa, landed in the south of Spain A. D. 711, A. H. 89; and within two months, Cordova, Granada, Jaen, Malaga, and Toledo, then the capital of Spain, were reduced, or opened their gates to the conquerors. The mosque of Cordova was finished by Hishám, A. D. 794.

† These were probably obtained from some Roman buildings that existed in the neighbourhood, as some of them have bases, so as to bring them to the required height, while others, which were too short, were lengthened by giving them tall capitals. In this building there are upwards of 900 columns.

attempt a short description of this model of pure Arabian architecture would only be an injustice to it, as no notion would thereby be conveyed of this extraordinary work; we therefore can only remark, that every part of the walls and ceilings is covered with a mass of ornament enriched with gold and the most brilliant colours, and which bears the strongest evidence of the high degree of refinement and luxury at which the Moors had arrived prior to their overthrow.* The whole of the ornaments are composed of stucco; and it has been observed, that no nation has constructed so many magnificent buildings without having recourse to the quarry.

Moorish architecture has several kinds of arches: the horse-shoe form, having the centre raised above the spring of the curve, which diminishes in width; the pointed arch, in which, likewise, the greatest width is above the impost or spring from which the curve commences. Some of these latter arches contain on the inside a succession of small cusps of a seg-mental form. The next example is that of the cuspid arch, strictly so termed, the outline being produced by intersecting semicircles, very similar to the trefoil heads of Gothic windows, with the exception that they are not circumscribed by a con-tinuous arch. Arches of this kind occur in the sanctuary of the great mosque at Cordova, where they rest upon columns. Another example, very unlike the preceding, is in the Court of Lions in the Alhambra, it being circular-headed and stilted, and considerably more than a semicircle: the part below the centre of the curve is vertical, and rests on small corbels that are fixed against panels wider than the slender pillars that support them.

The style is noted for the extremely slender proportions of its pillars, and for the fancy and diversity of invention shown in the devices of mosaics and pavements, many of which appear exceedingly elaborate, although, when analyzed, they

* For a full description, with views and the details represented in their original colours, the reader is referred to the work published by Mr. Owen Jones, which is truly worthy of the magnificence that it illustrates.

are found to be very simple in principle: some patterns, exhibiting octagons, stars, and other figures, are produced merely by a series of zig-zag lines intersecting each other at right angles; and different combinations are formed by turning the points in a contrary direction.

Amongst other features of this style is the honeycomb, fret-work, or pendents, which compose the ceilings of the buildings of the later dates, of which it is impossible to convey a notion without illustrations: in short, it is a cone-shaped covering, but ornated with a multiplicity of projecting forms, which render its first appearance perplexing; but, like the mosaics, it is extremely simple in principle. This is a style that, with all its beauties, scarcely admits of a revival in its original forms, except in detached portions, on account of the pro-digality of its enrichments and colour, which, if simplified, would rob it of its great attraction. The ornaments, though very conventional, are so beautifully combined as to be copied or studied with great advantage by those who study the art of decoration.

CHAPTER X.

DRUIDICAL, CELTIC, AND ANGLO-ROMAN ARCHITECTURE.

IN an inquiry like the present, intended to trace the origin of the arts in this country, it will only be necessary to take a cursory view of the earlier monuments of antiquity which still exist in different parts of Great Britain, without entertaining theories respecting their origin, from which no satisfactory conclusions can be arrived at, and which had no influence on buildings erected long after, when their purpose was but im-perfectly known, and the religion from which they sprung had passed away.

The earliest remains of a structural nature are the unhewn

stones which, in various forms, are found in different parts of the island. The introduction of those in the southern parts is chiefly attributed to the Phœnicians, or Canaanites of Tyre and Sidon, who were the most expert sailors of antiquity, and maintained a commerce with the southern parts of England.

It seems unquestionable but that their frequent adventurous voyages suggested the idea of planting a colony in this part of Britain, and that they then introduced the custom of erecting gigantic stones, which had been a practice in Asia from the earliest periods. These erections are varied, and may be classed as follows: 1, the single stone, or obelisk; 2, circles of stones of different numbers; 3, sacrificial stones; 4, cromlechs and cairns; 5, logan stones; 6, tolmen, or colossal stones.

The most remarkable of these monuments, both for its preservation and arrangement, is Stonehenge, on Salisbury Plain, in Wiltshire, which has been generally considered as a Druidical and Celtic work. It consists of concentric circles of large stones, placed upright in the ground like pillars, with another large stone resting upon them as an architrave or lintel, which is secured by mortises and tenons; thus indicating a regular principle of construction, although the stones themselves are not squared. The remains at Avebury, near Silbury Hill, are merely rude masses of stonework in the form of a circle, with smaller detached circles of stones within its area. The other classes are chiefly of unhewn stones in different positions, and are only interesting in an antiquarian point of view.

The earliest habitations of the Britons were of a circular form, and composed of wicker filled in with clay, and sometimes placed upon foundations of stone, although caves were much used at the same time. The very rude nature of their abodes must tend to convince us that their mechanical knowledge had considerably fallen off, if the works at Stonehenge were executed by them.

From the invasion of Julius Cæsar, in the year 55 B. C., may be dated the erection of solid buildings; for very shortly afterwards the Romans formed settlements and permanent stations, and erected temples, theatres, and public edifices within their walls. After the second invasion under Claudius, 44 A. D., the Britons learned the art of erecting substantial buildings, and were further encouraged by Agricola, who used every means to civilize and draw them from their former roaming and unsettled life to one more conducive to their comfort, and rendered them every assistance in erecting houses and public buildings. From the year 85 A. D. to the fourth century, architecture and the arts connected with it flourished greatly, and the same taste was introduced into Britain for convenient and ornamental buildings that had long prevailed in Italy. To the Romans may be justly attributed the conversion of this country from comparative barbarism; for every colony and city that they founded was adorned with palaces, halls, basilicæ, aqueducts, and other works, either for use or ornament.

These stations abounded throughout the country, and, engaging a large number of people, infused a spirit for building; and in the third century this island was celebrated for the number and skill of its artificers, some of whom went to Gaul to assist in similar works.

As the advent of the Romans to Britain was the period from which the knowledge of the arts and architecture commenced, so to their departure, in 410 A. D., may be attributed their sudden decline. It must, however, be admitted that for more than a century previous to this, their skill and arts of design had been gradually retrograding,—their uncertain position in this country, combined with the difficulties they experienced in resisting the opposing nations, rendered them negligent of the arts of peace, and careless of the style in which their buildings were erected or repaired.

Although the structures of the Romans, during their stay in Britain, were works on which great skill and industry were expended, and were of a very ornamental character, yet from the numerous vestiges of architecture that remain, we cannot consider them as good examples for study, or at all worthy to be compared with the best works that existed in the parent state ; indeed it can hardly be imagined that the edifices of a colony so far removed, and chiefly executed by people unused to building, could in any way cope with those on which the best talent of the period was engaged.

CHAPTER XI.

ANGLO-SAXON ARCHITECTURE.

THE little that remained of the art of building in the island was extinguished very shortly after the arrival of the Saxons in 449 A. D., as they, like the inhabitants of the other parts of Germany, were totally ignorant of all civilized modes of living, being accustomed only to dwell in hovels, built in the rudest manner with branches of trees and reeds : all knowledge of building, therefore, seems to have been lost for nearly two centuries afterwards. The idolatrous creed of the Saxons appears to have possessed no incentive to improvement in building temples; indeed, we find that, in 652 A. D., when the Christian religion had taken root, the churches were mostly built of wood and covered with reeds, which practice continued for some time afterwards.* The church built at Lindisfarne, or Holy Island, and also that at York, in which King Edwin was baptized, in 627 A. D., were built of timber, and the only parts composed of stone were the altars.†

---

* St. Augustin, who came to Britain in 597 A. D., found many of the heathen temples, which had been left by the Romans and afterwards used by the Saxons, still in existence : those which were substantially built, Gregory ordered to be consecrated and converted to the Christian service. —Bede's ' Historia Ecclesiastica.'

† Poole's ' Ecclesiastical Architecture of England,' p. 20.

Paulinus, the instructor to Edwin, and first Bishop of York, is said to have erected the earliest churches of stone, as, on the authority of Bede, he "rebuilt that of York, and built at Lincoln a stone church of beautiful workmanship."

It was not until the latter part of the 7th century that the art of building in stone was again practised in England. This has been attributed to the exertions of Wilfred, Bishop of York, who erected churches at Ripon and Hexham, which were the admiration of the age: that at the latter place obtained great celebrity. Bishop Hiscop seems to have been equally energetic and devoted to raising buildings worthy of their purpose as for the erection of the monasteries of Weremouth and Jarrow.* He collected masons from France to build after the Roman manner, whereof he was a great admirer; he likewise sent for manufacturers of glass, who were not at that time to be found in England. His agents were successful, having induced several artizans to accompany them. These not only executed the work assigned to them, but gave instructions to the English in the art of making glass for windows, lamps, and other uses.†

The numerous ecclesiastical and monastic buildings that sprung up in the latter part of the seventh as well as the three following centuries, were "built after the Roman manner," or in the debased Roman style which prevailed at that period throughout Germany and France, and has received the title of Anglo-Saxon. The continued internal wars, as well as the repeated incursions of the Danes, who everywhere plundered and burnt, must have tended considerably to retard advances in the arts of building. The destruction of the numerous edifices, which were magnificent for that period, and had been erected at great cost, must have given little encouragement to those pious donations, from which had arisen the churches and monasteries so numerously distributed throughout the country.

* Weremouth was founded 674 A. D., and Jarrow 684 A. D.
† Vide Bede.

On the authority of ancient records, as well as from the few existing examples, it appears that the plans ot the Anglo-Saxon churches differed considerably, and must have been regulated by their size. The ancient church of Abbendon is described as a building of 120 feet long, with circular recesses both at the eastern and western ends.* The cathedral of Hexham in Northumberland, erected in the 7th century, was "furnished with a central tower; from this proceeded four aisles, or four arms of a cross; it had deep crypts and oratories, with passages under the ground. The walls were of great length and height, and were divided into three tiers, supported by columns both square and circular, which, as well as the walls and the arch of the sanctuary, were of stone, decorated with images in relief, and painted of various colours. The body of the church was surrounded by aisles and chapels of exquisite workmanship: the galleries above were so disposed that persons might pass round the church without being seen by any one in the nave below."† The Saxon church at Hexham was, according to Eddius, superior in magnificence to any on this side of the Alps.

The account of the rebuilding of York cathedral, in A. D. 767, by Alcuin, one of the architects, describes it as "having pillars, arches, vaulted roofs, porticoes, galleries, and altars:" these are sufficient indications that architecture must have been cultivated and brought to a considerable degree of perfection at a time prior to the invasion of the Danes.

The abbey of Ramsey in Huntingdonshire, which was rebuilt in A. D. 974, is described as having two towers, one at the western end, and the other in the middle of the building, supported by four pillars and connected by arches: these extended to other adjoining arches, to prevent the former giving way.‡ This shows that the plan of the building must

* Monast. Angl.

† 'Tractatus de Statu et Episcopis Hagustaldensis Ecclesiæ,' by Richard, the prior of the cathedral.

‡ Hist. Ramesiensis.

have been cruciform, with side aisles, and somewhat similar to that of the cathedral at Hexham.

The Anglo-Saxon builders used to construct crypts beneath their most celebrated churches; those at Ripon, Hexham, York, and several of the Norman cathedrals, retain portions of the ancient crypts. Beneath the chancel of Repton church, Derbyshire, is perhaps the most perfect specimen of a crypt in the Anglo-Saxon style, with a vaulted roof supported by four piers of singular character, with a spiral band round each, and also the entasis, exhibiting the swell peculiar to the baluster shafts of the belfry windows of that period.* The buildings here noticed were some of the most celebrated, and therefore very elaborate in plan and arrangement. In the smaller churches the plans were extremely simple, and of an oblong form, the total length of which varied from three to four times the breadth, with the semicircular apsis at the east end. At rather more than half the entire length was placed the tower, which separated the nave from the chancel. In the earliest churches there were no towers, and the bells were suspended under stone arches and weatherings, above the western entrance. The towers of the Anglo-Saxon churches were generally placed at the west end, examples of which arrangement exist at Barton-upon-Humber, Lincolnshire; Brigsworth and Earl's Barton, in Northamptonshire. The latter more particularly is entitled to notice, from its possessing peculiarities of construction which clearly denote its being the work of the Anglo-Saxons, as they are nowhere found in the works of the Normans. The execution of this tower seems to bear a greater similarity to a timber than a stone erection: beyond the face of the walls, long thin stones project, placed vertically at nearly equal distances, which continue from one horizontal course or story to another, and in the spaces between are semicircular and diagonal pieces, which give it a greater similarity to wood quartering. The quoins are of the description of masonry which is always identi-

* Bloxam's 'Gothic Architecture.'

fied with the Anglo-Saxon style, and called long and short work, from their being arranged with stones of equal size, placed alternately in a vertical and horizontal position upon each other, thus bearing resemblance to debased rustic-work.

The walls of the tower of St. Peter's church, Barton-upon-Humber, are built in a similar manner to those just described, of rubble stone and grout, interspersed with a sort of framework of projecting freestone in compartments, and encasing the doors and windows. The openings of the windows in the upper story are covered by two stones, inclining together without any curvature.

The heads of the doorways of the Anglo-Saxon style are either triangular-arched or semicircular; the latter were more generally used, and those which are more ancient were constructed of large flat bricks or tiles placed on end, and the spaces between, which are nearly equal to them in width, filled in with coarse rubble-work; the jambs or imposts of the arches were generally of stone. The mode of forming these arches, as well as the walls in which tiles were introduced, either in horizontal layers or arranged herring-bone fashion, was undoubtedly copied from the later works of the Romans: one of the most perfect specimens of this kind of construction is to be found in the church at Brigsworth in Northamptonshire, which is undoubtedly one of the earliest erections of the Anglo-Saxons at present existing.

The triangular-arched head is of a later date, and possesses little constructive merit; the extreme of the triangle rests on a plain abacus, the impost in some cases projecting from the wall: instances of this kind of arch are to be seen at the churches of Barnack; at Barton-upon-Humber, Lincolnshire; and at the tower of Brigstock church, Northamptonshire. Arches similar in form are known to have been used for decoration in the earliest variations of Roman architecture, and may be seen on several sarcophagi in the catacombs of Rome.

To enumerate the several churches that retain traces of this style of building would be only to occupy space that for our object may be engaged more usefully; as it must be borne in mind that we do not attempt more than such general descriptions of buildings as may serve to assist our history of the various styles of architecture, and exemplify the numerous and gradual changes that have taken place in this art at different periods, and trace them, as far as possible, to their sources.

The prevailing character of the Anglo-Saxon style is massiveness, with only the occasional introduction of a moulding, which in most cases consists simply of a square-faced projection with a chamfer or splay on the upper or lower edge: the sculpture of that period was extremely rude, and rarely introduced.

The constant invasions of the Danes, and the consequent plunder and destruction of religious edifices, lasted until the country was totally conquered by Sweyn, in A.D. 1012; but it can scarcely be considered that the ecclesiastics felt themselves sufficiently secure to commence the work of reconstruction before the accession of Canute, in A.D. 1017, to the sovereignty of this realm. In the course of his reign, which lasted twenty-nine years, the churches that had been left in ruins were rebuilt, and many monasteries were founded: that at Bury, in honour of St. Edmund, is attributed solely to the piety of this prince.* After the deaths of Harold the First and Hardicanute, the sons of Canute, Edward the Confessor ascended the throne, who, in the course of a quiet reign, was a great benefactor to the monasteries that were rapidly springing up in every part of England. The abbey church at Westminster was rebuilt by him A.D. 1065, and is described as "having been designed and constructed in a novel style of architecture, and as furnishing an example from which many churches were subsequently built." †

* "Over the body of the most holy Edmund, whom the Danes of former times had killed, he built a church with princely magnificence, applied to it an abbot and monks, and conferred on it many large estates." —William of Malmsbury de Gestis Regum Anglorum, p. 41.
    † Matthew Paris and William of Malmsbury.

The church erected at Westminster by Edward the Confessor must in all probability have partaken of the style of architecture that was then practised in Normandy, as the art of building in that country was far in advance of that which prevailed in England at the same time. The long residence of this prince among the Normans doubtless gave him a prejudice in favour of their modes of construction, and caused him to bring over a great number of the workmen who were engaged in numerous large edifices in the southern and middle counties, which, by their dates being anterior to the Conquest, have been erroneously classed under the head of Anglo-Saxon; whereas, in fact, they are Anglo-Norman in style: want of space, however, hinders our giving a description of the churches to which these observations apply.

CHAPTER XII.

ANGLO-NORMAN STYLE.

It has been usual to commence the successive history of the art of architecture in England from the date of the Conquest by William of Normandy, in 1066: we shall therefore pursue the same course, as from that period architecture received an impulse unknown before in this country, and continued unchecked for more than four centuries, from which gradually sprung up those styles of building in which not the least vestige of their origin was perceptible. After the arrival of the Normans, and the establishment of William the Conqueror upon the throne, monasteries and churches were rapidly built in 'the new style' in almost every city and town; and within seventy years from the accession of Canute, in 1017, the number of churches had so increased, that on the compilation of the Doomsday Book, one thousand seven hundred were recorded in that survey as being then in existence.*

* Bloxam's 'Gothic Architecture,' p. 75.

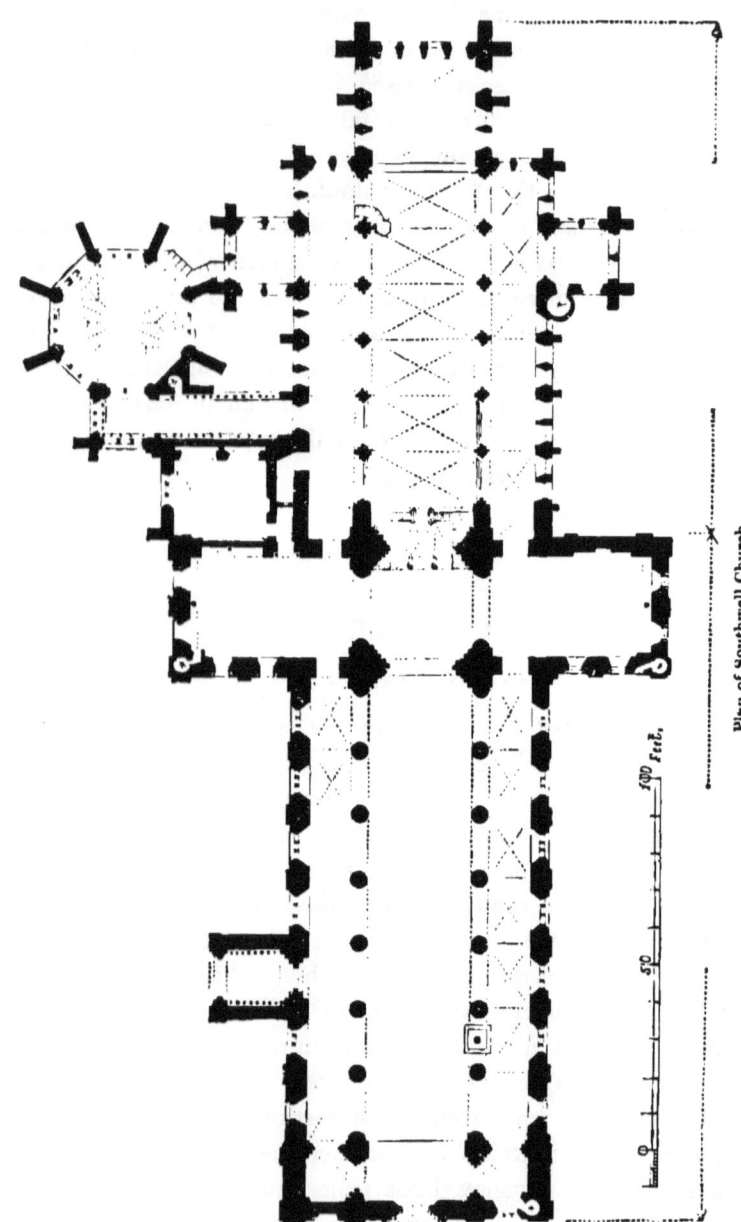

Plan of Southwell Church.

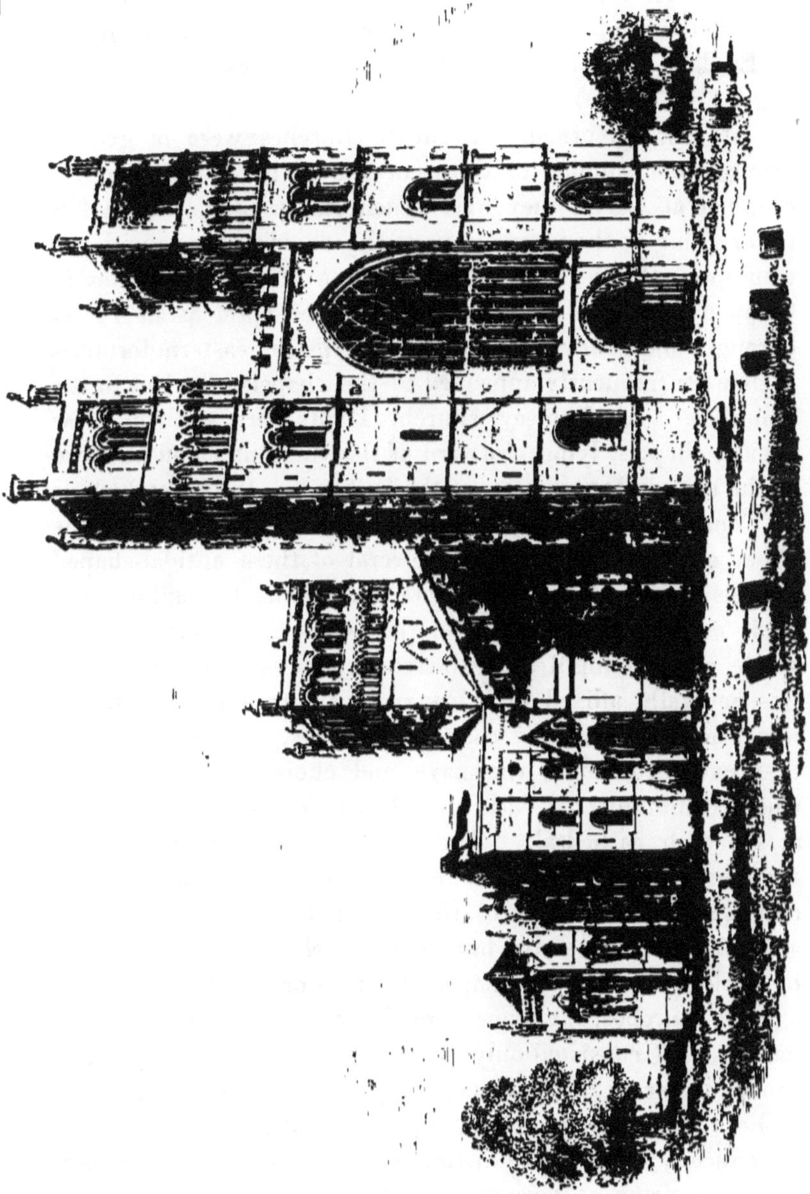

Southwell Church.

Southwell was distinguished at a remote period by the establishment of one of the three primitive Christian churches in England; namely, at York, Lincoln, and Southwell. (See pages 78, 79, 84.)

The Anglo-Norman conventual churches were in general arrangement similar to those of the Holy Trinity and St. Stephen at Caen: they were cruciform in plan, with a low tower rising at the intersection of the choir and nave with the transepts: the former, as in the case of some churches in Germany, terminated with a semicircular apse, as in Peterborough and Norwich cathedrals. Apsidal eastern terminations were frequently appended to the chapels attached to the churches. At Romsey church, Hants, are two of these apsidal chapels, lying eastward of the transepts, and also two at the eastern termination of the building. In the cathedrals of Canterbury, Norwich, and Gloucester, as well as in the abbey church of Tewkesbury, several of these apsidal-shaped chapels exist. The aisles were continuous throughout the choir as well as the nave, so that on solemn occasions the whole church might be traversed in processions. The altar was generally affixed to a low reredos screen or wall, which was placed between the easternmost piers. Above the aisles that extended round the nave and choir was a triforium, which communicated with chapels similar to those below, as at Norwich cathedral. The west, or principal front, was sometimes flanked with towers, in addition to that before named: at the angles of the transepts and porches were generally placed massive buttresses, or else turrets terminated by conical or polygonal-shaped cappings or pinnacles. In the smaller churches, the plans were similar to those of the Anglo-Saxons, and consisted only of a nave and chancel, with a low square tower at the junction, supported by bold semicircular arches: in these the apse at the east end is very frequently introduced; indeed it is a distinctive feature of that style which bears the name of Norman or Romanesque (derived from the ancient basilicæ), and never introduced after the style which was immediately received from the Continent, namely, the semicircular-arched, had passed away.

The Anglo-Norman style of architecture might be divided into three classes,—the Primitive, the Enriched, and the Transition: in the two former kinds, the principles are identical, although the mode of ornamentation that is used, unless considered in its various stages, appears to be the result of fresh impressions derived from some foreign source: as regards the latter, it explains itself, having features of a somewhat different character, which were the germs of a style totally dissimilar in principle.

The Norman style embraces the very plainest as well as the richest specimens of work, from that characterized by the low square and circular piers, so numerously distributed about the country, to the florid decoration with which many of our cathedrals and abbeys are embellished. The former of these exhibit but massive and clumsy remains of the classical principles, but they display a grandeur and solemnity of appearance from the solidity of the masonry and smallness of the openings. The piers in the earlier buildings were either entirely square, or else a succession of receding faces crowned by a plain square abacus, the lower edge of which was chamfered.* Isolated circular columns were likewise used in this country shortly after the Conquest, as at the chapel of the White Tower, London, (see page 82,) Great Malvern church, and the cathedrals of Gloucester, Peterborough, Durham, and Hereford,† besides several conventual and collegiate churches; among which latter class of buildings we may refer to Southwell (see page 78). At the later periods, portions of columns were attached to the square piers; those facing the nave or choir were carried up to the clerestory windows, and from their capitals sprung the ribs of

* The nave arches of St. Alban's abbey are of the nature here referred to.

† Fifteen of the twenty-two English cathedrals retain parts of their Norman erection, either in the crypts or superstructure.

St John's Chapel, White Tower.

the groining of the roof; the others carried a part of the
mouldings of the nave arches, as in Norwich and Peterborough
cathedrals.   In the latest instances, the square pier is entirely
discontinued, and the columns are connected together without
the angular pieces.

The arrangement of the interior compartments of the Norman cathedrals and larger churches is that from which nearly
all others of subsequent dates were copied; it consisted of
three tiers or stages.   The lower or larger opening was spanned
by a semicircular arch, which rested on the piers before de-

scribed, above which was a horizontal string-course: in the second story, or triforium, were two smaller arches, supported in the centre by a slender column; these were enclosed in a larger arch, the span of which was rather less than that below it; above this was another string-course: in the third, or clerestory, there were generally three arched openings divided by columns, that in the centre being higher and wider than the others, and forming either the window, or an opening before it, in the thickness of the wall. These three arches generally occupied a space equal to the arch below them, and were enclosed in the arch springing from the shaft which formed part of the semicircular stone groining with which the larger churches were usually vaulted.

In all the churches of the Anglo-Normans, without consideration as to their size, the western and southern doorways appear to have been the points on which they bestowed the greatest amount of enrichment: in buildings where every other part is simple in character, we find doorways decorated with a profusion of ornamental mouldings and sculpture. Many of these doorways are composed of a succession of receding semicircular arches, enriched on the edges and faces with bold mouldings, partly covered either with sculpture or with varieties of the zig-zag (an ornament peculiar to this style): beneath the abaci are ornamented columns, which fill up the angles of the receding space; the shafts, as well as the capitals, are sometimes covered with sculpture: those at the west and south sides of Iffley church, Oxfordshire; Ockendon church, Essex; on the south side of Earl's Barton church, Lincolnshire; at the west end of Hemel-Hempstead church, Herts: that inside the porch on the north side of Southwell collegiate church, and that of the southern porch of Malmsbury abbey church, are good specimens of their class.

Many of the Norman doorways have the arch heads filled up, forming that which is called the tympanum: this is frequently adorned by sculpture of the Saviour, angels, saints, or animals; the figure of our Lord is also sometimes enclosed in the vesica piscis,* as in the beautiful doorway on the south side of the nave of Ely cathedral: at other times the tympanum is ornamented by a representation of our Saviour in a sitting position, holding a book in his left hand, while the right is upheld as if in the attitude of benediction : † in other examples we find sculptures of St. George or St. Michael

Porch of Southwell Church.

combating the dragon : numerous instances are to be found of symbolical sculpture on the tympana of Norman doorways,

* This is a most ancient mystical figure, and is represented in several basilica mosaics and Saxon MSS.   Mr. Hope, p. 163, calls it " the rough outline of the fish."

† Thus placed in allusion to his words, " I am the door: by me if any man enter in, he shall be saved."—John x. 9.

Compartments of St. Bartholomew's choir.

as at Rochester cathedral, Malmsbury abbey church, Elstow church, Bedfordshire; Water Stratford church, Buckinghamshire; Barfreston church, Kent; and elsewhere.*

Amidst the alterations that were made to the Anglo-Norman churches, when so many of them were nearly rebuilt in a style quite at variance with their principles, the architects preserved the doorways, either from admiration of the workmanship, or reverence for the founders of the original buildings,— of whose piety they wished to retain some visible remembrance. In very many churches of a comparatively late date we find no remains to tell of their Norman origin but the doorway, which has remained undisturbed, although alterations to a very great extent have been effected in every succeeding style of architecture. In London, the churches of St. Bartholomew, West Smithfield, and that in the Temple, retain their original Norman doorways. (See also compartments of St. Bartholomew's choir, page 85.)

Another peculiarity in this style is that the arch is the feature on which the greatest amount of ornament and enrichment was bestowed, as there was scarcely any sculptured moulding then in use but had its origin in, and was applied to, the decoration of the arch. The first deviation from the square angles and receding faces was made by cutting a bead and hollow moulding on the arch, and this principle was carried out in the gradual development of its extreme richness. Among the instances that exist of the most elaborate work of the Anglo-Norman era, we may mention parts of Durham, Norwich, Oxford, (see page 87,) and Canterbury cathedrals; the chapter-house of Bristol cathedral; the college gateway, Bristol; St. Peter's church, Northampton; Steyning church, Sussex; and Castle Acre priory, Norfolk.†

Although in the Anglo-Norman style of architecture great

---

* Bloxam's 'Gothic Architecture.'

† Durham cathedral, begun about 1090; the choir of Norwich cathedral, between 1086 and 1101; Oxford cathedral, 1120; Canterbury cathedral, 1106; the chapter-house of Bristol cathedral, about 1156.

Oxford Cathedral.

richness was bestowed on some of the parts, yet, taking it as a whole, flatness, solidity, and massiveness were its chief features. The buttresses had little projection, the string-courses were generally small, and the window openings only sufficiently large to admit so much light to the interior of the buildings as might assist in producing the same impressions of solemnity which the general character of the exterior conveyed.

The decorative details and mouldings of this style, although numerous, are of a peculiar description, and appear to have been worked on the originally plain surface of the masonry, and, in many cases, re-worked at an after period to a greater degree of richness than they originally possessed. The chevron, or zig-zag, for instance, which is the most common or more generally used among the Anglo-Norman enrichments, has numerous stages of improvement: in the earlier instances its form is little more than indented on the plain face of the projection or wall; afterwards we find it partially beaded; then double-beaded with hollow; and in the latest examples it was completely cut away, and standing out in full relief, with a second series of mouldings carved on the backing. The billet-moulding likewise shows its origin in the bead, with spaces cut away to give variety of light and shade. The pellet, lozenge, and cable are very primitive in their composition. The star, nail-head, and embattled frette are likewise extremely simple. From these, and a few others that cannot be explained without illustrations, the whole of the ornamentation of this style is composed, which in some of the instances to which we have referred (with the aid of the receding faces) have produced effects of light and shadow unsurpassed by any later style.

The windows of the Anglo-Norman buildings were usually small and extremely simple, having no mouldings round them, but only a receding face on the outside, the inside being splayed, as at Romsey church, Hampshire, and Steyning church, Sussex.* Towards the beginning of the twelfth century, mouldings and columns were introduced in the

* This church is very interesting, and deserves attentive study: the exterior is extremely plain, while in the interior are some of the most elaborate details of Norman art.

jambs, and the semicircular heads were carved with the zig-
zag and other enrichments: about the year 1180, the highest
degree of ornamentation ever applied to Norman art was
arrived at: good examples exist at the churches of St. Cross,
Hampshire; Iffley, Oxfordshire; and Castle Rising, Norfolk.
The arrangement of the west front of the latter building is
very curious in its composition and details, and bears a
stronger resemblance to the ancient parochial churches of
Normandy than any other in this country: the window in
the centre of this façade is surmounted by three rows of
ornamental mouldings and columns; on either side are three
arches supported on columns, and from other columns in
front of these spring larger interlacing arches, encompassing
two of the others. This part of the church is supposed to
have been erected by Odo, Bishop of Bayeux, about 1090,
but from its arrangement and enrichments we are led to
suppose the date not to be earlier than 1170. The windows
of the later churches are much larger, and are sometimes
found introduced in pairs, with a shaft between them, and
enclosed in a larger arca: they were likewise grouped together in triplets, as at Iffley and Romsey churches. There
are very few circular windows remaining in this style; that at
the eastern transept of Canterbury cathedral, and also that at
Southwell minster, appear to be of this date.* There is one
at Chichester cathedral, erected about A. D. 1150, and another
at Barfreston church, Kent, A. D. 1180.

The Norman style, which had been gradually advancing, in
the richness of its arrangement and ornaments, from the period
of its introduction into this country up to the middle of the
twelfth century, began from that time to evince the germs of
different combinations and features, which were characterized
by the verticality of its principles, and a change from the semicircular to the pointed form of the arch. This has been called
the Transition, or Semi-Norman style, as in it we find the

* 'Glossary of Architecture.'

pointed arch in its incipient state, formed by the intersections of portions of a circle, whilst the details and accessories remained unaltered: thus was the pointed arch, for nearly fifty years, completely intermixed, more or less, in conjunction with the pure Norman style, without entirely superseding it, until the close of the twelfth century. We have already drawn the attention of our readers to some of the various theories respecting the direct origin of the pointed arch, and shall therefore offer no further observations on them, but merely consider this prominent feature as we find it introduced in our buildings, apparently resulting from new combinations, and as being the consequence, and not the cause, of a new style.

The Transition, or Semi-Norman style, which lasted during the reigns of Henry the Second and Richard the First, evinced, in its early stages, no other deviation from the Norman than that of the arches being pointed; but these were frequently introduced in situations where the old form was actually built with and even surmounting them. Thus we find them in the choir of the church of St. Cross, Hampshire: the lower arches here are pointed, whilst the arcade above, as well as the clerestory, is strictly Norman: the same arrangement exists at Malmsbury abbey church, with the exception of the upper story having been built nearly two centuries afterwards. In the transept of Romsey church, at the west end of Croyland abbey church, Lincolnshire, and in many other instances, the pointed arch is placed beneath the semicircular; and this has not been an after alteration, but is really the original work. The span of the arches at this time became greater, the columns higher and less massive, and the capitals began to be ornamented with a kind of foliage terminating in a volute or bulbous leaf.* The columns were frequently octagonal in form, and the bases had additional mouldings with an overlapping ornament at the angles, and were placed upon square plinths.

* The eastern part of Canterbury cathedral illustrates these peculiarities.

Although the alteration of the arch and diminution in the massiveness of the columns were at first the only indications of a transition from the style of the Normans, yet other peculiarities, which followed in gradual succession, bear testimony to the certain progress that was being made towards a more ornate and lighter style of architecture. The mouldings were more generally beaded and less massive, yet the use of the zig-zag, of various forms, was still retained. The columns of the doorways were frequently banded in the centre, and placed quite free in the receding angles and splays.

Examples of this period may be instanced in many of the Norman, as well as Early Pointed buildings: the great west tower and south wing of Ely cathedral are especially deserving of attention. Perhaps no finer specimen than this exists in the kingdom: the pointed arch, the trefoiled head, and other features of the next period in this example, here just begin to appear, although the whole aspect is decidedly Norman. The vastness of the surfaces, which are completely covered by arcading and sculpture, both within and without, from the ground to the very roofs, is almost bewildering to the eye: the date is about 1170.* Buildwas abbey, Shropshire; Malmsbury, Kirkstall, Fountains, and Croyland abbeys; the churches of New Shoreham; Rothwell, Northamptonshire; Walsoken, Norfolk; Ketton, Rutland; Bloxham, Oxfordshire; Little Snoring, Norfolk; retain portions of the work of this date. Trinity chapel, and the circular part called Becket's Crown, Canterbury cathedral, built A. D. 1175, are very interesting: St. Joseph's chapel, Glastonbury, erected at this period, is perhaps the richest specimen now remaining of the Semi-Norman, or Transition style, and remarkable for the profusion and beauty of its sculptured detail, as well as the close resemblance it presents in many parts to the succeeding styles.†

* Paley's 'Manual of Gothic,' p. 68.　　† Bloxam's Gothic.

CHAPTER XIII.

THE EARLY POINTED OR EARLY ENGLISH STYLE.

IT has been usual to date the introduction of the Pointed, or what has been denominated the Early English style,* to about A. D. 1200, although the vertical principles from which it sprung were not fully developed for thirty years afterwards. At its first appearance it retained much of the heaviness of the preceding style, but all resemblance to the Norman was speedily effaced by the development of its own peculiar and beautiful characteristics, which consisted in the high gables and roofs, the elongated window, the slender shaft, and the high pinnacles and spires. The lancet, as well as the equilateral shaped arch, was used at this period: the former prevails in Westminster abbey, A. D. 1215 (see page 93); while in Salisbury cathedral, which was commenced in 1220 and finished in 1258, the equilateral arch was principally adopted. The mouldings in general consist of alternate rounds and deeply cut hollows, producing a strong effect of light and shade: the tooth ornament is of frequent occurrence, and used only in the architecture of this date.

It is difficult to imagine a greater contrast than exists between the Early English style and that which preceded it; the whole composition of the buildings was changed,—from low to lofty, from heavy to the extreme of lightness, and from the horizontal to the vertical disposition of ornaments and mouldings. Although the progress in the new principles was very gradual, yet, when they were established, every detail and feature of the Norman style was carefully avoided, and an extravagant contrariety was indulged in, which, in many instances, by the too frequent introduction of the bead and

* This, as well as the Perpendicular, or Late Pointed, is peculiar to our country, as nothing similar is to be found in any buildings abroad.

North end of the Transept, Westminster Abbey.
The tracery and glass of the circular window is modern.)

hollow, produced a monotonous effect; and the deep shadows that the hollows presented tended to destroy the appearance of solidity which is so essential to all ecclesiastical buildings.

The features of this style which principally distinguish it from all others are, the lancet windows, the thin isolated and clustered shafts, the buttresses and pinnacles, the foliage, the mouldings, and the sculptured ornaments and figures; all of which must be studied with care in order to understand and appreciate fully its peculiarities, and will be found generally to determine the dates of the churches. The windows are of various kinds in the early period: the lancet windows, long and narrow, of one light, were most frequently used, with merely a small splay on the outside, and without any label moulding; afterwards they were surmounted by labels, which, being continued horizontally from window to window, formed a string-course between them. Two lancet windows under a single drip-stone are sometimes met with, but in the most beautiful specimens of this arrangement the jambs and the pier between the openings are ornamented with slender shafts, crowned by moulded capitals, and surmounted by the mouldings of the arches, over which are moulded double labels, as at Winchester and York cathedrals; St. Saviour's church, London; and many other places. The next arrangement is that of a triplet, or a combination of three windows together, that in the centre being higher, and in some cases larger than those at the side: the arrangement of columns in front of the piers and on the jambs, as well as the arch and label mouldings, is similar to the last noticed. These windows, in the smaller parochial churches, are most frequently placed at the east end of the chancels, and are only splayed, or very slightly decorated with mouldings, as at Wimborne minster, Dorset; Stanton Harcourt, Oxfordshire; and Warmington, Northamptonshire. Of the enriched kind, instances are found in Salisbury and York cathedrals, Beverley minster, Yorkshire, and the churches of the Temple and St. Saviour, London. The annexed view from the nave, now destroyed, of St. Mary Overy or St. Saviour's, is

St. Mary Overy, from the Nave, now destroyed.

also worth our observation. Four windows thus disposed, the two middlemost being the highest, are inserted in the east wall of the chancel at Repton,* and five lancets, rising in gradation to the centre, and comprised under a single label, occur at Oundle church, and at the east end of Irthlingborough church, Northamptonshire. In the interior of the richest buildings of this style we find detached shafts standing out in front of the piers and jambs, and supporting another combination of mouldings, as in Durham, Worcester, and Hereford cathedrals, and the chapter-house of Oxford cathedral. The combination that next demands our attention, in consequence of its evincing the germs of another class of Gothic architecture, and by its being the first approximation towards the introduction of tracery in the heads of windows, is that in which a part is pierced over a double lancet window, comprised within a single drip-stone. At Brownsover church, Warwickshire, is a very simple specimen; another likewise existed in the painted chamber at Westminster. A very interesting window of this kind is at Stone church, Kent; it has a quatre-foil opening on the out-side, which is repeated on a second moulded tracery within, supported by detached columns: the date is about 1260. Circular windows were frequently introduced during the preva-lence of this style, and were inserted above other windows within the angular part of gables: fine specimens remain in Beverley minster, and in the cathedrals of York, Lincoln, and Peterborough; others of the transition period exist at Barfres-ton and Patricksbourne, Kent.

The doorways of this style vary considerably both in form and in the arrangements of the arch mouldings and the sup-porting columns: in some cases the columns are single de-tached shafts, placed in a receding angle, whilst in others we find them in three or four receding spaces, and sometimes con-nected by bands or otherwise moulded: the upper mouldings of the capitals were mostly continuous, and from them sprung assemblages of small bead and hollow mouldings, in which the

* Bloxam.

tooth ornament was frequently introduced. At the cloisters of Salisbury cathedral; Warmington church, Northamptonshire (erected about A. D. 1250 and A. D. 1260); Byland abbey, Yorkshire, and elsewhere, are instances of a partial application of tracery to the openings of doorways: in the first of these, the head is cinquefoiled, and contained in an arched drip-stone; that at Warmington is rich in the arrangement of its receding columns and mouldings; within the two-centered arch is the trefoiled form, which is deeply moulded, and the hollows filled in with the tooth ornament. In the cathedrals and large conventual churches we meet with double doorways, divided by clustered columns or ornamented piers, and en-closed by a two-centered arch; the space above the openings being filled either with sculptured figures and ornaments, or else by moulded quatrefoiled tracery. Examples of these door-ways occur in the cloisters of Westminster abbey; at the south transept, Beverley minster; at Wells, Salisbury, and Lichfield cathedrals, and Higham Ferrers, Northamptonshire. In some of these the heads of the openings are cinquefoiled, and richly decorated with mouldings and sculpture. The west and tran-sept doors of Lichfield cathedral are particularly beautiful, and elaborately enriched.

The pillars usually consist of small shafts (often of Purbeck marble), arranged round a circular pier, and connected by a band of mouldings at half the height of the shafts, and at the capitals and bases: others of different kinds are to be found; a circular or octagonal pillar is common in country churches, which is crowned by moulded capitals, in which the nail-head and tooth ornaments, and also the rich flowing foliage of that style, are used. The buttresses of this date were often very prominent, and are frequently carried, with occasional weather-ings, to the tops of the parapets, and terminated either by high pyramidal cappings, as at Lincoln cathedral, or else by acutely pointed pediments, as at Beverley minster and Salis-bury cathedral. Buttresses at this period were seldom placed diagonally at the angles of the buildings, although such disposition in the succeeding style was very general. The angles of the buttresses were frequently chamfered, or else small shafts, not projecting beyond the face, were introduced. The carved foliage is very remarkable for boldness of effect, and was much used in capitals, brackets, bosses, crockets, and spandrils; it was often so much undercut as to be connected with the mouldings and backings only by the stalks and edges of the leaves. There is generally a stiffness and mannerism in the combinations of the sculpture of this era, but the effect of it is almost always so beautiful, that we overlook its unreality in the great flexibility and freedom both of the conception and execution. The prevailing leaf is a trefoil; this was also used to form the crockets, which had their origin in this style.

One of the principal structures erected at this period, and which demands our notice, is Salisbury cathedral, commenced by Bishop Poore in A.D. 1220, and finished in A.D. 1258: this building is the more interesting from the whole of it being erected in the same style, allowance being made for the advances that were yearly taking place in the art. The nave and transepts of Westminster abbey, commenced A.D. 1245, show a somewhat advanced stage. The greater portions of Lincoln and Worcester cathedrals are of this date, though many alterations have subsequently been made to both. The nave, lady-chapel, part of the transepts, and the west front of Wells cathedral, were erected at this period by Bishop Joceline, between A.D. 1213 and 1239: the west front is particularly rich in design, and is covered with arcades and trefoil-headed niches, in which are sculptured figures, remarkable for their freedom of design. The sculpture of this period is well worthy of note for the beauty, harmony, and elegance of its composition, whether in figures or ornaments, and was never surpassed, even during the fourteenth century, when mediæval art had reached its perfection.*

* The other cathedrals that retain portions of work of this date are,— Durham, the chapel of the nine altars; Carlisle, the choir and aisles, Winchester, the part east of the altar screen; Hereford, the lady-chapel;

We cannot bring this chapter to a conclusion, wherein (so far as our limits would permit) we have endeavoured to explain the general principles and characteristics of the style which boasts of the first introduction of the pointed arch, without drawing attention to the faith, piety, devotion, and zeal in church building, for which this age was so remarkable. This produced a spirit of rivalry and ambition amongst the clergy and religious orders to surpass each other in the grandeur and beauty of their edifices, as well as in the costliness of their vestments, altars, and sacred ornaments. During this period, viz. the reign of Henry the Third, the largest abbeys, priories, and religious houses, were founded, erected, and richly endowed: the great wealth of the clergy (or rather the piety and liberality of the laity whence that wealth was derived) furnished ample funds for the erection of the most magnificent structures, which were only retarded in their progress by an insufficient supply of workmen to execute them.*

Lichfield, the nave and lady-chapel; Oxford, the chapter-house; Peterborough, the west front; Canterbury, the transepts; York, the transepts; Ely, the presbytery; Rochester, the choir and transept. Of the conventual buildings of this period, we may refer to the following examples: Rivaulx, Yorkshire; Fountains; Whitby, Yorkshire; Netley, Hampshire; Tintern, Monmouthshire; Ripon and Beverley minsters; Milton abbey, Dorsetshire; the greater part of the nave, St. Alban's, Herts; Tynemouth, Northumberland; besides many others. Numerous examples exist of this style in parochial churches: Grantham, Lincolnshire; Higham Ferrers, Northamptonshire; Minster, Cobham, Maidstone, and Hythe, in Kent; as well as many in Lincolnshire, contain some interesting remains of this style.

* Great praise must be awarded to the Freemasons, for the regularity with which their body was governed; for to that must be attributed the prevalence of the same style, in its full purity, in different parts of the country, as well as all the improvements or advances that resulted from the union of men engaged heart and soul in the same good work. The energy with which their undertakings were carried on may be estimated by the fact, that no less than one hundred and fifty-seven abbeys and religious houses were built during this period.

What a contrast is here presented to the state of things in our own times! The labourers are now numerous, but the sources from which the funds come are comparatively few. Formerly, from the willing contributions of princes and nobles solely, were raised those glorious monuments which, though in ruins, and until lately unheeded, have remained to tell of the zealous liberality of men whose names have not been spared to us, but swept away with the institutions which they founded. These specimens of architecture were not raised merely to please the eye, and obtain the praise of man, or they would have been otherwise placed than in the marsh and the desert: the costly enrichments were lavished on temples for God's honour, in remote and secluded places, where none but the peaceful inmates, the wanderer, or houseless poor, could contemplate the noble product of labour and pious pains.

Such are the beautiful old abbeys, now ruined to rise no more; and may centuries yet to come pass over their remains, that their beauties may, if possible, be more fully and more generally appreciated, and be the means of causing others to follow the example of our forefathers in using their wealth, abilities, and talents, for the noblest of all purposes!

CHAPTER XIV.

THE DECORATED, OR GEOMETRIC MIDDLE POINTED STYLE.

The style at which we have arrived prevailed during the reigns of the first three Edwards, or from about A. D. 1274 to A. D. 1377, and has been generally distinguished by the term Decorated, though Geometric Middle Pointed has likewise been applied to it.* This, as well as that which preceded it, arrived at full development only by a gradual and almost imperceptible progression, and the stage of transition (as in that between the

---

* The former by Rickman, the latter by Paley.

Norman and Early English) might be considered as distinct
from, though partaking of, the peculiarities of both. This
period of transition has been the cause of a great confusion of
terms, as many buildings of a date prior to A.D. 1274 have
been described as decorated work, whereas that style did not
arrive at its distinctive and settled character until after A.D.
1290.

The Decorated style is of two characters, which can be easily
defined by the nature of the traceries of the windows, and
should be denominated 'early and late decorated.' In the
former, the geometrical figures prevail, consisting of combinations of circles, trefoils, quatrefoils, cinquefoils, and triangles.
It is remarkable for the harmony of its forms. The tracery
and cuspings were fully developed; and the uniting of several
openings as a whole under one arch, or a succession of concentric mouldings, marked an evident deviation from the arrangement and principles of the Early English architecture. This
Geometric Middle Pointed style may be considered to have been
in use until about A.D. 1327, or the beginning of the reign of
Edward the Third, when the compositions of the windows seem
to have undergone a change, and the flowing or wavy lines
succeeded, producing an almost endless variety of combinations. At the period to which we now refer, viz. from 1327 to
1377, the architecture of this country may justly be considered
to have attained its greatest excellence, both as regards graceful proportion and a luxuriant profusion of beautiful ornament
and mouldings. By very gradual progression, and almost imperceptible changes, had these principles of graceful design and
unequalled beauty of execution been arrived at; and it cannot
be denied but that the architectural art of this period was
neither equalled nor surpassed in any other country or in any
age.

The general plan of ecclesiastical and monastic buildings of
this era was little marked by any deviation from that which
preceded it : any change in the arrangement is to be attributed
more to the requirements of the situation than to any alteration

in the principles. To the details and parts of the combinations we must look for the distinguishing peculiarities. Throughout the century during which this style prevailed, the same kind of arch was generally used, and was either equilateral, obtuse-angled triangles, or segmental in form. The mouldings consisted chiefly of quarter or three-quarter rounds, with fillets, and in small churches double recessed splays alone were used: the deep hollows and unfilleted beads of the former style were quite discontinued.

The piers of this period, on which the nave arches rested, were frequently composed of half or three-quarter cylindrical shafts, which in some instances had small fillets at their greatest projection, and in others smaller shafts or filleted mouldings were placed at the junction of the large shafts: this arrangement differs from the Early English in the columns being more closely united. The octagonal, cylindrical, and circular pier is more generally to be found in small churches. The capitals are more frequently bell-shaped, crowned by quarter-rounds, fillets, and other mouldings, and having at the lower part a beaded or chamfered astragal. In the richer instances, or in large churches, the capitals were either numerously moulded, or ornamented with light elegant foliage, distributed completely over all parts of the capital but the abacus and the astragal: figures, battlements, and the ball-flower were frequently introduced on it. The bases of the piers differ from those of the preceding style in their being composed of two or more small round mouldings, with either a quarter-round or hollow below, and beneath it a splay or curved moulding was sometimes introduced. The ogee form was in some cases used, but it more frequently denoted a later period. In plan, the base mouldings take various forms, not always following that of the shaft, but changing from the circular to the octagonal, and from the octagonal to the square.

The windows of this style, as we have before stated, differ from those of the Early English style in having their openings connected and blended together either by geometrical or flowing tracery comprised under two-centered arch mouldings. They are generally large and of good proportion : those which were placed either at the east or west fronts, or at the transepts, varied from three to seven lights each, and were divided by mullions, which at the springing of the arch branched out into either geometrical or flowing combinations. The great variety of the traceries in windows of this style renders their description extremely difficult. In the best and most perfect instances, we find a principal and subordinate arrangement ; the extreme mouldings bounding the general forms, whilst the secondary or inside mouldings mark the disposition and form of the lights. It is scarcely necessary to observe that these harmonious arrangements of flowing lines were not produced solely from a correct perception of beautiful forms, but were grounded on that consummate skill and mathematical knowledge for which the Freemasons of this country were so eminent. One of the most elaborate and beautiful windows of this date is at Carlisle cathedral : the geometrical principles on which it was designed have with great care been illustrated by Mr. Billings in his interesting work on that cathedral : he has likewise given the primary, secondary, and tertiary mouldings by which the varied forms are enclosed. The western window of York cathedral is very rich and flowing ; the large and beautiful window in the south transept of Chichester cathedral is filled with geometrical tracery. That at the choir of Merton college chapel, and at the west end of Exeter cathedral, are likewise good examples. In some instances, as at the south aisle of Gloucester cathedral, and the tower of Salisbury cathedral, Badgworth church, Gloucestershire, St. Mary's tower, Oxford, and many churches in Lincolnshire, the mouldings of the mullions, jambs, and arches are enriched with small circular ornaments or ball-flowers : these windows are generally only of two lights, the tracery cinquefoiled, and that in the upper part of the arch very simple. Some curious windows of this date exist at Dorchester church, Oxfordshire : in one of these the genealogy of Jesse is represented ; on the mullions are projecting sculptured figures; these are connected by flowing foliated branches at different heights; the centre mullion springs from a recumbent figure of Jesse, and the whole is surmounted by the figure of our Lord. Ogee-headed windows are not uncommon in this style, as seen at Cracombe, Northamptonshire, 1320, and Great Bedwin, Wilts, 1300. Square-headed windows were very frequently employed, both in the aisles of the smaller churches and in the clerestories; in many of them the ball-flower is inserted into the hollows of the jambs and along the top mouldings, and sometimes it is introduced in the under moulding of the label: instances of this kind of window are to be found at Ashby Folville, Leicestershire, 1350, and Swinbrook church, Oxfordshire. Segmental, flat-headed and circular windows were likewise used: one of the largest and richest of the latter is to be found in the south transept of Lincoln cathedral. Windows of a triangular form, having the sides curved and filled in with tracery, are likewise peculiar to this date, and are used either to fill up the angle of a gable, or in clerestories, as at Barton Seagrave, Northamptonshire, and East Hendred, Berkshire. Square and diamond-shaped windows are sometimes introduced in churches of this period: of the former, a curious specimen is to be found at Whitby, filled in with four quatrefoils arranged angle-wise. The mullions of the windows of this era were very rarely divided between the sills and springings of the arches by any horizontal tracery or transom, which was one of the main features of the succeeding style. At the west front of York cathedral we have the mullions uninterrupted, whilst at the east end, which is of later date, or transition style, there are transoms. Pedimental labels, covered with crockets, and surmounted by rich double finials, were used over the more important windows, as well as to terminate niches. The tympanum above the windows, or the part between the arch mouldings and the angles, was filled in with rich flowing panelling, and sometimes with figures: some windows at York cathedral, and Howden church, are good examples of this arrangement.   It is unnecessary to cite any further instances, as with the general description we have already given, the careful student of Gothic architecture will be able to discern the more important characteristic features of the windows of this period.

The buttresses of this style are more varied in form and disposition than those which preceded : in the smaller buildings, they are generally of two stages, and frequently finished by gable-headed terminations, sometimes adorned with crockets and finials.   A gable is sometimes introduced at the middle weathering, and at the top there is only a succession of weatherings or moulded water tables, with a splay and half-round moulding at the nosing or greater projection ; as at Grendon, Warwickshire.   Those of Merton college chapel, Oxford, are good of their class.   Traceries and panels are frequently sunk within the faces of the buttresses of the large ecclesiastical buildings ; those of York and Howden are fine examples.   Niches were likewise made in some of those attached to parochial churches, as at St. Mary Magdalen, Oxford, and Witney church, Oxfordshire : the latter is very rich, having niches in both stages ; the lower is moulded and surrounded by an ogee head, with diaper-work in the angles ; the upper one is terminated by a crocketed gable, filled in with perforated tracery ; both niches have small pedestals.   Some of the buttresses at York cathedral and Beverley minster* are rich and free in their composition : they have moulded niches open on three sides, with arched and crocketed gables above ; these are surmounted by sunken panels, and terminated by pinnacles decorated with crockets and finials.   Except in large buildings, where the buttresses have pyramidal terminations, the gable heads are not carried above the parapets.   In many cases both the heads and set-offs are weathered and splayed without enrichment : the buttresses of this date were placed at the angles, or diagonally with the faces of the wall, an

---

* See Pugin's ‘ Specimens,’ and Britton's ‘ Chronological History.’

arrangement which was scarcely ever seen in the preceding style. Flying buttresses were used at this period, and are to be seen in Exeter cathedral, Beverley minster, and other large erections.

The early decorated doorways retain much of the arrangement of the former period, and had on each side engaged shafts with moulded and ornamented capitals: these were gradually abandoned, and the mouldings of the arches were carried down to within a short distance from the ground, and were finished either by bases, or else the mouldings terminated on splays. The arch mouldings were usually a combination of small rounds, filleted beads, and hollows, and were composed in two or three sets; in some instances the arch mouldings are lost or merge into larger jamb mouldings of a round or hollow form, uninterrupted by any horizontal moulding or capital: a good instance of this is at the west end of Tunstead church, Norfolk.* Ornaments of a square and four-leaved nature, as well as the ball-flower connected by stems, were applied to enrich the hollow mouldings of the jambs and arches. Crocketed canopies were sometimes used at the springing of the arch; the north door of Adderbury church, Oxfordshire, is particularly fine in this respect.† The doorways of the most important buildings of this date were particularly rich in arrangement and ornamental sculpture, and had a second label of a pedimental form covered with crockets: within this, a figure of the patron saint, or of the founder, was frequently sculptured in high relief, under a canopy, and surrounded by traceried panels or ornamental foliage: those at the west end of York cathedral are very good examples. The large doorways are sometimes divided by clustered shafts and mouldings into a double opening, as at the entrances of the chapter-houses of York and Wells cathedrals. The openings

---

* On the south door of this church there is some ornamental iron-work of this period, which for freedom of design and execution cannot be surpassed.

† Bloxam's 'Gothic Architecture.'

of the doorways were frequently cuspid or foiled ; that at the west end of Tintern abbey is beautifully composed. At Cley church, Norfolk, * there is a rich specimen of a single doorway with a foliated and traceried arch ; others, of different degrees of simplicity, exist at Ewerby church, Lincolnshire, and Higham Ferrers, Northamptonshire.

The niches of this period were generally surmounted by canopies of a pedimental or ogee form, and were of very elaborate workmanship, more particularly those of the latter part of Edward the Third's reign ; they frequently projected in front, either in a curved or splayed line, and were enriched with crockets or finials. Niches were frequently placed at the sides of the east window in the chancel ; though in some instances, as at Selby church, Yorkshire, we find only brackets with sculptured figures and ornaments, and above it a rich canopy, without any recess being made in the wall for the figure.

The parapets of this date were very frequently pierced with trefoil and quatrefoil openings ; that of a wavy flowing form was much used : examples are to be seen at Selby church, Yorkshire ; St. Mary Magdalen, Oxford ; and Brailes church, Warwickshire. Solid parapets are more general in the smaller churches. Gurgoyls, or grotesque figures projecting from the walls, were first employed to conduct the water from the gutters.

The crockets, finials, and enriched capitals were particularly graceful ; and the foliage or ornaments of which they were composed, were divested of the mannerism of the former period : they exhibited a more natural freedom, the leaves were more gracefully disposed, and were executed with great boldness : the oak, vine, ivy, and hazel foliage were more generally followed. The carving throughout York cathedral deserves notice and careful study.

The churches that retain portions of this very beautiful style of architecture are extremely numerous ; indeed, in the

* Illustrated in Brandon's ' Analysis.'

middle and northern parts of England there are few in which some feature of it is not left. Among the monasteries or larger buildings we must direct attention to the remains of the abbeys of Tintern and Guisborough, which are splendid specimens of the Geometric period. Selby and Howden churches, Yorkshire, of a later date and more florid character, are noble edifices of this style. The gateway of St. Augustin's, Canterbury, is particularly good in design. Queen Eleanor's crosses at Waltham, Northampton, and Geddington are likewise interesting. Amongst the cathedrals that retain portions of work of this date, we may draw particular attention to that of Lincoln, the choir of which is generally admitted to be the most perfect structure in England, both internally and externally, and is a model of the Geometric Pointed in its earliest form. The chapter-houses of York, Salisbury, and Wells cathedrals, as well as the abbey of St. Mary, at York, are of the same period, and contain valuable studies of their peculiar detail. The nave of York cathedral is of a richer class of decorated work, and of a later date. Winchester contains some good wood-work in the stalls. The lady-chapel and other parts of Lichfield cathedral, the centre tower and spire of Salisbury, and parts of Beverley minster, are of this period. Exeter cathedral contains portions of both the earlier and later dates. The cloisters of Norwich cathedral are very interesting, though they were not erected at one time; they were commenced in 1297, and not completed for upwards of a century.

CHAPTER XV.

THE PERPENDICULAR, FLORID, THIRD, OR LATE POINTED STYLE.

WE have now reached the third period of the Pointed Style, which may be dated from the latter part of the fourteenth century to the commencement of the sixteenth, or the early times of Henry the Eighth. To mark its architectural peculiarities, and the general features which distinguished it from that which preceded, the above titles have been applied. The appellation of Perpendicular,—which was bestowed on it by Rickman, and has since been very generally adopted,—is in some respects appropriate and descriptive; yet it by no means conveys an adequate idea of the distinguishing characteristics. It appears to be tolerably correct if we consider it only as regards the mullions or parts of the traceries of windows, and the upright forms of the ornamental panellings with which the surfaces of the most elaborate ecclesiastical buildings of this date were enriched: to these features we must admit a perpendicularity beyond that which the preceding style presented; but it is no less obvious, that with these exceptions, the term Perpendicular is equally, if not more, applicable to the first and second Pointed periods. With propriety might the term Horizontal be applied, as it would be equally or more appropriate of the two; since the mullions are crossed by numerous horizontal lines, and the divisions of the panellings are as positively marked. The tops of the doorways are enclosed by horizontal labels; the pointed character of the arch is in a great measure lost, and marked by a squareness of outline; the string-courses and base-mouldings are more numerous and strongly defined, even in buildings of comparatively small dimensions. Although the term Perpendicular is so very inefficient for the purpose of satisfactorily elucidating the numerous deviations from the former styles, yet no other single phrase can probably be found which would be more explanatory. The appellations of Third, or Late Pointed, are more comprehensive and explanatory as to the period of this style, and less likely to mislead, by causing the student to attach too much importance to some of its peculiarities, to the hindrance of a more careful study of the principles, which this class of architecture so much requires.

We have made the preceding remarks, less with a view of provoking controversy or to advance any term of our own, than to warn those in search of the true principles of design from attaching undue weight to conventional terms, however generally used: we shall now proceed with a description of the most important features of this style.

That the church architecture of this country reached its highest degree of excellence during the Decorated or Second Pointed period, is undeniable; yet, still we must not too readily believe (as some writers would persuade us) that a general debasement of style, and sudden retrogression in architectonic taste, were the natural consequences of the first deviation from its principles of composition; and that all works which were executed subsequently, presenting different combinations and details, were but so many rapid advances in the downward course of Gothic art, and therefore not entitled to consideration, much less to the admiration which, until lately, was so generally bestowed on them.

During the period of transition, and indeed throughout the greater part of the fifteenth century, works were executed which (although they may be somewhat at variance with the spirit of the pure style from which they originated) must ever be regarded by the unprejudiced as possessing unsurpassed excellence, in point of the execution of the sculpture and ornamental embellishments. The great variety of design, elegance of arrangement in the lace-like combinations of traceries on the walls and groinings, the delicate carving and almost magic intricacy which is displayed in the canopied niches, or tabernacle-work, in the screens or stalls, must in justice excuse the earlier examples of this period from that censure, which, by being justly bestowed on the ecclesiastical architecture of the last Henry, has, to a considerable extent, caused a veil to hang over the architectural excellences of the few preceding reigns.

In order to give a satisfactory elucidation of the elements of the Third Pointed, or Perpendicular style, we ought to consider it with reference to its precursor, and exhibit the numerous changes which are visible in its details and combinations. To accomplish this, and trace the progressive steps from one class of constituent principles to another, more space would be required than our limits admit of; for as the changes were more gradual than in the preceding styles, and the deviations were more frequently caused by fresh requirements in the arrangements, or a feeling for more general ornamentation, it would be necessary to analyze so many examples to explain fully our views, or to follow a successive course of inquiry.

It is essential that this should be borne in mind, and that we enter less on the transitions than the positive differences between the second and third classes of pointed architecture: our notice will therefore have reference more to the later than earlier periods. The chronological list of buildings, with which this book terminates, will include several which might be interesting as examples of transition work.

The general peculiarities of the fully developed style of the fifteenth century are chiefly visible in the increased expansion and the upright and square tendency of the tracery of the windows, the gorgeous fan-like tracery of the groinings, the four-centered arches and horizontal lines of the doorways, the excessive decoration of the wooden roofs, and in the introduction of heraldic enrichments and colour.

The strongest evidences which can be adduced to prove the charge of retrogression from the pure principles which pre-

ceded, are to be seen in the depressed form of the arches of
the later period, the low angle of the roofs and gables, and
the introduction of useless battlements instead of the pierced
parapet. As regards the two first of these objections, it is
obvious that they resulted from a desire to add to the richness
and beauty of the sacred edifices. The cause of the nave
arches being reduced in height was to give greater consequence to the clerestory windows, and increased opportunities for the display of the painted glass which at this period
was most lavishly used for the adornment of churches: the
flatness of the curvature of the heads of the west doorways
resulted partly from the same motive, viz. the enlargement of
the window, as well as to make the doorway compose with
it, by joining the label with the string-course, which was
usually just below the sill of the windows. The flatness
of the angle of the roofs was the natural consequence of
the increased height and size of the clerestory windows,
as the height of the nave walls was in all probability
sufficient, without making the roof a feature of importance:
besides, had it been constructed at the same slope as in
the earlier periods, the western tower, against which it usually
abutted, would have required a disproportionate and in other
respects unnecessary raising.

But we must likewise consider this subject independently
of these matters of detail: the principles on which the buildings of the fifteenth century were designed were different;
the same altitude was obtained, but by other means: in the
Decorated style, the roofs were made accessory to that object;
whereas in this they were only considered as coverings,
and therefore were concealed as much as possible behind the
stone-work. In three of the richest and most remarkable
buildings of this period, viz. Henry the Seventh's chapel,
Westminster; St. George's chapel, Windsor; and King's
college chapel, Cambridge,—the external roofs are so flat as
not to be seen from the ground, but are screened by enriched
parapets, which harmonize with and form a beautiful termi-

nation to the substructure. The introduction of battlements cannot be justified in an ecclesiastical edifice; the form was used simply to produce a more pleasing effect than that which an unbroken line of parapet would present, more particularly in the upper parts of the buildings.

Although to this style the depressed or four-centered arch was first applied, still it was not invariably used in churches, even at the latest periods: the two-centered, more or less obtuse, as well as the segmental form, are to be found in the same building. The compound arch must therefore not be considered as an essential ingredient in the Perpendicular work, as that style had developed itself at a period long before it was brought into use; but from the latter part of the fifteenth century, when it was first introduced, it gradually became flatter, until at last the arched form merged into two lines slightly inclining from the centre, and terminating in small curves.

The windows of this period exhibit in their traceries a most decided deviation from those of the Decorated class: in the latter, all the lines are flowing and curved, whereas in this the principal mullions are carried up perpendicularly to the enclosing arch, with curved or hori-zontal intersections: above the tre-foiled arches, which connect the mullions at the springings, other smaller mullions are introduced, thus making the openings only half the width of those below: these are united at two or three different heights by horizontal lines and smaller arches.

Window from Christchurch, Hants.

Segmental-arched as well as square-headed windows were frequently used, more particularly in the clerestories; and in some instances they are set so closely together as nearly to form a continuous perforation: numerous churches in Suffolk are peculiar in this respect; those at Long Melford, Lavenham, and Lowestoft are good examples, though it is nearly impossible to form an opinion of their original effect, from the absence of the stained glass with which they were filled, and for the introduction of which the windows were thus arranged.*

The groined ceilings of this period particularly deserve attention; in no other style is the fan-shaped or enriched radiating tracery to be found: the cloisters of several of our cathedrals retain some good examples; that of Gloucester is particularly fine. The buildings in which it is introduced on its largest scale, and in its greatest beauty, are Henry the Seventh's chapel (see pp. 115, 117); St. George's chapel, Windsor; and King's college chapel, Cambridge: in the former, the most profound skill has been displayed in the geometrical composition, in the luxuriancy of ornament, and in the scientific principles of its construction: the means by which the numerous large stone pendants are supported are beautifully disguised by the enrichments. The ceilings in the other buildings do not present the same variety or complexity of arrangement; they possess all the elegance for which the fan-like groining is so remarkable, and the whole surface of the stone is worked into a variety of radiating traceries. The construction of the latter differs from the others in one respect; there are no aisles to act as sustaining abutments to the lateral pressure, which is much greater than in Henry the Seventh's chapel, in consequence of the very depressed form of the

---

* In examining the ancient ecclesiastical buildings of this country, too much care cannot be bestowed in endeavouring to find out the motives of their designers; otherwise, from their mutilated remains, very erroneous conclusions will be arrived at. It is marvellous that so much has been spared to us of our churches: they have been exposed to sacrilegious spoliation, to fanatical desecration and partial destruction, and then left for two centuries neglected, unprotected, and unheeded; excepting in some cases, where the few remains of internal enrichment have been ignorantly or wantonly defaced. Limewash, pens,— or pews,— have indeed done their duty in the work of disfigurement; whilst, in some districts, dirt and cobwebs are most scrupulously retained, and, from habit, considered an essential feature in a church.

Henry the Seventh's Chapel.

vaulting. This was remedied by the introduction of massive
buttresses, carried out to a great extent beneath the lowest

weathering, which are judiciously connected by small chapels, thus disguising their necessary extreme projection.*

The piers, or detached pillars, from which the nave arches spring, were in the buildings of this period less solid than in the Decorated style, generally consisting of four small circular shafts, separated by deep hollows, which, towards the end of this style, were divided either by fillets, beads, or double ogee mouldings.   In plan, the general arrangement was that of a square, placed diagonally with the face of the walls: some-times, however, they were contracted in breadth, so as to become narrower between the arches, or from east to west, than in the opposite direction,—thus being diamond-shaped. These attached shafts rested on octagonal bases, and more generally were finished by moulded capitals of the same form : in some instances the mouldings of the piers were continued in an uninterrupted sweep to the apex of the arch, and some-times panelled, as at Sherborne, Dorsetshire : the hollows and the smaller members between the shafts were in most cases continued round the arches.   The spandrils of the nave arches

---

* Henry the Seventh's chapel, Westminster, styled by Leland 'orbis miraculum,' was commenced on the 24th of January, 1502 or 1503, and completed to the vaulting before the King's decease in 1509: the whole was finished by Christmas, 1519.   The design of this building has been attributed to Sir Reginald Bray, though he only lived to see the first stone laid; it was carried up and finished under Prior Bolton.   St. George's chapel, Windsor, was begun in 1476 by Edward the Fourth, who con-stituted Richard Beauchamp, Bishop of Salisbury, master and surveyor of the work: Sir Reginald Bray was engaged on it by Henry the Seventh: its completion, however, did not take place before the early part of the following reign.   King's college chapel, Cambridge, was founded by Henry the Sixth about the year 1446: it was proceeded with until the accession of Edward the Fourth in 1461, when a stop was put to it by a seizure of the revenues: the works were afterwards partially proceeded with, as the funds permitted.   In 1484, the east end of the chapel was only carried up to the top of the window ;—thus it remained until 1508, when Henry the Seventh engaged to finish it : this was not accomplished until July, 1515.

Henry the Seventh's Chapel.

were sometimes filled in with panelling; those of Winchester cathedral are remarkable in this respect. The shaft towards the nave was frequently carried up to the springing of the clerestory windows, and on the capital with which it was surmounted, the wall-pieces and arched portions of the roof rested: good examples of this arrangement are frequent in the Suffolk and Norfolk churches; those at Laven-

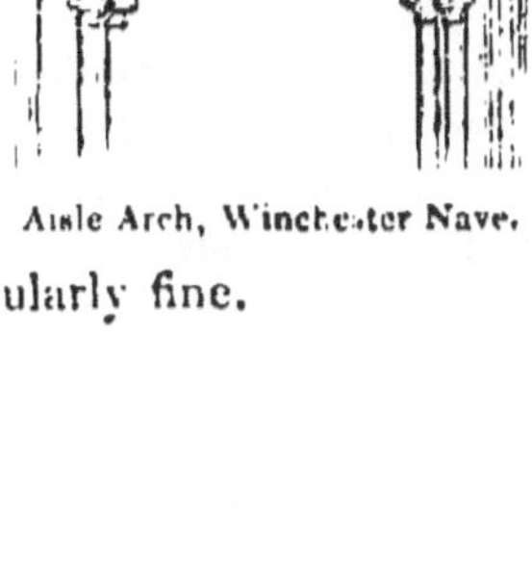

Aisle Arch, Winchester Nave.

ham and Bury St. Edmund's are particularly fine.

We have before observed that pointed arches of every curvature were used in this style : even in its last stages we meet the two-centered, and the depressed or Tudor arch, combined in the same building; therefore to the mouldings and general arrangement we must look, to form a conclusion as to the dates : the later the work, the more subdivided and thinner it becomes.

The doorways of this style, although they vary so much in the shape of the arched head, are generally included within square-headed mouldings, which are carried down the jambs to the base-mouldings; the spandrils or the corner spaces are enriched with panelling, quatrefoils, sculptured ornaments, and shields, on which the arms of the founders or benefactors were carved. The upper members of the base-mouldings are some-times carried with good effect up the sides, and along the top of the doorway, thereby serving as a label. On the sides of some of the western doorways, niches with canopies were introduced;—that at Fakenham church, Norfolk, is a very good example: many others are to be found in the same county, which is so very celebrated for the excessive richness of the buildings erected during this period. The wooden doors were generally covered with a profusion of panel-work, with deeply recessed mouldings, from which sprung traceried heads, increasing in richness to the apex of the arch.

This style is celebrated for the very ornamental character of its porches, which were often covered with traceried panels, and niches for the figures of the saints. Some porches were of large dimensions, and had a room over the groined entrance,* which frequently contained a piscina, and was used as a chapel; in some, a fire-place is provided, and served for a dwelling room for a priest.

Those of the churches of Northleach in Gloucestershire,

* This, in modern times, has been called a Parvise; although that name in ancient writings seems to refer more particularly to a porch or open area before the entrance to a church. The origin of the term is involved in obscurity.

Burford, Oxfordshire, and Oundle, Northamptonshire, are
celebrated for their size, as well as the elegant and elaborate
nature of their compositions. The top of that at Burford is
finished with a panelled and embattled parapet, with a rich
string-course beneath ; at the angles are buttresses with crocketed pinnacles: the interior is panelled, and the roof is
groined with fan tracery.

Other examples of porches, equally rich in design, are to be
seen at Gloucester and Canterbury cathedrals: those of the
churches in Norfolk are interesting from their being in many
instances covered with tracery, flush with the face of the wall,
without any relief, and the inside part filled in with split
flints, which very distinctly mark the forms by the contrast
of the colour. In some smaller porches, both the roof and
the walls are constructed of stone, as at West Hendred in
Berkshire, and Broughton church, Lincolnshire. The porches
of this style vary in detail and arrangement from extreme
plainness to excessive richness; they, however, retain the
general peculiarities of the style, and are easily distinguished.

The next features in the churches of this period, which
particularly mark them from that which preceded it, and
demand our attention, are the wooden roofs: these are very
numerous, and frequently found in buildings of a prior style,
where the original roofs, for want of repair, have been removed.
The pitch or slope of the roofs of the fifteenth century was,
as we have before observed, much lower than before, and (as
in the arches) approached gradually nearly to flatness: the
roofs were not visible outside, being concealed by the parapets.
They are generally divided into bays by tie-beams and trusses,
or larger rafters; these were faced with mouldings, ornaments,
and painting; the triangular part between the tie-beam and
rafters was filled in with perforated tracery; in the centre was
an ornamental king-post. Beneath the tie-beam, braces were
frequently placed, which rested on stone corbels, and carried
some of the weight from the top of the walls: the spandrils
were filled in with pierced tracery. The churches of Somer-

setshire, Norfolk, and Suffolk retain the finest examples of the various modes adopted by the architects of this period to ornament the construction of their roofs : every moulding and ornament, at the earlier period of this style, had its purpose, and necessity, more than a preponderating desire for enrichment, influenced their introduction. Towards the close of this style, we frequently find that the whole of the rafters are hidden by panelling and combinations of squares and parallelograms, with bosses at the intersections of the ribs. The roofs of the chapter-houses of Exeter and Canterbury cathedrals, those in the churches of St. Mary, Bury St. Edmund's, and St. Peter, Lavenham, Suffolk, and in New Walsingham, Norfolk, are good specimens of this description. Another class, peculiar to this style, is called the hammer-beam roof; this is of as lofty a pitch as that used during the Decorated period; it is so framed that the tie-beam is dispensed with. A horizontal timber, called a hammer-beam, on which the principal rafters rest, projects from the wall (about one-quarter the width of the nave) and is supported by wall-pieces and spandril braces; these sustain the queen-posts and struts, which connect the hammer-beams with the principal rafters. The rafters are tied together with collar-beams at about half their height; wind braces are likewise used to add strength to the framing. The ends of the hammer-beams are usually ornamented; in some cases the greater part is concealed by carved figures of angels bearing shields and scrolls. One of the most beautiful examples is that over the nave of St. Mary's, Bury St. Edmund's, and is only second to that of Westminster Hall. Another fine roof covers the nave and chancel of St. Peter Mancroft church, Norwich: in short, so very numerous are the varieties of arrangement and decoration of the roofs of this style, that they would engage an entire chapter if we could give them the description which they merit: this our space will not permit. Painting and gilding were much used, more particularly on that part which was nearest the altar: the ground of the panels was usually azure colour, and studded with gilt stars, to represent the firmament of heaven; it was often covered with ornaments and texts; the mouldings were likewise painted in different colours, and the heads striped or dotted with flowers: that of the nave of Aldenham church, Herts, retains its original colours; on the rafters and tie-beams, flowing ornaments are painted. It has been often stated that on this part of the church more expense and attention were bestowed than on any other: this is erroneous; the principles on which these buildings were designed differ widely from those of the present day; one part was not starved, to enrich another: where we now find roofs of exceeding richness, we may be assured that the other parts were uniformly elaborate; but the hand of the fanatic or the ignorant has destroyed those parts more immediately within its reach.

The screen-work of this period was particularly rich, and is to be distinguished from that of the thirteenth and fourteenth centuries (of which existing examples are rare) by the mullions, or divisions of the traceries, being moulded instead of consisting of cylindrical shafts, with capitals and bases. These screens generally separated the chancels from the body of the church, and supported rood-lofts, which were approached by small stone staircases in the walls; the front was richly panelled, and the under side formed into a large coved cornice, which connected it with the screen below. The lower part was not pierced, although the divisions of the upper or open part were continued down, and arranged into panels with traceried heads: on the sunken part, figures of the saints were often beautifully painted. Screens were likewise used to enclose portions of the east end of the aisles, as chantry chapels. Good examples are to be seen at Higham Ferrers, and in other churches in Northamptonshire and Norfolk.

The octagonal turrets of this style are frequently surmounted by ogee-headed terminations, on the angles of which crockets or carved animals project. They are constructed

F

as buttresses round Henry the Seventh's chapel: at Winchester cathedral, King's college chapel, Cambridge, and
St. George's chapel, Windsor, they are likewise to be found.

The towers of this era retain the peculiarities of elaborate panelling and decoration which were used throughout all
the other features of the buildings of this style, although
no distinct characteristic (besides the forms of the mouldings
and arches) is visible beyond that for which each county
is noted: varieties of design occur occasionally in the same
district, which must convince us that the ancient builders
were not so much fettered by fixed rules or single notions
in their combinations (as we seem to be at the present day),
but had the desire and ability to give fresh expression to the
prevailing style of details. The tower of St. Nicholas, Newcastle, is single and peculiar in its design. "From the base of
the octagonal turrets, which crown the angular buttresses,
spring four flying buttresses, on the intersection of which
is placed an elegant lantern crowned by a spire. The flying
buttresses are crocketed, and are particularly graceful in
form. This steeple is as fine a composition as any of
its date, and the lightness and boldness of the upper part
can hardly be exceeded." * It is Early Perpendicular, and
is the type of which there are various imitations: the best
known are those of St. Giles's, Edinburgh, the church at
Linlithgow, the college tower at Aberdeen, and its modern
imitation by Sir C. Wren, at St. Dunstan's in the East,
London: but all these fall far short of the original.

Spires at this period are not unfrequent; and although they
are considered as one of the main features of the preceding
style, yet many examples are found in Northamptonshire and
elsewhere, both with and without crockets at the angles ;—those
of Kettering, Rushden, and Oundle churches are of good proportion ;—those of Louth, in Lincolnshire, built between 1501
and 1518, and the earlier one of St. Michael's, Coventry, 1395,
are likewise celebrated.

* Rickman.

There is another termination which is perhaps peculiar to the towers of this date. The ordinary square tower is surmounted by an octagonal lantern of smaller dimensions, and is connected with the composition of the tower by flying buttresses from the bases of the angle pinnacles. That of Lowick in Northamptonshire is by far more graceful than that of Fotheringay, though perhaps the latter is better known; it has crocketed pinnacles at the angles, with light traceried windows between. That of Boston in Lincolnshire is one of the finest compositions of the style; the walls and buttresses are well arranged in panels, except the belfry story, in which the window is so large as nearly to occupy the whole width of the tower. The rich and elegant octagonal lantern rises from the tower, and is supported by flying buttresses from the four pinnacles; this lantern is panelled throughout, and each side is pierced with a large two-light window with double transoms. This composition gives to the upper part of the steeple a richness and lightness of appearance scarcely equalled in the kingdom.

Campanile towers are to be found: that at Evesham is interesting from its grouping with the adjacent churches: another fine example is to be seen near Norwich.

The most remarkable of our Perpendicular towers is that of Gloucester, erected about 1455 by Abbot Seabrook; it rises above two hundred feet from the ground, and about one hundred from the roof of the choir. It is of two stories, with two windows in each face, arranged within an elaborate composition of buttresses and panels of the very richest description, and flanked by four perforated turret-like pinnacles of the most delicate work, which have an appearance so light and graceful, almost beyond the natural capacity of stone-work. This has had its influence on the erections of others in the surrounding districts, as we find the same character prevailing in Somersetshire, and near Bristol. Some of the most important of these towers are St. Mary's, Taunton; St. John's, Glastonbury; St. Stephen's, Bristol; at North Pether-

ton, and Thornbury. The great peculiarity of the Somersetshire towers consists in the richly pierced parapets and
pinnacles, the open stone-work of the belfry windows, and
the ornamental feature which the external stair turret is
almost always made.

Perpendicular towers are very numerous in all parts of the
kingdom: among such as best deserve attention may be
mentioned those of Gloucester, York, and Canterbury cathedrals; Cirencester, Gloucestershire; Great Malvern, Worcestershire, and that of St. Mary Magdalen college, Oxford.

Magdalen College, Oxford.

Of the cathedrals which have had alterations made during
the period we are now concluding, we may instance those of
Winchester, Gloucester, Canterbury, Norwich, Bristol, Wells,
and Worcester.

In our description of Gothic architecture, we have been
under the necessity of confining ourselves solely to those parts
of the ecclesiastical buildings whose various modifications
constitute the most obvious distinctions between one style and
another. We have only presented a mere sketch of the
peculiarities, and enough of the principles to show that the

changes of style were gradual, and the results of a desire to
improve in general combinations and more enriched details.
To assert that all the works of the Gothic masons at any
date were perfect, and devoid of inconsistencies, would be
to mislead: it is however surprising that so little of the
defective should exist, when we consider the insufficient
number of architects and masons for the host of buildings
which were in the course of erection at the same periods.
Let the student of this class of art endeavour to discriminate
between that which is really good, and accidental or compulsory
peculiarities; and not attach undue importance to, or endeavour to imitate, features whose only recommendation is their
quaintness or picturesque effects, or the ingenuity displayed in
disguising that which is otherwise deficient in harmony or
arrangement.

CHAPTER XVI.

THE CASTELLATED AND DOMESTIC BUILDINGS OF ENGLAND, FROM THE NORMAN TO THE TUDOR PERIOD.

THE buildings of the Anglo-Saxon nobility, as well as those of
the burgesses and common people of this country, were of a
very humble character, and constructed of timber covered with
reeds and straw: the former, says William of Malmsbury,
"squandered their ample means in low and mean dwellings."
On the settlement of the Normans after the Conquest, the
kings, nobility, and prelates erected large and magnificent
palaces or castles, and the barons were equally jealous in
raising fortified castles, as were the prelates in the erection
of ecclesiastical buildings. This change, like all others in the
art of building, was the result of necessity: the Normans
found that although they had conquered, and intended to
retain possession of the country, yet they were surrounded by

vassals by whom they were detested, on account of the plunder and subjugation to which they had been compelled to submit.

To guard against an expulsion from the island, (which was far from improbable,) the Conqueror resolved to encourage his nobles and prelates in the erection of fortified places, and for that object made large grants of lands to such as had the power to build, either by their own means or exaction. Amongst the castles erected during the reign of the first Norman king, or shortly afterwards, may be mentioned, the Tower of London, the castles of Porchester, Canterbury, Rochester, Dover, Colchester, Norwich, Ludlow, Hedingham, Guildford, Oxford, Newcastle-upon-Tyne, Corfe, Bamborough, and Richmond;—these in plan were either square or oblong. Of the round or polygonal, the following are the most important: Arundel, Conisburgh, York, Tunbridge, Lincoln, Oxford, Windsor, Durham, and Berkeley.

William Rufus and Henry I. were as much addicted to the erection of castles as their father; but during the reign of Stephen, which lasted from 1135 to 1154, this practice had become so general, that in the short space of nineteen years no fewer than 1115 had been raised from their foundations; in fact, all those who had the ability or means built a stronghold or castle. A concise description of the general arrangement of these structures may be interesting. An eminence near a river was the situation generally chosen: the boundary walls were often of great extent, and in plan very irregular, their form being regulated by the nature of the position, or levels of the ground; the whole was surrounded by a broad ditch, called the fosse, which could be filled with water when required. The most advanced work beyond the fosse was the barbican or watch-tower; it was placed before the drawbridge and principal entrance as a protection from sudden assaults: these outworks were of great strength, and so planned, that if the gate was forced, those within could still annoy the assailants from the turrets and embrasures during their attack on the drawbridge entrance.* Within the ditch was a wall of great strength, frequently from 8 to 9 feet in thickness, and as much as 30 feet in height; towers were placed at the most commanding or principal positions of it, in which the principal officers of the castle resided: inside of the wall were the apartments of the retainers, servants, as well as storehouses and necessary offices. On the top of the wall was a platform extending the whole length and over the towers: the side towards the ditch was protected by battlements. The great gate was flanked on each side with a square or circular tower, and above the gateway were rooms which communicated with those in the towers. The mode of protecting this entrance was by a portcullis, or framework of wood faced with iron; it was fixed in a groove, and was raised or lowered by machinery: behind this were massive oak double doors, which were either covered with iron or large nail-heads. Within the external wall was a large open space or court, containing the chapel: in some instances another ditch and wall enclosed an inner court or ballium, where the dungeon or keep was placed. This great tower, the principal stronghold of the castle, was built on the most elevated spot, sometimes on an artificial mound, and varied from four to five stories in height. The walls were of great thickness, and in them the passages or stairs were built: the openings were small, and admitted but little light into the apartments. This building was used as the residence of the owner, or constable of the castle, and was provided with underground vaults for the confinement of prisoners. On the second floor was the state room or hall for entertainment, as well as a chapel. This mass of masonry was made to contain provisions and ammunition for a long defence, in the event of the rest of the castle being taken: the well was usually in the centre of the tower, and had openings to each floor.† The

* Instances of the barbican are to be seen at York, Scarborough castle, Yorkshire, and Carlisle castle, Cumberland.

† Those at Rochester and Conisburgh are still existing.

only admission to this tower was by a door at from 15 to 20 feet from the ground, approached by a steep external staircase. The whole of this strong building was surmounted by projecting battlements and machicolations, through the openings of which arrows, stones, and other missiles were thrown on the assailants.   One of the most interesting keep-towers is that of Conisburgh, Yorkshire, built by William de Warren in 1070,

Keep-tower, Conisburgh Castle.

during the reign of William of Normandy. It is circular inside, and divided into three stories or floors : beneath the lowest of these is an apartment, which was probably the dungeon ; it is arched over, and has no window or opening

but that in the floor of the room above, through which you
descend. The apartment on the first floor was used as a
store-room, and had no other external opening than the door;
above this was the great hall and other apartments.* The
keeps of the Anglo-Norman castles which are most perfect at

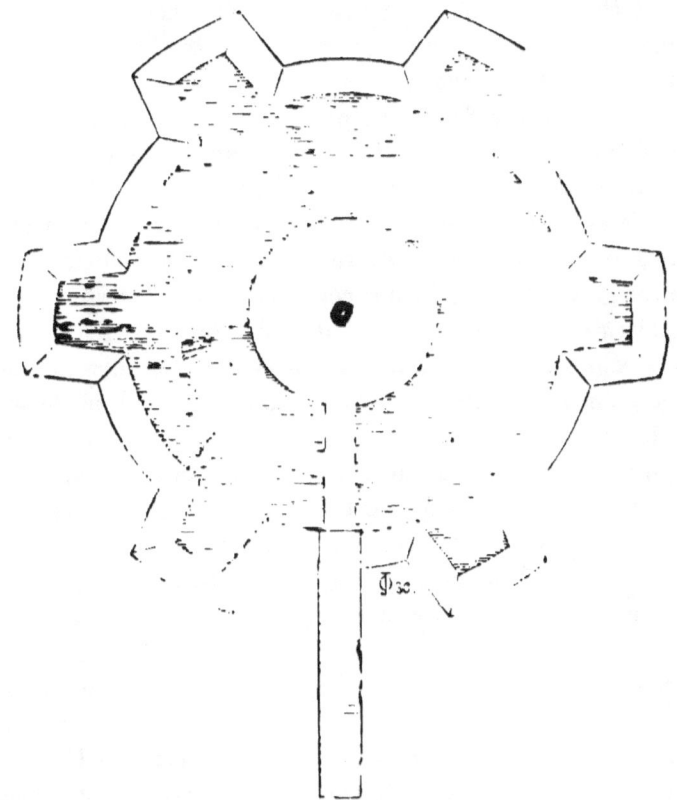

Plan of Conisburgh Castle.

the present time are those of the White Tower of London,
Rochester, Guildford, Norwich, and Hedingham.†

* The internal diameter is about 23 feet, and the walls are from 10 to
13 feet in thickness; the total height from the ground is about 90 feet.

† The first two were erected by Gundulph, Bishop of Rochester.

The arrangement of the early castles varied as the circumstances or situation required; but their massiveness remained nearly the same until the time of Edward I., when the castellated as well as the ecclesiastical architecture of this country acquired more varied forms and lighter details. The castles built by this monarch lost much of the stern gloominess of the stronghold, and assumed more the character of a fortified residence,—thus evincing an advance towards a greater refinement in the mode of living; for though the security of the owner of these fortresses was considered, yet in the castellated buildings of this and the following reigns a more commodious arrangement of the principal apartments was adopted, and the window openings were made larger. Caernarvon Castle, Wales, built by Edward I., was both a fortress and a palace; the King held his court in it, and Queen Eleanor gave birth to Edward II. within its walls, on April 25th, 1284. It was commenced by Edward immediately after his conquest of the country in 1282, and the fortifications and castle were completed within the space of one year by the labour of the peasants, and at the cost of the chieftains of the country, on whom the conqueror imposed the hateful task.* This castle was of great strength, and regular in plan: the towers are very beautiful, and in form are pentagonal, hexagonal, or octagonal. The eagle tower is fine, and has the addition of three slender turrets issuing from the top.

Among the castles erected by Edward I., those of Caernarvon, Conway, Beaumaris, Harlech, in Wales, are the most remarkable. Windsor Castle was nearly rebuilt by Edward III., who extended it to the present dimensions, and gave it the appearance of a castellated palace, instead of the fortress which preceded it.†

* Britton's ' Architectural Antiquities.'

† William de Wykeham was appointed to superintend the works which were in progress from the year 1357 to 1375. Many alterations were made by the successors of Edward III. The beautiful chapel of St. George was enlarged and rebuilt by Edward IV., and Henry VII. vaulted the roof

From the beginning of the fourteenth century, or from the time of Henry IV., the habitable castles gradually assumed a lighter and more pleasing character, until they changed into the castellated mansion, and were adapted to suit the improved domestic habits of each period. Those of Windsor, Warwick, and Raby are therefore remarkable; for, whilst they present the external features of feudal ages, their apartments are at once spacious and elegant: in the window openings, mullions and traceried heads were introduced.

Ragland Castle, Monmouthshire, erected in the reigns of Edward IV. and Henry VII. by the Earl of Worcester, at the close of the fifteenth century, is built of stone, and very interesting, from its combining the external requisites of a defensive castle with the internal arrangements of a mansion. The windows of the great hall, dining-room, bed-rooms, and indeed all those which look towards the court-yard, are divided by mullions and transoms, whilst the heads are traceried. The strength of this castle may be inferred from its having been garrisoned by eight hundred men during the civil wars: at length it surrendered to the parliamentary forces, was confiscated with the large estates of its loyal and venerable owner, and shared the same fate which befell so many similar buildings;—it was plundered and dismantled.

Thornbury Castle, Gloucestershire, commenced about 1511, is another example of the castellated mansion; it is celebrated for the elaborate and beautiful style of the windows, chimneys, and other ornaments. The parts at present existing were built in the reign of Henry VIII. by Edward Stafford, Duke of Buckingham, who was engaged on it for ten years. The completion of this magnificent design was prevented by its noble owner being sacrificed to the resentment of Cardinal Wolsey.*

---

of the choir: Henry VIII. rebuilt the great gate in the lower ward, and additions have been made by most succeeding monarchs.

* The Duke of Buckingham was arrested at Thornbury Castle, and

From what remains of this ducal edifice, it is evident that it was intended to have been built on a very spacious and magnificent scale, and to have rivalled in size and richness of decoration the palaces of Nonsuch, Richmond, and Hampton Court. This presumption may have been instrumental in provoking the enmity of the King, who looked with jealousy on those of his nobles who dared to emulate him in their mansions, and which was not lessened by the Duke being one of the most powerful and wealthy persons of his time.   .

The buildings which the Duke commenced remained unfinished, and were abandoned to ruin immediately after his attainder. Since that period, all the older parts of the castle, comprising a great many rooms, have been totally demolished, and much injury has been done to the windows and other ornamental parts within the last century.

The towers at the entrance to the inner court are bold in design; the projecting machicolations, still preserved, are very good examples. The bay windows of the great hall are beautifully composed; the plans of the upper and lower parts vary, the one being a combination of five semicircles of four lights in each, whilst the latter is angular, and more solid in construction. It is impossible to describe properly the great oriel window, the enriched chimney shafts, fire-places, and other features of interest, without the assistance of illustrations: we must therefore refer the reader to Pugin's 'Examples,' vol. ii., for further information on the details of this interesting and most ornamental specimen of the castellated mansion.

We cannot turn from the stone erections of this period without notice of Kenilworth Castle, long since dismantled,

---

conducted to London, where he was tried and declared guilty of high treason, chiefly on the evidence of Charles Knevet, who had been formerly steward to the Duke; and who, being dismissed for misconduct, sought revenge by betraying his master. Of course, the remorseless Henry consigned him to execution, and his head was struck off on Tower Hill, May 17th, 1521.—Pugin's 'Examples,' vol. ii.

and whose shattered halls and towers are gradually falling to the ground. This spacious and once magnificent pile was composed of buildings raised at different periods during five centuries, and consequently exhibited almost every variety of architecture that successively was practised from the Norman to that now commonly called the Elizabethan style. Geoffrey de Clinton, Lord Chamberlain and Treasurer to Henry I., was the founder of the castle, to which he annexed an extensive park or chase. In 1172, during the reign of Henry II., it was fortified and garrisoned by the King, when his eldest son raised a rebellion which involved the whole nation in tumult. Henry III. granted it to Simon de Montfort, Earl of Leicester, for life; it remained from that period until 1485 in the hands of the Crown, when Henry VI. transferred it to the possessions of the Duchy of Cornwall. In 1562, Queen Elizabeth, by letters patent, bestowed it on her favourite, Robert, Lord Dudley, afterwards Earl of Leicester. The costly festivities and splendid entertainments which took place here on the royal visit, as well as the history of the untimely end of its princely owner, have given an interest to this above all other castles. All the buildings were enclosed by an outward court, comprising seven acres, surrounded with massive walls, embattled, and strengthened with buttresses and towers. The richest and most perfect parts are the remains of the great hall and the rooms adjoining it, which appear of about the date of Henry VIII. The castles of Warwick, Bolton, and Middleham, Yorkshire, and many others, possess features of great interest both to the architect and antiquary.

The next class or section of defensive mansions may be termed fortified manor-houses, erected of bricks, either plain or ornamental, with an occasional introduction of stone: of these, Herst-Monceaux, in Sussex, is perhaps the most celebrated;—this may have been partly caused by its destruction, which is unaccountable. Mr. Wilson remarks that—"Had accidental fire, or a siege in the civil wars, reduced it to the mere shell we have now before us, our regret would have been softened by reflections on the inevitable fate that, sooner or later, attends all human grandeur. But what can be said of the sordid possessor of such a treasure, who deliberately pulls it to pieces?"—The right of property is unquestionable; but it would have been happy for the memory of the owner, had he considered that the possession of a building which the public admire and value is, in some sort, equivalent to a public trust, and its destruction is sure to be followed by the censure of posterity.

The castle was built A. D. 1440, in the nineteenth year of Henry VI., by Sir Roger Ficnes, who obtained a royal licence to enclose six hundred acres of land, and fortify his manor-house. It remained in the family until 1701, when this noble castle was purchased by George Naylor, Esq., from whom it descended to the Rev. Robert Hare, by whom it was completely gutted and reduced to a ruin in the year 1777.

All that now remains of Herst-Monceaux Castle are the gate-house and towers, with the whole of the external walls, which are nearly a square of about 200 feet: these are as perfect as when built, having octagonal towers at the angles, and three others between. The arrangement of the apartments seems, from the account in Grose's 'Antiquities,' to have been on an enlarged and magnificent scale of richness. The hall is spoken of as "resembling those at Oxford and Cambridge, with three handsome rooms at the eastern end, one of them 40 feet long; beyond these were the chapel, and parlours for common use, with rooms for the upper servants. The grand stairs, which lie beyond the hall, occupy an area of 40 feet square. The kitchen, as well as the hall and chapel, goes in height to the upper story of the house." The other chambers were large and numerous; the apartments on one floor were sufficient to lodge a garrison. The windows were of stone, and in every one was painted glass. The towers on each side of the gate-house on the south front are 84 feet high, and very fine in design. This castle, entirely built with brick, is one of the oldest edifices of that material in the kingdom (excepting those left by the Romans), as well as one of the most complete, no flaw or crack being observable in any part of it. The walls are of great thickness; the doorways, copings, water tables, and all moulded work, are of stone.

Another of the same class of defensive manor-house as the preceding, though of a later date, is Oxborough Hall, Norfolk; it was built in 1482 by Sir Edmund Bedingfield, a zealous adherent to the House of York, and in high favour with Edward IV., who granted him a licence to build towers and fortifications at his manor of Oxborough.

This mansion is constructed entirely of brick, with the exception of the larger windows and gateway in the entrance tower. The whole of the traceried panels, mouldings, and battlements are either of cut brick or moulded tiles. It is in plan nearly a square of 172 feet, with the buildings entirely surrounding a central court. The hall, 52 feet long and 29 feet broad, and also the principal apartments, were in the southern range, or facing the entrance: these, with the private dining-room and great kitchen, were taken down in the year 1778. The grand entrance gateway remains unchanged, and is a most interesting feature: it is flanked by two octagonal towers 80 feet in height, panelled in six stories, standing forward with a bold projection, and rising from the moat, which entirely surrounds the walls. The approach to the gates is by a bridge of three arches: an arch projecting from the face of the wall connecting the towers, and supporting the battlements, serves for the purpose of machicolations: windows of three and four openings light the rooms over the gateway. In the tower on the right hand of the entrance is a spiral staircase of brick, leading to the top of the building, and lighted by small quatrefoil apertures. The other tower is occupied by four rooms, three of which have covered brick roofs, with projecting ribs.

In its original state, Oxborough Hall exhibited a complete example of a fortified mansion, which, as we have before explained, succeeded, and was the last of a class having any similitude to the castles of the earlier times: it was designed with more regard to internal space, convenience, and the improved habits of living, although constructed of sufficient strength to resist any casual hostile assault. Many other examples of dismantled buildings of this date and character still exist in different parts of the country; but as we have chosen the best and most perfect, no advantage would be obtained by further descriptions.

CHAPTER XVII.

THE DOMESTIC AND CIVIL ARCHITECTURE OF ENGLAND OF THE TUDOR AND ELIZABETHAN PERIODS.

WE have now arrived at a class of architecture more pleasing in its contemplation than that described in our previous chapter: all the buildings there noticed were erected for a purpose more or less offensive or defensive;—the history of the country, the numerous wars or disputes between kings and nobles, and the unsettled or rather disordered state of society, are written in indelible characters on every stone and brick which remains. However we may be pleased by an antiquarian or historical research into these evidences of past events, and the ingenuity displayed in their erection, still, to the studious mind or to the philanthropist, they are so many monuments recording the sufferings of people by the tyranny of ambition, or else are the records of oppression, domestic broils, and anarchy. Their great attraction to the world at large is the picturesque appearance which their ruinous state presents; but it is to be questioned whether, in the under current of the mind's reflections, another feeling does not arise that imperceptibly assists the charm, viz.

congratulation at our more peaceful state, and the sub-
version of customs in which might was often considered
synonymous with right and justice. Nothing perhaps forms
a more beautiful picture than castellated ruins well covered
with vegetation, intermixed and surrounded by trees in all
their natural loveliness of form, unindebted to the hand of
man for planting or training, and more frequently growing,
as in mockery to the founder, in the great halls or state
chambers, where but a very few centuries since the frail repre-
sentative of humanity prided himself on the capabilities which
power gave him to persecute his fellow man.

The halls or manor-houses of the reigns of Henry the
Seventh and Henry the Eighth retained little of fortified
character beyond the battlements with which the walls were
surmounted, more for ornament than use (as we find in the
churches of this period). The thickness of the walls, size of
the windows, turrets, and buttresses, were influenced by their
situation or requirements, and without any idea of making the
mansion assume an appearance of more than necessary
strength. In the arrangement of the plans of the Tudor
houses, no systematic principle seems to have been considered,
and the position of the rooms was caused by local circumstances: in those of a large scale, the courts were generally
surrounded by buildings, as at Haddon Hall, Derbyshire;
whilst in others of less pretension there was a gate-house in
advance of the mansion, but connected with it by mantle walls:
the manor-house, East Barsham, Norfolk, has this appendage.

The style of architecture which prevailed during the latter
part of the fifteenth century is more extended, both for its
uses and modification, than any other we are acquainted with,
and was applied to domestic as well as ecclesiastical structures.
The preceding styles had been only employed in religious
buildings, with which the castellated ones of the same period
had little in common, and had so very few features wherein the
general style could at all exhibit itself: they must, therefore,
be considered as forming distinct classes of themselves.

In the ornamental domestic architecture of the fifteenth and sixteenth centuries, generally designated Tudor, (there are very few examples before that period,) we perceive the same style as that of the ecclesiastical buildings applied to another class, where, although the parts are somewhat differently composed, the style of ornament and detail is essentially the same. Some features, such as doorways and porches, are very little altered from those of churches; while others, unknown to the latter class of buildings, such as chimneys and projecting windows, became highly characteristic and decorative in this.* Oriel and bay windows are peculiar to this style: these terms are often used indiscriminately;—the former of these project out in the upper part of a building, and over-hang that below, being corbelled upon mouldings splaying downwards on every side: the latter may be similar in openings and ornament, but they rise immediately from the ground, and are connected with the building by the base and string-course mouldings. Oriels are both single and compound, that is, are either confined to one of the upper floors of the building, or carried up through all its stories: of the latter description is the singularly rich one in the entrance tower of Magdalen college, Oxford, built in 1475;—others are to be seen at Windsor. Of the former, we may refer to examples of varied character and degrees of richness at Balliol, St. John's, and All Souls' colleges, Oxford; Windsor Castle; Hengrave Hall, Suffolk; the Chancellor's house, Lincoln; the manor-houses of Great Chalfield and Wraxall, Wilts; the hall of the Vicar's close, Wells; the tribunal-house, Glastonbury; Thornbury Castle, Gloucestershire; and the Deanery, Wells.† Oriel windows are rarely to be found in any buildings but those of the period of Henry the Seventh or the early part of Henry the Eighth; whereas the bay window

---

* Projecting or bay windows have sometimes been misapplied to churches, as at Spetchley in Worcestershire, and Dorchester, Dorset.

† Illustrations of the greater part of these are to be found in Pugin's 'Examples of Gothic Architecture.'

was retained until the end of the reign of Elizabeth, and made one of the most important features in the compositions. Bay windows, so called from forming a bay or recess in a room, projecting from the wall either in a rectangular, semi-octagonal, or circular form, do not appear to have been used prior to the introduction of the Perpendicular style, when they were very frequently employed, particularly in halls, where they were invariably found at one end, and sometimes at both ends of the dais: the openings were generally longer than those of the other windows, so as to reach within about three feet from the floor. Some of the finest specimens of the Tudor period are to be found at Hampton Court Palace; the hall of the Palace at Eltham, Kent; Crosby Hall, London; Compton Winyate, Warwickshire; Thornbury Castle, Gloucestershire; Sutton Place, Surrey; Athelhampton, Dorsetshire; Kenilworth Castle, Warwickshire; and Haddon Hall, Derbyshire.

Chimney shafts, which until the latter part of the fifteenth century had not been made of importance, and were generally attached or in pairs, now became one of the principal features by being clustered together and very highly ornamented; they were executed both of stone and brick; examples of the latter material are very numerous; their form was either octagonal or circular: those at East Barsham manor-house, and Thorpland Hall, Norfolk, are richly ornamented with devices; other beautiful varieties exist at Gifford's Hall, Suffolk; Eton college, Buckinghamshire; Hampton Court, Middlesex; and Chesham, Buckinghamshire.

Although chimneys had been long invented, and were much in use for other rooms, our ancestors do not appear to have introduced them generally into their halls until the end of the fifteenth or the early part of the sixteenth century. The previously open hearth, on which the fire was made, was in the centre of the hall, and the smoke escaped through the louvre lantern in the roof: about this period they were added to many halls of an older date.

The general plan, as we have before observed, of the larger

mansions of the Tudor period was quadrangular, consisting of
an inner and base court, between which stood the gate-house:
on the side of the inner court facing the entrance, the principal apartments were placed; these consisted of the hall,
the chapel, the great chamber and dining-room, and were
connected with a gallery for amusements, running the whole
length of another side of the quadrangle.* Good examples
of this class of mansion are to be found, although many are so
altered as to retain but a slight expression of their original
state. Hannaker House, near Midhurst, Sussex, was built
round a court, with the entrance under an embattled gate-
house, flanked by small octagonal towers on the south. A
square tower was at the south-east angle; the chapel and other
apartments on the east; the hall and principal rooms on the
north: the latter contains carving and oak panelling of the
time of Henry the Eighth. In a compartment near the centre
are the arms of England: over the doors leading from the

* Warton, in 1783, thus describes "a most beautiful and genuine
model of a magnificent mansion of the reign of Henry the Eighth, built
by Sir Anthony Brown at Midhurst in Sussex:"

" We enter a spacious and lofty quadrangle of stone through a stately
Gothic tower, with four light angular turrets. The roof of the gateway is
a fine piece of old fret-work. There is a venerable old hall, with a noble
oak-raftered roof and a large high range of Gothic windows. Opposite
the screen is the arched portal of the buttery. Adjoining the hall is a
dining-room, the walls painted all over, (as was anciently the mode soon
after the beginning of the reign of Edward the Sixth,) chiefly with histories
(out of perspective) of Henry the Eighth: the roof is in flat compartments.
A gallery, with window recesses or oriels, occupies one side of the quadrangular court. A gallery on the opposite, of equal dimensions, has given
way to modern convenience, and is converted into bed-chambers. In the
centre of the court is a magnificent old fountain, with much imagery in
brass, and a variety of devices for shooting water. On the top of the hall
is the original louvre or lantern, adorned with a profusion of vanes. The
chapel, running at right angles with the hall, terminates in the garden
with three large Gothic windows."

The same Sir Anthony Brown built also Byfleet House, Surrey: he
died in 1548.

hall to the buttery and cellar are half-length figures of men holding cups: over the head of one, on a label, is LES · BIEN · VENUS; and over the other, COME · IN · AND · DRINGE.*

Hengrave Hall, Suffolk, built in 1538, is another of the fine old mansions with which that county abounds: the date of this is certain from an inscription on the outside of the curious oriel window. An open court occupies the centre of the buildings; this is surrounded on three sides by a gallery, with windows to the court, communicating with all the apartments: the hall (34 feet by 25) is on the other; the bay and two windows, by which it is lighted, look into the court. The apartments are numerous, and their arrangement is, perhaps, more in accordance with modern requirements than we generally find in buildings of this date. The principal front (which is about 160 feet in length) displays a fine picturesque character; indeed, the whole is a unique example of ancient domestic architecture. It is built of brick and stone; the gateway is peculiar and in high preservation; perhaps a more elegant specimen of the architecture of that age can scarcely be seen.

The great halls in the palaces, mansions, and colleges of this period were extremely lofty, frequently predominating over the surrounding buildings: the ceilings and roofs were very boldly constructed and elaborately ornamented.† The most deserving attention are those at Eltham Palace, Kent, built by Edward the Fourth about 1482;—and at Hampton Court, built by Cardinal Wolsey between 1520 and 1540, which is the most florid in its decorations of any in the kingdom, and measures 106 feet by 40, the walls being 45 feet high. That of Christ Church, Oxford, built likewise by Cardinal Wolsey a few years earlier, is much more simple, though scarcely less

---

* Hunt's 'Tudor Architecture.'

† For a full description of the constructive principles and peculiarities of the open timber roofs of this as well as the preceding style, the reader is referred to the 'Rudimentary Art of Building,' published in this series.

beautiful;—the size is 115 feet by 40, and 50 feet high. Beddington Hall, Surrey, is another fine example. The roof of Crosby Hall, London, built about 1470, cannot be exceeded in richness of effect, the details of which are of the pure styles of the florid Gothic, and unlike that of Hampton Court, where the Italian or transition style has been partially introduced. The interior of Crosby Hall measures 69 feet by 27 ; and the height in the centre of the roof about 38 feet. The noblest of the open timber roofs is that of Westminster Hall, erected by Richard the Second in 1395; the hammer-beam and arched rib are its peculiar constructive features : the length of this hall is 228 feet, breadth 66 feet, and height 92 feet. Many other open roofs, more or less ornamented, are to be found in the colleges at Oxford and Cambridge, the inns of court in London, besides others in the country, of which we mention Athelhampton Hall, Dorsetshire, Penshurst Place, and Cobham college, Kent.

The next description of manor-house is that where the buildings were not quadrangular, but arranged in one front, with projecting wings, or else having a porch-tower in the centre. In front of this was an irregular court, formed partly by the house, and by stables or other out-buildings : those of Great Chalfield and South Wraxall are thus arranged, with entrance gate-houses : the former is in a very perfect state, still retaining the elaborately carved oak screen of the banqueting-hall : it is altogether one of the best examples of the latter part of the reign of Henry the Sixth.*

The brick-built manor-houses of this period, so peculiar to the counties of Norfolk and Suffolk, deserve our notice : that at East Barsham exhibits an extraordinary specimen of skilful workmanship, being almost wholly composed of that material ; and it is much to be regretted that this curious and extensive fabric should have been suffered to fall into ruins, when a little expense and care bestowed on it, about a century since, would have preserved it : at present, more than half the

* See Pugin's 'Examples,' vol. iii.

Westminster Hall.

house is roofless, and reduced to a state so decayed and ruinous, that its original form cannot be exactly traced. It was commenced in the reign of Henry the Seventh, and finished in that succeeding. The walls of the principal front are nearly on one plane, being broken only by the porch in the centre; and octagonal turrets of different sizes are so distributed as to give a variety of outline to the combination. The hall is to the left of the porch by which it is entered: the great parlour and principal apartments are beyond, or at the back of it. The windows are large, and must have given the rooms a cheerful appearance. The building consists of only two stories, except in one part, where another is added as a tower. The upper string-courses are bold in moulding, and rich in cast ornaments and panels: these are surmounted by moulded battlements, with beautiful traceried panels. The stack of ten chimneys at the west end of the hall, and the turret terminations, are fine in design and execution.

The building, which measures 140 feet by 58 feet, has a gate-house tower about 40 feet in front of the porch (a paved court intervening): on this, if possible, a greater degree of moulding and enrichment has been bestowed;—figures, armorial bearings, battlements, and panelling, are all executed in brick in a surprising manner.

Thorpland Hall, within two miles of East Barsham, is evidently of the same date, and erected by the same party: although it will not bear any comparison as to scale, yet the details and ornaments are in no way inferior. It is a valuable example of the class, and exhibits features well suited to modern imitation. The parsonage-house, Great Snoring, in the immediate vicinity of Thorplands, likewise built of brick, is celebrated for its peculiar richness of design.

In many towns there are considerable remains of houses built during the fifteenth century, both of stone as well as of timber and ornamental plaster: of the former, an inn and tribunal-house at Glastonbury, and another at Grantham, are noted for their elaborate and beautiful arrangement: of the latter class, numerous instances still exist in most of the old cities, Coventry, Winchester, York, Norwich, and at Hadleigh, Lavenham, Ipswich, and many other places in Suffolk and Norfolk.

We have little evidence of the way in which houses were fitted up until late in the fifteenth century. Tapestries were much in use, but very few specimens remain; those at St. Mary's Hall, Coventry, representing Henry VI. and his court, and Queen Margaret, are good early examples, and in a comparatively perfect state of preservation. Oak panelling generally lined the walls of the halls and larger rooms to one-third of their height; paintings of ornaments, figures, and armorial bearings were likewise adopted for decoration, but few examples remain.* The ceilings of this period were usually of timber, divided into squares, with carved flowers at the intersections, as at Sherborne Abbey, Dorset. Another, at the Deanery, Worcester, has the whole of the mouldings relieved in colour, and on the ground of the square panels roses are painted. The hall at Great Chalfield has its ceiling divided into squares by the main timbers, and at the intersections are plaster bosses, composed of foliage and devices.

Towards the close of the fifteenth century Italian features were continually increasing, and consequently greater variations were observable in the ornamental details at the beginning of the following century. Wainscot came much in fashion: the panels were small, and mostly of what is called the linen pattern; but they were also carved with great variety

* Painting on the walls of rooms is of high antiquity. Henry III., who was a great encourager of the fine arts, kept several painters in his service. One chamber in the palace of Winchester was painted green, with stars of gold, and the whole history of the Old and New Testament. A room at Westminster, and another in the Tower of London, were embellished with the history of the expedition of Richard I. into the Holy Land. The coronation, wars, and marriage of Edward I. were painted on the walls of the great hall in the episcopal palace at Lichfield, in 1312.

"In the famous royal palace of England is a celebrated chamber, on whose walls all the warlike histories of the Bible are painted, and explained by a regular series of texts." During Edward the Third's time, the taste for painting was so great and general, that even the walls of the bed-chambers of private gentlemen were ornamented with historical pictures.

of design, mixed more or less with Italian details, and frequently in the upper line of panels fanciful heads, placed in
wreaths, were carved in high relief. "A great deal of this
kind of work yet remains at Tolleshunt Darcy, Essex; Thame
Park, Oxford; Boughton Malherbe, Kent; Syon House,
Middlesex; and in many other places. Towards the end of
this century, planer panels were introduced, sometimes with
gilding, as at a house at Hollingbourne, Kent, and also
arabesques, &c., in painting, as at Boughton Malherbe.
Sometimes the walls had rude paintings, as at Eastbury
House, Essex."*

In the early part of this century the main divisions of the
ceilings were formed by the girders of the floor above, which
were either chamfered or moulded at the angles; and the joists
were either bare, but ornamented with mouldings and carved,
or else concealed by panels with ribs of oak, divided into various
figures, the ground of which, or the spaces between, were both
of wood and plaster: of the former class, the ceiling of the old
Star Chamber was a beautiful example. At Layer Marney,
Essex, Hever and Allington Castles, Kent, instances of the
latter are to be found. Ornamental staircases and galleries do
not occur until the end of this century.

The timber houses, both in the country and towns, erected
during the latter part of the sixteenth and the succeeding
century, are often very splendid. The town-halls of Hereford
and Leominster, and a house in Ludlow, are very perfect
examples of street buildings. The towns of Chester, Shrewsbury, Leicester, Warwick, and Ipswich contain others more or
less perfect. The counties of Cheshire and Shropshire are
noted for country mansions of this class. Moreton Hall, built
about 1559, is a particularly fine example of the arrangement
of the timber buildings of this period, and almost wholly composed of wood and plaster. At present it encloses three sides
of a spacious court, the south side of which has never been
completed, or has been taken down. The bay and projecting

* 'Remarks on Domestic Architecture,' by William Twopenny, Esq.

windows, surmounted by carved gables, are arranged to form
very picturesque features, and filled with ornamental glazing
and stained glass. Park Hall, near Oswestry, Shropshire,
presents many peculiarities in the plan and decoration of the
exterior, differing from the preceding example: it is more
uniform in its arrangement, having a projecting central porch
and wings at each end: bay windows are here introduced: the
centre of the building, as well as the greater part of the wings
on the ground and first floors, comprises one continuous
window, interrupted only by the projections and mullions,
but having no piers: the portions not used as openings display the ornamental framing filled in with plaster. Ockwells,
Berks, near Windsor, is a most interesting specimen of the half-
timbered mansions of the time of Henry VI. and Edward IV.
The windows are less united than those of the later date,
and the mullions are connected by arched heads; the gables
in particular are very beautiful. Bramhall Hall, Cheshire, is
another of these remarkable buildings, retaining the peculiarity
of the front presenting the appearance of one continuous window
on each floor: the glazing is very varied in pattern, and enriched by circles of stained glass.

As multiplying examples of buildings retaining similar features and combinations would not assist our inquiry, we shall
proceed to the consideration of the styles which succeeded.

Scarcely any English sovereign, with the exception of the
first two Georges, did less in direct patronage of the arts and
architecture than the Queen whose name has been attached
to a style which has been more generally followed in this
country for domestic buildings than any other; for, with the
exception of the royal gallery at Windsor, she herself, in a
forty years' reign, did actually nothing. Elizabeth, therefore,
does not appear to have inherited any taste or passion for
architecture from her father; or, if she did, the thought that
her father had done sufficient in building palaces might have
hindered her from exercising it: of one thing we are certain,

she at least encouraged the nobles of her court in great expenditure on their residences ;* and their example was so generally
followed, that in this reign more ornamental and substantial
houses were erected than in any other before or since.

The decline and ultimate extinction of the Pointed style of
architecture, and the introduction of a class of art hitherto
unknown in England, cannot justly be attributed either to the
dissolution of religious houses, the alteration in ceremonies, or
even to the suppression of the ancient faith, as some would
make us believe.   It must be borne in mind that a positive
change in the arts of design, as applied to ecclesiastical buildings, had taken place in France and Germany, where the
religion remained unchanged, at least half a century before it
was visible in our own country.   We are free to admit that,
whilst art was in the hands of the Catholic clergy of this
country, it flourished vigorously; still its expression and ornamentation were constantly varying.   The Perpendicular style
had its transitions, and some which must clearly convince us
that even when there was no prospect of a change of the forms
of religion, the style was becoming debased, and the principles
of Gothic art neglected.

Architecture and the arts had revived in Italy in the fifteenth
century, and the style most adopted there was enriched with
imaginary and fantastic representations of animals, birds, fruit,
and foliage; the walls were covered with designs of an ornamental nature, in which fancy was occasionally excited to its
utmost scope; in short, every variety of detail and general
design was introduced.   The immense patronage which the
arts received at this period in all parts of Italy had the effect
of producing an extraordinary amount of talent, which became
celebrated throughout Europe, and originated a demand for
that style of architecture which hitherto had not been practised
north of the Alps.

* The Earl of Leicester expended on Kenilworth alone no less a sum
than £ 60,000.

The desire for change and variety seems nearly inseparable from the human mind, and mutability has been the rule of all things under the sun, since first the earth was gladdened by its rays; yet still progression or retrogression has more generally been gradual: unfortunately, in the history of art and architecture, the latter has invariably been marked by additional speed towards its end. This most assuredly was the case with the architecture of the last Pointed period; a century had been taken to perfect it, and less than a quarter of one was only needed for its debasement and total extinction in this country.

The constant intercourse with the Continent during the reign of Henry VIII. had its influence on the arts of design. At this period, in France, the Netherlands and Germany, styles were practised having the features of the cinque cento; or the renaissance of Italy, blended on the class of architecture which had previously prevailed in each country. Thus arose three new styles;—that in France, during the reign of Francis I. retained the features of Gothic designs, but was enriched with Italian details, and has been deservedly celebrated for the elegance and excellence of its forms, and the exquisite execution of its ornaments. From this source came much of the classic detail so perceptible in the latter works of Henry the Eighth's reign.

The reign of Elizabeth is remarkable for the introduction of a style of domestic architecture more systematic in plan, more commodious in its arrangements, and imposing in its effects, than any preceding. Up to this period the mansions of the nobles were only one story in height, and in plan greatly deficient in the requirements incidental to the improved social condition. Indeed, the domestic architecture under Elizabeth had assumed a more scientific character, and we have ample evidence that no building was now undertaken without the previous arrangement of a well-considered plan. Books on the arts of design and construction were now published, and architects had begun to act upon a system in the construction of the palatial houses of the aristocracy. The principal deviation from the plans of the Tudor houses was in the frequent introduction of bay windows; the improvement in the galleries, which were now generally lofty, wide, and more than 100 feet in length; that of staircases, from being small and inconvenient, to occupying a considerable portion of the mansion, and communicating with the entrance or staircase halls of spacious dimensions. The exteriors of the porticoes and parapets were greatly enriched with carved entablatures, columns, pilasters, figures, armorial bearings, and every variety of device which the most fantastic imagination could supply.

To houses of this date, terraces of great grandeur were generally attached, connected with each other by broad flights of steps;—they were bounded by richly perforated parapets or balustrades. The windows retain more of the Gothic character than any other feature; they were divided by mullions and transoms, although their height, as well as width, was generally much increased: in some examples there are three and four tiers of openings, diminishing in height as they ascend.

The Italian Orders are much introduced, but their classic proportions not attended to: the columns, pilasters, and piers are usually banded in several courses by square blocks, which are constantly decorated with diamond or jewel-shaped projections: this ornament is of very frequent occurrence, and may be considered as a distinct characteristic of this style. The entablatures are more usually broken, either by projecting profiles or scrolled and voluted ornaments. The bay windows, parapets, and gables are terminated in general by perforated ornaments of either a square, circular, or scroll form.

This singular manner of designing must be examined to be well understood; no description can possibly convey a just idea of its complex forms and elaborate ornaments. There perhaps is no class of English architecture more compounded of inconsistencies, defects, and beauties, than this mixture of Gothic and Italian; but to be properly appreciated, it should be studied with a mind unbiassed alike by the tendencies of a previous education and the indiscriminating caprices of fashion. The application of this style to country mansions is unquestionably not to be equalled by any other, as its varied forms of plan and outline will either harmonize or contrast beautifully with scenery of any description.

One of the most celebrated architects of the reigns of Elizabeth and her successor was John Thorpe, who designed and erected most of the principal palatial edifices of the time. The general form of his plans is that of three sides of a quadrangle, and the portico in the centre. When the quadrangles were used, they are surrounded by an open arcade or corridor. As his designs are not distinguished by any peculiarity differing from those already described, we will only mention the names of some of his principal works: Holland House, Middlesex; Longford Castle, Wilts; Wollaton Hall, Notts; Audley End, Essex; Kirby, and Burleigh House. Bernard Adams and Lawrence Bradshaw, Robert and Huntingdon Smithson, were also eminent architects of this period.

The best architecture of this style may be seen at Westwood, Audley End, Hatfield, Wollaton, Burleigh, and Hardwick Hall; very many more buildings have beautiful and most elaborate features: in some, the staircases and screens; in others, the entrances. The plaster ceilings of the Elizabethan date are particularly deserving of attention, on account of their richness and beautiful arrangement: the fire-places, panelling, cornices, friezes, and ornaments of the principal apartments were extremely varied, and generally good in design. Crew Hall, Bramshill, and Knowle, retain good examples of these.

CHAPTER XVIII.

THE INTRODUCTION OF ITALIAN ARCHITECTURE INTO ENGLAND.

FROM JAMES I. TO THE PRESENT PERIOD.

THE early part of the seventeenth century, during the reign of James the First, is the period of the introduction of unmixed Italian architecture into England : it is to be attributed to the genius of Inigo Jones, who, in the early part of his professional career, had erected and altered several large buildings in the mixed style, which continued to prevail until his masterly designs of the Venetian school caused a general admiration and adoption of this class of art. Little is known of Inigo Jones or his

Inigo Jones.

works as an architect previous to 1605, when James the First visited the university of Oxford, at which time he was employed on the quadrangle at St. John's college, and had been to Italy : from that time until his second visit the buildings on which he was engaged were of a mixed or transition character ; when by a careful study of the works of Palladio, he perfected his taste, ripened his judgment, and laid the foundation for his future well-merited reputation. On his return to England he was appointed to the office of Surveyor of Public Buildings, and from that time his fame and practice rapidly increased.

The banqueting-house at Whitehall, begun in 1619 and completed in two years, is justly considered one of the most

Banqueting-House, Whitehall.

beautifully proportioned buildings in Europe. It is of the pure Italian style, and was but an inconsiderable portion of a magnificent design for a palace, which in magnitude would have exceeded the palace of Diocletian. In plan it was an oblong square, subdivided into seven courts; and would have extended from the park to the river: the latter front of 720 feet, as well as that towards Charing Cross extending 1152 feet, would from their scale alone have been imposing. The banqueting-house (the only part finished), now used as a chapel, is the largest room in England (Westminster Hall excepted), it being 115 feet in length, 60 in breadth, and 55 in height.

The garden front of old Somerset House, erected in 1623, was a work of great beauty, (and on its demolition was partially copied by Sir W. Chambers for the street front of the present edifice.) The portico of old St. Paul's, London (p. 154), built in 1633, was likewise his design; and although we may question the taste of adding a Roman portico (however well proportioned) to a Gothic cathedral, still it is perhaps less objectionable than attempting a style whose beauties and principles even the genius of Jones could not appreciate.

Jones also erected the York Stairs at the end of Buckingham Street in the Strand, (formerly in the gardens of the Duke of Buckingham,) in 1626. The façades of this building were of the Tuscan Order, divided into three openings: that in the centre, used for the passage and stairs, is wider than the other: on the river side, four half-columns are attached to the walls, and support an entablature, which is broken above the capitals: over the archway is a segmental pediment, having its tympanum ornamented with a shield. The façade next the street is similar in its combination, with the exception that the piers are ornamented with pilasters instead of columns. This building, though small in dimensions, is much admired for its boldness and propriety of character.

The church of St. Paul, in Covent Garden, built from the designs of Jones, is interesting from

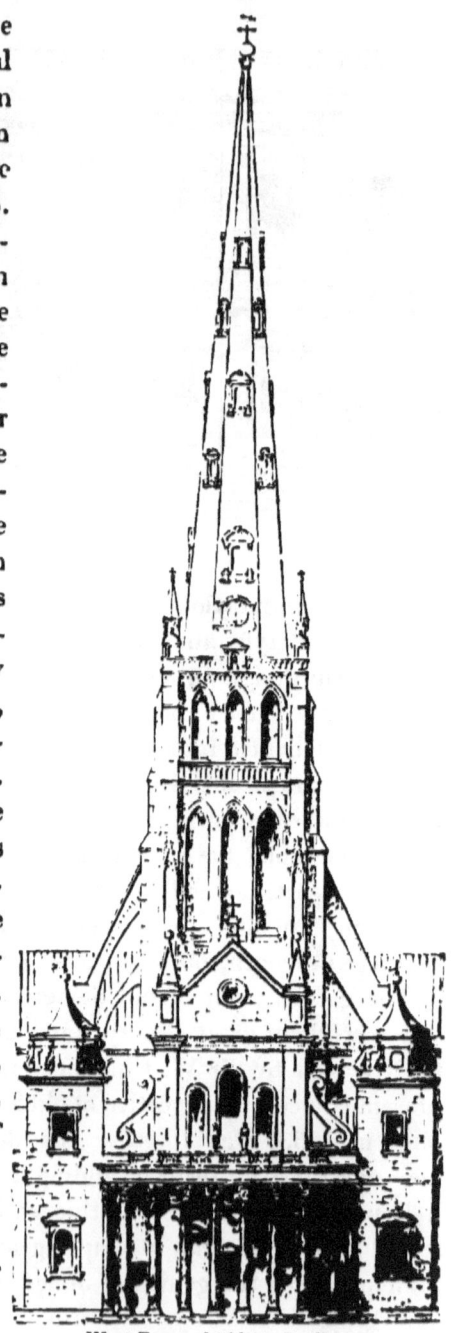

West Front of Old St. Paul's.

its being the only specimen of the Tuscan Order similarly applied, and is intended to exhibit the proportions of the temples of that class as they are described by Vitruvius: the whole building is of a very massive character, and may be considered as particularly applicable to its situation. The plan is rectangular,—of 133 feet long, including the portico, and 66 feet wide; the height from the ground to the cornice is 35 feet. The façade consists of a pedimental portico, supported by two columns of the Tuscan Order, between the antæ pilasters.

The numerous works executed by Jones have received, at different times, both praise and severe criticism: it must be admitted that his admiration of Palladian architecture sometimes led him to adopt plans and arrangements for houses not altogether suited to our climate or habits, and to aim at a splendour of design, which, under circumstances, could not be accomplished. The combination of his windows was Italian, and the piers between them were frequently so large as to offer too much obstruction to the admission of sufficient light. Objections have been offered to the height of his roofs, and the unmeaning, as well as useless, introduction of porticoes in the centres of his façades. The encouragement received by Inigo Jones was brought to a close by the misfortunes of his royal patron: art or artists found so little favour or encouragement during the time of the Commonwealth, that, unmindful of his talents, he had to pay £545 as a penalty for being a Roman Catholic. Disappointment and trouble accelerated his death, which took place in 1651.

The fire of 1666, which destroyed nearly the whole of London, was the occasion to which Sir Christopher Wren was indebted for the opportunities of displaying his skill in architecture and constructive science. One of his first designs was that for the rebuilding the city on a regular plan, which unfortunately was never carried wholly into effect,—and is the more to be regretted, as we then should have been spared the inconvenience resulting from our present bad arrangement.

The task of re-erecting the cathedral of St. Paul and the greater part of the churches in the city was intrusted to Wren, whose distinguished talents were fully equal to the stupendous undertakings. No architect, before or since his time, has possessed such a variety of knowledge, both in design and construction : the multiplicity and magnitude of his works proclaim the universality of his genius. The same hand produced the noblest of modern cathedrals, the largest palace, hospitals, and numberless public and private buildings, besides twenty-five churches in the city of London. Great length of days were bestowed on him : "he lived to enrich the reigns of several princes, and disgraced the last of them;"—(at the advanced age of 86 he was removed by George I. from the office of Surveyor-General ;)—"he restored London, and recorded its fall;"—he designed and lived to complete a building which is the boast of England and the admiration of the world, of which a general description is all that we can give.

The cathedral church of St. Paul stands on a greater portion of the site of the old one; the designs were approved by Charles II., and the warrant issued for the execution of the works on the 1st of May, 1675. The first stone was laid on the 21st of June, 1675 : within ten years the walls of the choir and aisles and the north and south porticoes were finished, and the piers of the dome were brought up to the same height. The highest stone on the top of the lantern, which was the last, was laid by the son of the architect, in 1710. The whole edifice was completed in thirty-five years, having only one architect, one master-mason, and the see being occupied the whole time by one bishop.

The plan of St. Paul's is a Latin cross, measuring from east to west 480 feet ; its general breadth on the exterior is 125 feet, and from the north to the south ends of the transepts 280 feet. The western end of the edifice is flanked by towers on the same plan as the walls, but projecting 27 feet beyond the north and south walls, thus making the whole width of

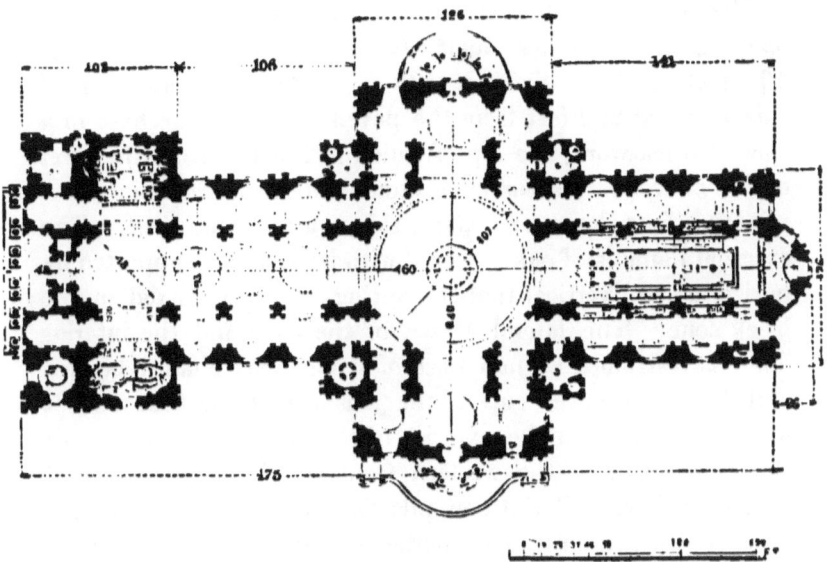

Plan of St. Paul's.

the façade 180 feet.   The exterior of the building consists of
two Orders;—the lower, or Corinthian, stands on a basement
10 feet above the ground, which is the level of the church,
which on the western side is approached by a magnificent flight
of marble steps, extending nearly the whole breadth of the
front.   From this level to the top of the entablature, or the
whole height of the Order, is 50 feet; and from this to the
upper part of the second Order, which is Composite, is 40 feet;
thus making the whole height of the body of the church 100
feet from the ground.   A magnificent portico, of the two Orders
in height, ornaments the western front; the lower story consists of twelve coupled columns, and the upper of eight,
besides four pilasters: this portico is surmounted by a pediment, on whose tympanum the subject of the conversion of St.
Paul is sculptured in high relief.   At the ends of the transepts
are porticoes, in form of a segment of a circle, round which are
six fluted Corinthian columns; this is crowned by a half-
dome, resting against the wall of the building.

The height of the cathedral, from the pavement to the opening of the inner dome (which is of brick-work), is 168 feet, and its diameter 100 feet. On the haunches of this dome, at 200 feet from the pavement, rests the base of a cone of brick-work, the top of which is 285 feet from the level of the church : this carries a stone lantern 55 feet high, terminating in a dome, and above this is a ball and cross. The external dome is of oak, covered with lead, and is supported by horizontal and vertical timbers resting on corbels fixed in the brick cone. The lateral thrust of the cone and the interior dome is restrained by four tiers of strong iron chains, bedded with lead in grooves cut in the masonry at the base and at different heights on the exterior of the dome. The towers at the extremities of the western front are 220 feet high, and ornamented with Corinthian pilasters, terminating above the roof of the church in open lanterns, and covered with domes. On the exterior of the building, the intervals of the columns and pilasters are occupied by niches or windows with semi-circular or horizontal heads, and crowned by pediments. In the upper Order of the north and south sides there are no windows, as it is merely a screening wall to the nave.

This edifice may, for elegance of design, bear comparison with any in Europe, not even excepting St. Peter's at Rome, though it is far from being so large. It must be admitted, however, that the interior faces of the walls present a naked appearance, and require much embellishment from ornamental sculpture before they will harmonize with the richness of the exterior. A great defect also arises, in the interior, from the want of connection which is caused by the arcades interrupting the entablatures. Sir Christopher Wren appears to have surpassed all those who preceded him in the skill required for raising a building on the minimum of foundation. Some criterion may be drawn of the comparative skill employed in the construction of other buildings somewhat similar, by comparing the ratio between the area of the whole plan and that of the sum of the areas of the whole of the piers, walls,

Western view of St. Paul's, from Ludgate Steeple.

and pillars which serve to support the superincumbent mass. To produce the greatest effect by the smallest means is one of the first qualifications of an architect, and the similarity of four churches affords a criterion of their respective merits as to the least amount of solid for area.*

Sir Christopher Wren.

Wren lived to complete St. Paul's (which cost £736,752, exclusive of the stone and iron enclosures round it, which cost £11,202): he died in 1723, at the age of 91, and was buried under the fabric,—with four words—

SI QUÆRAS MONUMENTUM CIRCUMSPICE.

To describe the works of Sir Christopher Wren would occupy much space we must therefore content ourselves with a notice of some of his principal buildings. Besides the great work just mentioned, he designed or executed most of the public edifices of his time: that upon which his fame is as justly founded as St. Paul's itself, is St. Stephen's church, Walbrook, remarkable for the elegance of its interior ornament. Its plan is a rectangle, 82 feet long by 59 broad, with a semicircular recess at the eastern end. It is divided longi-

* We borrow Mr. Joseph Gwilt's table of their proportionate areas.

Church.	Whole area in English feet.	Area of points of support.	Ratio.
St. Peter's at Rome	227,069	59,308	1 : 0·261
Sta. Maria del Fiore, Florence .	84,802	17,030	1 : 0·201
St. Paul's, London	84,025	14,311	1 : 0·170
St. Genevieve (Pantheon), Paris	60,287	9,269	1 : 0·154

tudinally into five aisles by four rows of Corinthian columns on pedestals; but near the centre, the places of four columns are unoccupied, and on the entablatures of the columns which are left, eight semicircular arches are turned, on the spandrils of which are pendentives forming the circular base of a dome, which rises in the shape of a segment of a sphere; and on the top of the dome is an elegant lantern. This church owes its reputation to the merit of the interior : the confined situation of the building among the neighbouring houses rendered an ornamental exterior unnecessary.

The lofty tower and spire, so peculiar to the Gothic churches, appears to have been considered by Wren as an essential characteristic and ornament of an ecclesiastical edifice; he therefore, in the greater part of his city churches, adopted their vast height and pyramidal form, to which he gave Italian details and features, so as to accord with the architectural combinations of the body of the building. The most remarkable of these towers is that of St. Bride's church in Fleet Street, which is 226 feet in height, and exceeds that of any other church executed according to the Roman Orders of architecture, and indeed most of the Gothic ones in this country. Its height was 234 feet, before it was struck by lightning in 1764, when, in repairing, it was reduced to its present dimensions. Bow church, likewise by Wren, has a tower and spire of noble proportions : the entire height from the ground is 197 feet, the tower alone being 32 feet broad and 83 feet in height. The upper part of the tower of the church of St. Dunstan in the East is remarkable for its being similar to that of the Gothic churches of St. Nicholas, Newcastle, and the High Church, Edinburgh.

The Monument of London, erected between the years 1671 and 1677, is a well-proportioned work, and exceeds in loftiness any of the historical columns of the ancients : its height is 202 feet, the lower diameter on the upper part of the base is 15 feet, and the pedestal is 21 feet square.

The works of this extraordinary architect are numerous

and varied in design, and we here give a list of his principal buildings and churches:

	Begun.	Completed.
Palace of Greenwich	1663	
Theatre at Oxford	1663	1669
The Monument	1671	1677
Temple Bar	1670	1672
St. Paul's Cathedral	1675	1710
Library at Trinity College, Cambridge .	1679	
Campanile of Christ Church, Oxford .	1681	1682
Ashmolean Museum, Oxford	1682	
Palace at Winchester	1683	unfinished.
College of Physicians, (the old) . . .	1689	
College at Chelsea	1690	
Palace of Hampton Court	1690	1694
Towers of Westminster Abbey . . .	1696	
Greenwich Hospital.		

CHURCHES.	Time of erection.	Cost. £.
Allhallows the Great	1697	5641
Allhallows, Lombard Street	1694	8058
St. Andrew Wardrobe	1692	7060
St. Andrew, Holborn	1687	9000
St. Antholin	1682	5685
St. Bride	1680	11,430
Christ Church, Newgate Street . . .	1687	11,778
St. Clement Dane's	1680	8786
St. Dionis Backchurch	1674	5737
St. Edmund the King	1690	5207
St. James, Garlick Hill	1683	3357
St. James, Westminster	1689	8500
St. Lawrence Jewry	1677	11,870
St. Michael Royal	1694	7555
St. Martin's, Ludgate	1684	5378
St. Mary-le-Bow	1673	8071
,, The Steeple	1680	1388

CHURCHES.	Time of erection.	Cost. £.
St. Margaret, Lothbury	1690	5340
St. Mary, Somerset	1695	6579
St. Mary, Aldermanbury	1677	5237
St. Olave Jewry	1673	5580
St. Magnus, London Bridge	1676	9579
St. Peter, Cornhill	1681	5647
St. Swithin, Cannon Street	1679	4687
St. Nicholas, Cole-abbey	1677	5052
St. Vedast, Foster Lane	1674	
St. Dunstan's in the East.*		

Front of Christ Church College, Oxford.

---

* A description of some of the churches in London, including those of Sir Christopher Wren, and of his successors, Hawksmoor and Gibbs, with several illustrations, is given as an Appendix to the present edition of this work

FROM THE TIME OF GEORGE I.

The beginning of the eighteenth century was remarkable for the introduction of a style of building quite at variance with that previously practised; its author, Sir John Vanbrugh, was evidently determined not to be controlled by any rules of architectural composition, but to give an expression in accordance with his own convictions. His buildings were combinations of novel forms and peculiarities, which were imperfectly understood by the world at large, and therefore have been subjected to more severe criticism than the works of any other architect.

Sir Joshua Reynolds, however, looked on the censured buildings with the feelings of a painter, and praised the composition of forms, the effects of light and shade, and the magnificence and picturesque character of the architecture of Vanbrugh.

Blenheim House, Oxfordshire, erected in 1715, is the principal work of this architect, and may be considered as a specimen of the style of building of which we have been speaking. The prevailing defect of this edifice is a want of unity and harmony of design; each feature of the principal elevation is distinct in character, and thereby, in composition, disconnected from the others: its immense scale and massiveness may give it an appearance of grandeur, but at the same time a monumental solemnity, somewhat out of place in a palatial residence or nobleman's mansion.* The whole extent in length is 350 feet, and its breadth 200 feet.

Castle Howard, in Yorkshire, likewise by Vanbrugh, was commenced in 1702, and possesses much greater simplicity in the design than Blenheim. He likewise erected spacious mansions at Eastbury in Dorsetshire; King's Weston, near Bristol; and at Grimsthorpe in Lincolnshire.

* It is recorded as "a *monument* of the victories of Marlborough, raised by a grateful nation:" this has been successfully carried into effect.

It is somewhat extraordinary that Wren, during an extensive professional practice, lengthened beyond that of any other architect, should have imparted so little of his precepts or talents: whatever may have been the number of his pupils, but one only became celebrated, and that pupil was Nicholas Hawksmoor, who had assisted his master in some of his buildings, and afterwards practised on his own account. The church on which the skill of Hawksmoor has been most successfully displayed is that of St. Mary Woolnoth, Lombard Street,—commenced in 1716, and finished three years afterwards,—the design of which has been considered to be scarcely inferior to the best productions of his master. The plan is nearly a square; in the western angles are the stairs to the galleries. The external appearance is very bold in character, and the rusticated niches good in proportion: in point of construction, there is an undue ratio of points of support to the superficies, and consequently an unnecessary employment of materials. St. George's, Bloomsbury, was not so happy a production; for by making George I. really the head of the church, in placing him on the top of the steeple, with lions and unicorns scrambling at the corners, the architect has subjected his design to much severe criticism. Hawksmoor likewise erected the churches of Christ-church, Spitalfields; St. George, Middlesex; St. Anne, Limehouse; part of All Souls' college, Oxford, and the new quadrangle at Queens' college, besides many private works, and was associated with Vanbrugh at Blenheim, and Castle Howard: he died at the age of seventy, in the year 1736.

About the same period the genius of the Earl of Burlington was displayed in the improvements of the mansion in Piccadilly which bears his name, the erection of a villa at Chiswick, &c. He directed his studies to the remains of the ancient architecture of Italy, and the works of Palladio: his designs were not numerous, but very correct in taste: he died in 1753.

The next architect of any note was James Gibbs, to

whom London is indebted for several harmonious and good
proportioned churches,—who, if he had not the genius of
some architects who had preceded him, was most assuredly
an artist of very considerable talent.   The church of St.
Martin in the Fields, completed in 1726, is the most distinguished monument of his taste and skill:* the length is
137 feet, not including the portico, which is 24 feet deep, and
the extreme external width 79 feet. The Corinthian Order
has been followed throughout the portico, which projects
boldly, is well designed, and is unequalled in London : attached pilasters of the same Order ornament the exterior of the
side walls, and stand on a plinth level with the pavement of
the portico, which is approached by a flight of steps.   The
churches erected by Gibbs are subject to one objection, which
is in the tower and steeple being raised over the body of the
building, so that it appears to stand on the roof, instead of
resting on the ground : the propriety of this structure may be
questioned ; but when a portico is introduced, it is difficult to
point out any other arrangement which would display the
same uniformity. The church of St. George, Hanover Square,
by the same artist, resembles externally that of St. Martin,
to which it is equal, but the interior composition is not quite
so satisfactory. The church of St. Mary-le-Strand, although
carefully designed, is too much cut up by detail, and wants
breadth of effect. The Radcliffe Library, at Oxford, which
was completed in 1747, tended to increase the fame of Gibbs,
as he afterwards received at that university the degree of
Master of Arts.   St. Bartholomew's Hospital, London, was
likewise one of his works.

  We will briefly draw attention to the architects who succeeded Gibbs, and whose works are deserving of notice. Colin
Campbell, who published three volumes on the principal
buildings in England, entitled ' Vitruvius Britannicus,' was an
artist of merit, and erected Wansted House, Essex, in 1715.
William Kent, who died in 1748, was an architect of some

* The cost of this building was £ 33,017.

celebrity: among his public works we may mention the Horse Guards, and the buildings in Margaret Street, Westminster, now containing the law courts. His greatest work was Holkham Hall, Norfolk, erected for the late Earl of Leicester.

Passing over some names little known, we arrive at the reign of George III., during which period architecture was much cultivated, although it cannot be attributed to the direct encouragement given to architects by the sovereign or to any show of taste or study of their art. The first, in point of date, of the successful professors of the art, was Robert Taylor (afterwards knighted), who retained for a long time an exalted reputation; but as his talents were chiefly devoted to numerous private buildings and some mansions which are little known to the public generally, we shall not enumerate them. Sir Robert Taylor died in the year 1778.

The celebrated authors of the well-known ' Antiquities of Athens,' Stuart and Revett, were contemporaneous with the last-named artist, and by their labours gave a more correct knowledge of the buildings of Greece, as regards their composition and ornamental arrangement; but unfortunately it is to be doubted whether the science of architecture was not injured, and its progress much retarded, by the fashion for everything Greek which followed this publication. It is certain that, without any consideration as to the nature of the building, or its purpose, absurd and diminutive imitations of the porticoes of the temples of Greece were for a time considered by the public at large as necessary appendages; and when they could not possibly be introduced on the ground floor, absurdity was carried to the extreme by placing them in front of the floor above. The lengths to which this error was carried were so palpable, that it corrected itself, and so-called Greek designs were no longer required.

The chapel and infirmary to Greenwich Hospital, Lord Anson's house in St. James's Square; Belvedere, in Kent: part of Lord Spencer's house in St. James's Place, and a house in Portman Square, where the chief architectural works of James Stuart, who died in 1788. Revett was less successful; a few additions of porticoes to mansions, and a church in Hertfordshire, were the extent of his practice.

As a contrast to the pure style which the last-named architects had endeavoured to introduce into the edifices of this country, we have to mention that which was brought into fashion by Robert Adams, whose corrupt taste had invented a style which contained all the worst peculiarities of the worst class of ornamentation and composition: this had its numerous admirers, and unfortunately it was extensively practised. In some happy hour he is stated to have made one design of merit for Lord Scarsdale, viz. Kedlestone, which he carried into execution, and as a whole it is considered to be a splendid composition. He likewise was engaged at Luton for the Earl of Bute, for Lord Mansfield at Hampstead, and other places: he died in 1792, at the age of ninety-four.

The only architect of the past generation to whom, in concluding this chapter, we propose to direct attention is Sir William Chambers, who was unquestionably the most eminent artist of his day; and in his capacity of instructor in the fine arts to George III., used his utmost endeavours to direct the taste of that monarch so as to obtain for his profession the royal patronage. Unfortu-

Sir William Chambers.

nately, the wars in which this country was constantly engaged may have hindered a proper consideration of the arts of peace. Sir William Chambers, however, was extensively employed in all parts of Great Britain; but his noblest effort was Somerset House, which was magnificently conceived and evinced, more than any other of his works, his consummate skill in the art of design.

This building stands on an area of 800 feet in width by 500 feet in depth, and is disposed on the four sides of a rectangular court, (with a street running from north to south on the eastern and western sides,) the interior length of which is 319 feet from north to south, and 224 feet in breadth : the façade towards the Strand is 133 feet long, and consists of three stories : nine arches are assigned to the basement, whereof the three in the centre are open, and lead to the great court, besides having entrances to the apartments of the societies : the other rusticated arches are occupied by windows decorated with pilasters, entablatures, and pediments. Above this story are two tiers of windows, of which those in the lower tier have entablatures, supported by Ionic columns : the upper windows are square, and are surrounded by square architraves. Between these windows, the walls are ornamented with three-quarter columns of the Corinthian Order, standing on pedestals : the height of the Order, without the pedestals, is 23 feet, and that of the entablature is 5 feet. Over the three central compartments of this façade is an attic story, with oval windows and statues in front : the entire height from the ground is 62 feet. The front towards the river Thames is 350 feet long, and presents a magnificent appearance. Its arrangement corresponds with that of the quadrangle, but a superior boldness of character has been adopted in its centre wings, where disengaged columns with pilasters are introduced. The centre part of this building is crowned by a cupola. Before this façade is a terrace 50 feet wide, supported by a lofty arcade, and protected by a balustrade. In the centre is one great semicircular arch, for the admission of vessels from the river ; and near each extremity is a water-gate of a similar form, the piers of which are ornamented with rusticated columns. This terrace was originally intended to have extended 1100 feet.

To Sir William Chambers we are indebted for one of the

H

best written works on the decorative part of civil architecture, published in 1759, in which a variety of designs for the different members of an edifice are exhibited and described. In the edition of 1825, by Mr. Joseph Gwilt, an outline of Grecian architecture has been added, thus rendering the original work complete. This work has been deservedly popular, and continues to be a text-book for the student. Chambers commenced Somerset House in 1776, and died in 1796.*

Towards the close of the 18th century, a very observable change in both architectural opinion and practice began to manifest itself. The taste of the Burlington Palladian school, which, it must be acknowledged, was, if correct, not a little feeble and tame, had all but completely waned away. The passion for rearing such ambitiously palatial patrician country residences, almost the chief architectural works of their time, as Houghton and Holkham, Wanstead, Wentworth, and Worksop, was rapidly declining. A comparison of the subjects in the original Vitruvius Britannicus, by Campbell, with those in the 'New' one by Richardson, renders strikingly evident that taste had passed from one extreme to the other. Improvement in some respect there was, yet of little more than a very negative kind: many obvious faults had been *subtracted*, but scarcely any fresh beauties *added* to design, which, if purified, became impoverished also.

A very mistaken kind of simplicity, not even aiming at artistic quality, for it consisted in nothing better than baldness

---

* After being for about forty years a disfigurement to Waterloo Bridge and its approach, the back of the west range of buildings, which, until the bridge was erected, was entirely shut out from view, is being converted into a very handsome, and certainly very conspicuous façade, in which Mr. Pennethorne has judiciously adhered to the character of the original, at the same time that he has introduced into his design some effective touches of his own. Thus, Chambers' noble pile will at length be worthily completed.

and blankness, had become the order of the day. If inoffensive, it was also insipid and flavourless. James Wyatt (1746-1813), who had all at once been brought into vogue by his first work, the Pantheon, in Oxford Street,* had become, in the strictest sense of the term, the 'fashionable' architect of the day. Employed in almost every county in England in erecting country-houses, whose character might be best expressed by the epithet 'genteel,' he fell into a sort of *improvisatore* method. On the other hand, he had no small share in forwarding that decided change in architectural feeling, or fashion, in favour of Gothic, which came up about that time (1780-90). Till then there had been no question as to what style ought to be followed. Before Stuart's Athens and the Ionian Antiquities appeared, no one ever thought of looking to other than Roman or Italian models; and, paradoxical as it may sound, it was perhaps the spirit of historical enquiry and research to which the above named works gave rise, that first directed attention to mediæval architecture. Horace Walpole's 'Gothic' plaything, Strawberry Hill, now spoken of only with contempt, was regarded as a wonder in its way,† and what had been called a 'monkish,' was considered almost a 'modish' style of building.

Some little professional practice there had indeed been in that style, but it had not extended beyond necessary repairs and restorations, for whose details the respective buildings furnished authority. James Essex, of Cambridge, where he was much employed in similar work, restored the lantern at

---

* That celebrated place of amusement was first opened in 1772, but as the whole interior was destroyed by fire twenty years afterwards, and no designs of it were ever published, it is impossible now to judge how far it really deserved the reputation it obtained for consummate taste and refined elegance. From such prints of it as still exist, the Great Room does not appear to have been by any means faultless.

† Even Dallaway has not scrupled to assert, in his observations or English Architecture, that Strawberry Hill "exhibits all that is fascinating in the Gothic style."

Ely cathedral, and executed considerable repairs at Lincoln. He died in 1784, at about which time Wyatt began to be applied to on similar occasions, although it is not very clear whether it was merely on the strength of his reputation generally, or because he had manifested any attachment to Gothic. After being engaged upon some of the buildings of several colleges at Oxford, he was appointed to restore Salisbury cathedral, but so greatly exceeded the bounds of legitimate restoration, that, while he *re*paired the structure, he greatly *im*paired its original character and effect by sweeping away all the chapels, and some other parts, which sacrilegious proceeding incurred for him and his employers something like vituperation from antiquaries. Nevertheless he was a few years afterwards (1795) commissioned by Mr. Beckford, then considered a second Aladdin (who summoned Wyatt as his geni), to rear up the towering pile of Fonthill, regardless of expense. The jealous secrecy with which the structure was carried on, and inaccessibility to it afterwards, magnified Fonthill Abbey into a marvel of surpassing splendour, till people could behold it with their own eyes, when it was discovered to be a pompous mistake. A few years later Wyatt commenced Ashridge for the Earl of Bridgewater : he made also some alterations at Windsor Castle, and had begun to erect a Gothic palace or castle for George III. at Kew, of which the little that was done has since disappeared. At all events, James Wyatt forms a kind of epoch in modern English architecture; he stands at what may be called a turning point in it; and, although it has since become the fashion to speak of him very slightingly, nay, even contemptuously, he ought in fairness to be judged of according to the standard of his own time, not of ours. When he began to take up Gothic, that style was scarcely understood at all, except by a few industrious antiquaries, and even by them only imperfectly, and almost exclusively with reference to ecclesiastical examples. The aids to professional study which have since been so amply provided did not then exist. Certainly there were the same buildings then as now to consult;

but it would have taken an individual a lifetime to examine a sufficient number of them to gain any tolerably clear insight into a style, or rather such a series of styles, as are those comprehended under the general title of Gothic. All things considered, Wyatt may be more readily forgiven for his failures in Gothic, than for his feebleness and effeminate taste in that style to which he had been educated. At all events, he has left one important lesson behind him, which is, that the reputation arising out of popular vogue, be it ever so brilliant, carries with it no pledge for permanency, but is in danger of being succeeded by either oblivion or obloquy.

We must now go back a little to speak of some other contemporaries of Chambers, the chief of whom were Sir Robert Taylor, George Dance, son of the architect of the Mansion House, and Henry Holland. The first of these (1714-88), though educated as a sculptor, did not show any disposition to encourage sculptural decoration in his buildings. His practice, if not his taste, inclined far more to plainness than enrichment. The wings which he added to the Bank of England have been since expunged by his successor, Soane, as has likewise nearly all his other work. To Dance belongs the credit of having produced one of the finest and most expressive pieces of design, and the disgrace of perpetrating one of the most execrable, viz. Newgate Prison and the front of Guildhall, which last is still permitted to remain a monument of that taste which relishes nothing so much as city dinners and turtle soup. Of Holland's works, the two by which he was most known to the public no longer exist: his Drury Lane Theatre was, like Wyatt's Pantheon, destroyed by fire, and Carlton House has been demolished: the portico of the latter was the richest example of Corinthianism that had been produced in this country, and, though carped at by small-witted critics, the Ionic screen colonnade in front produced a strikingly scenic effect; it was indeed only a piece of decoration, its real fault therefore was that it was not sufficiently ornate. The little screen façade which he added to Melbourne House,

Whitehall, is a most charming composition, but unfortunately shows itself to very great disadvantage, its want of size causing it to appear insignificant in comparison with neighbouring objects. After being so long attributed to Jupp, who was only the E. I. Company's surveyor, it is now ascertained beyond all doubt that the India House was designed by Holland. What he did at the Pavilion at Brighton was altogether so unworthy of him, that it is unlucky the memory of such an abortion should be preserved, by its having been singled out by Richardson for one of the subjects in his Vitruvius. Holland was one of the first who adopted the Greek Ionic.

Having again come down to the present century, we find Soane at the commencement startling criticism by his additions to the Bank, which were then assuming importance. Even now, it is no easy matter for criticism to form a decided opinion of him, so strangely were original merits, and faults—that might also be called original,—were beauties and blemishes mixed up together in all his works. In arrangement of plan and in contrivance he has been equalled by few—surpassed by none ; of invention, he possessed a more than ordinary degree, but it was so ill-regulated that it frequently showed no better than caprice, and that too of a rather pitiful kind. An eye for the picturesque he certainly had, and was most exemplarily studious of scenic effect in interiors, which he sometimes heightened by the mellowing glow of coloured glass. He would show to most advantage in a volume of ' Elegant Extracts' from his buildings, containing only those ideas to be found in them—and they are not a few, which may be studied with advantage. Pre-eminent among them would be that truly fascinating composition, the loggia at the north-west angle of the Bank.

The destruction of Covent Garden by fire in 1808, was a fortunate accident for Smirke (now Sir Robert), for whom the new edifice obtained the same sudden acquisition of a popular name as the Pantheon had for Wyatt. It seems also to have done somethiug more, as it caused Greek,—'done to order,'—to be for a while the reigning architectural fashion of the day. Prompted to call it 'classical,' people did not perceive how prosaically and unartistically it was treated, though they at length sickened of the style, when they discovered that it amounted to no more than a wearisome repetition of the same Doric or Ionic columns, which were besides made nearly the all-in-all of design and composition also. Even Bethlehem Hospital (begun in 1812) has an Ionic portico, and Newgate would no doubt have had a similar classical appendage had it been erected at that time. If choice and admirably executed Greek details were all that is required to produce what should have besides some distinct merits of its own, St. Pancras' Church deserves to be rated very highly indeed. Since then the mania for Greek 'neat as imported' has subsided, which may perhaps account for the indifference with which the last of the numerous works, by the architect of Covent Garden Theatre, has been received. When the British Museum was first begun, architectural taste was altogether different from what it is now, as is indeed strikingly evident, from the very un-Greek character of the railing erected before the Museum itself.

The termination of the war in 1815, enabled the Prince Regent to promote undertakings connected with architecture, upon a scale that it might not otherwise have been prudent to propose. Regent Street was, accordingly, not only projected but forthwith realised; and, although its 'grandeur' consisted of nothing better than the merest common place, and even vulgarity of design, it pioneered the way to better things. Had it not been for Nash's 'lath and plaster,' we should not perhaps even yet have forsaken the humdrum of mere brick and mortar. An impulse was then given, whose influence has spread far and wide, and is now manifesting itself not only in various parts of the metropolis, but in our chief provincial cities and towns. That regard to architectural appearance, which in the last century was only exceptional, has become almost the universal rule; for banking houses, club houses, the offices of insurance companies, &c., which before used to be scarcely distinguishable from other houses, some sort of architecture is now considered quite necessary: and they have, besides, so greatly multiplied in some parts of the city, as to form a series of various façades ; some of which exhibit a degree of propriety as well as ornateness very far superior, as regards quality of design, to the productions of what may be called the column-and-pilaster school, as exhibited, not in Regent Street alone, but in the earlier erected of our modern club-houses. It was a club-house that set an example which infused fresh spirit into our architecture, and awakened it from its indolent self-complacency and torpor. Barry's Travellers' made what the newspapers call 'a sensation' ; it charmed every one who could appreciate finished elegance and refined simplicity. It is impossible for verbal description to do justice to its beauties, or even convey any idea of them ; or, even if it were, it is quite out of the question here. It has obtained description of a far more satisfactory kind in an illustrated monograph,* which has enabled those who could else only have viewed the building more or less attentively, to study leisurely all its details,—and most worthy of study they are. Nor has the lesson given by that work of Barry's, and the published studies of it, been thrown away. Until the Travellers' was erected, the cornicione (large and deep cornice) was not known in this country, or if known, as it must have been to those of our architects who had visited Italy, was not adopted by them here at home. In Astylar composition, the cornice is a most important feature, and even as the termination and completion of a columnar ordinance, it is what will bear to be exaggerated rather freely than at all diminished. Not to mention others, the decorated 'string course' is another important element of design in that mode of it which, although

---

* Plans, elevations, sections, and details of this building are published in a work entitled The Travellers' Club House, by Chas. Barry, Architect, with text by W. H. Leeds.

now distinguished by the name of *Astylar* (from the absence
of an ordinance of either columns or pilasters) might itself be
called decorated, or decorated-astylar. *Richness* was by no
means a characteristic quality in even the best productions of
the Anglo-Palladian and Anglo-classic schools; whatever of
such quality there was in them was confined to the order itself,
or else produced by means of such ornamental accessories as
statues, vases, festoons, &c., while such essential features as
doors and windows were comparatively plain, certainly mea-
gre, and almost stereotyped likewise, the same dressings to
them, with scarcely any attempt at variety being employed by
different architects as a sort of common property. By those
of the Adam and the Wyatt school, plainness was exaggerated
into poverty; which was rendered all the more offensive by
pretensiousness to design in other respects. The building
which has given rise to these remarks furnishes a most convincing proof that richness and simplicity are perfectly com-
patible with each other.

Independently of other merits, that example and the adjoining building belonging to the Reform Club, by the same architect, showed a laudable attention to keeping and consistency;
and further rendered the other clubs so ambitious of making
architectural display that Pall-Mall, at least the 'shady side' of
it, has been all but entirely transformed into a line of *palazzi*,
all the more dignified because they cannot be suspected of
being other than they are, but are utterly free from that expression of littleness in largeness which is inseparable from
monster warehouses and railway hotels, however pretensiously
they may be tricked out.

Barry's two club-houses led at once to what may be called
greater generosity in architecture, and attention began to be
paid to matters that had previously been regarded as of little
moment. The principal club-houses have, undeniably, contributed not a little to enliven street architecture in the locality
where they congregate, and if one or two of them are not quite
unexceptionable in point of design, all erected subsequently to

the Reform have, like that, an unmistakeable aristocratic air, which is more than is affected by even our wealthier nobility in their town residences,—owing, no doubt, to the circumstance of so few of them being hereditary family mansions. To the scanty list of the buildings of that class, which are noticeable as architecture, two have of late been added that are really important architectural objects, viz., Bridgewater House and the new Dorchester, *alias* Holford House in Park Lane. The former, by Barry, is almost the *ne plus ultra* of decorated Italian astylar ; as far as artistic design is concerned, it humbles into utter insignificance, such arrant insipidities as Stafford House and Apsley House. As to Buckingham Palace, the less that is said of it, perhaps, the better. It was poor enough, and had too much of Regent Street in its constitution when it first came out of Nash's hands, and it has been rather damaged than improved by the handiwork of Blore. Windsor Castle is the only English palace that does any credit to royal taste ; and even that would, probably, be several degrees better, had it to be done at the present day.

In October, 1834, Vulcan, *alias* fire, rendered an important service to architecture by destroying the Houses of Parliament, and again, in less than four years afterwards, by burning the old Royal Exchange. With respect to the first-mentioned, it is to be regretted that as the site was to be retained, that the new structure—its river front at least, was not raised upon a lofty terrace, like Somerset House and the Adelphi. Yet, notwithstanding all the objections which criticism has advanced against it,—some of which are not to be contradicted,—Barry's New Palace of Westminster is a magnificent undertaking worthily carried out, in which, what error there is, has been not on the side of short-coming but overdoing. That national and monumental work has helped to promote all those arts which minister to architecture for its adornment. One important, though indirect, result of the fire at Westminster is, that in consequence of public competition, till then almost unknown among us, being adopted as the safest and most impartial mode of obtaining a good design, by selecting the best out of many, that course has been pursued ever since on similar occasions, and is now resorted to even on the most trivial ones. Excellent in principle, in practice, competition is liable to be grossly abused. Committees composed of persons, perhaps, wholly unqualified, or else, not known to be qualified to judge of designs, and, moreover, quite irresponsible to any one for their doings, are quite as likely to decide wrong as right. They may, indeed, decide honestly, and according to the best of their judgment, yet, if that best be bad—unless they happen to be suddenly inspired at the moment,—the mischief is not mended. At any rate, there is one thing which they ought to decide upon beforehand, namely, what is to be the style of the intended building, for there are now so many styles and varieties of them practised, that the leaving style optional is no better than a perplexing inconvenience to competitors. Carried to the extent it now is, the system imposes upon the profession no small quantity of labour that must of necessity be unrequited. Taking the average, there are, at least, twenty designs prepared, when only a single one can be executed; and that the chosen one is sometimes very far from the best, is rendered mortifyingly evident by rejected ones afterwards exhibited.

Of three competitions, however, the results have proved satisfactory, viz., the Fitzwilliam Museum, Cambridge, by Basevi; the Royal Exchange, by Tite; and St. George's Hall, Liverpool, by H. L. Elmes; which last far excels the only edifice in the metropolis that admits of comparison with it, it being decidedly superior to the British Museum, both with regard to originality of conception and artistic treatment.*

* In one respect it is less fortunate, for the principal façade suffers from the disadvantage of an east aspect, which, somewhat remarkably, is also the case with the river front of the Palace of Westminster, the new Treasury Buildings, Covent Garden Theatre, and, not to mention other instances, the façade and piquantly-planned portico of the Fitzwilliam Museum.

The interior of the Liverpool Hall, completed after Elmes' death by Cockerell, presents even a lavish display of ornamentation, whose magnificence contrasts very forcibly with the homeliness, as it would now be thought, of Burlington's once-famed Great Assembly Room at York. Colour, which in the last century was all but ignored in architectural decoration, and at best applied very timidly and sparingly, has now come to be considered almost a *sine-qua-non* in internal design, as giving it emphasis. Polychromy has, in fact, become nearly a study in itself,—has certainly engaged much attention since it was discovered, that, quite contrary to all established notions of classic taste, the Greeks employed it even externally, though whether they did so to anything like to the extent that some have conjectured—for, after all, there is more of conjecture than proof in the matter—may very well be questioned.

Although not to be compared with the one at Liverpool, several town-halls and other public edifices for various purposes—all making pretension to rank as works of architecture, and some of them of considerable merit, have within the last few years been erected, or else are now in progress in the more important provincial towns. Never, in fact, has architecture found among us, in modern times, more abundant employment than at present. Railways have raised up an entirely new class of buildings in immediate connection with them, either as terminuses and stations, with all their dependencies, or as hotels, which, though apart from, are attached to them. The colleges, schools, institutes, music halls, concert rooms, museums, hospitals, alms-houses, together with a nondescript *et cetera*, that have of late years been erected, may be conveniently reckoned up as being innumerable. Some of them are assuredly no great prizes, but they all help to indicate the movement which has taken place as regards attention to architectural appearance, though it must be confessed that the limits of propriety are too frequently overleaped, as when a Union-workhouse is made to assume externally the semblance of an aristocratic Elizabethan mansion, or a Manchester warehouse that of a pompously pretentious, though not precisely palace-like, pile. If not exactly to be called deception, such practices partake of unreality, and, besides causing distinctive character to be disregarded, tend in some measure to lower the assumed character, if not to deter from the adoption of it where it would be appropriate.

The architects of our own day have been taunted more than once with the remark, that their art does not at all keep pace with the improvements visible in most of the mechanical arts, including those which are immediately connected with and auxiliary to architecture itself. They are reproached for not having yet produced a nineteenth century style! Admitting that a decidedly new style is to be looked for every century,—which, however, admits of considerable doubt,—the reproach is justly deserved; but then, on whom ought it to fall? Surely, quite as much upon, or even more upon, the public; that is, those who employ architects, than on architects themselves. So far from seeking to promote advance in the art, it appears to be the main object of those who affect to take especial interest in it to retard, or rather altogether hinder advance, and to resist all suggested improvement as innovation,—any deviation from precedent as so illegitimate that it ought to be made illegal. It must be somewhat amusing to mere bystanders to hear architects abused for not getting forward, and those who have the power of dictating to them commended, almost in the same breath, for exerting themselves strenuously to pull them back. While architecture is of all the fine arts the one most dependent upon public taste and its caprices, it is also the one with which the public are the least acquainted, and even the little they do know of it enables them only to insist upon close adherence to some previous style. Employers keep down architects to their own level: original talent has small chance of being appreciated, or of making its way through the prejudices opposed against it. Where the most servile copyism is looked upon as a merit, any attempt at breaking away from it is looked at askance, as showing a dangerous disregard of established rules, and disaffection to that 'good old' system which, by substituting mere got-by-heart rules for æsthetic principles, saves no small amount of troublesome thinking, not only to architects themselves, but to those also who set up for architectural critics, yet whose brains oftener than not unconsciously exhibit nothing better than 'a beggarly account of empty boxes,' even those among them who speak to the public through the 'Times' itself. To say the truth, and it is by no means a very pleasant one, the generality of architectural criticism, or what has passed itself off and been accepted as such, is what would now hardly be tolerated in any other department of either literature or art; which proves but too plainly the real indifference, however it may be disguised, prevailing with regard to that one of the fine arts which, were it properly understood, would have a most salutary influence upon all that is connected with æsthetics and taste.

We are beginning, however, to perceive one or two fundamental mistakes in modern practice during nearly three centuries, the main one being that of conventional dogmatism repeated by rote, sometimes in utter ignorance of the very nature of architecture, and in such manner as to deny it all further plastic power. At length, Ferguson, Garbett, Huggins, Petit, and some other writers, have come to its rescue, earnestly deprecating the present injurious system of servile, literal copyism, which has all but completely reduced what ought to be recognised in its potentiality as a Fine—certainly a noble—Art, to the level of a mechanical pursuit. Copyism has proved a convenient but a fatal opiate; it has soothed, but it has also stupified. It puts all nearly upon the same level: so far from encouraging, it virtually prohibits artistic study. Æsthetic feeling and artistic talent are left quite out of the question in deciding whether some not over-bright youth shall become architect, or auctioneer and house-agent. The Roman epigrammatist's ironical advice

> "Si duri puer ingeni videtur,
> Præconem facias vel *architectum*,"

has not yet lost its point. Yet let us hope that it will do so ere very long, and that the claims of architecture, as art, will be not only, as heretofore, asserted, but substantiated; and that, followed worthily and with generous spirit by the profession, it will be honoured by obtaining from the public that equally intelligent and generous sympathy upon which its advancement so greatly depends.

APPENDIX:

CONTAINING SOME REMARKS ON THE CHURCHES OF

SIR CHRISTOPHER WREN,

AND THOSE OF HIS SUCCESSORS, HAWKSMOOR AND GIBBS.

St. Stephen's, Walbrook, is considered the most original
and beautiful of the fifty parochial churches rebuilt by Wren
in consequence of the great fire in 1666. In many, perhaps
most, of these structures, the doggedness of the authorities
confined him rigidly to the Catholic routine of nave and aisles,
and in these, of course, he could do little. The more licence
he could obtain to deviate from this everlasting mimic basilica,
the better he succeeded; and to say that this is the building
in which the greatest deviation therefrom was allowed, is
tantamount to pronouncing it his masterpiece. * * * *
Though a simple cell enclosed by four walls, the tame-
ness of that form wholly disappears behind the unique and
varied arrangement of its sixteen columns. They reproduce
and unite almost every beauty of plan to be found in all the
cathedrals of Europe. Now they form the Latin cross, with
its nave, transept, and chancel; anon they divide the whole
space into five aisles, regularly diminishing from the centre to
the sides; again we perceive, in the midst, a square apartment
with recesses on all its sides—a square, nay, an octagon—no,
a circle. It changes at every glance, as we view the entablature, or the arches above it, or the all-uniting dome. With
the same harmonious variety, we have every form of ceiling
brought together at once—flat, camerated, groined, pendentive,
domical—yet no confusion. The fitness to its destination is
perfect; every eye can see the minister, and every ear is within
hearing distance of him, in every part of the service. It is

St. Vedast's.

Christ Church.

the most beautiful of preaching-rooms; and though only a sketch, and executed only in counterfeit building, would, if carried out in Wren's spirit instead of his employers', form the most perfect of Protestant temples.

St. James's, Piccadilly, is about the largest of Wren's churches, but at the same time the most meanly built, everything about it indicating such extreme parsimony, that he seems to have given up the exterior in despair, bestowing on it only a few of his favourite cherubs' heads. It has lately been improved by the addition of a cornice, which it much wanted.

Christ Church, Newgate Street (see p. 187), is very similar to the last, but with an elliptic central ceiling, and is one of the best-proportioned churches on the basilican plan, with galleries.

St. Anne and Agnes, north of the Post Office; St. Martin's, Ludgate; St. Antholin's, Budge Row; and St. Swithin's, Cannon Street, are among those which display the greatest originality of plan.

In nothing was the fertility of Wren's invention so strikingly displayed as in the belfries of his churches, which, being frequently the only parts visible at all from a right distance, received much attention; and their extraordinary diversity of forms (as seen from either of the eastern bridges) has no parallel in any other city, and contrasts strangely with the monotonous repetition of two round temples and an attic, pervading the other parts of London, or the everlasting mock-Early-English pyramid that now succeeds them.

The steeples of Wren all rise from the ground, and not from the roof of a building; they all have a regular increase of decoration, from the plain and solid basement to the broken and fanciful finish; they are all square and undiminished up to half their entire height, often more, but perhaps always to the middle of that portion expected to be generally visible above the houses; and in all, except those of St. Paul's, the upper or pyramidal portion is so arranged that in almost every view its outlines may touch (and be confined by) two straight lines meeting at the summit. In later times all these rules have generally been reversed, especially the last, our modern steeples affecting a convexity of outline whose prominent points are limited by the form of a pointed arch instead of a triangle. Wren employed this convex outline in the belfries of St. Paul's alone, plainly showing his sense of its fitness to a situation requiring more breadth and majesty; in fact, a character altogether distinct from that of parochial steeples, where he has given a lighter and more feminine expression by the triangular outline. The proportions of his triangle vary from an equilateral to one whose height is six times its base.

St. Mary-le-Bow, commonly called Bow Church, Cheapside, and St. Bride's, Fleet Street (p. 186); Christ Church, Newgate Street, and St. Vedast's, Foster Lane (p. 187), have the steeples of the tallest proportion; and the two former are the tallest in London, having been apparently intended to equal exactly those of St. Paul's, or about 235 feet, but St. Bride's has been reduced a few feet. The diversity of these four steeples is admirable. Bow has been the general favourite, probably from the variety of plan in its different stories. In the other three, one plan, different in each, is preserved throughout the pyramid : in Christ Church, a square; in St. Bride's, an octagon; in St. Vedast's, a figure of four concave quadrants. The depth of hollowing in this last does not, in an English climate, form a sufficient substitute for thorough piercing or detached members, so that the whole is too solid and flat, but would answer well in Italian sunshine. Christ Church has one great merit, that of more connection and mutual dependence between the stories than usual; but its outline has been destroyed by the removal of a few vases. St. Bride's is, considered by itself, far from the happiest of Wren's works, and, if it stood alone, would be justly called puerile, but it adds a pleasing variety to the general assemblage; and though one design on this principle is enough,

St. Michael's, Cornhill.

St. Dunstan's.

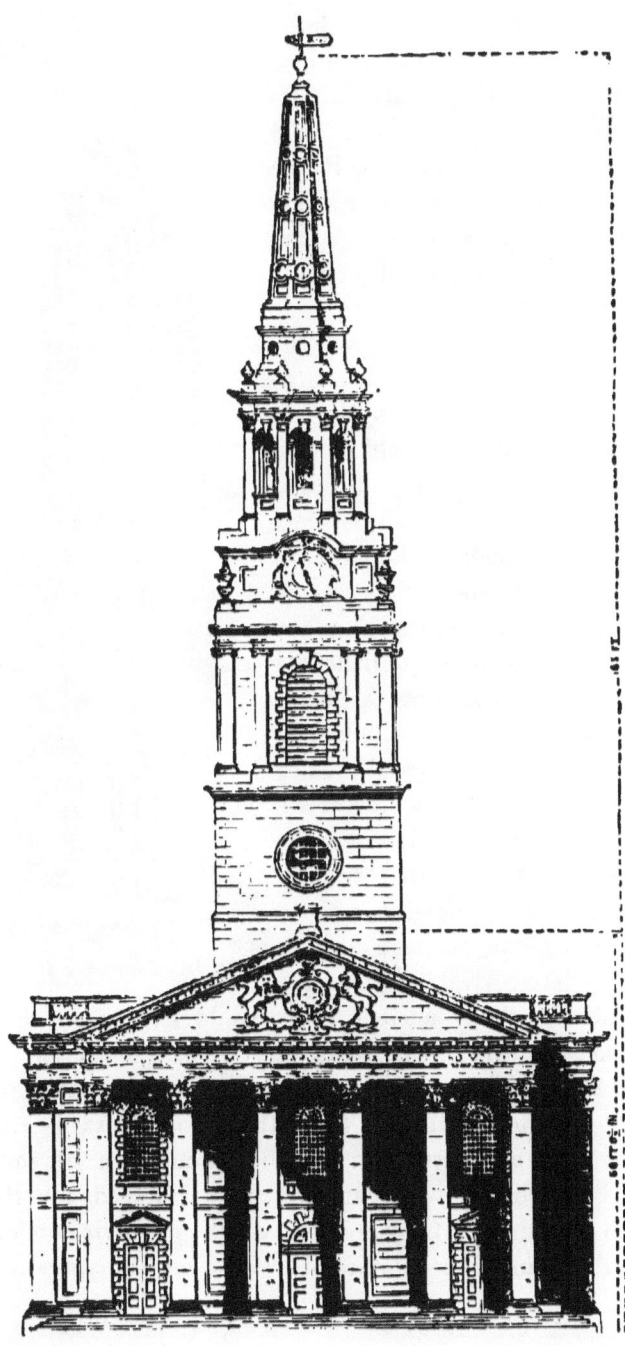

that one required to be on a large
scale to carry out the idea thoroughly.

St. James's, Garlick Hill; St. Michael's, College Hill; St. Stephen's,
Walbrook; and St. Bennet's, Paul's
Wharf, are some of the finest of his
numerous steeples, whose upper part
is limited by a pyramid of a lower
proportion.

St. Michael's, Cornhill, and St.
Dunstan's, near the Custom House (p.
190), present in their belfries, Wren's
nearest approaches to the old Gothic
style; for his works present every
shade of intermediate design between
these and pure Italian. His faults, in
the Gothic, are precisely the same as
when following his usual style; but
the flatness, shallowness, and littleness
of mouldings, become here far more
glaring, simply because his tendency
this way is not restrained by rules
and proportional measures, such as the
Italian systematizers had laid down.

It will be observed, that though
Wren's constant profession was to
imitate the ancients, such an idea as
that of the mere revival, or histrionic

St. James's, Garlick Hill.

representation, of any ancient style, could never have been
entertained by him; otherwise, his great admiration of
Salisbury Cathedral and Westminster Abbey, and long employment on the repairs of both those matchless fabrics,
could not but have led him to the production of some
mock-Early-English, which, however, was reserved for this
nineteenth century. His words, if taken in their modern
sense, would strangely contradict his works, for his expressions

ıf reverence for antiquity, and endeavour to follow its rules, could not have been more modest if St. Paul's had been only a sham temple, like the Madeleine or Walhalla.

The churches erected by Wren's successors, Hawksmoor and Gibbs, were more liberally built and far more more ornate than those of the great architect himself, especially their exteriors, which, however, were not, as in later times, enriched *at the expense of the interior.*

Five churches by these masters are worthy of notice :

St. Mary's, Woolnoth, in Lombard Street, is the master-piece of Wren's pupil, Hawksmoor, and by far the most original work erected since his time. The exterior seems to have been designed with a view towards the foreseen open-ing of a new street, which has since taken place; and both the north and west faces are well fitted, the former to its aspect, and the latter to its present situation. The interior is unique for a church, and apparently imitates Vitruvius's description of one sort of ancient atrium. Its great merit is, that the galleries, though very capacious, are not offensive. It seems incredible, did we not see proof of it on every side, that a problem of daily requirement in modern times should, though solved more than once, be now given up in despair.

St. George's, Bloomsbury, by the same architect, is remark-able for the picturesque grouping of its front, and majestic effect of its portico, which is on the principle of the ancient Roman ones, which style, indeed, this artist seems to have studied more than the modern Italian. The crowning of the tower, however, by a pyramid of steps, is a sad mistake. That form is (or represents) the most massive and solid in all archi-tecture, therefore the most unfit form possible for a finish, and it should be replaced by some light open composition, enclosing and sheltering the statue, instead of hoisting it aloft to the storms.

St. Mary-le-Strand, the first church erected by Gibbs, shows, altogether, a very tawdry taste, and is remarkable for the very singular conceit of making a single apartment appear

ı

externally of two stories.   Even counterfeit littleness, however, is perhaps better than counterfeit greatness.

St. George's, Hanover Square, is the best, or rather the least faulty, of the works of James, who introduced the fashion of

St. Botolph, Bishopsgate.

placing the belfry centrally behind a. portico; which in this case was, perhaps, from the peculiar plan of the neighbourhood, its only good position, for it falls nearly in the axis of three streets, Grosvenor and Maddox Streets, and Harewood Place, and, seen from the latter, forms part of one of the very few groups in London that can be called picturesque. This belfry is also well fitted to its novel situation, and not too high for the portico below. The north side shows by its boldness, that *aspect* was still considered, and allowed to influence architectural composition, which, perhaps, it has never since done.

St. Martin's in the Fields (see p. 181), now in Trafalgar Square, and the most conspicuous church in London, is by Gibbs, and, though shining like a gem among more modern works, cannot be considered an improvement on anything preceding it. The steeple is here too much for the portico, and should have been placed elsewhere. The whole air is pompous and ostentatious, and the enrichment, which was now almost turned out from the interior to the exterior of churches, seems working itself to the surface, and introducing us to an age in which beauty should not even be skin-deep. The interior is in a style only fit for a theatre.

St. Botolph's, Bishopsgate, is a favourable specimen of the less pretending churches of the same age (that of George I.). It is the only known work of its architect, James Gold.

CHRONOLOGICAL TABLE*

OF THE

STYLES OF ARCHITECTURE,

From the earliest to the present Period,—illustrative especially of those practised in England.

---

* The pages are referred to where each subject is treated in the volume.

DATE.
A. D.   PAGE

1357—1375. Great part of Windsor castle pulled down and rebuilt: the works were
    commenced under the direction of William of Wykeham . . . 130, 131
1361. The choir of York cathedral commenced by Archbishop John de Thoresby . 107
1361. The spire of Norwich cathedral rebuilt by Bishop Thomas Percy.
1362. The college of Cobham, Kent, founded by John, Lord Cobham . . 142
1363. The Vicar's college, or close, at Wells, founded by Ralph of Shrewsbury . 137
1377. The cathedral of Ulm commenced 37
1381—1412. The cloisters of Gloucester cathedral completed between these periods
    by Abbot Walter Froucester 123
1390—1392. The great east window of Exeter cathedral reconstructed.
1391—1411. The chapter-house at Canterbury repaired and partly rebuilt.
1394—1410. The greater part of the nave and aisles of Winchester cathedral
    remodelled by William of Wykeham 117
1395. The open timber roof of Westminster Hall constructed by Richard II. . 142
1395. St. Michael's church, Coventry, built 122
1420—1437. The west front and south porch of Gloucester cathedral built by
    Abbot John Morwent 119
1420—1440. The ceiling of the choir, the windows of the aisles, and a rich monu-
    mental chapel, in St. Alban's abbey, built by Abbot John de Wheathamstead.
1422. The college of Higham Ferrers founded by Henry Chicheley, Archbishop of
    Canterbury.
1424. The transept and tower of Merton college chapel, Oxford, being finished,
    was in this year re-dedicated 105
427—1455. The upper part of the chapter-house of Exeter cathedral rebuilt by
    Bishop Edmund de Lacy 120
1430. The cloisters of Norwich cathedral completed by Bishop William Alnwyk . 124
1435 Fotheringay church, Northamptonshire, built 123
1437. Thierry de Moers carried up the southern tower of Cologne cathedral to the
    third story 36
1439. The cathedral of Strasburg brought to its present state . . . 35
1439. The Beauchamp chapel at Warwick begun, and also the monument of
    Richard de Beauchamp, Earl of Warwick.
1440. Herst-Monceaux manor-house, Sussex, built by Sir Roger Fienes . 133, 134
1441—1522. Eton college 138
1446. Rosslyn chapel, Scotland, commenced by William St. Clair, Earl of Orkney.
1446—1515. King's college chapel, Cambridge, begun by Henry VI. and finished
    in the reign of Henry VIII. 116
1450—1472. Norwich cathedral: the roof of the nave and the rood-loft screen built
    by Bishop Walter Lyhart.
1455—1457. The central tower of Gloucester cathedral built by Abbot Thomas
    Seabroke, the finishing of which he committed, on his death, to Robert
    Tulley 123
1457—1498. The lady-chapel in Gloucester cathedral begun by Abbot Richard
    Hanley, and finished by his successor Abbot William Farleigh . . 124
1458. The nave of Northbleach church, Gloucestershire, built by John Forley, wool-
    merchant 118
1460. The sepulchral chapel of Abbot Wheathamstead in St. Alban's abbey church.
1465—1491. The choir of the church of Stratford on Avon, Warwickshire, built by
    Thomas Balsall.
1468—1477. The northern tower of the west front of Rouen cathedral erected, with
    the exception of the base.
1470. Crosby Hall, London, built by Sir John Crosby 142
1470. Lavenham church, Suffolk, built by Thomas Spring . . . 120
1470—1524. The lady-chapel of Winchester cathedral rebuilt by Th. Hunton and
    Th. Silkslede 124
1475—1480. Magdalen college, Oxford, built by William of Waynflect, Bishop of
    Winchester . . . . ib.
1476—1484. The altar-screen in St. Alban's abbey church.
1476. St. George's chapel, Windsor, begun by Edward IV. . . . 116
1480. Ratisbon cathedral was built (about) 37
1480—1492. The stone vault of the choir of Norwich cathedral, the upper windows,
    and flying buttresses of the same, built by Bishop James Goldwell . . 124
1482. Eltham Palace, Kent, built by Edward IV. (about) . . . 141
1482. Oxborough Hall, Norfolk, built by Sir Edmund Bedingfield . . 135
1492—1505. The tower of Magdalen college, Oxford 124
1493—1499. The Palais de Justice, at Rouen, built.
1500—1539. Bath abbey church.

INDEX.

THE END.

VIRTUE AND CO., PRINTERS, CITY ROAD, LONDON

A NEW LIST

OF

WEALE'S
RUDIMENTARY SCIENTIFIC, EDUCATIONAL, AND CLASSICAL SERIES.

These popular and cheap Series of Books, now comprising nearly Three Hundred distinct works in almost every department of Science, Art, and Education, are recommended to the notice of Engineers. Architects, Builders, Artisans, and Students generally, as well as to those interested in Workmen's Libraries, Free Libraries Literary and Scientific Institutions, Colleges, Schools, Science Classes, &c., &c.

N.B.—In ordering from this List it is recommended, as a means of facilitating business and obviating error, to quote the numbers affixed to the volumes, as well as the titles and prices.

** The books are bound in limp cloth, unless otherwise stated.

RUDIMENTARY SCIENTIFIC SERIES.

ARCHITECTURE, BUILDING, ETC.

No.

16. *ARCHITECTURE—ORDERS*—The Orders and their Æsthetic Principles. By W. H. LEEDS. Illustrated. 1s. 6d.

17. *ARCHITECTURE—STYLES*—The History and Description of the Styles of Architecture of Various Countries, from the Earliest to the Present Period. By T. TALBOT BURY, F.R.I.B.A., &c. Illustrated. 2s.
** ORDERS AND STYLES OF ARCHITECTURE, *in One Vol.,* 3s. 6d.

18. *ARCHITECTURE—DESIGN*—The Principles of Design in Architecture, as deducible from Nature and exemplified in the Works of the Greek and Gothic Architects. By E. L. GARBETT, Architect. Illustrated. 2s.
** *The three preceding Works, in One handsome Vol., half bound, entitled* "MODERN ARCHITECTURE," *Price* 6s.

22. *THE ART OF BUILDING*, Rudiments of. General Principles of Construction, Materials used in Building, Strength and Use of Materials, Working Drawings, Specifications, and Estimates. By EDWARD DOBSON, M.R.I.B.A., &c. Illustrated. 1s. 6d.

23. *BRICKS AND TILES*, Rudimentary Treatise on the Manufacture of; containing an Outline of the Principles of Brickmaking. By EDW. DOBSON, M.R.I.B.A. With Additions by C. TOMLINSON, F.R.S. Illustrated. 3s.

25. *MASONRY AND STONECUTTING*, Rudimentary Treatise on; in which the Principles of Masonic Projection and their application to the Construction of Curved Wing-Walls, Domes, Oblique Bridges, and Roman and Gothic Vaulting, are concisely explained. By EDWARD DOBSON, M.R.I.B.A., &c. Illustrated with Plates and Diagrams. 2s. 6d.

44. *FOUNDATIONS AND CONCRETE WORKS*, a Rudimentary Treatise on; containing a Synopsis of the principal cases of Foundation Works, with the usual Modes of Treatment, and Practical Remarks on Footings, Planking, Sand, Concrete, Béton, Pile-driving, Caissons, and Cofferdams. By E. DOBSON, M.R.I.B.A., &c. Third Edition, revised by GEORGE DODD, C.E. Illustrated. 1s. 6d.

LOCKWOOD AND CO., 7, STATIONERS' HALL COURT, E.C.

Architecture, Building, etc., *continued.*

CIVIL ENGINEERING, ETC.

13. *CIVIL ENGINEERING,* the Rudiments of; for the Use of Beginners, for Practical Engineers, and for the Army and Navy. By HENRY LAW, C.E. Including a Section on Hydraulic Engineering, by GEORGE R. BURNELL, C.E. 5th Edition, with Notes and Illustrations by ROBERT MALLET, A.M., F.R.S. Illustrated with Plates and Diagrams. 5s.

29. *THE DRAINAGE OF DISTRICTS AND LANDS.* By G. DRYSDALE DEMPSEY, C.E. New Edition, revised and enlarged. Illustrated. 1s. 6d.

30. *THE DRAINAGE OF TOWNS AND BUILDINGS.* By G. DRYSDALE DEMPSEY, C.E. New Edition. Illustrated. 2s. 6d.
*** With "*Drainage of Districts and Lands,*" in One Vol., 3s. 6d.

31. *WELL-DIGGING, BORING, AND PUMP-WORK.* By JOHN GEORGE SWINDELL, Assoc. R.I.B.A. New Edition, revised by G. R. BURNELL, C.E. Illustrated. 1s.

35. *THE BLASTING AND QUARRYING OF STONE,* Rudimentary Treatise on; for Building and other Purposes, with the Constituents and Analyses of Granite, Slate, Limestone, and Sandstone: to which is added some Remarks on the Blowing up of Bridges. By Gen. Sir JOHN BURGOYNE, Bart., K.C.B. Illustrated. 1s. 6d.

43. *TUBULAR AND OTHER IRON GIRDER BRIDGES.* Particularly describing the BRITANNIA and CONWAY TUBULAR BRIDGES. With a Sketch of Iron Bridges, and Illustrations of the Application of Malleable Iron to the Art of Bridge Building. By G. D. DEMPSEY, C.E., Author of "The Practical Railway Engineer," &c., &c. New Edition, with Illustrations. 1s. 6d.

46. *CONSTRUCTING AND REPAIRING COMMON ROADS,* Papers on the Art of. Containing a Survey of the Metropolitan Roads, by S. HUGHES, C.E.; The Art of Constructing Common Roads, by HENRY LAW, C.E.; Remarks on the Maintenance of Macadamised Roads, by Field-Marshal Sir JOHN F. BURGOYNE, Bart., G.C.B., Royal Engineers, &c., &c. Illustrated. 1s. 6d.

62. *RAILWAY CONSTRUCTION,* Elementary and Practical Instruction on the Science of. By Sir MACDONALD STEPHENSON, C.E., Managing Director of the East India Railway Company. New Edition, revised and enlarged by EDWARD NUGENT, C.E. Plates and numerous Woodcuts. 3s.

62*. *RAILWAYS;* their Capital and Dividends. With Statistics of their Working in Great Britain, &c., &c. By E. D. CHATTAWAY. 1s.
*** 62 and 62*, in One Vol., 3s. 6d.

80*. *EMBANKING LANDS FROM THE SEA,* the Practice of. Treated as a Means of Profitable Employment for Capital. With Examples and Particulars of actual Embankments, and also Practical Remarks on the Repair of old Sea Walls. By JOHN WIGGINS, F.G.S. New Edition, with Notes by ROBERT MALLET, F.R.S. 2s.

81. *WATER WORKS,* for the Supply of Cities and Towns. With a Description of the Principal Geological Formations of England as influencing Supplies of Water; and Details of Engines and Pumping Machinery for raising Water. By SAMUEL HUGHES, F.G.S., C.E. New Edition, revised and enlarged, with numerous Illustrations. 4s.

82**. *GAS WORKS,* and the Practice of Manufacturing and Distributing Coal Gas. By SAMUEL HUGHES, C.E. New Edition, revised by W. RICHARDS, C.E. Illustrated. 3s.

117. *SUBTERRANEOUS SURVEYING;* an Elementary and Practical Treatise on. By THOMAS FENWICK. Also the Method of Conducting Subterraneous Surveys without the Use of the Magnetic Needle, and other modern Improvements. By THOMAS BAKER, C.E. Illustrated. 2s. 6d.

118. *CIVIL ENGINEERING IN NORTH AMERICA,* a Sketch of. By DAVID STEVENSON, F.R.S.E., &c. Plates and Diagrams. 3s.

Civil Engineering, etc., *continued.*

120. *HYDRAULIC ENGINEERING*, the Rudiments of. By G. R. Burnell, C.E., F.G.S. Illustrated. 3s.

121. *RIVERS AND TORRENTS.* With the Method of Regulating their Courses and Channels. By Professor Paul Frisi, F.R.S., of Milan. To which is added, AN ESSAY ON NAVIGABLE CANALS. Translated by Major-General John Garstin, of the Bengal Engineers. Plates. 2s. 6d.

MECHANICAL ENGINEERING, ETC.

33. *CRANES*, the Construction of, and other Machinery for Raising Heavy Bodies for the Erection of Buildings, and for Hoisting Goods. By Joseph Glynn, F.R.S., &c. Illustrated. 1s. 6d.

34. *THE STEAM ENGINE*, a Rudimentary Treatise on. By Dr. Lardner. Illustrated. 1s.

59. *STEAM BOILERS:* Their Construction and Management. By R. Armstrong, C.E. Illustrated. 1s. 6d.

63. *AGRICULTURAL ENGINEERING:* Farm Buildings, Motive Power, Field Machines, Machinery, and Implements. By G. H. Andrews, C.E. Illustrated. 3s.

67. *CLOCKS, WATCHES, AND BELLS*, a Rudimentary Treatise on. By Sir Edmund Beckett (late Edmund Beckett Denison, LL.D., Q.C.)

** *A New, Revised, and considerably Enlarged Edition of the above Standard Treatise, with very numerous Illustrations, is now ready, price 4s. 6d.*

77*. *THE ECONOMY OF FUEL*, particularly with Reference to Reverbatory Furnaces for the Manufacture of Iron, and to Steam Boilers. By T. Symes Prideaux. 1s. 6d.

82. *THE POWER OF WATER*, as applied to drive Flour Mills, and to give motion to Turbines and other Hydrostatic Engines. By Joseph Glynn, F.R.S., &c. New Edition, Illustrated. 2s.

98. *PRACTICAL MECHANISM*, the Elements of; and Machine Tools. By T. Baker, C.E. With Remarks on Tools and Machinery, by J. Nasmyth, C.E. Plates. 2s. 6d.

114. *MACHINERY*, Elementary Principles of, in its Construction and Working. Illustrated by numerous Examples of Modern Machinery for different Branches of Manufacture. By C. D. Abel, C.E. 1s. 6d.

115. *ATLAS OF PLATES.* Illustrating the above Treatise. By C. D. Abel, C.E. 7s. 6d.

125. *THE COMBUSTION OF COAL AND THE PREVENTION* OF SMOKE, Chemically and Practically Considered. With an Appendix. By C. Wye Williams, A.I.C.E. Plates. 3s.

139. *THE STEAM ENGINE*, a Treatise on the Mathematical Theory of, with Rules at length, and Examples for the Use of Practical Men. By T. Baker, C.E. Illustrated. 1s.

162. *THE BRASS FOUNDER'S MANUAL;* Instructions for Modelling, Pattern-Making, Moulding, Turning, Filing, Burnishing, Bronzing, &c. With copious Receipts, numerous Tables, and Notes on Prime Costs and Estimates. By Walter Graham. Illustrated. 2s. 6d.

164. *MODERN WORKSHOP PRACTICE*, as applied to Marine, Land, and Locomotive Engines, Floating Docks, Dredging Machines, Bridges, Cranes, Ship-building, &c., &c. By J. G. Winton. Illustrated. 3s.

165. *IRON AND HEAT*, exhibiting the Principles concerned in the Construction of Iron Beams, Pillars, and Bridge Girders, and the Action of Heat in the Smelting Furnace. By J. Armour, C.E. Numerous Woodcuts. 2s. 6d.

Mechanical Engineering, etc., *continued*.

166. *POWER IN MOTION:* Horse-Power, Motion, Toothed-Wheel Gearing, Long and Short Driving Bands, Angular Forces. By JAMES ARMOUR, C.E. With 73 Diagrams. 2s. 6d.

167. *THE APPLICATION OF IRON TO THE CONSTRUCTION* OF BRIDGES, GIRDERS, ROOFS, AND OTHER WORKS. Showing the Principles upon which such Structures are designed, and their Practical Application. By FRANCIS CAMPIN, C.E. Numerous Woodcuts. 2s.

171. *THE WORKMAN'S MANUAL OF ENGINEERING* DRAWING. By JOHN MAXTON, Engineer, Instructor in Engineering Drawing, Royal School of Naval Architecture and Marine Engineering, South Kensington. Illustrated with 7 Plates and nearly 350 Woodcuts. 3s.6d.

SHIPBUILDING, NAVIGATION, MARINE ENGINEERING, ETC.

51. *NAVAL ARCHITECTURE*, the Rudiments of; or, an Exposition of the Elementary Principles of the Science, and their Practical Application to Naval Construction. Compiled for the Use of Beginners. By JAMES PEAKE, School of Naval Architecture, H.M. Dockyard, Portsmouth. Fourth Edition, corrected, with Plates and Diagrams. 3s. 6d.

53*. *SHIPS FOR OCEAN AND RIVER SERVICE*, Elementary and Practical Principles of the Construction of. By HAKON A. SOMMERFELDT, Surveyor of the Royal Norwegian Navy. With an Appendix. 1s.

53**. *AN ATLAS OF ENGRAVINGS* to Illustrate the above. Twelve large folding plates. Royal 4to, cloth. 7s. 6d.

54. *MASTING, MAST-MAKING, AND RIGGING OF SHIPS*, Rudimentary Treatise on. Also Tables of Spars, Rigging, Blocks; Chain, Wire, and Hemp Ropes, &c., relative to every class of vessels. Together with an Appendix of Dimensions of Masts and Yards of the Royal Navy of Great Britain and Ireland. By ROBERT KIPPING, N.A. Thirteenth Edition. Illustrated. 1s. 6d.

54*. *IRON SHIP-BUILDING*. With Practical Examples and Details for the Use of Ship Owners and Ship Builders. By JOHN GRANTHAM, Consulting Engineer and Naval Architect. Fifth Edition, with important Additions. 4s.

54**. *AN ATLAS OF FORTY PLATES* to Illustrate the above. Fifth Edition. Including the latest Examples, such as H.M. Steam Frigates "Warrior," "Hercules," "Bellerophon;" H.M. Troop Ship "Serapis," Iron Floating Dock, &c., &c. 4to, boards. 38s.

55. *THE SAILOR'S SEA BOOK:* A Rudimentary Treatise on Navigation. I. How to Keep the Log and Work it off. II. On Finding the Latitude and Longitude. By JAMES GREENWOOD, B.A., of Jesus College, Cambridge. To which are added, Directions for Great Circle Sailing; an Essay on the Law of Storms and Variable Winds; and Explanations of Terms used in Ship-building. Ninth Edition, with several Engravings and Coloured Illustrations of the Flags of Maritime Nations. 2s.

80. *MARINE ENGINES, AND STEAM VESSELS*, a Treatise on. Together with Practical Remarks on the Screw and Propelling Power, as used in the Royal and Merchant Navy. By ROBERT MURRAY, C.E., Engineer-Surveyor to the Board of Trade. With a Glossary of Technical Terms, and their Equivalents in French, German, and Spanish. Fifth Edition, revised and enlarged. Illustrated. 3s.

83*bis*. *THE FORMS OF SHIPS AND BOATS:* Hints, Experimentally Derived, on some of the Principles regulating Ship-building. By W. BLAND. Sixth Edition, revised, with numerous Illustrations and Models. 1s. 6d.

99. *NAVIGATION AND NAUTICAL ASTRONOMY*, in Theory and Practice. With Attempts to facilitate the Finding of the Time and the Longitude at Sea. By J. R. YOUNG, formerly Professor of Mathematics in Belfast College. Illustrated. 2s. 6d.

Shipbuilding, Navigation, etc., *continued.*

100*. *TABLES* intended to facilitate the Operations of Navigation and Nautical Astronomy, as an Accompaniment to the above Book. By J. R. Young. 1s. 6d.

106. *SHIPS' ANCHORS*, a Treatise on. By George Cotsell, N.A. Illustrated. 1s. 6d.

149. *SAILS AND SAIL-MAKING*, an Elementary Treatise on. With Draughting, and the Centre of Effort of the Sails. Also, Weights and Sizes of Ropes ; Masting, Rigging, and Sails of Steam Vessels, &c., &c. Ninth Edition, enlarged, with an Appendix. By Robert Kipping, N.A., Sailmaker, Quayside, Newcastle. Illustrated. 2s. 6d.

155. *THE ENGINEER'S GUIDE TO THE ROYAL AND* MERCANTILE NAVIES. By a Practical Engineer. Revised by D. F. M'Carthy, late of the Ordnance Survey Office, Southampton. 3s.

PHYSICAL SCIENCE, NATURAL PHILO-SOPHY, ETC.

1. *CHEMISTRY*, for the Use of Beginners. By Professor George Fownes, F.R.S. With an Appendix, on the Application of Chemistry to Agriculture. 1s.

2. *NATURAL PHILOSOPHY*, Introduction to the Study of; for the Use of Beginners. By C. Tomlinson, Lecturer on Natural Science in King's College School, London. Woodcuts. 1s. 6d.

4. *MINERALOGY*, Rudiments of; a concise View of the Properties of Minerals. By A. Ramsey, Jun. Woodcuts and Steel Plates. 3s.

6. *MECHANICS*, Rudimentary Treatise on; Being a concise Exposition of the General Principles of Mechanical Science, and their Applications. By Charles Tomlinson, Lecturer on Natural Science in King's College School, London. Illustrated. 1s. 6d.

7. *ELECTRICITY;* showing the General Principles of Electrical Science, and the purposes to which it has been applied. By Sir W. Snow Harris, F.R.S., &c. With considerable Additions by R. Sabine, C.E., F.S.A. Woodcuts. 1s. 6d.

7*. *GALVANISM*, Rudimentary Treatise on, and the General Principles of Animal and Voltaic Electricity. By Sir W. Snow Harris. New Edition, revised, with considerable Additions, by Robert Sabine, C.E., F.S.A. Woodcuts. 1s. 6d.

8. *MAGNETISM;* being a concise Exposition of the General Principles of Magnetical Science, and the Purposes to which it has been applied. By Sir W. Snow Harris. New Edition, revised and enlarged by H. M. Noad, Ph.D., Vice-President of the Chemical Society, Author of "A Manual of Electricity," &c., &c. With 165 Woocuts. 3s. 6d.

11. *THE ELECTRIC TELEGRAPH;* its History and Progress; with Descriptions of some of the Apparatus. By R. Sabine, C.E., F.S.A., &c. Woodcuts. 3s

12. *PNEUMATICS*, for the Use of Beginners. By Charles Tomlinson. Illustrated. 1s. 6d.

72. *MANUAL OF THE MOLLUSCA ;* a Treatise on Recent and Fossil Shells. By Dr. S. P. Woodward, A.L.S. With Appendix by Ralph Tate, A.L.S., F.G.S. With numerous Plates and 300 Woodcuts, 6s. 6d. Cloth boards, 7s. 6d.

79**. *PHOTOGRAPHY*, Popular Treatise on; with a Description of the Stereoscope, &c. Translated from the French of D. Van Monckhoven, by W. H. Thornthwaite, Ph.D. Woodcuts. 1s. 6d.

96. *ASTRONOMY*. By the Rev. R. Main, M.A., F.R.S., &c. New and enlarged Edition, with an Appendix on "Spectrum Analysis." Woodcuts. 1s. 6d.

Physical Science, Natural Philosophy, etc., *continued*.

97. *STATICS AND DYNAMICS*, the Principles and Practice of; embracing also a clear development of Hydrostatics, Hydrodynamics, and Central Forces. By T. BAKER, C.E. 1s. 6d.

138. *TELEGRAPH*, Handbook of the; a Manual of Telegraphy, Telegraph Clerks' Remembrancer, and Guide to Candidates for Employment in the Telegraph Service. By R. BOND. Fourth Edition, revised and enlarged: to which is appended, QUESTIONS on MAGNETISM, ELECTRICITY, and PRACTICAL TELEGRAPHY, for the Use of Students, by W. McGREGOR, First Assistant Superintendent, Indian Gov. Telegraphs. Woodcuts. 3s.

143. *EXPERIMENTAL ESSAYS.* By CHARLES TOMLINSON. I. On the Motions of Camphor on Water. II. On the Motion of Camphor towards the Light. III. History of the Modern Theory of Dew. Woodcuts. 1s.

173. *PHYSICAL GEOLOGY*, partly based on Major-General PORTLOCK's "Rudiments of Geology." By RALPH TATE, A.L.S., &c. Numerous Woodcuts. 2s.

174. *HISTORICAL GEOLOGY*, partly based on Major-General PORTLOCK's "Rudiments." By RALPH TATE, A.L.S., &c. Woodcuts. 2s. 6d.

173 & 174. *RUDIMENTARY TREATISE ON GEOLOGY*, Physical and Historical. Partly based on Major-General PORTLOCK's "Rudiments of Geology." By RALPH TATE, A.L.S., F.G.S., &c., &c. Numerous Illustrations. In One Volume. 4s. 6d.

183 & 184. *ANIMAL PHYSICS*, Handbook of. By DIONYSIUS LARDNER, D.C.L., formerly Professor of Natural Philosophy and Astronomy in University College, London. With 520 Illustrations. In One Volume, cloth boards. 7s. 6d.

⁎ *Sold also in Two Parts, as follows :—*

183. ANIMAL PHYSICS. By Dr. LARDNER. Part I., Chapter I—VII. 4s.
184. ANIMAL PHYSICS. By Dr. LARDNER. Part II. Chapter VIII—XVIII. 3s.

MINING, METALLURGY, ETC.

117. *SUBTERRANEOUS SURVEYING*, Elementary and Practical Treatise on, with and without the Magnetic Needle. By THOMAS FENWICK, Surveyor of Mines, and THOMAS BAKER, C.E. Illustrated. 2s. 6d.

133. *METALLURGY OF COPPER ;* an Introduction to the Methods of Seeking, Mining, and Assaying Copper, and Manufacturing its Alloys. By ROBERT H. LAMBORN, Ph.D. Woodcuts. 2s.

134. *METALLURGY OF SILVER AND LEAD.* A Description of the Ores; their Assay and Treatment, and valuable Constituents. By Dr. R. H. LAMBORN. Woodcuts. 2s.

135. *ELECTRO-METALLURGY;* Practically Treated. By ALEXANDER WATT, F.R.S.S.A. New Edition. Woodcuts. 2s.

172. *MINING TOOLS*, Manual of. For the Use of Mine Managers, Agents, Students, &c. Comprising Observations on the Materials from, and Processes by which, they are manufactured; their Special Uses, Applications, Qualities, and Efficiency. By WILLIAM MORGANS, Lecturer on Mining at the Bristol School of Mines. 2s. 6d.

172*. *MINING TOOLS, ATLAS* of Engravings to Illustrate the above, containing 235 Illustrations of Mining Tools, drawn to Scale. 4to. 4s. 6d.

176. *METALLURGY OF IRON*, a Treatise on the. Containing Outlines of the History of Iron Manufacture, Methods of Assay, and Analyses of Iron Ores, Processes of Manufacture of Iron and Steel, &c. By H. BAUERMAN, F.G.S., Associate of the Royal School of Mines. Fourth Edition, revised and enlarged, with numerous Illustrations. 4s. 6d.

Mining, Metallurgy, etc., *continued*.

180. *COAL AND COAL MINING:* A Rudimentary Treatise on. By WARINGTON W. SMYTH, M.A., F.R.S., &c., Chief Inspector of the Mines of the Crown and of the Duchy of Cornwall. Second Edition, revised and corrected. With numerous Illustrations. 3s. 6d.

EMIGRATION.

154. *GENERAL HINTS TO EMIGRANTS.* Containing Notices of the various Fields for Emigration. With Hints on Preparation for Emigrating, Outfits, &c., &c. With Directions and Recipes useful to the Emigrant. With a Map of the World. 2s.

157. *THE EMIGRANT'S GUIDE TO NATAL.* By ROBERT JAMES MANN, F.R.A.S., F.M.S. Second Edition, carefully corrected to the present Date. Map. 2s.

159. *THE EMIGRANT'S GUIDE TO AUSTRALIA, New South Wales, Western Australia, South Australia, Victoria, and Queensland.* By the Rev. JAMES BAIRD, B.A. Map. 2s. 6d.

160. *THE EMIGRANT'S GUIDE TO TASMANIA and NEW ZEALAND.* By the Rev. JAMES BAIRD, B.A. With a Map. 2s.

159 & *THE EMIGRANT'S GUIDE TO AUSTRALASIA.* By the 160. Rev. J. BAIRD, B.A. Comprising the above two volumes, 12mo, cloth boards. With Maps of Australia and New Zealand. 5s.

AGRICULTURE.

29. *THE DRAINAGE OF DISTRICTS AND LANDS.* By G. DRYSDALE DEMPSEY, C.E. Illustrated. 1s. 6d.
   * With " *Drainage of Towns and Buildings,*" *in One Vol.,* 3s.

63. *AGRICULTURAL ENGINEERING:* Farm Buildings, Motive Powers and Machinery of the Steading, Field Machines, and Implements. By G. H. ANDREWS, C.E. Illustrated. 3s.

66. *CLAY LANDS AND LOAMY SOILS.* By Professor DONALDSON. 1s.

131. *MILLER'S, MERCHANT'S, AND FARMER'S READY RECKONER,* for ascertaining at sight the value of any quantity of Corn, from One Bushel to One Hundred Quarters, at any given price, from £1 to £5 per quarter. Together with the approximate values of Millstones and Millwork, &c. 1s.

140. *SOILS, MANURES, AND CROPS* (Vol. 1. OUTLINES OF MODERN FARMING.) By R. SCOTT BURN. Woodcuts. 2s.

141. *FARMING AND FARMING ECONOMY,* Notes, Historical and Practical on. (Vol. 2. OUTLINES OF MODERN FARMING.) By R. SCOTT BURN. Woodcuts. 3s.

142. *STOCK; CATTLE, SHEEP, AND HORSES.* (Vol. 3. OUTLINES OF MODERN FARMING.) By R. SCOTT BURN. Woodcuts. 2s. 6d.

145. *DAIRY, PIGS, AND POULTRY,* Management of the. By R. SCOTT BURN. With Notes on the Diseases of Stock. (Vol. 4. OUTLINES OF MODERN FARMING.) Woodcuts. 2s.

146. *UTILIZATION OF SEWAGE, IRRIGATION, AND RECLAMATION OF WASTE LAND.* (Vol. 5. OUTLINES OF MODERN FARMING.) By R. SCOTT BURN. Woodcuts. 2s. 6d.
   * Nos. 140-1-2-5-6, in One Vol., handsomely half-bound, entitled " OUTLINES OF MODERN FARMING." By ROBERT SCOTT BURN. Price 12s.

177. *FRUIT TREES;* The Scientific and Profitable Culture of. From the French of DU BREUIL, Revised by GEO. GLENNY. 187 Woodcuts. 3s. 6d.

FINE ARTS.

20. *PERSPECTIVE FOR BEGINNERS.* Adapted to Young Students and Amateurs in Architecture, Painting, &c. By GEORGE PYNE, Artist. Woodcuts. 2s.

27. *A GRAMMAR OF COLOURING*, applicable to House Painting, Decorative Architecture, and the Arts, for the Use of Practical Painters and Decorators. By GEORGE FIELD, Author of "Chromatics; or, The Analogy, Harmony, and Philosophy of Colours," &c. Enlarged by ELLIS A. DAVIDSON. Coloured Illustrations. 2s. 6d.

40. *GLASS STAINING;* or, Painting on Glass, The Art of. Comprising Directions for Preparing the Pigments and Fluxes, laying them upon the Glass, and Firing or Burning in the Colours. From the German of Dr. GESSERT. To which is added, an Appendix on THE ART OF ENAMELLING, &c. 1s.

41. *PAINTING ON GLASS*, The Art of. From the German of EMANUEL OTTO FROMBERG. 1s.

69. *MUSIC*, A Rudimentary and Practical Treatise on. With numerous Examples. By CHARLES CHILD SPENCER. 2s.

71. *PIANOFORTE*, The Art of Playing the. With numerous Exercises and Lessons. Written and Selected from the Best Masters, by CHARLES CHILD SPENCER. 1s. 6d.

181. *PAINTING POPULARLY EXPLAINED*, including Fresco, Oil, Mosaic, Water Colour, Water-Glass, Tempera, Encaustic, Miniature, Painting on Ivory, Vellum, Pottery, Enamel, Glass, &c. With Historical Sketches of the Progress of the Art by THOMAS JOHN GULLICK, assisted by JOHN TIMBS, F.S.A. Third Edition, revised and enlarged, with Frontispiece and Vignette. 5s.

ARITHMETIC, GEOMETRY, MATHEMATICS, ETC.

32. *MATHEMATICAL INSTRUMENTS*, a Treatise on; in which their Construction, and the Methods of Testing, Adjusting, and Using them are concisely Explained. By J. F. HEATHER, M.A., of the Royal Military Academy, Woolwich. Original Edition, in 1 vol., Illustrated. 1s. 6d.

*** *In ordering the above, be careful to say, "Original Edition," or give the number in the Series* (32) *to distinguish it from the Enlarged Edition in 3 vols.* (*Nos.* 168-9-70).

60. *LAND AND ENGINEERING SURVEYING*, a Treatise on; with all the Modern Improvements. Arranged for the Use of Schools and Private Students; also for Practical Land Surveyors and Engineers. By T. BAKER, C.E. New Edition, revised by EDWARD NUGENT, C.E. Illustrated with Plates and Diagrams. 2s.

61*. *READY RECKONER FOR THE ADMEASUREMENT OF LAND*. By ABRAHAM ARMAN, Schoolmaster, Thurleigh, Beds. To which is added a Table, showing the Price of Work, from 2s. 6d. to £1 per acre, and Tables for the Valuation of Land, from 1s. to £1,000 per acre, and from one pole to two thousand acres in extent, &c., &c. 1s. 6d.

76. *DESCRIPTIVE GEOMETRY*, an Elementary Treatise on; with a Theory of Shadows and of Perspective, extracted from the French of G. MONGE. To which is added, a description of the Principles and Practice of Isometrical Projection; the whole being intended as an introduction to the Application of Descriptive Geometry to various branches of the Arts. By J. F. HEATHER, M.A. Illustrated with 14 Plates. 2s.

178. *PRACTICAL PLANE GEOMETRY:* giving the Simplest Modes of Constructing Figures contained in one Plane and Geometrical Construction of the Ground. By J. F. HEATHER, M.A. With 215 Woodcuts. 2s.

179. *PROJECTION:* Orthographic, Topographic, and Perspective: giving the various Modes of Delineating Solid Forms by Constructions on a Single Plane Surface. By J. F. HEATHER, M.A. [*In preparation.*

*** *The above three volumes will form a* COMPLETE ELEMENTARY COURSE OF MATHEMATICAL DRAWING.

Arithmetic, Geometry, Mathematics, etc., *continued*.

83. *COMMERCIAL BOOK-KEEPING.* With Commercial Phrases and Forms in English, French, Italian, and German. By JAMES HADDON, M.A., Arithmetical Master of King's College School, London. 1s.

84. *ARITHMETIC*, a Rudimentary Treatise on : with full Explanations of its Theoretical Principles, and numerous Examples for Practice. For the Use of Schools and for Self-Instruction. By J. R. YOUNG, late Professor of Mathematics in Belfast College. New Edition, with Index. 1s. 6d.

84.* A KEY to the above, containing Solutions in full to the Exercises, together with Comments, Explanations, and Improved Processes, for the Use of Teachers and Unassisted Learners. By J. R. YOUNG. 1s. 6d.

85. *EQUATIONAL ARITHMETIC*, applied to Questions of Interest,
85*. Annuities, Life Assurance, and General Commerce; with various Tables by which all Calculations may be greatly facilitated. By W. HIPSLEY. In Two Parts, 1s. each ; or in One Vol. 2s.

86. *ALGEBRA*, the Elements of. By JAMES HADDON, M.A., Second Mathematical Master of King's College School. With Appendix, containing miscellaneous Investigations, and a Collection of Problems in various parts of Algebra. 2s.

86* A KEY AND COMPANION to the above Book, forming an extensive repository of Solved Examples and Problems in Illustration of the various Expedients necessary in Algebraical Operations. Especially adapted for Self-Instruction. By J. R. YOUNG. 1s. 6d.

88. *EUCLID*, THE ELEMENTS OF : with many additional Propositions
89. and Explanatory Notes: to which is prefixed, an Introductory Essay on Logic. By HENRY LAW, C.E. 2s. 6d.

** Sold also separately, viz. :—

88. EUCLID, The First Three Books. By HENRY LAW, C.E. 1s.

89. EUCLID, Books 4, 5, 6, 11, 12. By HENRY LAW, C.E. 1s. 6d.

90. *ANALYTICAL GEOMETRY AND CONICAL SECTIONS*, a Rudimentary Treatise on. By JAMES HANN, late Mathematical Master of King's College School, London. A New Edition, re-written and enlarged by J. R. YOUNG, formerly Professor of Mathematics at Belfast College. 2s.

91. *PLANE TRIGONOMETRY*, the Elements of. By JAMES HANN, formerly Mathematical Master of King's College, London. 1s.

92. *SPHERICAL TRIGONOMETRY*, the Elements of. By JAMES HANN. Revised by CHARLES H. DOWLING, C.E. 1s.

** Or with "The Elements of Plane Trigonometry," in One Volume, 2s.

93. *MENSURATION AND MEASURING*, for Students and Practical Use. With the Mensuration and Levelling of Land for the Purposes of Modern Engineering. By T. BAKER, C.E. New Edition, with Corrections and Additions by E. NUGENT, C.E. Illustrated. 1s. 6d.

94. *LOGARITHMS*, a Treatise on; with Mathematical Tables for facilitating Astronomical, Nautical, Trigonometrical, and Logarithmic Calculations; Tables of Natural Sines and Tangents and Natural Cosines. By HENRY LAW, C.E. Illustrated. 2s. 6d.

101*. *MEASURES, WEIGHTS, AND MONEYS OF ALL NATIONS*, and an Analysis of the Christian, Hebrew, and Mahometan Calendars. By W. S. B. WOOLHOUSE, F.R.A.S., &c. 1s. 6d.

102. *INTEGRAL CALCULUS*, Rudimentary Treatise on the. By HOMERSHAM COX, B.A. Illustrated. 1s.

103. *INTEGRAL CALCULUS*, Examples on the. By JAMES HANN, late of King's College, London. Illustrated. 1s.

101. *DIFFERENTIAL CALCULUS*, Examples of the. By W. S. B. WOOLHOUSE, F.R.A.S., &c. 1s. 6d.

104. *DIFFERENTIAL CALCULUS*, Examples and Solutions of the. By JAMES HADDON, M.A. 1s.

LONDON : LOCKWOOD AND CO.,

Arithmetic, Geometry, Mathematics, etc., *continued*.

105. *MNEMONICAL LESSONS.* — GEOMETRY, ALGEBRA, AND TRIGONOMETRY, in Easy Mnemonical Lessons. By the Rev. THOMAS PENYNGTON KIRKMAN, M.A. 1s. 6d.

136. *ARITHMETIC*, Rudimentary, for the Use of Schools and Self-Instruction. By JAMES HADDON, M.A. Revised by ABRAHAM ARMAN. 1s. 6d.

137. A KEY TO HADDON'S RUDIMENTARY ARITHMETIC. By A. ARMAN. 1s. 6d.

147. *ARITHMETIC*, STEPPING-STONE TO; Being a Complete Course of Exercises in the First Four Rules (Simple and Compound), on an entirely new principle. For the Use of Elementary Schools of every Grade. Intended as an Introduction to the more extended works on Arithmetic. By ABRAHAM ARMAN. 1s.

148. A KEY TO STEPPING-STONE TO ARITHMETIC. By A. ARMAN. 1s.

158. *THE SLIDE RULE, AND HOW TO USE IT;* Containing full, easy, and simple Instructions to perform all Business Calculations with unexampled rapidity and accuracy. By CHARLES HOARE, C.E. With a Slide Rule in tuck of cover. 3s.

168. *DRAWING AND MEASURING INSTRUMENTS.* Including—I. Instruments employed in Geometrical and Mechanical Drawing, and in the Construction, Copying, and Measurement of Maps and Plans. II. Instruments Used for the purposes of Accurate Measurement, and for Arithmetical Computations. By J. F. HEATHER, M.A., late of the Royal Military Academy, Woolwich, Author of "Descriptive Geometry," &c., &c. Illustrated. 1s. 6d.

169. *OPTICAL INSTRUMENTS.* Including (more especially) Telescopes, Microscopes, and Apparatus for producing copies of Maps and Plans by Photography. By J. F. HEATHER, M.A. Illustrated. 1s. 6d.

170. *SURVEYING AND ASTRONOMICAL INSTRUMENTS.* Including—I. Instruments Used for Determining the Geometrical Features of a portion of Ground. II. Instruments Employed in Astronomical Observations. By J. F. HEATHER, M.A. Illustrated. 1s. 6d.

_{*} *The above three volumes form an enlargement of the Author's original work,* "*Mathematical Instruments: their Construction, Adjustment, Testing, and Use,*" *the Eleventh Edition of which is on sale, price 1s. 6d. (See No. 32 in the Series.)*

168.⎫ *MATHEMATICAL INSTRUMENTS.* By J. F. HEATHER,
169.⎬ M.A. Enlarged Edition, for the most part entirely re-written. The 3 Parts as
170.⎭ above, in One thick Volume. With numerous Illustrations. Cloth boards. 5s.

LEGAL TREATISES.

50. *THE LAW OF CONTRACTS FOR WORKS AND SERVICES.* By DAVID GIBBONS. Third Edition, Enlarged. 3s.

107. *COUNTY COURT GUIDE*, Plain Guide for Suitors in the County Court. By a BARRISTER. 1s. 6d.

108. *THE METROPOLIS LOCAL MANAGEMENT ACT*, 18th and 19th Vict., c. 120; 19th and 20th Vict., c. 112; 21st and 22nd Vict., c. 104; 24th and 25th Vict., c. 61; also, the last Pauper Removal Act., and the Parochial Assessment Act. 1s. 6d.

108*. *THE METROPOLIS LOCAL MANAGEMENT AMENDMENT ACT*, 1862, 25th and 26th Vict., c. 120. Notes and an Index. 1s.
_{*} *With the Local Management Act, in One Volume, 2s. 6d.*

151. *A HANDY BOOK ON THE LAW OF FRIENDLY, INDUSTRIAL & PROVIDENT BUILDING & LOAN SOCIETIES.* With copious Notes. By NATHANIEL WHITE, of H.M. Civil Service. 1s.

163. *THE LAW OF PATENTS FOR INVENTIONS*; and on the Protection of Designs and Trade Marks. By F. W. CAMPIN, Barrister-at-Law. 2s.

MISCELLANEOUS VOLUMES.

36. *A DICTIONARY OF TERMS used in ARCHITECTURE, BUILDING, ENGINEERING, MINING, METALLURGY, ARCHÆOLOGY, the FINE ARTS, &c.* With Explanatory Observations on various Subjects connected with Applied Science and Art. By JOHN WEALE. Fourth Edition, with numerous Additions. Edited by ROBERT HUNT, F.R.S., Keeper of Mining Records, Editor of Ure's " Dictionary of Arts, Manufactures, and Mines." Numerous Illustrations. 5s.

112. *MANUAL OF DOMESTIC MEDICINE.* Describing the Symptoms, Causes, and Treatment of the most common Medical and Surgical Affections. By R. GOODING, B.A., M.B., The whole intended as a Family Guide in all Cases of Accident and Emergency. 2s.

112*. *MANAGEMENT OF HEALTH.* A Manual of Home and Personal Hygiene. Being Practical Hints on Air, Light, and Ventilation; Exercise, Diet, and Clothing; Rest, Sleep, and Mental Discipline; Bathing and Therapeutics. By the Rev. JAMES BAIRD, B.A. 1s.

113. *FIELD ARTILLERY ON SERVICE, on the Use of.* With especial Reference to that of an Army Corps. For Officers of all Arms. By TAUBERT, Captain, Prussian Artillery. Translated from the German by Lieut.-Col. HENRY HAMILTON MAXWELL, Bengal Artillery. 1s. 6d.

113*. *SWORDS, AND OTHER ARMS* used for Cutting and Thrusting, Memoir on. By Colonel MAREY. Translated from the French by Colonel H. H. MAXWELL. With Notes and Plates. 1s.

150. *LOGIC,* Pure and Applied. By S. H. EMMENS. Third Edition. 1s. 6d.

152. *PRACTICAL HINTS FOR INVESTING MONEY.* With an Explanation of the Mode of Transacting Business on the Stock Exchange. By FRANCIS PLAYFORD, Sworn Broker. 1s.

153. *SELECTIONS FROM LOCKE'S ESSAYS ON THE HUMAN UNDERSTANDING.* With Notes by S. H. EMMENS. 2s.

EDUCATIONAL AND CLASSICAL SERIES.

HISTORY.

1. **England, Outlines of the History of;** more especially with reference to the Origin and Progress of the English Constitution. A Text Book for Schools and Colleges. By WILLIAM DOUGLAS HAMILTON, F.S.A., of Her Majesty's Public Record Office. Fourth Edition, revised and brought down to 1872. Maps and Woodcuts. 5s.; cloth boards, 6s. Also in Five Parts, 1s. each.

5. **Greece, Outlines of the History of;** in connection with the Rise of the Arts and Civilization in Europe. By W. DOUGLAS HAMILTON, of University College, London, and EDWARD LEVIEN, M.A., of Balliol College, Oxford. 2s. 6d.; cloth boards, 3s. 6d.

7. **Rome, Outlines of the History of;** From the Earliest Period to the Christian Era and the Commencement of the Decline of the Empire. By EDWARD LEVIEN, of Balliol College, Oxford. Map, 2s. 6d.; cl. bds. 3s. 6d.

9. **Chronology of History, Art, Literature, and Progress,** from the Creation of the World to the Conclusion of the Franco-German War. The Continuation by W. D. HAMILTON, F.S.A., of Her Majesty's Record Office. 3s.; cloth boards, 3s. 6d.

50. **Dates and Events in English History,** for the use of Candidates in Public and Private Examinations. By the Rev. EDGAR RAND, B.A. 1s.

ENGLISH LANGUAGE AND MISCEL-LANEOUS.

11. **Grammar of the English Tongue,** Spoken and Written. With an Introduction to the Study of Comparative Philology. By HYDE CLARKE, D.C.L. Third Edition. 1s.

11*. **Philology:** Handbook of the Comparative Philology of English, Anglo-Saxon, Frisian, Flemish or Dutch, Low or Platt Dutch, High Dutch or German, Danish, Swedish, Icelandic, Latin, Italian, French, Spanish, and Portuguese Tongues. By HYDE CLARKE, D.C.L. 1s.

12. **Dictionary of the English Language,** as Spoken and Written. Containing above 100,000 Words. By HYDE CLARKE, D.C.L. 3s. 6d.; cloth boards, 4s. 6d.; complete with the GRAMMAR, cloth bds., 5s. 6d.

48. **Composition and Punctuation,** familiarly Explained for those who have neglected the Study of Grammar. By AUSTIN BRENAN. 16th Edition. 1s.

49. **Derivative Spelling-Book:** Giving the Origin of Every Word from the Greek, Latin, Saxon, German, Teutonic, Dutch, French, Spanish, and other Languages; with their present Acceptation and Pronunciation. By J. ROWBOTHAM, F.R.A.S. Improved Edition. 1s. 6d.

51. **The Art of Extempore Speaking:** Hints for the Pulpit, the Senate, and the Bar. By M. BAUTAIN, Vicar-General and Professor at the Sorbonne. Translated from the French. Fifth Edition, carefully corrected. 2s. 6d.

52. **Mining and Quarrying,** with the Sciences connected therewith. First Book of, for Schools. By J. H. COLLINS, F.G.S., Lecturer to the Miners' Association of Cornwall and Devon. 1s. 6d.

53. **Places and Facts in Political and Physical Geography,** for Candidates in Public and Private Examinations. By the Rev. EDGAR RAND, B.A. 1s.

54. **Analytical Chemistry,** Qualitative and Quantitative, a Course of. To which is prefixed, a Brief Treatise upon Modern Chemical Nomenclature and Notation. By WM. W. PINK, Practical Chemist, &c., and GEORGE E. WEBSTER, Lecturer on Metallurgy and the Applied Sciences, Nottingham. 2s.

THE SCHOOL MANAGERS' SERIES OF READING BOOKS,

Adapted to the Requirements of the New Code. Edited by the Rev. A. R. GRANT, Rector of Hitcham, and Honorary Canon of Ely; formerly H.M. Inspector of Schools.

	s.	d.					s.	d.
INTRODUCTORY PRIMER	0	3	THIRD STANDARD	.	.	.	1	0
FIRST STANDARD	0	6	FOURTH ,,	.	.	.	1	2
SECOND ,,	0	10	FIFTH ,,	.	.	.	1	6

*** *A Sixth Standard in Preparation.*

LESSONS FROM THE BIBLE. Part I. Old Testament. 1s.
LESSONS FROM THE BIBLE. Part II. New Testament, to which is added THE GEOGRAPHY OF THE BIBLE, for very young Children. By Rev. C. THORNTON FORSTER. 1s. 2d. *** Or the Two Parts in One Volume. 2s.

FRENCH.

24. **French Grammar.** With Complete and Concise Rules on the Genders of French Nouns. By G. L. STRAUSS, Ph.D. 1s.

25. **French-English Dictionary.** Comprising a large number of New Terms used in Engineering, Mining, on Railways, &c. By ALFRED ELWES. 1s. 6d.

French, *continued.*

26. **English–French Dictionary.** By ALFRED ELWES. 2s.
25,26. **French Dictionary** (as above). Complete, in One Vol., 3s.; cloth boards, 3s. 6d. *** Or with the GRAMMAR, cloth boards, 4s. 6d.
47. **French and English Phrase Book:** Containing Introductory Lessons, with Translations, for the convenience of Students; several Vocabularies of Words, a Collection of suitable Phrases, and Easy Familiar Dialogues. 1s.

GERMAN.

39. **German Grammar.** Adapted for English Students, from Heyse's Theoretical and Practical Grammar, by Dr. G. L. STRAUSS. 1s.
40. **German Reader:** A Series of Extracts, carefully culled from the most approved Authors of Germany; with Notes, Philological and Explanatory. By G. L. STRAUSS, Ph.D. 1s.
41. **German Triglot Dictionary.** By NICHOLAS ESTERHAZY, S. A. HAMILTON. Part I. English-German-French. 1s.
42. **German Triglot Dictionary.** Part II. German-French-English. 1s.
43. **German Triglot Dictionary.** Part III. French-German-English. 1s.
41-43. **German Triglot Dictionary** (as above), in One Vol., 3s.; cloth boards, 4s. *** Or with the GERMAN GRAMMAR, cloth boards, 5s.

ITALIAN.

27. **Italian Grammar,** arranged in Twenty Lessons, with a Course of Exercises. By ALFRED ELWES. 1s.
28. **Italian Triglot Dictionary,** wherein the Genders of all the Italian and French Nouns are carefully noted down. By ALFRED ELWES. Vol. 1. Italian-English-French. 2s.
30. **Italian Triglot Dictionary.** By A. ELWES. Vol. 2. English-French-Italian. 2s.
32. **Italian Triglot Dictionary.** By ALFRED ELWES. Vol. 3. French-Italian-English. 2s.
28,30, **Italian Triglot Dictionary** (as above). In One Vol., 6s.;
32.   cloth boards, 7s. 6d. *** Or with the ITALIAN GRAMMAR, cloth bds., 8s. 6d.

SPANISH.

34. **Spanish Grammar,** in a Simple and Practical Form. With a Course of Exercises. By ALFRED ELWES. 1s.
35. **Spanish–English and English–Spanish Dictionary.** Including a large number of Technical Terms used in Mining, Engineering, &c., with the proper Accents and the Gender of every Noun. By ALFRED ELWES. 4s.; cloth boards, 5s. *** Or with the GRAMMAR, cloth boards, 6s.

HEBREW.

46*. **Hebrew Grammar.** By Dr. BRESSLAU. 1s.
44. **Hebrew and English Dictionary,** Biblical and Rabbinical; containing the Hebrew and Chaldee Roots of the Old Testament Post-Rabbinical Writings. By Dr. BRESSLAU. 6s. *** Or with the GRAMMAR, 7s.
46. **English and Hebrew Dictionary.** By Dr. BRESSLAU. 3s.
44,46. **Hebrew Dictionary** (as above), in Two Vols., complete, with
46*.   the GRAMMAR, cloth boards, 12s.

LATIN.

19. **Latin Grammar.** Containing the Inflections and Elementary Principles of Translation and Construction. By the Rev. Thomas Goodwin, M.A., Head Master of the Greenwich Proprietary School. 1s.

20. **Latin-English Dictionary.** Compiled from the best Authorities. By the Rev. Thomas Goodwin, M.A. 2s.

22. **English-Latin Dictionary;** together with an Appendix of French and Italian Words which have their origin from the Latin. By the Rev. Thomas Goodwin, M.A. 1s. 6d.

20,22. **Latin Dictionary** (as above). Complete in One Vol., 3s. 6d.; cloth boards, 4s. 6d. *⁎* Or with the Grammar, cloth boards, 5s. 6d.

LATIN CLASSICS. With Explanatory Notes in English.

1. **Latin Delectus.** Containing Extracts from Classical Authors, with Genealogical Vocabularies and Explanatory Notes, by Henry Young, lately Second Master of the Royal Grammar School, Guildford. 1s.

2. **Cæsaris Commentarii de Bello Gallico.** Notes, and a Geographical Register for the Use of Schools, by H. Young. 2s.

12. **Ciceronis Oratio pro Sexto Roscio Amerino.** Edited, with an Introduction, Analysis, and Notes Explanatory and Critical, by the Rev. James Davies, M.A. 1s.

14. **Ciceronis Cato Major, Lælius, Brutus, sive de Senectute, de Amicitia, de Claris Oratoribus Dialogi.** With Notes by W. Brownrigg Smith, M.A., F.R.G.S. 2s

3. **Cornelius Nepos.** With Notes. Intended for the Use of Schools. By H. Young. 1s.

6. **Horace;** Odes, Epode, and Carmen Sæculare. Notes by H. Young. 1s. 6d.

7. **Horace;** Satires, Epistles, and Ars Poetica. Notes by W. Brownrigg Smith, M.A., F.R.G.S. 1s. 6d.

21. **Juvenalis Satiræ.** With Prolegomena and Notes by T. H. S. Escott, B.A., Lecturer on Logic at King's College, London. 1s. 6d.

16. **Livy:** History of Rome. Notes by H. Young and W. B. Smith, M.A. Part 1. Books i., ii., 1s. 6d.

16*. —————— Part 2. Books iii., iv., v., 1s. 6d.

17. —————— Part 3. Books xxi. xxii., 1s. 6d.

8. **Sallustii Crispi Catalina et Bellum Jugurthinum.** Notes Critical and Explanatory, by W. M. Donne, B.A., Trinity College, Cambridge. 1s. 6d.

10. **Terentii Adelphi Hecyra, Phormio.** Edited, with Notes, Critical and Explanatory, by the Rev. James Davies, M.A. 2s.

9. **Terentii Andria et Heautontimorumenos.** With Notes, Critical and Explanatory, by the Rev. James Davies, M.A. 1s. 6d.

11. **Terentii Eunuchus, Comœdia.** Edited, with Notes, by the Rev. James Davies, M.A. 1s. 6d. Or the Adelphi, Andria, and Eunuchus, 3 vols. in 1, cloth boards, 6s.

4. **Virgilii Maronis Bucolica et Georgica.** With Notes on the Bucolics by W. Rushton, M.A., and on the Georgics by H. Young. 1s. 6d.

5. **Virgilii Maronis Æneis.** Notes, Critical and Explanatory, by H. Young. 2s.

19. **Latin Verse Selections,** from Catullus, Tibullus, Propertius, and Ovid. Notes by W. B. Donne, M.A., Trinity College, Cambridge. s.

20. **Latin Prose Selections,** from Varro, Columella, Vitruvius, Seneca, Quintilian, Florus, Velleius Paterculus, Valerius Maximus Suetonius, Apuleius, &c. Notes by W. B. Donne, M.A. 2s.

GREEK.

14. **Greek Grammar,** in accordance with the Principles and Philological Researches of the most eminent Scholars of our own day. By HANS CLAUDE HAMILTON. 1s.

15,17. **Greek Lexicon.** Containing all the Words in General Use, with their Significations, Inflections, and Doubtful Quantities. By HENRY R. HAMILTON. Vol. 1. Greek-English, 2s.; Vol. 2. English-Greek, 2s. Or the Two Vols. in One, 4s.: cloth boards, 5s.

14,15. **Greek Lexicon** (as above). Complete, with the GRAMMAR, in 17.   One Vol., cloth boards, 6s.

GREEK CLASSICS.   With Explanatory Notes in English.

1. **Greek Delectus.** Containing Extracts from Classical Authors, with Genealogical Vocabularies and Explanatory Notes, by H. YOUNG. New Edition, with an improved and enlarged Supplementary Vocabulary, by JOHN HUTCHISON, M.A., of the High School, Glasgow. 1s.

30. **Æschylus: Prometheus Vinctus: The Prometheus Bound.** From the Text of DINDORF. Edited, with English Notes, Critical and Explanatory, by the Rev. JAMES DAVIES, M.A. 1s.

32. **Æschylus: Septem Contra Thebes: The Seven against Thebes.** From the Text of DINDORF. Edited, with English Notes, Critical and Explanatory, by the Rev. JAMES DAVIES, M A. 1s.

40. **Aristophanes: Acharnians.** Chiefly from the Text of C. H. WEISE. With Notes, by C. S. T. TOWNSHEND, M.A. 1s. 6d.

26. **Euripides: Alcestis.** Chiefly from the Text of DINDORF. With Notes, Critical and Explanatory, by JOHN MILNER, B.A. 1s.

23. **Euripides: Hecuba and Medea.** Chiefly from the Text of DINDORF. With Notes, Critical and Explanatory, by W. BROWNRIGG SMITH, M.A., F.R.G.S. 1s. 6d.

14-17. **Herodotus, The History of,** chiefly after the Text of GAISFORD. With Preliminary Observations and Appendices, and Notes, Critical and Explanatory, by T. H. L. LEARY, M.A., D.C.L.
> Part 1. Books i., ii. (The Clio and Euterpe), 1s. 6d.
> Part 2. Books iii., iv. (The Thalia and Melpomene), 1s. 6d.
> Part 3. Books v.-vii. (The Terpsichore, Erato, and Polymnia) 1s. 6d.
> Part 4. Books viii., iv. (The Urania and Calliope) and Index, 1s. 6d.

5-12. **Homer, The Works of.** According to the Text of BAEUMLEIN. With Notes, Critical and Explanatory, drawn from the best and latest Authorities, with Preliminary Observations and Appendices, by T. H. L. LEARY, M.A., D.C.L.

THE ILIAD: Part 1. Books i. to vi., 1s. 6d. | Part 3. Books xiii. to xviii., 1s. 6d.
Part 2. Books vii. to xii., 1s. 6d. | Part 4. Books xix. to xxiv., 1s. 6d.

THE ODYSSEY: Part 1. Books i. to vi., 1s. 6d. | Part 3. Books xiii. to xviii., 1s. 6d.
Part 2. Books vii. to xii., 1s. 6d. | Part 4. Books xix. to xxiv., and Hymns, 2s.

4. **Lucian's Select Dialogues.** The Text carefully revised, with Grammatical and Explanatory Notes, by H YOUNG. 1s.

13. **Plato's Dialogues:** The Apology of Socrates, the Crito, and the Phædo. From the Text of C. F. HERMANN. Edited with Notes, Critical and Explanatory, by the Rev. JAMES DAVIES, M.A. 2s.

18. **Sophocles: Œdipus Tyrannus.** Notes by H. YOUNG. 1s.

20. **Sophocles: Antigone.** From the Text of DINDORF. Notes, Critical and Explanatory, by the Rev. JOHN MILNER, B.A. 2s.

41. **Thucydides:** History of the Peloponnesian War. Notes by H. YOUNG. Book 1. 1s.

2, 3. **Xenophon's Anabasis;** or, The Retreat of the Ten Thousand. Notes and a Geographica Register, by H. YOUNG. Part 1. Books i. to iii., 1s. Part 2. Books iv. to vii., 1s.

42. **Xenophon's Panegyric on Agesilaus.** Notes and Introduction by LL. F. W. JEWITT. 1s. 6d.

LONDON, *May*, 1875.

𝔄 Catalogue of Books

INCLUDING MANY

NEW & STANDARD WORKS

IN

ENGINEERING, ARCHITECTURE, AGRICULTURE, MATHEMATICS, MECHANICS, SCIENCE, &c. &c.

PUBLISHED BY

LOCKWOOD & CO.,

7, STATIONERS'-HALL COURT, LUDGATE HILL, E.C.

. ENGINEERING, SURVEYING, &c.

—◆—

Humber's New Work on Water-Supply.

A COMPREHENSIVE TREATISE on the WATER-SUPPLY of CITIES and TOWNS. By WILLIAM HUMBER, Assoc. Inst. C.E., and M. Inst. M.E. Author of "Cast and Wrought Iron Bridge Construction," &c. &c. This work, it is expected, will contain about 50 Double Plates, and upwards of 300 pages of Text. Imp. 4to, half bound in morocco. [*In the press.*

*** *In accumulating information for this volume, the Author has been very liberally assisted by several professional friends, who have made this department of engineering their special study. He has thus been in a position to prepare a work which, within the limits of a single volume, will supply the reader with the most complete and reliable information upon all subjects, theoretical and practical, connected with water supply. Through the kindness of Messrs. Anderson, Bateman, Hawksley, Homersham, Baldwin Latham, Lawson, Milne, Quick, Rawlinson, Simpson, and others, several works, constructed and in course of construction, from the designs of these gentlemen, will be fully illustrated and described.*

AMONGST OTHER IMPORTANT SUBJECTS THE FOLLOWING WILL BE TREATED IN THE TEXT :—

Historical Sketch of the means that have been proposed and adopted for the Supply of Water.—Water and the Foreign Matter usually associated with it.—Rainfall and Evaporation.—Springs and Subterranean Lakes.—Hydraulics.—The Selection of Sites for Water Works.—Wells.—Reservoirs.—Filtration and Filter Beds.—Reservoir and Filter Bed Appendages.—Pumps and Appendages.—Pumping Machinery.—Culverts and Conduits, Aqueducts, Syphons, &c.—Distribution of Water.—Water Meters and general House Fittings.—Cost of Works for the Supply of Water.—Constant and Intermittent Supply.—Suggestions for preparing Plans, &c. &c., together with a Description of the numerous Works illustrated, viz :—Aberdeen, Bideford, Cockermouth, Dublin, Glasgow, Loch Katrine, Liverpool, Manchester, Rotherham, Sunderland, and several others ; with copies of the Contract, Drawings and Specification in each case.

Humber's Modern Engineering.   First Series.

A RECORD of the PROGRESS of MODERN ENGINEER-ING, 1863. Comprising Civil, Mechanical, Marine, Hydraulic, Railway, Bridge, and other Engineering Works, &c. By WILLIAM HUMBER, Assoc. Iust. C.E., &c. Imp. 4to, with 36 Double Plates, drawn to a large scale, and Photographic Portrait of John Hawkshaw, C.E., F.R.S., &c. Price 3*l.* 3*s.* half morocco.

List of the Plates.

NAME AND DESCRIPTION.	PLATES.	NAME OF ENGINEER.
Victoria Station and Roof—L. B.& S. C. Rail.	1 to 8	Mr. R. Jacomb Hood, C.E.
Southport Pier	9 and 10	Mr. James Brunlees, C.E.
Victoria Station and Roof—L. C. & D. & G.W. Railways	11 to 15A	Mr. John Fowler, C.E.
Roof of Cremorne Music Hall	16	Mr. William Humber, C.E.
Bridge over G. N. Railway	17	Mr. Joseph Cubitt, C.E.
Roof of Station—Dutch Rhenish Railway	18 and 19	Mr. Euschedi, C.E.
Bridge over the Thames—West London Extension Railway	20 to 24	Mr. William Baker, C.E.
Armour Plates	25	Mr. James Chalmers, C.E.
Suspension Bridge, Thames	26 to 29	Mr. Peter W. Barlow, C.E.
The Allen Engine	30	Mr. G. T. Porter, M.E.
Suspension Bridge, Avon	31 to 33	Mr. John Hawkshaw, C.E. and W. H. Barlow, C.E.
Underground Railway	34 to 36	Mr. John Fowler, C.E.

With copious Descriptive Letterpress, Specifications, &c.

" Handsomely lithographed and printed. It will find favour with many who desire to preserve in a permanent form copies of the plans and specifications prepared for the guidance of the contractors for many important engineering works."—*Engineer.*

Humber's Modern Engineering.   Second Series.

A RECORD of the PROGRESS of MODERN ENGINEER-ING, 1864; with Photographic Portrait of Robert Stephenson, C.E., M.P., F.R.S., &c. Price 3*l.* 3*s.* half morocco.

List of the Plates.

NAME AND DESCRIPTION.	PLATES.	NAME OF ENGINEER.
Birkenhead Docks, Low Water Basin	1 to 15	Mr. G. F. Lyster, C.E.
Charing Cross Station Roof—C. C. Railway.	16 to 18	Mr. Hawkshaw, C.E.
Digswell Viaduct—Great Northern Railway.	19	Mr. J. Cubitt, C.E.
Robbery Wood Viaduct—Great N. Railway.	20	Mr. J. Cubitt, C.E.
Iron Permanent Way	20a	
Clydach Viaduct—Merthyr, Tredegar, and Abergavenny Railway	21	Mr. Gardner, C.E.
Ebbw Viaduct ditto ditto ditto	22	Mr. Gardner, C.E.
College Wood Viaduct—Cornwall Railway	23	Mr. Brunel.
Dublin Winter Palace Roof	24 to 26	Messrs. Ordish & Le Feuvre.
Bridge over the Thames—L. C. & D. Railw.	27 to 32	Mr. J. Cubitt, C.E.
Albert Harbour, Greenock	33 to 36	Messrs. Bell & Miller.

With copious Descriptive Letterpress, Specifications, &c.

" A *resumé* of all the more interesting and important works lately completed in Great Britain; and containing, as it does, carefully executed drawings, with full working details, it will be found a valuable accessory to the profession at large."—*Engineer.*

"Mr. Humber has done the profession good and true service, by the fine collection of examples he has here brought before the profession and the public."—*Practical Mechanics' Journal.*

Humber's Modern Engineering. Third Series.

A RECORD of the PROGRESS of MODERN ENGINEER-
ING, 1865. Imp. 4to, with 40 Double Plates, drawn to a large
scale, and Photographic Portrait of J. R. M'Clean, Esq., late President of the Institution of Civil Engineers. Price 3*l.* 3*s.* half
morocco.

List of Plates and Diagrams.

MAIN DRAINAGE, METROPOLIS.

NORTH SIDE.

Map showing Interception of Sewers.
Middle Level Sewer. Sewer under Re-
gent's Canal.
Middle Level Sewer. Junction with Fleet
Ditch.
Outfall Sewer. Bridge over River Lea.
Elevation.
Outfall Sewer. Bridge over River Lea.
Details.
Outfall Sewer. Bridge over River Lea.
Details.
Outfall Sewer. Bridge over Marsh Lane,
North Woolwich Railway, and Bow and
Barking Railway Junction.
Outfall Sewer. Bridge over Bow and
Barking Railway. Elevation.
Outfall Sewer. Bridge over Bow and
Barking Railway. Details.
Outfall Sewer. Bridge over Bow and
Barking Railway. Details.
Outfall Sewer. Bridge over East London
Waterworks' Feeder. Elevation.
Outfall Sewer. Bridge over East London
Waterworks' Feeder. Details.
Outfall Sewer. Reservoir. Plan.
Outfall Sewer. Reservoir. Section.
Outfall Sewer. Tumbling Bay and Outlet.
Outfall Sewer. Penstocks.

SOUTH SIDE.

Outfall Sewer. Bermondsey Branch.
Outfall Sewer. Bermondsey Branch.
Outfall Sewer. Reservoir and Outlet.
Plan.

MAIN DRAINAGE, METROPOLIS,
continued—

Outfall Sewer. Reservoir and Outlet.
Details.
Outfall Sewer. Reservoir and Outlet.
Details.
Outfall Sewer. Reservoir and Outlet.
Details.
Outfall Sewer. Filth Hoist.
Sections of Sewers (North and South
Sides).

THAMES EMBANKMENT.

Section of River Wall.
Steam-boat Pier, Westminster. Elevation.
Steam-boat Pier, Westminster. Details.
Landing Stairs between Charing Cross
and Waterloo Bridges.
York Gate. Front Elevation.
York Gate. Side Elevation and Details.
Overflow and Outlet at Savoy Street Sewer.
Details.
Overflow and Outlet at Savoy Street Sewer.
Penstock.
Overflow and Outlet at Savoy Street Sewer.
Penstock.
Steam-boat Pier, Waterloo Bridge. Eleva-
tion.
Steam-boat Pier, Waterloo Bridge. De-
tails.
Steam-boat Pier, Waterloo Bridge. De-
tails.
Junction of Sewers. Plans and Sections.
Gullies. Plans and Sections.
Rolling Stock.
Granite and Iron Forts.

With copious Descriptive Letterpress, Specifications, &c.

Opinions of the Press.

"Mr. Humber's works—especially his annual 'Record,' with which so many of our
readers are now familiar—fill a void occupied by no other branch of literature. . . . .
The drawings have a constantly increasing value, and whoever desires to possess clear
representations of the two great works carried out by our Metropolitan Board will
obtain Mr. Humber's last volume."—*Engineering.*

"No engineer, architect, or contractor should fail to preserve these records of works
which, for magnitude, have not their parallel in the present day, no student in the
profession but should carefully study the details of these great works, which he may be
one day called upon to imitate."—*Mechanics' Magazine.*

"A work highly creditable to the industry of its author. . . . . The volume is quite
an encyclopædia for the study of the student who desires to master the subject of
municipal drainage on its scale of greatest development."—*Practical Mechanics
Journal.*

Humber's Modern Engineering. Fourth Series.

A RECORD of the PROGRESS of MODERN ENGINEER-ING, 1866. Imp. 4to, with 36 Double Plates, drawn to a large scale, and Photographic Portrait of John Fowler, Esq., President of the Institution of Civil Engineers.   Price 3*l*. 3*s*. half-morocco.

List of the Plates and Diagrams.

NAME AND DESCRIPTION.	PLATES.	NAME OF ENGINEER.
Abbey Mills Pumping Station, Main Drainage, Metropolis	1 to 4	Mr. Bazalgette, C.E.
Barrow Docks	5 to 9	Messrs. M'Clean & Stillman, [C. E.
Manquis Viaduct, Santiago and Valparaiso Railway	10, 11	Mr. W. Loyd, C.E.
Adams' Locomotive, St. Helen's Canal Railw.	12, 13	Mr. H. Cross, C.E.
Cannon Street Station Roof, Charing Cross Railway	14 to 16	Mr. J. Hawkshaw, C.E.
Road Bridge over the River Moka	17, 18	Mr. H. Wakefield, C.E.
Telegraphic Apparatus for Mesopotamia	19	Mr. Siemens, C.E.
Viaduct over the River Wye, Midland Railw.	20 to 22	Mr. W. H. Barlow, C.E.
St. Germans Viaduct, Cornwall Railway	23, 24	Mr. Brunel, C.E.
Wrought-Iron Cylinder for Diving Bell	25	Mr. J. Coode, C.E.
Millwall Docks	26 to 31	Messrs. J. Fowler, C.E., and William Wilson, C.E.
Milroy's Patent Excavator	32	Mr. Milroy, C.E.
Metropolitan District Railway	33 to 38	Mr. J. Fowler, Engineer-in-Chief, and Mr. T. M. Johnson, C.E.
Harbours, Ports, and Breakwaters	A to C	

The Letterpress comprises—

A concluding article on Harbours, Ports, and Breakwaters, with Illustrations and detailed descriptions of the Breakwater at Cherbourg, and other important modern works ; an article on the Telegraph Lines of Mesopotamia ; a full description of the Wrought-iron Diving Cylinder for Ceylon, the circumstances under which it was used, and the means of working it ; full description of the Millwall Docks ; &c., &c., &c.

Opinions of the Press.

"Mr. Humber's 'Record of Modern Engineering' is a work of peculiar value, as well to those who design as to those who study the art of engineering construction. It embodies a vast amount of practical information in the form of full descriptions and working drawings of all the most recent and noteworthy engineering works.   The plates are excellently lithographed, and the present volume of the 'Record' is not a whit behind its predecessors."—*Mechanics' Magazine.*

"We gladly welcome another year's issue of this valuable publication from the able pen of Mr. Humber.   The accuracy and general excellence of this work are well known, while its usefulness in giving the measurements and details of some of the latest examples of engineering, as carried out by the most eminent men in the profession, cannot be too highly prized."—*Artizan.*

"The volume forms a valuable companion to those which have preceded it, and cannot fail to prove a most important addition to every engineering library."—*Mining Journal.*

"No one of Mr. Humber's volumes was bad ; all were worth their cost, from the mass of plates from well-executed drawings which they contained.   In this respect, perhaps, this last volume is the most valuable that the author has produced."—*Practical Mechanics' Journal.*

Humber's Great Work on Bridge Construction.

A COMPLETE and PRACTICAL TREATISE on CAST and WROUGHT-IRON BRIDGE CONSTRUCTION, including Iron Foundations. In Three Parts—Theoretical, Practical, and Descriptive. By WILLIAM HUMBER, Assoc. Inst. C.E., and M. Inst. M.E. Third Edition, revised and much improved, with 115 Double Plates (20 of which now first appear in this edition), and numerous additions to the Text. In 2 vols. imp. 4to., price 6l. 16s. 6d. half bound in morocco.

"A very valuable contribution to the standard literature of civil engineering. In addition to elevations, plans, and sections, large scale details are given, which very much enhance the instructive worth of these illustrations. No engineer would willingly be without so valuable a fund of information."—*Civil Engineer and Architect's Journal.*

"The First or Theoretical Part contains mathematical investigations of the principles involved in the various forms now adopted in bridge construction. These investigations are exceedingly complete, having evidently been very carefully considered and worked out to the utmost extent that can be desired by the practical man. The tables are of a very useful character, containing the results of the most recent experiments, and amongst them are some valuable tables of the weight and cost of cast and wrought-iron structures actually erected. The volume of text is amply illustrated by numerous woodcuts, plates, and diagrams ; and the plates in the second volume do great credit to both draughtsmen and engravers. In conclusion, we have great pleasure in cordially recommending this work to our readers."—*Artizan.*

"Mr. Humber's stately volumes lately issued—in which the most important bridges erected during the last five years, under the direction of the late Mr. Brunel, Sir W. Cubitt, Mr. Hawkshaw, Mr. Page, Mr. Fowler, Mr. Hemans, and others among our most eminent engineers, are drawn and specified in great detail."—*Engineer.*

Weale's Engineers' Pocket-Book.

THE ENGINEERS', ARCHITECTS', and CONTRACTORS' POCKET-BOOK (LOCKWOOD & Co.'s ; formerly WEALE'S). Published Annually. In roan tuck, gilt edges, with 10 Copper-Plates and numerous Woodcuts. Price 6s.

"A vast amount of really valuable matter condensed into the small dimensions of a book which is, in reality, what it professes to be—a pocket-book. . . . We cordially recommend the book to the notice of the managers of coal and other mines; to them it will prove a handy book of reference on a variety of subjects more or less intimately connected with their profession."—*Colliery Guardian.*

"Every branch of engineering is treated of, and facts, figures, and data of every kind abound."—*Mechanics' Mag.*

"It contains a large amount of information peculiarly valuable to those for whose use it is compiled. We cordially commend it to the engineering and architectural professions generally."—*Mining Journal.*

Iron Bridges, Girders, Roofs, &c.

A TREATISE on the APPLICATION of IRON to the CONSTRUCTION of BRIDGES, GIRDERS, ROOFS, and OTHER WORKS ; showing the Principles upon which such Structures are Designed, and their Practical Application. Especially arranged for the use of Students and Practical Mechanics, all Mathematical Formulæ and Symbols being excluded. By FRANCIS CAMPIN, C.E. With numerous Diagrams. 12mo., cloth boards, 3s.

"For numbers of young engineers the book is just the cheap, handy, first guide they want."—*Middlesborough Weekly News.*

"Invaluable to those who have not been educated in mathematics."—*Colliery Guardian.*

"Remarkably accurate and well written."—*Artizan.*

Barlow on the Strength of Materials, enlarged.

A TREATISE ON THE STRENGTH OF MATERIALS, with Rules for application in Architecture, the Construction of Suspension Bridges, Railways, &c. ; and an Appendix on the Power of Locomotive Engines, and the effect of Inclined Planes and Gradients. By PETER BARLOW, F.R.S. A New Edition, revised by his Sons, P. W. BARLOW, F.R.S., and W. H. BARLOW, F.R.S., to which are added Experiments by HODGKINSON, FAIR-BAIRN, and KIRKALDY ; an Essay (with Illustrations) on the effect produced by passing Weights over Elastic Bars, by the Rev. ROBERT WILLIS, M.A., F.R.S. And Formulæ for Calculating Girders, &c. The whole arranged and edited by W. HUMBER, Assoc. Inst. C.E., Author of " A Complete and Practical Treatise on Cast and Wrought-Iron Bridge Construction," &c. &c. Demy 8vo, 400 pp., with 19 large Plates, and numerous woodcuts, price 18s. cloth.

" Although issued as the sixth edition, the volume under consideration is worthy of being regarded, for all practical purposes, as an entirely new work . . . the book is undoubtedly worthy of the highest commendation."—*Mining Journal.*

" An increased value has been given to this very valuable work by the addition of a large amount of information, which cannot prove otherwise than highly useful to those who require to consult it. . . . . The arrangement and editing of this mass of information has been undertaken by Mr. Humber, who has most ably fulfilled a task requiring special care and ability to render it a success."—*Mechanics' Magazine.*

" The best book on the subject which has yet appeared. . . . . We know of no work that so completely fulfils its mission."—*English Mechanic.*

" There is not a pupil in an engineering school, an apprentice in an engineer's or architect's office, or a competent clerk of works, who will not recognise in the scientific volume newly given to circulation, an old and valued friend."—*Building News.*

" The standard treatise upon this particular subject."—*Engineer.*

Strains, Formulæ & Diagrams for Calculation of.

A HANDY BOOK for the CALCULATION of STRAINS in GIRDERS and SIMILAR STRUCTURES, and their STRENGTH ; consisting of Formulæ and Corresponding Diagrams, with numerous Details for Practical Application, &c. By WILLIAM HUMBER, Assoc. Inst. C.E., &c. Fcap. 8vo, with nearly 100 Woodcuts and 3 Plates, price 7s. 6d. cloth.

" The arrangement of the matter in this little volume is as convenient as it well could be. . . . . The system of employing diagrams as a substitute for complex computations is one justly coming into great favour, and in that respect Mr. Humber's volume is fully up to the times."—*Engineering.*

" The formulæ are neatly expressed, and the diagrams good."—*Athenæum.*

" We heartily commend this really *handy* book to our engineer and architect readers."—*English Mechanic.*

Mechanical Engineering.

A PRACTICAL TREATISE ON MECHANICAL ENGINEERING : comprising Metallurgy, Moulding, Casting, Forging, Tools, Workshop Machinery, Mechanical Manipulation, Manufacture of the Steam Engine, &c. &c. With an Appendix on the Analysis of Iron and Iron Ore, and Glossary of Terms. By FRANCIS CAMPIN, C.E. Illustrated with 91 Woodcuts and 28 Plates of Slotting, Shaping, Drilling, Punching, Shearing, and Riveting Machines—Blast, Refining, and Reverberatory Furnaces—Steam Engines, Governors, Boilers, Locomotives, &c. 8vo, cloth, 12s.

Strains.

THE STRAINS ON STRUCTURES OF IRONWORK; with Practical Remarks on Iron Construction. By F. W. SHEILDS, M. Inst. C.E. Second Edition, with 5 plates. Royal 8vo, 5s. cloth.

CONTENTS.—Introductory Remarks; Beams Loaded at Centre; Beams Loaded at unequal distances between supports; Beams uniformly Loaded; Girders with triangular bracing Loaded at centre; Ditto, Loaded at unequal distances between supports; Ditto, uniformly Loaded; Calculation of the Strains on Girders with triangular Basings; Cantilevers; Continuous Girders; Lattice Girders; Girders with Vertical Struts and Diagonal Ties; Calculation of the Strains on Ditto; Bow and String Girders; Girders of a form not belonging to any regular figure; Plate Girders; Apportionments of Material to Strain; Comparison of different Girders; Proportion of Length to Depth of Girders; Character of the Work; Iron Roofs.

Construction of Iron Beams, Pillars, &c.

IRON AND HEAT, Exhibiting the Principles concerned in the Construction of Iron Beams, Pillars, and Bridge Girders, and the Action of Heat in the Smelting Furnace. By JAMES ARMOUR, C.E. Woodcuts, 12mo, cloth boards, 3s. 6d.; cloth limp, 2s. 6d.

" A very useful and thoroughly practical little volume, in every way deserving of circulation amongst working men."—*Mining Journal.*

" No ironworker who wishes to acquaint himself with the principles of his own trade can afford to be without it."—*South Durham Mercury.*

Power in Motion.

POWER IN MOTION: Horse Power, Motion, Toothed Wheel Gearing, Long and Short Driving Bands, Angular Forces, &c. By JAMES ARMOUR, C.E. With 73 Diagrams. 12mo, cloth boards, 3s. 6d. [*Recently published.*

" Numerous illustrations enable the author to convey his meaning as explicitly as it is perhaps possible to be conveyed. The value of the theoretic and practical knowledge imparted cannot well be over estimated."—*Newcastle Weekly Chronicle.*

Metallurgy of Iron.

A TREATISE ON THE METALLURGY OF IRON: containing Outlines of the History of Iron Manufacture, Methods of Assay, and Analyses of Iron Ores, Processes of Manufacture of Iron and Steel, &c. By H. BAUERMAN, F.G.S., Associate of the Royal School of Mines. With numerous Illustrations. Fourth Edition, revised and much enlarged. 12mo., cloth boards, 5s. 6d. [*Just published.*

" Carefully written, it has the merit of brevity and conciseness, as to less important points, while all material matters are very fully and thoroughly entered into."—*Standard.*

Trigonometrical Surveying.

AN OUTLINE OF THE METHOD OF CONDUCTING A TRIGONOMETRICAL SURVEY, for the Formation of Geographical and Topographical Maps and Plans, Military Reconnaissance, Levelling, &c., with the most useful Problems in Geodesy and Practical Astronomy, and Formulæ and Tables for Facilitating their Calculation. By LIEUT-GENERAL FROME, R.E., late Inspector-General of Fortifications, &c. Fourth Edition, Enlarged, thoroughly Revised, and partly Re-written. By CAPTAIN CHARLES WARREN, R.E., F.G.S. With 19 Plates and 115 Woodcuts, royal 8vo, price 16s. cloth.

Hydraulics.

HYDRAULIC TABLES, CO-EFFICIENTS, and FORMULÆ for finding the Discharge of Water from Orifices, Notches, Weirs, Pipes, and Rivers. With New Formulæ, Tables, and General Information on Rain-fall, Catchment-Basins, Drainage, Sewerage, Water Supply for Towns and Mill Power. By JOHN NEVILLE, Civil Engineer, M.R.I.A. Third Edition, carefully revised, with considerable Additions. Numerous Illustrations. Crown 8vo, 14s. cloth.   [Now ready.

Drawing for Engineers, &c.

THE WORKMAN'S MANUAL OF ENGINEERING DRAWING. By JOHN MAXTON, Instructor in Engineering Drawing, South Kensington. Second Edition, carefully revised. With upwards of 300 Plates and Diagrams. 12mo, cloth, strongly bound, 4s. 6d.

"Even accomplished draughtsmen will find in it much that will be of use to them. A copy of it should be kept for reference in every drawing office."—*Engineering.*
"An indispensable book for teachers of engineering drawing." — *Mechanics' Magazine.*

Levelling.

A TREATISE on the PRINCIPLES and PRACTICE of LEVELLING; showing its Application to Purposes of Railway and Civil Engineering, in the Construction of Roads; with Mr. TELFORD'S Rules for the same. By FREDERICK W. SIMMS, F.G.S., M. Inst. C.E. Fifth Edition, very carefully revised, with the addition of Mr. LAW'S Practical Examples for Setting out Railway Curves, and Mr. TRAUTWINE'S Field Practice of Laying out Circular Curves. With 7 Plates and numerous Woodcuts. 8vo, 8s. 6d. cloth.   ** TRAUTWINE on Curves, separate, price 5s.

"One of the most important text-books for the general surveyor, and there is scarcely a question connected with levelling for which a solution would be sought but that would be satisfactorily answered by consulting the volume."—*Mining Journal.*
"The text-book on levelling in most of our engineering schools and colleges."—*Engineer.*
"The publishers have rendered a substantial service to the profession, especially to the younger members, by bringing out the present edition of Mr. Simms's useful work."—*Engineering.*

Earthwork.

EARTHWORK TABLES, showing the Contents in Cubic Yards of Embankments, Cuttings, &c., of Heights or Depths up to an average of 80 feet. By JOSEPH BROADBENT, C.E., and FRANCIS CAMPIN, C.E. Cr. 8vo. oblong, 5s. cloth.   [*Just Published.*

"Creditable to both the authors and the publishers. . . . The way in which accuracy is attained, by a simple division of each cross section into three elements, two of which are constant and one variable, is ingenious."—*Athenæum.*
"Likely to be of considerable service to engineers."—*Building News.*
"Practical illustrations of the tabulated quantities are given, which make the working of the tables easy to the most inexperienced. The work is excellently got up, and the type is remarkably clear; and contractors, builders, and engineers should not be without it."—*Builders' Weekly Reporter.*
"Two additions, one subtraction, and four multiplications, with the use of the tables, suffice to determine the quantity with considerable accuracy in any piece of earthwork; and, as the tables are of pocket-book size and very legibly printed, they cannot fail to come into general use."—*Mining Journal.*

Strength of Cast Iron, &c.

A PRACTICAL ESSAY on the STRENGTH of CAST IRON and OTHER METALS. By the late THOMAS TREDGOLD, Mem. Inst. C.E., Author of "Elementary Principles of Carpentry," &c. Fifth Edition, Edited by EATON HODGKINSON, F.R.S. ; to which are added EXPERIMENTAL RESEARCHES on the STRENGTH and OTHER PROPERTIES of CAST IRON. By the EDITOR. The whole Illustrated with 9 Engravings and numerous Woodcuts. 8vo, 12s. cloth.

₄ HODGKINSON'S EXPERIMENTAL RESEARCHES ON THE STRENGTH AND OTHER PROPERTIES OF CAST IRON may be had separately. With Engravings and Woodcuts. 8vo, price 6s. cloth.

The High-Pressure Steam Engine.

THE HIGH-PRESSURE STEAM ENGINE ; an Exposition of its Comparative Merits, and an Essay towards an Improved System of Construction, adapted especially to secure Safety and Economy. By Dr. ERNST ALBAN, Practical Machine Maker, Plau, Mecklenberg. Translated from the German, with Notes, by Dr. POLE, F.R.S., M. Inst. C.E., &c. &c. With 28 fine Plates, 8vo, 16s. 6d. cloth.

"A work like this, which goes thoroughly into the examination of the high-pressure engine, the boiler, and its appendages, &c., is exceedingly useful, and deserves a place in every scientific library."—*Steam Shipping Chronicle.*

Steam Boilers.

A TREATISE ON STEAM BOILERS : their Strength, Construction, and Economical Working. By ROBERT WILSON, late Inspector for the Manchester Steam Users' Association for the Prevention of Steam Boiler Explosions, and for the Attainment of Economy in the Application of Steam. 12mo, cloth boards, 328 pages, price 6s.

Tables of Curves.

TABLES OF TANGENTIAL ANGLES and MULTIPLES for setting out Curves from 5 to 200 Radius. By ALEXANDER BEAZELEY, M. Inst. C.E. Printed on 48 Cards, and sold in a cloth box, waistcoat-pocket size, price 3s. 6d.

"Each table is printed on a small card, which, being placed on the theodolite, leaves the hands free to manipulate the instrument—no small advantage as regards the rapidity of work. They are clearly printed, and compactly fitted into a small case for the pocket—an arrangement that will recommend them to all practical men."—*Engineer.*

"Very handy : a man may know that all his day's work must fall on two of these cards, which he puts into his own card-case, and leaves the rest behind."—*Athenæum.*

Laying Out Curves.

THE FIELD PRACTICE of LAYING OUT CIRCULAR CURVES for RAILROADS. By JOHN C. TRAUTWINE, C.E. (Extracted from SIMMS's Work on Levelling). 8vo, 5s. sewed.

Estimate and Price Book.

THE CIVIL ENGINEER'S AND CONTRACTOR'S ESTIMATE AND PRICE BOOK for Home or Foreign Service : in reference to Roads, Railways, Tramways, Docks, Harbours, Forts, Fortifications, Bridges, Aqueducts, Tunnels, Sewers, Waterworks, Gasworks, Stations, Barracks, Warehouses, &c. &c. &c. With Specifications for Permanent Way, Telegraph Materials, Plant, Maintenance, and Working of a Railway ; and a Priced List of Machinery, Plant, Tools, &c. By W. D. HASKOLL, C.E. Plates and Woodcuts. Published annually. 8vo, cloth, 6s.

"As furnishing a variety of data on every conceivable want to civil engineers and contractors, this book has ever stood perhaps unrivalled."—*Architect.*

Surveying (Land and Marine).

LAND AND MARINE SURVEYING, in Reference to the Preparation of Plans for Roads and Railways, Canals, Rivers, Towns' Water Supplies, Docks and Harbours ; with Description and Use of Surveying Instruments. By W. DAVIS HASKOLL, C.E., Author of "The Engineer's Field Book," "Examples of Bridge and Viaduct Construction," &c. Demy 8vo, price 12s. 6d. cloth, with 14 folding Plates, and numerous Woodcuts.

"A most useful and well arranged book for the aid of a student. . . . . We can strongly recommend it as a carefully-written and valuable text-book."—*Builder.*

"Mr. Haskoll has knowledge and experience, and can so give expression to it as to make any matter on which he writes, clear to the youngest pupil in a surveyor's office."—*Colliery Guardian.*

"A volume which cannot fail to prove of the utmost practical utility. . . . . It is one which may be safely recommended to all students who aspire to become clean and expert surveyors."—*Mining Journal.*

Engineering Fieldwork.

THE PRACTICE OF ENGINEERING FIELDWORK, applied to Land and Hydraulic, Hydrographic, and Submarine Surveying and Levelling. Second Edition, revised, with considerable additions, and a Supplementary Volume on WATERWORKS, SEWERS, SEWAGE, and IRRIGATION. By W. DAVIS HASKOLL, C.E. Numerous folding Plates. Demy 8vo, 2 vols. in one, cloth boards, 1l. 1s. (published at 2l. 4s.)

Mining, Surveying and Valuing.

THE MINERAL SURVEYOR AND VALUER'S COMPLETE GUIDE, comprising a Treatise on Improved Mining Surveying, with new Traverse Tables ; and Descriptions of Improved Instruments ; also an Exposition of the Correct Principles of Laying out and Valuing Home and Foreign Iron and Coal Mineral Properties: to which is appended M. THOMAN'S (of the Crédit Mobilier, Paris) TREATISE on COMPOUND INTEREST and ANNUITIES, with LOGARITHMIC TABLES. By WILLIAM LINTERN, Mining and Civil Engineer. 12mo, strongly bound in cloth boards, with four Plates of Diagrams, Plans, &c., price 10s. 6d.

"Contains much valuable information given in a small compass, and which, as far as we have tested it, is thoroughly trustworthy."—*Iron and Coal Trades Review.*

"The matter, arrangement, and illustration of this work are all excellent, and make it one of the best of its kind."—*Standard.*

Fire Engineering.

FIRES, FIRE-ENGINES, AND FIRE BRIGADES. With a History of Fire-Engines, their Construction, Use, and Management; Remarks on Fire-Proof Buildings, and the Preservation of Life from Fire; Statistics of the Fire Appliances in English Towns; Foreign Fire Systems; Hints on Fire Brigades, &c., &c. By CHARLES F. T. YOUNG, C.E. With numerous Illustrations, handsomely printed, 544 pp., demy 8vo, price 1l. 4s. cloth.

"We can most heartily commend this book. . . . . It is really the only English work we now have upon the subject."—*Engineering.*

'We strongly recommend the book to the notice of all who are in any way interested in fires, fire-engines, or fire-brigades."—*Mechanics' Magazine.*

Manual of Mining Tools.

MINING TOOLS. For the use of Mine Managers, Agents, Mining Students, &c. By WILLIAM MORGANS, Lecturer on Practical Mining at the Bristol School of Mines. Volume of Text. 12mo. With an Atlas of Plates, containing 235 Illustrations. 4to. Together, price 9s. cloth boards.   [*Recently published.*

"Students in the Science of Mining, and not only they, but subordinate officials in mines, and even Overmen, Captains, Managers, and Viewers may gain practical knowledge and useful hints by the study of Mr. Morgans's Manual."—*Colliery Guardian.*

"A very valuable work, which will tend materially to improve our mining literature."—*Mining Journal.*

Gas and Gasworks.

A TREATISE on GASWORKS and the PRACTICE of MANUFACTURING and DISTRIBUTING COAL GAS. By SAMUEL HUGHES, C.E. Fourth Edition, revised by W. RICHARDS, C.E. With 68 Woodcuts, bound in cloth boards, 12mo, price 4s.

Waterworks for Cities and Towns.

WATERWORKS for the SUPPLY of CITIES and TOWNS, with a Description of the Principal Geological Formations of England as influencing Supplies of Water. By SAMUEL HUGHES, F.G.S., Civil Engineer. New and enlarged edition, 12mo, cloth boards, with numerous Illustrations, price 5s.

"One of the most convenient, and at the same time reliable works on a subject, the vital importance of which cannot be over-estimated."—*Bradford Observer.*

Coal and Coal Mining.

COAL AND COAL MINING: a Rudimentary Treatise on. By WARINGTON W. SMYTH, M.A., F.R.S., &c., Chief Inspector of the Mines of the Crown and of the Duchy of Cornwall. New edition, revised and corrected. 12mo., cloth boards, with numerous Illustrations, price 4s. 6d.

"Every portion of the volume appears to have been prepared with much care, and .. an outline is given of every known coal-field in this and other countries, as well as of the two principal methods of working, the book will doubtless interest a very large number of readers."—*Mining Journal.*

"Certainly experimental skill and rule-of-thumb practice would be greatly enriched by the addition of the theoretical knowledge and scientific information which Mr. Warington Smyth communicates in combination with the results of his own experience and personal research."—*Colliery Guardian.*

Field-Book for Engineers.

THE ENGINEER'S, MINING SURVEYOR'S, and CON-
TRACTOR'S FIELD-BOOK. By W. DAVIS HASKOLL, Civil
Engineer. Third Edition, much enlarged, consisting of a Series
of Tables, with Rules, Explanations of Systems, and Use of Theodolite for Traverse Surveying and Plotting the Work with minute
accuracy by means of Straight Edge and Set Square only; Levelling
with the Theodolite, Casting out and Reducing Levels to Datum,
and Plotting Sections in the ordinary manner; Setting out Curves
with the Theodolite by Tangential Angles and Multiples with Right
and Left-hand Readings of the Instrument; Setting out Curves
without Theodolite on the System of Tangential Angles by Sets of
Tangents and Offsets; and Earthwork Tables to 80 feet deep, calculated for every 6 inches in depth. With numerous wood-cuts,
12mo, price 12s. cloth.

"A very useful work for the practical engineer and surveyor. Every person
engaged in engineering field operations will estimate the importance of such a work
and the amount of valuable time which will be saved by reference to a set of reliable
tables prepared with the accuracy and fulness of those given in this volume."—*Railway News.*

"The book is very handy, and the author might have added that the separate tables
of sines and tangents to every minute will make it useful for many other purposes, the
genuine traverse tables existing all the same."—*Athenæum.*

"The work forms a handsome pocket volume, and cannot fail, from its portability
and utility, to be extensively patronised by the engineering profession."—*Mining
Journal.*

"We strongly recommend this second edition of Mr. Haskoll's 'Field Book' to all
classes of surveyors."—*Colliery Guardian.*

Earthwork, Measurement and Calculation of.

A MANUAL on EARTHWORK. By ALEX. J. S. GRAHAM,
C.E., Resident Engineer, Forest of Dean Central Railway. With
numerous Diagrams. 18mo, 2s. 6d. cloth.

"As a really handy book for reference, we know of no work equal to it; and the
railway engineers and others employed in the measurement and calculation of earth
work will find a great amount of practical information very admirably arranged, and
available for general or rough estimates, as well as for the more exact calculations
required in the engineers' contractor's offices."—*Artizan.*

Harbours.

THE DESIGN and CONSTRUCTION of HARBOURS: A
Treatise on Maritime Engineering. By THOMAS STEVENSON,
F.R.S.E., F.G.S., M.I.C.E. Second Edition, containing many
additional subjects, and otherwise generally extended and revised.
With 20 Plates and numerous Cuts. Small 4to, 15s. cloth.

Mathematical and Drawing Instruments.

A TREATISE ON THE PRINCIPAL MATHEMATICAL
AND DRAWING INSTRUMENTS employed by the Engineer,
Architect, and Surveyor. By FREDERICK W. SIMMS, M. Inst.
C.E., Author of "Practical Tunnelling," &c. Third Edition, with
numerous Cuts. 12mo, price 3s. 6d. cloth.

Bridge Construction in Masonry, Timber, & Iron.

EXAMPLES OF BRIDGE AND VIADUCT CONSTRUC-
TION OF MASONRY, TIMBER, AND IRON ; consisting of
46 Plates from the Contract Drawings or Admeasurement of select
Works.   By W. DAVIS HASKOLL, C.E.   Second Edition, with
the addition of 554 Estimates, and the Practice of Setting out Works,
illustrated with 6 pages of Diagrams.   Imp. 4to, price 2*l.* 12*s.* 6*d.*
half-morocco.

" One of the very few works extant descending to the level of ordinary routine, and
treating on the common every-day practice of the railway engineer. . . . A work of
the present nature by a man of Mr. Haskoll's experience, must prove invaluable to
hundreds.   The tables of estimates appended to this edition will considerably enhance
its value."—*Engineering.*

Mathematical Instruments, their Construction, &c.

MATHEMATICAL INSTRUMENTS : THEIR CONSTRUC-
TION, ADJUSTMENT, TESTING, AND USE; comprising
Drawing, Measuring, Optical, Surveying, and Astronomical Instruments.   By J. F. HEATHER, M.A., Author of "Practical Plane
Geometry," "Descriptive Geometry," &c.   Enlarged Edition, for
the most part entirely rewritten.   With numerous Wood-cuts.
12mo, cloth boards, price 5*s.*

Oblique Arches.

A PRACTICAL TREATISE ON THE CONSTRUCTION of
OBLIQUE ARCHES.   By JOHN HART.   Third Edition, with
Plates.   Imperial 8vo, price 8*s.* cloth.

Oblique Bridges.

A PRACTICAL and THEORETICAL ESSAY on OBLIQUE
BRIDGES, with 13 large folding Plates.   By GEO. WATSON
BUCK, M. Inst. C.E.   Second Edition, corrected by W. H.
BARLOW, M. Inst. C.E.   Imperial 8vo, 12*s.* cloth.

"The standard text-book for all engineers regarding skew arches, is Mr. Buck's
treatise, and it would be impossible to consult a better."—*Engineer.*

Pocket-Book for Marine Engineers.

A POCKET BOOK FOR MARINE ENGINEERS.   Con-
taining useful Rules and Formulæ in a compact form.   By FRANK
PROCTOR, A.I.N.A.   Second Edition, revised and enlarged.
Royal 32mo, leather, gilt edges, with strap, price 4*s.*

"We recommend it to our readers as going far to supply a long-felt want."—
Naval Science.
" A most useful companion to all marine engineers."—*United Service Gazette.*
" Scarcely anything required by a naval engineer appears to have been for-
gotten.—*Iron.*
" A very valuable publication . . . a means of saving much time and labour."—
New York Monthly Record.

Weale's Dictionary of Terms.

A DICTIONARY of TERMS used in ARCHITECTURE,
BUILDING, ENGINEERING, MINING, METALLURGY,
ARCHÆOLOGY, the FINE ARTS, &c.   By JOHN WEALE.
Fourth Edition, enlarged and revised by ROBERT HUNT, F.R.S.,
Keeper of Mining Records, Editor of " Ure's Dictionary of Arts,"
&c.   12mo, cloth boards, price 6*s.*

Grantham's Iron Ship-Building, enlarged.

ON IRON SHIP-BUILDING; with Practical Examples and Details. Fifth Edition. Imp. 4to, boards, enlarged from 24 to 40 Plates (21 quite new), including the latest Examples. Together with separate Text, 12mo, cloth limp, also considerably enlarged. By JOHN GRANTHAM, M. Inst. C.E., &c.   Price 2*l.* 2*s.* complete.

Description of Plates.

1. Hollow and Bar Keels, Stem and Stern Posts.   [Pieces.
2. Side Frames, Floorings, and Bilge
3. Floorings *continued*—Keelsons, Deck Beams, Gunwales, and Stringers.
4. Gunwales *continued* — Lower Decks, and Orlop Beams.
4*a.* Gunwales and Deck Beam Iron.
5. Angle-Iron, T Iron, Z Iron, Bulb Iron, as Rolled for Building.
6. Rivets, shown in section, natural size; Flush and Lapped Joints, with Single and Double Riveting.
7. Plating, three plans; Bulkheads and Modes of Securing them.
8. Iron Masts, with Longitudinal and Transverse Sections.
9. Sliding Keel, Water Ballast, Moulding the Frames in Iron Ship Building, Levelling Plates.
10. Longitudinal Section, and Half-breadth Deck Plan of Large Vessels on a reduced Scale.
11. Midship Sections of Three Vessels.
12. *Large Vessel,* showing Details—*Fore End* in Section, and End View, with Stern Post, Crutches, &c.
13. *Large Vessel,* showing Details—*After End* in Section, with End View, Stern Frame for Screw, and Rudder.
14. *Large Vessel,* showing Details—*Midship Section,* half breadth.
15. *Machines* for Punching and Shearing Plates and Angle-Iron, and for Bending Plates; Rivet Hearth.
15*a.* Beam-Bending Machine, Independent Shearing, Punching and Angle-Iron Machine.
15*b.* Double Lever Punching and Shearing Machine, arranged for cutting Angle and T Iron, with Dividing Table and Engine.
16. *Machines.*—Garforth's Riveting Machine, Drilling and Counter-Sinking Machine.
16*a.* Plate Planing Machine.
17. *Air Furnace* for Heating Plates and Angle-Iron: Various Tools used in Riveting and Plating.
18. *Gunwale;* Keel and Flooring; Plan for Sheathing with Copper.
18*a.* Grantham's Improved Plan of Sheathing Iron Ships with Copper.
19. Illustrations of the Magnetic Condition of various Iron Ships.
20. Gray's Floating Compass and Binnacle, with Adjusting Magnets, &c.
21. Corroded Iron Bolt in Frame of Wooden Ship; Jointing Plates.
22-4. *Great Eastern*—Longitudinal Sections and Half-breadth Plans—Midship Section, with Details—Section in Engine Room, and Paddle Boxes.
25-6. Paddle Steam Vessel of Steel.
27. *Scarbrough*—Paddle Vessel of Steel.
28-9. Proposed Passenger Steamer.
30. *Persian*—Iron Screw Steamer.
31. Midship Section of H.M. Steam Frigate, *Warrior.*
32. Midship Section of H.M. Steam Frigate, *Hercules.*
33. Stem, Stern, and Rudder of H.M. Steam Frigate, *Bellerophon.*
34. Midship Section of H.M. Troop Ship, *Serapis.*
35. Iron Floating Dock.

"A thoroughly practical work, and every question of the many in relation to iron shipping which admit of diversity of opinion, or have various and conflicting personal interests attached to them, is treated with sober and impartial wisdom and good sense. . . . . As good a volume for the instruction of the pupil or student of iron naval architecture as can be found in any language."—*Practical Mechanics' Journal.*

"A very elaborate work. . . . . It forms a most valuable addition to the history of iron shipbuilding, while its having been prepared by one who has made the subject his study for many years, and whose qualifications have been repeatedly recognised, will recommend it as one of practical utility to all interested in shipbuilding."—*Army and Navy Gazette.*

Steam.

THE SAFE USE OF STEAM: containing Rules for Unprofessional Steam Users. By an ENGINEER.

N. B.—*This little work should be in the hands of every person having to deal with a Steam Engine of any kind.*

"If steam-users would but learn this little book by heart, and then hand it to their stokers to do the same, and see that the latter do it, boiler explosions would become sensations by their rarity."—*English Mechanic.*

ARCHITECTURE, &c.

Construction.

THE SCIENCE of BUILDING: An Elementary Treatise on the Principles of Construction. By E. WYNDHAM TARN, M.A., Architect. Illustrated with 47 Wood Engravings. Demy 8vo, price 8s. 6d. cloth. [Recently published.

"A very valuable book, which we strongly recommend to all students."—Builder.

"While Mr. Tarn's valuable little volume is quite sufficiently scientific to answer the purposes intended, it is written in a style that will deservedly make it popular. The diagrams are numerous and exceedingly well executed, and the treatise does credit alike to the author and the publisher."—Engineer.

"No architectural student should be without this hand-book of constructional knowledge."—Architect.

"The book is very far from being a mere compilation; it is an able digest of information which is only to be found scattered through various works, and contains more really original writing than many putting forth far stronger claims to originality."—Engineering.

Beaton's Pocket Estimator.

THE POCKET ESTIMATOR FOR THE BUILDING TRADES, being an easy method of estimating the various parts of a Building collectively, more especially applied to Carpenters' and Joiners' work, priced according to the present value of material and labour. By A. C. BEATON, Author of 'Quantities and Measurements.' 33 Woodcuts. Leather. Waistcoat-pocket size. 2s.

Beaton's Builders' and Surveyors' Technical Guide.

THE POCKET TECHNICAL GUIDE AND MEASURER FOR BUILDERS AND SURVEYORS: containing a Complete Explanation of the Terms used in Building Construction, Memoranda for Reference, Technical Directions for Measuring Work in all the Building Trades, with a Treatise on the Measurement of Timbers, and Complete Specifications for Houses, Roads, and Drains. By A. C. BEATON, Author of 'Quantities and Measurements.' With 19 Woodcuts. Leather. Waistcoat-pocket size. 2s.

Villa Architecture.

A HANDY BOOK of VILLA ARCHITECTURE; being a Series of Designs for Villa Residences in various Styles. With Detailed Specifications and Estimates. By C. WICKES, Architect, Author of "The Spires and Towers of the Mediæval Churches of England," &c. First Series, consisting of 30 Plates; Second Series, 31 Plates. Complete in 1 vol. 4to, price 2l. 10s. half morocco. Either Series separate, price 1l. 7s. each, half morocco.

"The whole of the designs bear evidence of their being the work of an artistic architect, and they will prove very valuable and suggestive to architects, students, and amateurs."—Building News.

The Architect's Guide.

THE ARCHITECT'S GUIDE; or, Office and Pocket Companion for Engineers, Architects, Land and Building Surveyors, Contractors, Builders, Clerks of Works, &c. By W. DAVIS HASKOLL, C.E., R. W. BILLINGS, Architect, F. ROGERS, and P. THOMPSON. With numerous Experiments by G. RENNIE, C.E., &c. Woodcuts, 12mo, cloth, price 3s. 6d.

Architecture, Ancient and Modern.

RUDIMENTARY ARCHITECTURE, Ancient and Modern. Consisting of VITRUVIUS, translated by JOSEPH GWILT, F.S.A., &c., with 23 fine copper plates; GRECIAN Architecture, by the EARL of ABERDEEN; the ORDERS of Architecture, by W. H. LEEDS, Esq.; The STYLES of Architecture of Various Countries, by T. TALBOT BURY; The PRINCIPLES of DESIGN in Architecture, by E. L. GARBETT. In one handsome volume, half-bound (pp. 1,100), copiously illustrated, price 12s.

₊ *Sold separately, in two vols., as follows, price 6s. each, hf.-bd.*
ANCIENT ARCHITECTURE. Containing Gwilt's Vitruvius and Aberdeen's Grecian Architecture.

N.B.—*This is the only edition of VITRUVIUS procurable at a moderate price.*
MODERN ARCHITECTURE. Containing the Orders, by Leeds; The Styles, by Bury; and Principles of Design, by Garbett.

The Young Architect's Book.

HINTS TO YOUNG ARCHITECTS. By GEORGE WIGHTWICK, Architect, Author of "The Palace of Architecture," &c. &c. New Edition, revised and enlarged. By G. HUSKISSON GUILLAUME, Architect. With numerous illustrations. 12mo. cloth boards, 4s. [*Just Published.*

Drawing for Builders and Students.

PRACTICAL RULES ON DRAWING for the OPERATIVE BUILDER and YOUNG STUDENT in ARCHITECTURE. By GEORGE PYNE, Author of a "Rudimentary Treatise on Perspective for Beginners." With 14 Plates, 4to, 7s. 6d., boards.
CONTENTS.—I. Practical Rules on Drawing—Outlines. II. Ditto—the Grecian and Roman Orders. III. Practical Rules on Drawing—Perspective. IV. Practical Rules on Light and Shade. V. Practical Rules on Colour, &c. &c.

Cottages, Villas, and Country Houses.

DESIGNS and EXAMPLES of COTTAGES, VILLAS, and COUNTRY HOUSES; being the Studies of several eminent Architects and Builders; consisting of Plans, Elevations, and Perspective Views; with approximate Estimates of the Cost of each. In 4to, with 67 plates, price 1l. 1s., cloth.

Builder's Price Book.

LOCKWOOD & CO.'S BUILDER'S AND CONTRACTOR'S PRICE BOOK—with which is incorporated ATCHLEY's, and portions of the late G. R. BURNELL's Builders' Price Books—for 1875, containing the latest prices of all kinds of Builders' Materials and Labour, and of all Trades connected with Building; with many useful and important Memoranda and Tables; Lists of the Members of the Metropolitan Board of Works, of Districts, District Officers, and District Surveyors, and the Metropolitan Bye-laws. The whole revised and edited by FRANCIS T. W. MILLER, Architect and Surveyor. Fcap. 8vo, strongly half-bound, price 4s.

Handbook of Specifications.

THE HANDBOOK OF SPECIFICATIONS ; or, Practical
Guide to the Architect, Engineer, Surveyor, and Builder, in drawing
up Specifications and Contracts for Works and Constructions.
Illustrated by Precedents of Buildings actually executed by eminent
Architects and Engineers. Preceded by a Preliminary Essay, and
Skeletons of Specifications and Contracts, &c., &c., and explained
by numerous Lithograph Plates and Woodcuts. By Professor
THOMAS L. DONALDSON, President of the Royal Institute of British
Architects, Professor of Architecture and Construction, University
College, London, M.I.B.A., Member of the various European
Academies of the Fine Arts. With A REVIEW OF THE LAW OF
CONTRACTS, and of the Responsibilities of Architects, Engineers,
and Builders. By W. CUNNINGHAM GLEN, Barrister-at-Law, of
the Middle Temple. 2 vols., 8vo, with upwards of 1100 pp. of
text, and 33 Lithographic Plates, cloth, 2*l.* 2*s.* (Published at 4*l.*)

" In these two volumes of 1,100 pages 'together', forty-four specifications of executed
works are given, including the specifications for parts of the new Houses of Parliament,
by Sir Charles Barry, and for the new Royal Exchange, by Mr. Tite, M.P.
"Amongst the other known buildings, the specifications of which are given, are
the Wiltshire Lunatic Asylum (Wyatt and Brandon) ; Tothill Fields Prison (R. Abraham) ; the City Prison, Holloway (Bunning) ; the High School, Edinburgh (Hamilton) ;
Clothworkers' Hall, London (Angel) ; Wellington College, Sandhurst (J. Shaw) ;
Houses in Grosvenor Square, and elsewhere ; St. George's Church, Doncaster
(Scott) ; several works of smaller size by the Author, including Messrs. Shaw's Ware-
house in Fetter Lane, a very successful elevation ; the Newcastle-upon-Tyne Railway
Station (J. Dobson) ; new Westminster Bridge (Page) ; the High Level Bridge, Newcastle (R. Stephenson) ; various works on the Great Northern Railway (Brydone) ;
and one French specification for Houses in the Rue de Rivoli, Paris (MM. Armand,
Hittorff, Pellechet, and Rohault de Fleury, architects). The majority of the specifications have illustrations in the shape of elevations and plans.
"About 140 pages of the second volume are appropriated to an exposition of the
law in relation to the legal liabilities of engineers, architects, contractors, and builders,
by Mr. W. Cunningham Glen, Barrister-at-law. Donaldson's Handbook of Specifications must be bought by all architects."—*Builder.*

Specifications for Practical Architecture.

SPECIFICATIONS FOR PRACTICAL ARCHITECTURE:
A Guide to the Architect, Engineer, Surveyor, and Builder ; with
an Essay on the Structure and Science of Modern Buildings. By
FREDERICK ROGERS, Architect. With numerous Illustrations.
Demy 8vo, price 15*s.*, cloth. (Published at 1*l.* 10*s.*)

*** A volume of specifications of a practical character being greatly required, and the
old standard work of Alfred Bartholomew being out of print, the author, on the basis
of that work, has produced the above. Some of the specifications he has so altered
as to bring in the now universal use of concrete, the improvements in drainage, the
use of iron, glass, asphalte, and other material. He has also inserted specifications
of works that have been erected in his own practice.

The House-Owner's Estimator.

THE HOUSE-OWNER'S ESTIMATOR ; or, What will it
Cost to Build, Alter, or Repair? A Price-Book adapted to the
Use of Unprofessional People as well as for the Architectural
Surveyor and Builder. By the late JAMES D. SIMON, A.R.I.B.A.
Edited and Revised by FRANCIS T. W. MILLER, Surveyor. With
numerous Illustrations. Second Edition, with the prices carefully
revised to 1875. Crown 8vo, cloth, price 3*s.* 6*d.*

CARPENTRY, TIMBER, &c.

Tredgold's Carpentry, new, enlarged, and cheaper Edition.

THE ELEMENTARY PRINCIPLES OF CARPENTRY : a Treatise on the Pressure and Equilibrium of Timber Framing, the Resistance of Timber, and the Construction of Floors, Arches, Bridges, Roofs, Uniting Iron and Stone with Timber, &c. To which is added an Essay on the Nature and Properties of Timber, &c., with Descriptions of the Kinds of Wood used in Building ; also numerous Tables of the Scantlings of Timber for different purposes, the Specific Gravities of Materials, &c. By THOMAS TREDGOLD, C.E. Edited by PETER BARLOW, F.R.S. Fifth Edition, corrected and enlarged. With 64 Plates (11 of which now first appear in this edition), Portrait of the Author, and several Woodcuts. In 1 vol., 4to, published at 2l. 2s., reduced to 1l. 5s., cloth.

" ' Tredgold's Carpentry' ought to be in every architect's and every builder's library, and those who do not already possess it ought to avail themselves of the new issue."—*Builder.*

"A work whose monumental excellence must commend it wherever skilful carpentry is concerned. The Author's principles are rather confirmed than impaired by time, and, as now presented, combine the surest base with the most interesting display of progressive science. The additional plates are of great intrinsic value."—*Building News.*

Grandy's Timber Tables.

THE TIMBER IMPORTER'S, TIMBER MERCHANT'S, and BUILDER'S STANDARD GUIDE. By RICHARD E. GRANDY. Comprising :—An Analysis of Deal Standards, Home and Foreign, with comparative Values and Tabular Arrangements for Fixing Nett Landed Cost on Baltic and North American Deals, including all intermediate Expenses, Freight, Insurance, Duty, &c., &c. ; together with Copious Information for the Retailer and Builder. 12mo, price 7s. 6d. cloth.

" Everything it pretends to be : built up gradually, it leads one from a forest to a treenail, and throws in, as a makeweight, a host of material concerning bricks, columns, cisterns, &c.—all that the class to whom it appeals requires."—*English Mechanic.*

" The only difficulty we have is as to what is NOT in its pages. What we have tested of the contents, taken at random, is invariably correct."—*Illustrated Builder's Journal.*

Tables for Packing-Case Makers.

PACKING-CASE TABLES ; showing the number of Superficial Feet in Boxes or Packing-Cases, from six inches square and upwards. Compiled by WILLIAM RICHARDSON, Accountant. Oblong 4to, cloth, price 3s. 6d.

"Will save much labour and calculation to packing-case makers and those who use packing-cases."—*Grocer.*   " Invaluable labour-saving tables."—*Ironmonger.*

Nicholson's Carpenter's Guide.

THE CARPENTER'S NEW GUIDE ; or, BOOK of LINES for CARPENTERS : comprising all the Elementary Principles essential for acquiring a knowledge of Carpentry. Founded on the late PETER NICHOLSON'S standard work. A new Edition, revised by ARTHUR ASHPITEL, F.S.A., together with Practical Rules on Drawing, by GEORGE PYNE. With 74 Plates, 4to, 1l. 1s. cloth.

Dowsing's Timber Merchant's Companion.

THE TIMBER MERCHANT'S AND BUILDER'S COM-PANION ; containing New and Copious Tables of the Reduced Weight and Measurement of Deals and Battens, of all sizes, from One to a Thousand Pieces, and the relative Price that each size bears per Lineal Foot to any given Price per Petersburgh Standard Hundred ; the Price per Cube Foot of Square Timber to any given Price per Load of 50 Feet ; the proportionate Value of Deals and Battens by the Standard, to Square Timber by the Load of 50 Feet ; the readiest mode of ascertaining the Price of Scantling per Lineal Foot of any size, to any given Figure per Cube Foot. Also a variety of other valuable information. By WILLIAM DOWSING, Timber Merchant. Second Edition. Crown 8vo, 3s. cloth.

"Everything is as concise and clear as it can possibly be made. There can be no doubt that every timber merchant and builder ought to possess it."—*Hull Advertiser.*

Timber Freight Book.

THE TIMBER IMPORTERS' AND SHIPOWNERS' FREIGHT BOOK : Being a Comprehensive Series of Tables for the Use of Timber Importers, Captains of Ships, Shipbrokers, Builders, and all Dealers in Wood whatsoever. By WILLIAM RICHARDSON, Timber Broker, author of " Packing Case Tables," &c. Crown 8vo, cloth, price 6s.

MECHANICS, &c.

Horton's Measurer.

THE COMPLETE MEASURER ; setting forth the Measurement of Boards, Glass, &c., &c. ; Unequal-sided, Square-sided, Octagonal-sided, Round Timber and Stone, and Standing Timber. With just allowances for the bark in the respective species of trees, and proper deductions for the waste in hewing the trees, &c.; also a Table showing the solidity of hewn or eight-sided timber, or of any octagonal-sided column. Compiled for the accommodation of Timber-growers, Merchants, and Surveyors, Stonemasons, Architects, and others. By RICHARD HORTON. Second edition, with considerable and valuable additions, 12mo, strongly bound in leather, 5s.

"The office of the architect, engineer, building surveyor, or land agent that is without this excellent and useful work cannot truly be considered perfect in its furnishing."—*Irish Builder.*

"We have used the improved and other tables in this volume, and have not observed any unfairness or inaccuracy."—*Builder.*

"The tables we have tested are accurate. . . . . To the builder and estate agents this work will be most acceptable."—*British Architect.*

"Not only are the best methods of measurement shown, and in some instances illustrated by means of woodcuts, but the erroneous systems pursued by dishonest dealers are fully exposed. . . . . The work must be considered to be a valuable addition to every gardener's library.—*Garden.*

Superficial Measurement.

THE TRADESMAN'S GUIDE TO SUPERFICIAL MEASUREMENT. Tables calculated from 1 to 200 inches in length, by 1 to 108 inches in breadth. For the use of Architects, Surveyors, Engineers, Timber Merchants, Builders, &c. By JAMES HAWKINGS. Fcp. 3s. 6d. cloth.

Mechanic's Workshop Companion.

THE OPERATIVE MECHANIC'S WORKSHOP COM-
PANION, and THE SCIENTIFIC GENTLEMAN'S PRAC-
TICAL ASSISTANT; comprising a great variety of the most
useful Rules in Mechanical Science; with numerous Tables of Practical Data and Calculated Results. By W. TEMPLETON, Author
of "The Engineer's, Millwright's, and Machinist's Practical Assistant." Eleventh Edition, with Mechanical Tables for Operative
Smiths, Millwrights, Engineers, &c.; together with several Useful
and Practical Rules in Hydraulics and Hydrodynamics, a variety
of Experimental Results, and an Extensive Table of Powers and
Roots. 11 Plates. 12mo, 5s. bound.

"As a text-book of reference, in which mechanical and commercial demands are
judiciously met, TEMPLETON'S COMPANION stands unrivalled."—*Mechanics' Magazine.*
"Admirably adapted to the wants of a very large class. It has met with great
success in the engineering workshop, as we can testify; and there are a great many
men who, in a great measure, owe their rise in life to this little work."—*Building News.*

Engineer's Assistant.

THE ENGINEER'S, MILLWRIGHT'S, and MACHINIST'S
PRACTICAL ASSISTANT; comprising a Collection of Useful
Tables, Rules, and Data. Compiled and Arranged, with Original
Matter, by W. TEMPLETON. 5th Edition. 18mo, 2s. 6d. cloth.

"So much varied information compressed into so small a space, and published at a
price which places it within the reach of the humblest mechanic, cannot fail to command the sale which it deserves. With the utmost confidence we commend this book
to the attention of our readers. *Mechanics' Magazine.*

"Every mechanic should become the possessor of the volume, and a more suitable
present to an apprentice to any of the mechanical trades could not possibly be made."
—*Building News.*

Designing, Measuring, and Valuing.

THE STUDENT'S GUIDE to the PRACTICE of MEA-
SURING, and VALUING ARTIFICERS' WORKS; containing
Directions for taking Dimensions, Abstracting the same, and bringing
the Quantities into Bill, with Tables of Constants, and copious
Memoranda for the Valuation of Labour and Materials in the respective Trades of Bricklayer and Slater, Carpenter and Joiner,
Painter and Glazier, Paperhanger, &c. With 43 Plates and Woodcuts. Originally edited by EDWARD DOBSON, Architect. New
Edition, re-written, with Additions on Mensuration and Construction, and useful Tables for facilitating Calculations and Measurements. By E. WYNDHAM TARN, M.A., 8vo, 10s. 6d. cloth.

"This useful book should be in every architect's and builder's office. It contains
a vast amount of information absolutely necessary to be known."—*The Irish Builder.*

"We have failed to discover anything connected with the building trade, from ex-
cavating foundations to bell-hanging, that is not fully treated upon in this valuable
work."—*The Artizan.*

"Mr. Tarn has well performed the task imposed upon him, and has made many
further and valuable additions, embodying a large amount of information relating to
the technicalities and modes of construction employed in the several branches of the
building trade."—*Colliery Guardian.*

"Altogether the book is one which well fulfils the promise of its title-page, and we
can thoroughly recommend it to the class for whose use it has been compiled. Mr.
Tarn's additions and revisions have much increased the usefulness of the work, and
have especially augmented its value to students."—*Engineering.*

MATHEMATICS, &c.

Gregory's Practical Mathematics.

MATHEMATICS for PRACTICAL MEN ; being a Common-place Book of Pure and Mixed Mathematics. Designed chiefly for the Use of Civil Engineers, Architects, and Surveyors. Part I. PURE MATHEMATICS—comprising Arithmetic, Algebra, Geometry, Mensuration, Trigonometry, Conic Sections, Properties of Curves. Part II. MIXED MATHEMATICS—comprising Mechanics in general, Statics, Dynamics, Hydrostatics, Hydrodynamics, Pneumatics, Mechanical Agents, Strength of Materials. With an Appendix of copious Logarithmic and other Tables. By OLINTHUS GREGORY, LL.D., F R.A.S. Enlarged by HENRY LAW, C.E. 4th Edition, carefully revised and corrected by J. R. YOUNG, formerly Profes-sor of Mathematics, Belfast College ; Author of "A Course of Mathematics," &c. With 13 Plates. Medium 8vo, 1l. 1s. cloth.

" As a standard work on mathematics it has not been excelled."—*Artizan.*

" The engineer or architect will here find ready to his hand, rules for solving nearly every mathematical difficulty that may arise in his practice. As a moderate acquaint-ance with arithmetic, algebra, and elementary geometry is absolutely necessary to the proper understanding of the most useful portions of this book, the author very wisely has devoted the first three chapters to those subjects, so that the most ignorant may be enabled to master the whole of the book, without aid from any other. The rules are in all cases explained by means of examples, in which every step of the process is clearly worked out."—*Builder.*

" One of the most serviceable books to the practical mechanics of the country. . . The edition of 1847 was fortunately entrusted to the able hands of Mr. Law, who revised it thoroughly, re-wrote many chapters, and added several sections to those which had been rendered imperfect by advanced knowledge. On examining the various and many improvements which he introduced into the work, they seem almost like a new structure on an old plan, or rather like the restoration of an old ruin, not only to its former substance, but to an extent which meets the larger requirements of modern times. . . . . In the edition just brought out, the work has again been revised by Professor Young. He has modernised the notation throughout, introduced a few paragraphs here and there, and corrected the numerous typographical errors which have escaped the eyes of the former Editor. The book is now as complete as it is possible to make it. . . . . We have carried our notice of this book to a greater length than the space allowed us justified, but the experiments it contains are so interesting, and the method of describing them so clear, that we may be excused for overstepping our limit. It is an instructive book for the student, and a Text-book for him who having once mastered the subjects it treats of, needs occasionally to refresh his memory upon them."—*Building News.*

The Metric System.

A SERIES OF METRIC TABLES, in which the British Standard Measures and Weights are compared with those of the Metric System at present in use on the Continent. By C. H. DOWLING, C. E. Second Edition, revised and enlarged. 8vo, 10s. 6d. strongly bound.

" Mr. Dowling's Tables, which are well put together, come just in time as a ready reckoner for the conversion of one system into the other."—*Athenæum.*

" Their accuracy has been certified by Professor Airy, the Astronomer-Royal."—*Builder.*

" Resolution 8.—That advantage will be derived from the recent publication of Metric Tables, by C. H. Dowling, C.E."—*Report of Section F, British Association, Bath.*

Inwood's Tables, greatly enlarged and improved.

TABLES FOR THE PURCHASING of ESTATES, Freehold, Copyhold, or Leasehold; Annuities, Advowsons, &c., and for the Renewing of Leases held under Cathedral Churches, Colleges, or other corporate bodies; for Terms of Years certain, and for Lives; also for Valuing Reversionary Estates, Deferred Annuities, Next Presentations, &c., together with Smart's Five Tables of Compound Interest, and an Extension of the same to Lower and Intermediate Rates. By WILLIAM INWOOD, Architect. The 19th edition, with considerable additions, and new and valuable Tables of Logarithms for the more Difficult Computations of the Interest of Money, Discount, Annuities, &c., by M. FÉDOR THOMAN, of the Société Crédit Mobilier of Paris.   12mo, 8s. cloth.

₊ *This edition (the 19th) differs in many important particulars from former ones. The changes consist, first, in a more convenient and systematic arrangement of the original Tables, and in the removal of certain numerical errors which a very careful revision of the whole has enabled the present editor to discover; and secondly, in the extension of practical utility conferred on the work by the introduction of Tables now inserted for the first time. This new and important matter is all so much actually added to INWOOD'S TABLES; nothing has been abstracted from the original collection: so that those who have been long in the habit of consulting INWOOD for any special professional purpose will, as heretofore, find the information sought still in its pages.*

" Those interested in the purchase and sale of estates, and in the adjustment of compensation cases, as well as in transactions in annuities, life insurances, &c., will find the present edition of eminent service."—*Engineering.*

Geometry for the Architect, Engineer, &c.

PRACTICAL GEOMETRY, for the Architect, Engineer, and Mechanic; giving Rules for the Delineation and Application of various Geometrical Lines, Figures and Curves. By E. W. TARN, M.A., Architect, Author of "The Science of Building," &c. With 164 Illustrations.   Demy 8vo.   12s. 6d.

" No book with the same objects in view has ever been published in which the clearness of the rules laid down and the illustrative diagrams have been so satisfactory."—*Scotsman.*

Compound Interest and Annuities.

THEORY of COMPOUND INTEREST and ANNUITIES; with Tables of Logarithms for the more Difficult Computations of Interest, Discount, Annuities, &c., in all their Applications and Uses for Mercantile and State Purposes. With an elaborate Introduction. By FÉDOR THOMAN, of the Société Crédit Mobilier, Paris.   12mo, cloth, 5s.

" A very powerful work, and the Author has a very remarkable command of his subject."—*Professor A. de Morgan.*

" We recommend it to the notice of actuaries and accountants."—*A[illegible].*

SCIENCE AND ART.

The Military Sciences.

AIDE-MÉMOIRE to the MILITARY SCIENCES. Framed from Contributions of Officers and others connected with the different Services. Originally edited by a Committee of the Corps of Royal Engineers. Second Edition, most carefully revised by an Officer of the Corps, with many additions; containing nearly 350 Engravings and many hundred Woodcuts. 3 vols. royal 8vo, extra cloth boards, and lettered, price 4*l*. 10*s*.

"A compendious encyclopædia of military knowledge, to which we are greatly indebted."—*Edinburgh Review*.

"The most comprehensive work of reference to the military and collateral sciences. Among the list of contributors, some seventy-seven in number, will be found names of the highest distinction in the services."—*Volunteer Service Gazette*.

Field Fortification.

A TREATISE on FIELD FORTIFICATION, the ATTACK of FORTRESSES, MILITARY, MINING, and RECONNOITRING. By Colonel I. S. MACAULAY, late Professor of Fortification in the R. M. A., Woolwich. Sixth Edition, crown 8vo, cloth, with separate Atlas of 12 Plates, price 12*s*. complete.

Naval Science.

NAVAL SCIENCE: a Quarterly Magazine for Promoting the Improvement of Naval Architecture, Marine Engineering, Steam Navigation, Seamanship. Edited by E. J. REED, C.B., M.P., and late Chief Constructor of the Navy, and JOSEPH WOOLLEY, M.A., LL.D., F.R.A.S. Copiously illustrated. Price 2*s*. 6*d*. Now ready, Vols. II. & III., each containing 4 Nos. cloth boards, price 12*s*. 6*d*. each.

*** *The Contributors include the most Eminent Authorities in the several branches of the above subjects.*

Dye-Wares and Colours.

THE MANUAL of COLOURS and DYE-WARES: their Properties, Applications, Valuation, Impurities, and Sophistications. For the Use of Dyers, Printers, Dry Salters, Brokers, &c. By J. W. SLATER. Post 8vo, cloth, price 7*s*. 6*d*.

"A complete encyclopædia of the *materia tinctoria*. The information given respecting each article is full and precise, and the methods of determining the value of articles such as these, so liable to sophistication, are given with clearness, and are practical as well as valuable."—*Chemist and Druggist*.

Electricity.

A MANUAL of ELECTRICITY; including Galvanism, Magnetism, Diamagnetism, Electro-Dynamics, Magno-Electricity, and the Electric Telegraph. By HENRY M. NOAD, Ph.D., F.C.S., Lecturer on Chemistry at St. George's Hospital. Fourth Edition, entirely rewritten. Illustrated by 500 Woodcuts. 8vo, 1*l*. 4*s*. cloth.

"The commendations already bestowed in the pages of the *Lancet* on the former editions of this work are more than ever merited by the present. The accounts given of electricity and galvanism are not only complete in a scientific sense, but, which is a rarer thing, are popular and interesting."—*Lancet*.

Text-Book of Electricity.

THE STUDENT'S TEXT-BOOK OF ELECTRICITY: including Magnetism, Voltaic Electricity, Electro-Magnetism, Diamagnetism, Magneto-Electricity, Thermo-Electricity, and Electric Telegraphy. Being a Condensed Résumé of the Theory and Application of Electrical Science, including its latest Practical Developments, particularly as relating to Aërial and Submarine Telegraphy. By HENRY M. NOAD, Ph.D., Lecturer on Chemistry at St. George's Hospital. Post 8vo, 400 Illustrations, 12s. 6d. cloth.

"We can recommend Dr. Noad's book for clear style, great range of subject, a good index, and a plethora of woodcuts."—*Athenæum.*

"A most elaborate compilation of the facts of electricity and magnetism, and of the theories which have been advanced concerning them."—*Popular Science Review.*

"Clear, compendious, compact, well illustrated, and well printed."—*Lancet.*

"We can strongly recommend the work, as an admirable text-book, to every student —beginner or advanced—of electricity."—*Engineering.*

"Nothing of value has been passed over, and nothing given but what will lead to a correct, and even an exact, knowledge of the present state of electrical science."—*Mechanics' Magazine.*

"We know of no book on electricity containing so much information on experimental facts as this does, for the size of it, and no book of any size that contains so complete a range of facts."—*English Mechanic.*

Rudimentary Magnetism.

RUDIMENTARY MAGNETISM: being a concise exposition of the general principles of Magnetical Science, and the purposes to which it has been applied. By Sir W. SNOW HARRIS, F.R.S. New and enlarged Edition, with considerable additions by Dr. NOAD, Ph.D. With 165 Woodcuts. 12mo, cloth, 4s. 6d.

"There is a good index, and this volume of 412 pages may be considered the best possible manual on the subject of magnetism."—*Mechanics' Magazine.*

"As concise and lucid an exposition of the phenomena of magnetism as we believe it is possible to write."—*English Mechanic.*

"Not only will the scientific student find this volume an invaluable book of reference, but the general reader will find in it as much to interest as to inform his mind. Though a strictly scientific work, its subject is handled in a simple and readable style."—*Illustrated Review.*

Chemical Analysis.

THE COMMERCIAL HANDBOOK of CHEMICAL ANALYSIS; or Practical Instructions for the determination of the Intrinsic or Commercial Value of Substances used in Manufactures, in Trades, and in the Arts. By A. NORMANDY, Author of "Practical Introduction to Rose's Chemistry," and Editor of Rose's "Treatise of Chemical Analysis." *New Edition.* Enlarged, and to a great extent re-written, by Henry M. Noad, Ph. D., F.R.S. With numerous Illustrations. Crown 8vo, 12s. 6d. cloth.

[Just ready.)

"We recommend this book to the careful perusal of every one; it may be truly affirmed to be of universal interest, and we strongly recommend it to our readers as a guide, alike indispensable to the housewife as to the pharmaceutical practitioner."—*Medical Times.*

"The very best work on the subject the English press has yet produced."—*Mechanics' Magazine.*

Clocks, Watches, and Bells.

RUDIMENTARY TREATISE on CLOCKS, WATCHES, and BELLS. By Sir EDMUND BECKETT, Bart. (late E. B. Denison), LL.D., Q.C., F.R.A.S., Author of "Astronomy without Mathematics," &c. Sixth edition, thoroughly revised and enlarged, with numerous Illustrations. Limp cloth (No. 67, Weale's Series), 4s. 6d.; cloth boards, 5s. 6d.

"As a popular, and, at the same time, practical treatise on clocks and bells, it is unapproached." *English Mechanic.*

"The best work on the subject probably extant . . . . S far as we know it has no competitor worthy of the name. The treatise on bells is undoubtedly the best in the language. It shows that the author has contributed very much to their modern improvement, if indeed he has not revived this art, which was decaying here . . . . To call it a rudimentary treatise is a misnomer, at least as respects clocks and bells. It is something more. It is the most important work of its kind in English."—*Engineering.*

"The only modern treatise on clock-making."—*Horological Journal.*

"Without having any special interest in the subject, and even without possessing any general aptitude for mechanical studies, a reader must be very unintelligent who cannot find matter to engage his attention in this work. The little book now appears revised and enlarged, being one of the most praiseworthy volumes in Weale's admirable scientific and educational series."—*Daily Telegraph.*

"We do not know whether to wonder most at the extraordinary cheapness of this admirable treatise on clocks, by the most able authority on such a subject, or the thorough completeness of his work even to the minutest details. The chapter on bells is singular and amusing, and will be a real treat even to the uninitiated general reader. The illustrations, notes, and indices, make the work completely perfect of its kind."—*Standard.*

"There is probably no book in the English language on a technical subject so easy to read, and to read through, as the treatise on clocks, watches, and bells, written by the eminent Parliamentary Counsel, Mr. E. B. Denison—now Sir Edmund Beckett, Bart."—*Architect.*

Science and Scripture.

SCIENCE ELUCIDATIVE OF SCRIPTURE, AND NOT ANTAGONISTIC TO IT; being a Series of Essays on—1. Alleged Discrepancies; 2. The Theory of the Geologists and Figure of the Earth; 3. The Mosaic Cosmogony; 4. Miracles in general—Views of Hume and Powell; 5. The Miracle of Joshua—Views of Dr. Colenso: The Supernaturally Impossible; 6. The Age of the Fixed Stars—their Distances and Masses. By Professor J. R. YOUNG, Author of "A Course of Elementary Mathematics," &c. &c. Fcap. 8vo, price 5s. cloth lettered.

"Professor Young's examination of the early verses of Genesis, in connection with modern scientific hypotheses, is excellent."—*English Churchman.*

"Distinguished by the true spirit of scientific inquiry, by great knowledge, by keen logical ability, and by a style peculiarly clear, easy, and energetic."—*Nonconformist.*

"No one can rise from its perusal without being impressed with a sense of the singular weakness of modern scepticism."—*Baptist Magazine.*

"A valuable contribution to controversial theological literature."—*City Press.*

Practical Philosophy.

A SYNOPSIS of PRACTICAL PHILOSOPHY. By the Rev. JOHN CARR, M.A., late Fellow of Trin. Coll., Cambridge. Second Edition. 18mo, 5s. cloth.

Dr. Lardner's Museum of Science and Art.

THE MUSEUM OF SCIENCE AND ART. Edited by DIONYSIUS LARDNER, D.C.L., formerly Professor of Natural Philosophy and Astronomy in University College, London. CONTENTS: The Planets ; are they inhabited Worlds ?—Weather Prognostics—Popular Fallacies in Questions of Physical Science—Latitudes and Longitudes—Lunar Influences—Meteoric Stones and Shooting Stars — Railway Accidents — Light—Common Things :—Air—Locomotion in the United States—Cometary Influences—Common Things : Water—The Potter's Art—Common Things : Fire—Locomotion and Transport, their Influence and Progress—The Moon—Common Things : The Earth—The Electric Telegraph—Terrestrial Heat—The Sun—Earthquakes and Volcanoes—Barometer, Safety Lamp, and Whitworth's Micrometric Apparatus—Steam—The Steam Engine—The Eye—The Atmosphere—Time—Common Things : Pumps—Common Things : Spectacles, the Kaleidoscope—Clocks and Watches—Microscopic Drawing and Engraving—Locomotive—Thermometer—New Planets : Leverrier and Adams's Planet—Magnitude and Minuteness—Common Things : The Almanack—Optical Images—How to observe the Heavens—Common Things : the Looking-glass—Stellar Universe—The Tides — Colour — Common Things : Man — Magnifying Glasses—Instinct and Intelligence—The Solar Microscope—The Camera Lucida—The Magic Lantern—The Camera Obscura—The Microscope—The White Ants : their Manners and Habits—The Surface of the Earth, or First Notions of Geography—Science and Poetry—The Bee — Steam Navigation — Electro-Motive Power—Thunder, Lightning, and the Aurora Borealis—The Printing Press—The Crust of the Earth—Comets—The Stereoscope—The Pre-Adamite Earth—Eclipses—Sound. With upwards of 1200 Engravings on Wood. In 6 Double Volumes, handsomely bound in cloth, gilt, price £1 1s.

"The 'Museum of Science and Art' is the most valuable contribution that has ever been made to the Scientific Instruction of every class of society."—*Sir David Brewster in the North British Review.*

"Whether we consider the liberality and beauty of the illustrations, the charm of the writing, or the durable interest of the matter, we must express our belief that there is hardly to be found among the new books, one that would be welcomed by people of so many ages and classes as a valuable present."—*Examiner.*

*** *Separate books formed from the above, suitable for Workmen's Libraries, Science Classes, &c.*

COMMON THINGS EXPLAINED. With 233 Illustrations, 5s. cloth.

THE ELECTRIC TELEGRAPH POPULARIZED. 100 Illustrations, 1s. 6d. cloth.

THE MICROSCOPE. With 147 Illustrations, 2s. cloth.

POPULAR GEOLOGY. With 201 Illustrations, 2s. 6d. cloth.

POPULAR PHYSICS. With 85 Illustrations. 2s. 6d. cloth.

POPULAR ASTRONOMY. With 182 Illustrations, 4s. 6d. cloth.

STEAM AND ITS USES. With 89 Illustrations, 2s. cloth.

THE BEE AND WHITE ANTS. With 135 Illustrations, cloth, 2s.

DR. LARDNER'S SCIENTIFIC HANDBOOKS.

Astronomy.

THE HANDBOOK OF ASTRONOMY. By DIONYSIUS
LARDNER, D.C.L., formerly Professor of Natural Philosophy and
Astronomy in University College, London. Third Edition. Revised and Edited by EDWIN DUNKEN, F.R.A.S., Superintendent
of the Altazimuth Department, Royal Observatory, Greenwich.
With 37 plates and upwards of 100 Woodcuts. In 1 vol., small
8vo, cloth. 550 pages, price 7s. 6d.
"We can cordially recommend it to all those who desire to possess a complete
manual of the science and practice of astronomy."—*Astronomical Reporter.*

Optics.

THE HANDBOOK OF OPTICS. New Edition. Edited by
T. OLVER HARDING, B.A. Lond., of University College, London.
With 298 Illustrations. Small 8vo, cloth, 448 pages, price 5s.

Electricity.

THE HANDBOOK of ELECTRICITY, MAGNETISM, and
ACOUSTICS. New Edition. Edited by GEO. CAREY FOSTER,
B.A., F.C.S. With 400 Illustrations. Small 8vo, cloth, price 5s.
"The book could not have been entrusted to any one better calculated to preserve
the terse and lucid style of Lardner, while correcting his errors and bringing up his
work to the present state of scientific knowledge."—*Popular Science Review.*

Mechanics.

THE HANDBOOK OF MECHANICS.   [*Reprinting.*

Hydrostatics.

THE HANDBOOK of HYDROSTATICS and PNEUMATICS.
New Edition, Revised and Enlarged by BENJAMIN LOEWY,
F.R.A.S. With numerous Illustrations. 5s.   [*Just published.*

Heat.

THE HANDBOOK OF HEAT. New Edition, Re-written and
Enlarged. By BENJAMIN LOEWY, F.R.A.S.   [*Preparing.*

Animal Physics.

THE HANDBOOK OF ANIMAL PHYSICS. With 520
Illustrations. New edition, small 8vo, cloth, 7s. 6d. 732 pages.
                                            [*Just published.*

Electric Telegraph.

THE ELECTRIC TELEGRAPH. New Edition. Revised
and Re-written by E. B. BRIGHT, F.R.A.S. 140 Illustrations.
Small 8vo, 2s. 6d. cloth.
"One of the most readable books extant on the Electric Telegraph."—*Eng. Mechanic.*

NATURAL PHILOSOPHY FOR SCHOOLS. By DR. LARDNER.
328 Illustrations. Fifth Edition. 1 vol. 3s. 6d. cloth.
"A very convenient class-book for junior students in private schools. It is intended to convey, in clear and precise terms, general notions of all the principal
divisions of Physical Science."—*British Quarterly Review.*

ANIMAL PHYSIOLOGY FOR SCHOOLS. By DR. LARDNER.
With 190 Illustrations. Second Edition. 1 vol. 3s. 6d. cloth.
"Clearly written, well arranged, and excellently illustrated."—*Gardeners' Chronicle.*

Geology and Genesis Harmonised.

THE TWIN RECORDS of CREATION; or, Geology and Genesis, their Perfect Harmony and Wonderful Concord. By GEORGE W. VICTOR LE VAUX. With numerous Illustrations. Fcap. 8vo, price 5s. cloth.

"We can recommend Mr. Le Vaux as an able and interesting guide to a popular appreciation of geological science."—*Spectator*.

"The author combines an unbounded admiration of science with an unbounded admiration of the Written Record. The two impulses are balanced to a nicety; and the consequence is, that difficulties, which to minds less evenly poised, would be serious, find immediate solutions of the happiest kinds."—*London Review*.

"Vigorously written, reverent in spirit, stored with instructive geological facts, and designed to show that there is no discrepancy or inconsistency between the Word and the works of the Creator. The future of Nature, in connexion with the glorious destiny of man, is vividly conceived."—*Watchman*.

"No real difficulty is shirked, and no sophistry is left unexposed."—*The Rock*.

Geology, Physical.

PHYSICAL GEOLOGY. (Partly based on Major-General Portlock's Rudiments of Geology.) By RALPH TATE, A.L.S., F.G.S. Numerous Woodcuts. 12mo, 2s.   [*Ready*.

Geology, Historical.

HISTORICAL GEOLOGY. (Partly based on Major-General Portlock's Rudiments of Geology.) By RALPH TATE, A.L.S., F.G.S. Numerous Woodcuts. 12mo, 2s. 6d.   [*Ready*.

₊ Or PHYSICAL *and* HISTORICAL GEOLOGY, *bound in One Volume, price 5s.*

Wood-Carving.

INSTRUCTIONS in WOOD-CARVING, for Amateurs; with Hints on Design. By A LADY. In emblematic wrapper, handsomely printed, with Ten large Plates, price 2s. 6d.

"The handicraft of the wood-carver, so well as a book can impart it, may be learnt from 'A Lady's' publication."—*Athenæum*.

"A real *practical guide*. It is very complete."—*Literary Churchman*.

"The directions given are plain and easily understood, and it forms a very good introduction to the practical part of the carver's art."—*English Mechanic*.

Popular Work on Painting.

PAINTING POPULARLY EXPLAINED; with Historical Sketches of the Progress of the Art. By THOMAS JOHN GULLICK, Painter, and JOHN TIMBS, F.S.A. Second Edition, revised and enlarged. With Frontispiece and Vignette. In small 8vo, 6s. cloth.

₊ *This Work has been adopted as a Prize-book in the Schools of Art at South Kensington.*

"A work that may be advantageously consulted. Much may be learned, even by those who fancy they do not require to be taught, from the careful perusal of this unpretending but comprehensive treatise."—*Art Journal*.

"A valuable book, which supplies a want. It contains a large amount of original matter, agreeably conveyed, and will be found of value, as well by the young artist seeking information as by the general reader. We give a cordial welcome to the book, and augur for it an increasing reputation."—*Builder*.

"This volume is one that we can heartily recommend to all who are desirous of understanding what they admire in a good painting."—*Daily News*.

Delamotte's Works on Illumination & Alphabets.

A PRIMER OF THE ART OF ILLUMINATION ; for the use of Beginners : with a Rudimentary Treatise on the Art, Practical Directions for its Exercise, and numerous Examples taken from Illuminated MSS., printed in Gold and Colours. By F. DELAMOTTE. Small 4to, price 9s. Elegantly bound, cloth antique.

"A handy book, beautifully illustrated ; the text of which is well written, and calculated to be useful. . . . The examples of ancient MSS. recommended to the student, which, with much good sense, the author chooses from collections accessible to all, are selected with judgment and knowledge, as well as taste."—*Athenæum.*

ORNAMENTAL ALPHABETS, ANCIENT and MEDIÆVAL ; from the Eighth Century, with Numerals ; including Gothic, Church-Text, large and small, German, Italian, Arabesque, Initials for Illumination, Monograms, Crosses, &c. &c., for the use of Architectural and Engineering Draughtsmen, Missal Painters, Masons, Decorative Painters, Lithographers, Engravers, Carvers, &c. &c. &c. Collected and engraved by F. DELAMOTTE, and printed in Colours. Royal 8vo, oblong, price 4s. cloth.

"A well-known engraver and draughtsman has enrolled in this useful book the result of many years' study and research. For those who insert enamelled sentences round gilded chalices, who blazon shop legends over shop-doors, who letter church walls with pithy sentences from the Decalogue, this book will be useful."—*Athenæum.*

EXAMPLES OF MODERN ALPHABETS, PLAIN and ORNAMENTAL ; including German, Old English, Saxon, Italic, Perspective, Greek, Hebrew, Court Hand, Engrossing, Tuscan, Riband, Gothic, Rustic, and Arabesque ; with several Original Designs, and an Analysis of the Roman and Old English Alphabets, large and small, and Numerals, for the use of Draughtsmen, Surveyors, Masons, Decorative Painters, Lithographers, Engravers, Carvers, &c. Collected and engraved by F. DELAMOTTE, and printed in Colours. Royal 8vo, oblong, price 4s. cloth.

"To artists of all classes, but more especially to architects and engravers, this very handsome book will be invaluable. There is comprised in it every possible shape into which the letters of the alphabet and numerals can be formed, and the talent which has been expended in the conception of the various plain and ornamental letters is wonderful."—*Standard.*

MEDIÆVAL ALPHABETS AND INITIALS FOR ILLUMINATORS. By F. DELAMOTTE, Illuminator, Designer, and Engraver on Wood. Containing 21 Plates, and Illuminated Title, printed in Gold and Colours. With an Introduction by J. WILLIS BROOKS. Small 4to, 6s. cloth gilt.

"A volume in which the letters of the alphabet come forth glorified in gilding and all the colours of the prism interwoven and intertwined and intermingled, sometimes with a sort of rainbow arabesque. A poem emblazoned in these characters would be only comparable to one of those delicious love letters symbolized in a bunch of flowers well selected and cleverly arranged."—*Sun.*

THE EMBROIDERER'S BOOK OF DESIGN ; containing Initials, Emblems, Cyphers, Monograms, Ornamental Borders, Ecclesiastical Devices, Mediæval and Modern Alphabets, and National Emblems. Collected and engraved by F. DELAMOTTE, and printed in Colours. Oblong royal 8vo, 2s. 6d. in ornamental boards.

AGRICULTURE, &c.

Youatt and Burn's Complete Grazier.

THE COMPLETE GRAZIER, and FARMER'S and CATTL
BREEDER'S ASSISTANT. A Compendium of Husband
By WILLIAM YOUATT, ESQ., V.S. 11th Edition, enlarged
ROBERT SCOTT BURN, Author of "The Lessons of My Farm," &
One large 8vo volume, 784 pp. with 215 Illustrations. 1*l*. 1*s*. half-l

"The standard and text-book, with the farmer and grazier."—*Farmer's Magazi*
"A valuable repertory of intelligence for all who make agriculture a pursuit, r
especially for those who aim at keeping pace with the improvements of the age.
Bell's Weekly Messenger.
"A treatise which will remain a standard work on the subject as long as Brit
agriculture endures."—*Mark Lane Express.*
"One of the best books of reference that can be contained in the agriculturis
library. The word 'complete' expresses its character; since every detail of i
subject finds a place, treated upon, and explained, in a clear, comprehensive, a
practical manner."—*Magnet.*

Spooner on Sheep.

SHEEP; THE HISTORY, STRUCTURE, ECONOM
AND DISEASES OF. By W. C. SPOONER, M.R.V.C., &
Third Edition, considerably enlarged; with numerous fine engr
vings, including some specimens of New and Improved Bree
Fcp. 8vo. 366 pp., price 6*s*. cloth. *(Just published.)*

"The book is decidedly the best of the kind in our language."—*Scotsman.*
"A reliable text-book."—*Stamford Mercury.*
"Mr. Spooner has conferred upon the agricultural class a lasting benefit by e
bodying in this work the improvements made in sheep stock by such men
Humphreys, Rawlence, Howard, and others."—*Hampshire Advertiser.*
"The work should be in possession of every flock-master."—*Banbury Guardia*
"We can confidently recommend the work as useful and reliable, and of mu
practical utility to the class for whom it is intended."—*Salisbury and Winches.
Journal.*
"Mr. Spooner has conferred a boon on agriculturists generally, and the farme
library will be incomplete which does not include so admirable a guide to a ve
important branch of the business."—*Dorset County Chronicle.*

Scott Burn's System of Modern Farming.

OUTLINE OF MODERN FARMING. By R. SCOTT BUR
Soils, Manures, and Crops—Farming and Farming Econom
Historical and Practical—Cattle, Sheep, and Horses—Manageme
of the Dairy, Pigs, and Poultry, with Notes on the Diseases
Stock—Utilisation of Town-Sewage, Irrigation, and Reclamatio
of Waste Land. New Edition. In 1 vol. 1250 pp., half-boun
profusely Illustrated, price 12*s*.

"There is sufficient stated within the limits of this treatise to prevent a farm
from going far wrong in any of his operations. . . . The author has had gre
personal experience, and his opinions are entitled to every respect."—*Observer.*

Horton's Underwood and Woodland Tables.

TABLES FOR PLANTING AND VALUING UNDER
WOOD AND WOODLAND; also Lineal, Superficial, Cubica
Wages, Marketing, and Decimal Tables. Together with Tabl
for Converting Land-measure from one denomination to anothe
and instructions for Measuring Round Timber. By RICHAR
HORTON. 12mo. 2*s*. strongly bound in leather.

nd Improvers' Pocket-Book.

D IMPROVERS' POCKET-BOOK OF FOR-
BLES, and MEMORANDA, required in any Com-
ting to the Permanent Improvement of Landed Pro-
IN EWART, Land Surveyor and Agricultural Engineer.
oblong, leather, gilt edges, with elastic band, 4s.

ong required by land surveyors, agricultural engineers, &c."—

alculated to serve the purpose for which it was intended."—

nd handy little volume . . . admirably arranged, and can
xceedingly useful to the class of professional men for whom it
tor.
densed form the essence of many a treatise, and will be found
e land agent and measurer."—*Newcastle Daily Journal.*
dustrious compilation, containing everything requisite for com-
he permanent improvement of landed property ; it is a perfect
'veyor."—*John Bull.*

ibles for Land Valuers.

) VALUER'S BEST ASSISTANT : being Tables,
much improved Plan, for Calculating the Value of
which are added, Tables for reducing Scotch, Irish,
al Customary Acres to Statute Measure ; also, Tables
asure, and of the various Dimensions of an Acre in
Yards, by which the Contents of any Plot of Ground
tained without the expense of a regular Survey ; &c.
ON, C.E. New Edition, royal 32mo. oblong, leather,
th elastic band, 4s.

includes tables for ascertaining the value of leases for any term
wing how to lay out plots of ground of certain acres in forms,
ith valuable rules for ascertaining the probable worth of standing
; and is of incalculable value to the country gentleman and pro-
mer's Journal.

rricultural Surveyors' Pocket-Book.

) VALUER'S AND LAND IMPROVER'S COM-
CKET-BOOK ; consisting of the above two works
er, leather, gilt edges, with strap, 7s. 6d.

*bove forms an unequalled and most compendious Pocket
for the Land Agent and Agricultural Engineer.*
lson's book to be the best ready-reckoner on matters relating to
and crops we have ever seen, and its combination with Mr.
r enhances the value and usefulness of the latter-mentioned . .
a manual for reference to those for whom it is intended."—
'armer.

s Introduction to Farming.

ONS of MY FARM : a Book for Amateur Agricul-
an Introduction to Farm Practice, in the Culture of
eeding of Cattle, Management of the Dairy, Poultry,
l in the Keeping of Farm-work Records. By ROBERT
. With numerous Illustrations. Fcp. 6s. cloth.

introduction to the whole round of farming practice."—*John*

"*A Complete Epitome of the Laws of this Country.*"

EVERY MAN'S OWN LAWYER; a Handy-Book of the Principles of Law and Equity. By A BARRISTER. 12th Edition, carefully revised, including a Summary of The Building Societies Act, The Infants' Relief Act, The Married Women's Property Act, The Real Property Limitation Act, The Betting Act, The Hosiery Manufacture Act, a Summary of the Supreme Court of Judicature Act, &c., &c. With Notes and References to the Authorities. 12mo, price 6s. 8d. (saved at every consultation), strongly bound.

COMPRISING THE LAWS OF

BANKRUPTCY—BILLS OF EXCHANGE—CONTRACTS AND AGREEMENTS—COPYRIGHT—DOWER AND DIVORCE—ELECTIONS AND REGISTRATION—INSURANCE—LIBEL AND SLANDER—MORTGAGES—SETTLEMENTS—STOCK EXCHANGE PRACTICE—TRADE MARKS AND PATENTS—TRESPASS, NUISANCES, ETC.—TRANSFER OF LAND, ETC.—WARRANTY—WILLS AND AGREEMENTS, ETC. Also Law for Landlord and Tenant—Master and Servant—Workmen and Apprentices—Heirs, Devisees, and Legatees—Husband and Wife—Executors and Trustees—Guardian and Ward—Married Women and Infants—Partners and Agents—Lender and Borrower—Debtor and Creditor—Purchaser and Vendor—Companies and Associations—Friendly Societies—Clergymen, Churchwardens—Medical Practitioners, &c.—Bankers—Farmers—Contractors—Stock and Share Brokers—Sportsmen and Gamekeepers—Farriers and Horse-Dealers—Auctioneers, House-Agents—Innkeepers, &c.—Pawnbrokers—Surveyors—Railways and Carriers, &c. &c.

"*No Englishman ought to be without this book.*"—*Engineer.*

"It is a complete code of English Law, written in plain language which all can understand . . . should be in the hands of every business man, and all who wish to abolish lawyers' bills."—*Weekly Times.*

"A useful and concise epitome of the law."—*Law Magazine.*

"What it professes to be—a complete epitome of the laws of this country, thoroughly intelligible to non-professional readers."—*Bell's Life.*

Auctioneer's Assistant.

THE APPRAISER, AUCTIONEER, BROKER, HOUSE AND ESTATE AGENT, AND VALUER'S POCKET ASSISTANT, for the Valuation for Purchase, Sale, or Renewal of Leases, Annuities, and Reversions, and of property generally; with Prices for Inventories, &c. By JOHN WHEELER, Valuer, &c. Third Edition, enlarged, by C. NORRIS. Royal 32mo, cloth, 5s.

"A neat and concise book of reference, containing an admirable and clearly-arranged list of prices for inventories, and a very practical guide to determine the value of furniture, &c."—*Standard.*

Pawnbrokers' Legal Guide.

THE PAWNBROKERS', FACTORS', and MERCHANTS' GUIDE to the LAW of LOANS and PLEDGES. With the Statutes and a Digest of Cases on Rights and Liabilities, Civil and Criminal, as to Loans and Pledges of Goods, Debentures, Mercantile, and other Securities. By H. C. FOLKARD, Esq., of Lincoln's Inn, Barrister-at-Law, Author of the "Law of Slander and Libel," &c. 12mo, cloth boards, price 7s.

The Laws of Mines and Mining Companies.

A PRACTICAL TREATISE on the LAW RELATING to MINES and MINING COMPANIES. By WHITTON ARUNDELL, Attorney-at-Law. Crown 8vo. 4s. cloth.

Bradbury, Agnew, & Co., Printers, Whitefriars, London.

www.ingramcontent.com/pod-product-compliance
Lightning Source LLC
Chambersburg PA
CBHW030640030726
47497CB00006B/1880